Dervla McTiernan's debut novel, *The Ruin*, is a critically acclaimed international bestseller which was shortlisted in two categories for the 2018 Irish Book Awards, and was named on the Amazon US Best Book of the Year list 2018.

Dervla was born in County Cork, Ireland, to a family of seven. She studied corporate law at the National University of Ireland, Galway, and the Law Society of Ireland, and practised as a lawyer for twelve years. Following the global financial crisis, she moved with her family to Western Australia, where she now lives with her husband and two children. An avid fan of crime and detective novels from childhood, Dervla now writes full-time.

Also by Dervla McTiernan

The Ruin

THE SCHOLAR

DERVLA McTIERNAN

sphere

SPHERE

First published in Australia in 2019 by Harper Collin
First published in Great Britain in 2019 by Harper Collins
This paperback edition published in 2019 by Sphere

1 3 5 7 9 10 8 6 4 2

A CIP catalogue record for this book
is available from the British Library.

ISBN 978-0-7515-6933-9

Printed and bound in Great Britain by
Clays Ltd, Elcograf S.p.A.

Papers used by Sphere are from well-managed forests
and other responsible sources.

MIX
Paper from
responsible sources
FSC® C104740

Sphere
An imprint of
Little, Brown Book Group
Carmelite House
50 Victoria Embankment
London EC4Y ODZ

An Hachette UK Company
www.hachette.co.uk

www.littlebrown.co.uk

For Mum, for all the words.

For Dad, for the songs.

Dublin, Ireland

February 2006

PROLOGUE

Carline was eating watermelon and pancakes in Laila Barrett's kitchen when she heard about her father's death. They were on a playdate – though at twelve Carline and Laila thought they were too old to have their social lives arranged for them. It was one of the few things they agreed on. Laila's au pair Alice was watching the news on the television. A blonde journalist in a ski jacket and a hat spoke directly to the camera.

'Eoghan Darcy, son of John Darcy and heir to the multinational pharmaceutical company Darcy Therapeutics, was killed yesterday in an avalanche. Mr Darcy was skiing with a small group of friends in the Glacier du Pisaillas area of the Val d'Isère resort. The glacier had been closed due to avalanche risk. There were no survivors.'

Carline swallowed and put her fork down. On the TV the journalist gestured towards a distant mountain that was all but obscured by falling snow. She was still speaking, but Carline couldn't hear the words through a sudden roaring in her ears. Alice stood up, fumbled with the remote control, pressing buttons until the screen changed to show a soccer match, then pressing again until the screen finally went black. They sat for a moment in frozen silence. Carline closed her eyes. The roaring in her ears faded, and she could hear her own breathing, the distant sounds of traffic, the spatter of rain on the window panes.

'My dad isn't dead,' she said. But when she opened her eyes and looked straight at Alice, Alice just looked afraid. Laila was staring at her, eyes wide and mouth slightly open, as if it were her father the journalist had been talking about. As if she didn't have a mother and a father safe somewhere in the city, along with two older sisters, and a younger brother who was right at that moment playing in the other room. Laila didn't even want Carline there. She'd told Carline that herself. Her mother had made her ask Carline over and she had been angry because she'd really wanted to ask Aoife.

'I want to go home,' Carline said. 'Please can I go home now?'

Carline and Laila waited in the front room for Marie to pick her up. It seemed to take a long time.

'I'm sorry about your dad,' Laila said eventually.

Carline shook her head.

'You can cry if you want to,' Laila said.

Carline stared straight ahead and after a while Laila got up and left the room. Carline sat as still as she could on the couch, as if by staying quiet she could keep the dark thoughts at bay. Her father couldn't be dead. Maybe he had been knocked down the mountain by the avalanche. Maybe he was lost somewhere and they hadn't found him yet. Or he could be unconscious in a hospital and the doctors didn't know who he was. Yet one thought forced its way into her head, crowding everything else out. They wouldn't have said it on the television if it wasn't true, would they? Carline leaned forward and pushed the palms of her hands into her eyes. She pushed hard, but the tears came anyway.

Marie got to the house at six o'clock. She said it was traffic. Traffic was terrible. She gave Carline a long hug and kept her arm about her all the way to the car and when they got back to the house, she made them both tea. Then they sat together at the big table in the kitchen.

'I'm so sorry that you had to find out that way. From the news,' Marie said. 'I didn't know, you see. No one called me to tell me.'

Carline looked at her plate. 'Do you think he's really dead?' she asked. 'Not just missing?'

Marie put her hand on Carline's and squeezed. And then she told Carline that there was no doubt. That her father had been carrying a geolocator, and his body had been found. The avalanche was just too big. Once it started none of them had a chance, but it would have been very quick, and her father wouldn't have suffered.

Carline thought about what her father must have felt when he saw the tsunami of snow barrelling towards him, felt its brutal weight bearing him down, burying him. And then the realisation that he was under the snow, the panic as he tried to claw his way out. The cold, the snow in his mouth and then his lungs. Suddenly her own breathing felt constricted. She opened her mouth, took a single gasping breath, then another. Tears burned in her eyes. She wrapped her arms around her body and found that she was rocking herself and crying, feeling like she might never be able to stop. Marie came around the table and hugged her hard, and they sat together like that until her tears ran dry.

That night Carline's sleep was broken. The shadows in her bedroom were unfriendly. It was cold and she needed her quilt for warmth but the weight of it troubled her. For much of the night she lay, dry eyed and staring at the ceiling, thinking about her dad. He loved to ski. He loved to drive fast cars and he loved to travel. *Work hard, play hard.* That's what he said when he ruffled her hair as he left for another trip, left her with Marie or the au pair before Marie or the one before that. Why couldn't he just have stayed home? All night long Carline thought about what she could have done to prevent him from leaving, and it was only when the sun came up that she realised how stupid she had been. All through the night she had thought about her father and never once about what would happen next. But she should have. She should have been thinking about that because she was only twelve, and that meant she had to live with someone until she grew up. And there weren't very many options.

She needed to do something before it was too late. She got up and went to the bathroom. She brushed her teeth extra carefully, tied her hair neatly in a French plait, and dressed in a clean pair of jeans and a bright blue jumper that her father had once said brought out her eyes. Then she found her best coat and boots, put them on, and let herself quietly out of the back door.

Once, Carline had watched a movie about a girl whose parents had decided to divorce. The girl loved her parents and was determined to stop them. She did all sorts of crazy things to try to keep them together, to make them realise that they still loved each other. In the end they didn't get back together but they did become friends again and the girl was sad but accepting. Nothing about the scenario had been familiar to Carline. For starters, her parents had never lived together. Carline had always lived with her father in Dublin, and her mother, Evangeline, had always lived in Monaco. Carline saw Evangeline only twice a year, when they would have afternoon tea in Evangeline's rented suite at the Shelbourne hotel. Visits always started with a stiff hug and a kiss on the cheek. Afternoon tea would always come with a bottle of champagne. Evangeline would ask Carline questions, but her eyes would be on Carline's father. And then the bottle of champagne would be gone and maybe another one would follow, or there would be too many trips to the bathroom and the atmosphere in the room would become more dangerous. Then there would be more hugs, and kisses that were too wet, and after that the anger would come with shouting and horrible, horrible words. Carline had never for a moment wanted her parents to live together. She'd felt nothing but relief each time her father stood, took her hand, and told her it was time to go.

The train from Blackrock to Dalkey took exactly fourteen minutes. Carline usually liked taking the Dart. She liked to look at the people, and at the sea, even when it was a grey day and the sea looked sulky and dangerous. But that day she could not look at the water, because the waves made her think of a wall of snow bearing down, and she could not look at the people because she felt as if she were wide open, and they could see her all the way through. So she looked down at her feet, and told herself not to think about anything at all.

She got off the train in Dalkey and walked straight out towards the Vico Road. Her grandfather lived in a house on the top of a cliff overlooking the ocean. She'd never been in the house, but she knew where it was. She followed the Ardeevin Road. It was very pretty. The road was narrow, but it had a footpath that she could walk on and there were nice houses and lots of trees. It was good to have a few minutes to think, to try to plan what she might say. Most important of all, she knew, was that she mustn't cry. Her grandfather wouldn't like it. The road climbed as it curved, bringing her higher and higher, and when she was halfway there the view opened out and she could see a vast expanse of ocean spread out far beneath her. From her position high on the cliff road the water was different. At this distance the waves were muted, the water seemed still, and she felt safe.

Her grandfather's house was hidden behind high, cut-stone walls and protected by ornate wrought-iron gates. There was an intercom button on the right-hand gate post and Carline pressed the button firmly and waited. After a moment there was an answering buzz and a woman's voice said, 'Yes?'

'I'm Carline Darcy.' Carline made her voice as strong as she could. 'I'd like to speak to my grandfather.'

There was an uncomfortably long pause, then a buzz and the gate swung open. Carline walked through and down the drive towards the house. A woman opened the door. She had a nice face. She had grey hair, tied back, and was a bit thin. For a moment Carline wondered if this was the grandmother she had never met, and then she dismissed the idea. The woman looked nervous, perhaps, but not hostile.

'Could I see him, please?' Carline said, and this time her voice caught a little. She cleared her throat, straightened her shoulders.

'Your grandfather isn't here at the moment. Is he expecting you?'

Carline shook her head, and the woman pressed her lips together.

'I'll call him,' she said. 'I'll let him know you're here.'

Carline waited in the dining room for quite a long time. The room was at the front of the house so there was no view of the sea. The windows looked out instead on a small courtyard garden, its shrubs and ornamental trees a little ragged in the winter sunshine. There were twelve chairs around the long dining table, and an empty fireplace. The heating was turned off and it was cold, so Carline kept her coat on and put her hands in her pockets. She took them out again and sat up straighter when she heard her grandfather's car pull up, then his voice in the hall. He came in after a few minutes, leaving the door open behind him. He sat down in the chair opposite her and regarded her without warmth or affection. They had met only a handful of times, always at her father's insistence. Carline's grandmother had refused those meetings, her grandfather had attended only under duress. She wished that he didn't look so much like her father.

'Well?' he said.

Carline opened her mouth to speak but nothing came out. His eyes were on her. After a minute he let out a sigh and looked at his watch.

'I would like not to live with my mother, please,' Carline said, and if her voice was scratchy there were no tears at least.

She clenched her fists under the table. 'I would like very much to live in my own house with Marie, or with another au pair if Marie has to go home.'

'I see,' said her grandfather. 'And why don't you want to live with your mother?'

Carline closed her eyes. She had to, to get the words out. 'She doesn't like me,' she said, then shook her head. That wasn't it. It was true, but it wasn't what she had come here to say. She swallowed, forced herself to speak again. 'I'm afraid of her.'

Carline's grandfather said nothing. Carline heard the front door open, heard Marie's voice, loud and worried. Her eyes felt as heavy as bricks as she forced herself to raise them up and meet her grandfather's cold gaze. His eyes were paler than her father's, pale blue ice chips that looked right through her.

'Very well,' he said.

Marie brought Carline home. They stopped along the way to buy takeout for lunch. Carline waited in the car. She felt so strange, sort of shaky and achy and she wanted to cry again but to laugh as well. They brought their lunch home and ate it in the kitchen with the television on and then Carline got sick in the bathroom. Three days later they went to her father's funeral.

And after the funeral her mother came for her.

Galway, Ireland

Friday 25 April 2014

CHAPTER ONE

Carrie O'Halloran's phone stayed stubbornly silent. She'd expected a call from Ciarán so the girls could say goodnight. When that hadn't happened, she'd held out for a post-bedtime update. Nine o'clock came and went and her phone screen remained dark. She could have called him, she knew that, but she didn't have the energy for another one of those conversations. Instead she put her phone in the drawer and turned again to the mound of paper on her desk.

The case she was working on needed all her attention. It should have been a slam dunk – Rob Henderson had been caught red-handed – but the case showed distressing signs of slipping out of her control. She couldn't allow that to happen. Carrie had interviewed Lucy Henderson but had failed to make a connection. Now she was reviewing the statements of colleagues and extended family members, looking for the lever she could use to open Lucy up to the fact that her husband was a murderous bastard.

An hour passed before Carrie put her pen down and sat back from her desk. She took her phone from the drawer and woke the screen. No messages, no missed calls. Damnit. She didn't want to go home. The girls would be asleep, the kitchen a tip, and Ciarán pissed off and sulking. It would be easier to just go down to the basement, find an empty cell, and sleep there. She'd have to be back by six the next day anyway if she was going to finish her Henderson prep on time.

Carrie shut down her computer, stood, and took her jacket from the back of her chair. She looked around. There were plenty of occupied desks, but nobody else in the room had started their shift at seven that morning. Fuck's sake. It would be one thing if it was a one-off, but it had been like this for months. When she'd made sergeant she'd been thrilled at the thought of managing her own time. She would report to Murphy, yes, but looked forward to the broad autonomy sergeants had to run their own cases and to manage the gardaí reporting to them. The reality was nowadays she had less control than ever. As a uniformed garda she'd been able to go in, work her shift, and go home. There was always someone to take her place. She'd worked overtime, but only as needed, and in this day and age of budget cuts, as needed was a rare thing. Now she was one of only three sergeants working out of Mill Street Garda Station, and she never went home because if she did the work would never get done.

Carrie walked out of the room, along the corridor to the stairs, started down, then stopped. She'd started to dread going home, and dread going to work. This was bullshit. This was not who she was. How long was she going to let this go on before she tackled it? Carrie stood on the stairs and thought about Mel Hackett on holiday in the south of France, about Cormac Reilly walking out of the station at six o'clock, as he had every day this week. She turned on her heel and made for the Superintendent's office. Murphy wouldn't usually be in the station this late, preferring to leave the long shifts and antisocial hours to his juniors, but she knew he was there. He'd been at meetings in Dublin all day and had come directly to the station on his return to Galway. She knocked on his door.

'A moment, sir?'

Brian Murphy was engrossed in whatever was on his computer screen. His mouse hand clicked twice before he looked up. It was after hours; he was probably posting on *triathletenow.com* again. Not for the first time, Carrie tried to think of a way to drop a hint that Murphy's posts weren't as anonymous as he thought. Somehow, someone in vice had found out his user handle, and it was now known across the station. The night that *TopCopTriGuy* had engaged in a detailed discussion of haemorrhoid problems in older cyclists had resulted in station-wide hilarity, and the placing of cushions on meeting room chairs whenever Murphy was likely to appear. He couldn't possibly be as oblivious as he seemed, could he?

He gestured to her to take a seat. 'I've read your report on the Henderson case. Where are we with the assessment?'

Within an hour of being taken into custody, Rob Henderson had adopted an escalating pattern of behaviour that indicated either a serious mental illness, or exceptional acting skills. He was currently in the Central Mental Hospital in Dublin, undergoing assessment.

'Nothing formal yet, that will take a few more days, but I've been pushing, and I get the impression that they don't know what to make of him yet. Personally, I think it's all bullshit. He's faking.'

'And the wife?'

'Still in denial. I've a meeting with her again tomorrow. I'm going to push her harder this time.'

'Update me afterwards,' Murphy said. 'Let me know if you make any progress.'

Carrie nodded. She would have done so without the request. The case was high profile, and Murphy had been all over it from the beginning. He looked at her expectantly, waiting for more. She hesitated, almost let it go.

'Sir, I've got too much on,' Carrie blurted. 'Too many cases, I mean.'

Murphy started tapping the desk with his index finger, never a good sign.

'I've six active cases. Seven more going to court within the next few months.' Meanwhile Mel Hackett had what, two? Three max. And Reilly nothing current at all. 'It's not sustainable. If I keep working like this I'll make mistakes.'

'It's not a nine-to-five job, Carrie. I made that clear to you when I offered you the promotion.'

She ignored that, going straight to what she knew would motivate him. 'I've had a look at the stats. Our timeframe to clearance is running long. And we've two missing persons not yet traced.' Stats were a regular and contentious point of discussion at the station. The Commissioner had set a zero target for untraced missing persons that year and hitting that target would be top of Murphy's priority list.

Murphy leaned back in his chair. 'Hackett is due back next week,' he said. 'We'll sit down then and do a case review, see what can be redistributed.'

'Sir, I talked to Mel before she went on holiday. She's positive she doesn't have the capacity to take on anything more.' Which was bollox, but that was beside the point.

Murphy rubbed his jaw, compressed his lips, and said nothing.

'Cormac Reilly …' Carrie started.

'Reilly is fully engaged,' Murphy said. 'He's caught up in a cold case review that takes all of his time.'

Carrie made no attempt to hide her frustration. 'Christ sir, when do you want me to get it done? In my sleep?'

'This is the job, Carrie.'

'Sir, what I'm telling you is that you've got three sergeants working for you, and the least experienced of them is doing seventy per cent of the work load.' Because Hackett was an old hand at managing the system, and Cormac Reilly wasn't let near anything that looked like a real case. 'Reilly is a bloody good detective,' Carrie continued. 'I've heard about some of the cases he's run and won. We're lucky to have him. And it's madness to keep him working pissy little cold cases that aren't going to go anywhere. You need to put him

on active cases, or replace him with someone you can use.'
Carrie stopped, waited for Murphy to show her the door.

'One of those pissy little cold cases, as you so colourfully
call them, has resulted in a major arrest.'

'That's one case,' Carrie said quickly, hiding her relief.
'And it's all but put to bed.'

There was a long pause, during which the last few police
in the building could be heard talking loudly about pints and
weekend plans. It was all so bloody stupid. Did he really think
that Reilly would throw in the towel if he was frozen out for
long enough? He was a career cop, it was in his DNA. Reilly
was going nowhere, unless of course he transferred back to
Dublin. He might already have done that if it wasn't for the
girlfriend. Partner. Whatever.

'It wasn't his fault, sir. The shooting.'

'I never suggested it was.'

Carrie hesitated. The part of her that was interested in
self-preservation and career advancement wanted her to shut
up. The part of her that was desperate for a weekend off,
some time with her kids, and at least a chance of saving her
marriage, said to press on. The little bit of her that believed
Cormac Reilly had been treated unfairly tipped the balance.

'It's not going to work,' Carrie said quietly. 'He's not going
to go anywhere, and people are talking. It's been over a year.
The uniforms aren't stupid. They know about his previous
success rate. Internal affairs cleared him in the shooting case,
on paper he's back on active duty, but in practice he gets
nothing. They're asking why. They're saying there's no smoke
without fire. Sooner or later Reilly will have to do something.
What if he calls in the union? Or worse, a lawyer?'

'If you're suggesting that Cormac Reilly has been
treated unfavourably because of what happened last year,
O'Halloran, you're out of line. Reilly gets his cases in rotation
like everyone else.'

Carrie said nothing more, waited. Let the lie hang in the air between them. She looked at Murphy, caught his gaze and held it.

He was the first to look away. When he spoke it was very quietly. 'You're sure about this, Carrie? There's no going back.'

She hesitated. 'I'm sure.'

Without looking at her he turned to his computer screen, moved and clicked his mouse. Read something that Carrie couldn't see.

'Give Reilly the Durkan case.' Another click of the keys. 'Nesbitt too.' A pause. 'And give him Henderson.'

Carrie had been on the point of smiling in relief, but at Murphy's last word she froze, opened her mouth to protest. 'Sir, I …'

'I read the transcript of your last interview with Lucy Henderson. You're not getting anywhere with her. Let Reilly see where he can take it. She strikes me as the type who'd respond better to a man.'

His tone made it clear that the meeting was at an end.

Shit.

'Thank you, sir.' She waited, but he didn't react. She had reached the door when he spoke again.

'O'Halloran. I hope this isn't a mistake.' His tone was pointed, his expression distant, and the message was clear. Carrie had been granted a favour, and that favour had been noted in his little book of services owed and given. He would call it in too. He always did.

'Yes sir.'

Cormac was surprised, but not unpleasantly so, to receive a text message from Carrie O'Halloran asking if he was free for a quick drink. He was in town anyway, as it happened, having a pint and waiting for Emma. He texted Carrie back, ordering himself another drink and a glass of red for her while he waited.

He liked Carrie. She was a good cop, a good sergeant, and he trusted her. The year before, when an investigation had led Cormac to a violent confrontation with a colleague, Carrie had done what she could to ensure that the powers that be didn't scapegoat him. Since then they'd had coffee or lunch together a handful of times, but they weren't on the kind of terms that included Friday night drinks. Something must be up.

She arrived five minutes later, made her way through the bar and found him in his corner booth. He watched her as she approached, noted the signs of tiredness around her eyes. She was still wearing the tailored pants and jacket he'd seen her in earlier that day. She clocked the wine as soon as she sat down.

'Thanks,' she said. 'But I should probably have coffee.' Still, she reached out and picked up the glass, took a sip. 'I haven't been home before ten o'clock any night this week. I worked the last two weekends and worked three last month. I'm overloaded. I've spoken to Murphy and he's told me to transfer some cases to you.'

Cormac nodded slowly. 'That makes sense,' he said. He couldn't quite read her – had she wanted this? 'Which cases?'

'Durkan. Nesbitt. And Henderson.'

'Right.' The first two he'd heard nothing about, assumed were standard fare. But the Henderson case. He'd heard enough about it to know she'd been working it passionately. It was almost certainly the case that had kept her at the station all hours for the past week.

'Henderson,' Cormac said. 'Are you all right about that?'

'No,' she said baldly. She sipped her wine, then turned to him. 'Murphy wasn't too pleased with me putting him under pressure. I gave him an earful about you working cold cases.

Said he needed to shit or get off the pot. Well, not in so many words.'

'And Henderson was his way of saying ...'

'His way of saying thank you, yes.' She put her glass down on the table. 'It's an important case to get right,' she said, and he could tell that she was picking her words carefully. 'Lucy Henderson is a hard read.'

'Right,' Cormac said. He took a drink from his pint, buying time. He wanted the case. If he was honest with himself he knew he was desperate for it, desperate for the challenge. But getting it like this was not ideal – picking up something that already had someone else's fingerprints all over it, someone else's method, particularly when that someone resented handing it over.

'Let's talk to Murphy on Monday. Decide which cases are at a good stage to unload. You keep Henderson. I'll take whatever you think you should pass over. If we present Murphy with a fait accompli he'll have to take it.'

She looked surprised, then considering, then reluctantly shook her head. Took a longer sip from her wine. 'He's right, though I hate to admit it. I've made no progress with the wife. She might respond better to you. And the hearing will almost certainly clash with one of my other cases. I think you're going to have to take it.' She still looked tired but some of the tension had gone from her voice. 'There's an interview tomorrow morning, which is why I needed to catch you tonight.'

Cormac sat back. 'Carrie, I've no wish to fall out with you.'

She waved him off. 'No. Sorry. It's me. I was a bit pissed off, but that's just the tiredness speaking. I should go home. Get some sleep.' She made no move to stand.

A phone vibrated against the table and they both looked down. Cormac picked it up.

'That's Emma. It's too late for dinner but we can order a bite at the bar. Why don't you hang on? Have something to eat before you drive home.' Before Carrie could respond, Cormac answered the call. 'Em? You finished? I'm in Buskers. The back bar.' The half-smile on Cormac's face dropped away, and he stood, putting a hand to his ear to block the noise of the bar. He locked eyes with Carrie.

'Where are you? Emma. Stop. Take a breath.' Cormac's face was tense but his tone was very controlled. 'Tell me where you are.'

And then he was moving.

CHAPTER TWO

Cormac stalked up Kirwan's Lane. When he reached Cross Street he broke into a run, making for the taxi rank, aware that Carrie was a step behind him. He opened the door of the closest car, pulled out his ID and flashed it at the driver.

'I want the university. The chapel car park. Take Presentation Road and let's get there fast, okay?' He took the passenger seat, and Carrie, asking no questions, sat in the back. The driver, a twenty-something with acne scars on his cheeks, just shrugged.

'You're the boss.' Then he pulled out, and drove carefully, keeping just under the speed limit, down Bridge Street and on to Presentation Road.

'What is it?' Carrie asked. 'Is Emma all right?'

'I'm not sure,' Cormac said shortly. 'She's upset, but she said she's okay.' He glanced at the driver, who was listening with interest to the conversation. 'I'll fill you in when we get there,' he said to Carrie, then turned to the driver. 'Can you pick up the pace?'

The driver shook his head. 'It's a fifty zone here. Worth my licence to go over.'

Cormac was already regretting the taxi. He should have run the extra couple of hundred metres to the station and had a uniform drive them in a marked car with lights and siren.

'Look, just drive, all right? This is garda business.'

Mr Conscientious didn't need to be told twice. He grinned and put his foot to the floor, accelerated up to 70, then 80. He took the lights at University Road very late, then ran straight through a pedestrian crossing flashing amber. Cormac said nothing, just gritted his teeth.

They turned off onto Distillery Road. It was a narrow road flanked by 1960s houses that had once been homes, all long bought up by the university for use as offices and tutorial rooms. You could follow Distillery Road down to the river, which was where the private laboratories were located, or you could take a sharp right that would lead you past the university chapel and onward to the entrances to the library, the larger university canteen and coffee shop, and the concourse. Cormac knew the campus well. Over the past year, and in stark contrast to how things had been in Dublin, he'd had more than enough time to drive out and meet Emma regularly for lunch.

'Slow down,' Cormac said. 'I want you to stop at the corner.' He put his hand on the driver's shoulder and squeezed, making sure that the message was heard. The driver hit the brakes hard, and Cormac had his door open before the car came to a complete halt. He saw Emma's car straightaway. It was parked in the middle of the road, hazards flashing, blocking the way. As he approached, the driver's door opened and Emma stepped out. She walked towards him, hands pushed deep into her cardigan pockets.

'Are you hurt? What's happened?' Cormac reached out for her, ran his hands from her shoulders to her elbows and back. She was shivering. It could be shock. Christ, this was all she needed.

'I'm fine. I'm fine, Corm. It's not me.'

Carrie joined them. 'Are you okay?' she asked.

Emma nodded, and took a step back, out of reach. It was late, after eleven o'clock now, and the moon was hidden by heavy, low-hanging cloud. The distant streetlamps cast only an orange-tinged suggestion of light, and Emma's features were smudged, indistinct in the darkness.

'I found a body. A girl. Someone's killed her. I think she was hit by a car.'

Cormac wanted to reach out to Emma again, but with the barest shake of her head she asked him not to. She was just about holding it together, maybe, and anything more from him might send her over the edge. Fuck. Fuck fuck fuck. She'd been doing so well.

'Emma, we haven't met. I'm Carrie O'Halloran. I work with Cormac.' Carrie's voice was professional, calm, in control. 'Can you bring me to this girl? Are you sure that she's dead?'

'Yes.' Emma gave another hard shiver. 'Yes. She has to be dead. You'll understand when you see her.'

'Okay Em,' Cormac said. 'Show us where, all right?' He glanced at Carrie and opened his mouth to ask her to call an ambulance, but she was ahead of him, already dialling.

Emma led the way down the narrow road. The road was flanked on the left-hand side by trees and on the right by a footpath which bounded the chapel car park, and beyond that the chapel itself. The only streetlamps were on the far side of the car park, away from the road, and the rest of the campus seemed to be in darkness. There should have been a glow of lights from the library. The car park was all but empty – he counted only three cars, which struck him as odd. Wasn't it exam season? Shouldn't they all be studying late?

Emma, her arms tightly crossed and her shoulders a little hunched, led them about fifteen metres towards the library, then came to a stop. Cormac could just make out a crumpled heap on the road.

'She's there,' Emma said.

'Stay here.' Cormac looked at her to make sure she wasn't going to argue, waited for her nod. Then he walked carefully onward, conscious that if this was a crime scene he risked contaminating evidence, but aware that he had little choice. He needed to confirm that the woman was dead. The light was so poor that he was nearly on the body before he could distinguish shape from shadow, and could make out the pool of blood, mahogany dark, spread out from a spill of long blond hair. He took his phone from his pocket, shone the light on the scene. A woman, arms thrown back, a tyre print in cherry red painted across a white T-shirt, worn under a cardigan that had fallen open. Cormac took another step closer. The girl's chest was crushed, her pelvis twisted. And her face. Christ. There was nothing left but an open sore of blood and flesh. A gleam of white in the darkness that could be bone or tooth. Cormac swallowed, took a final careful step closer, and pressed two fingers to her neck. No pulse. Her skin was soft, and held a hint of warmth.

'She is dead, isn't she?'

Emma stood behind him on the footpath. Carrie was somewhere in the darkness, making phone calls. Cormac went to Emma, hugged her for a long moment, until she began to disentangle herself. He let her go, but walked her back along the footpath, away from the body.

'What happened?' he asked.

'I was working at home all day. I only came in to check on something in the lab.' Another shudder racked her body. 'I saw her on the road as soon as I turned the corner. I didn't know it was a person until I was closer, and then I thought she might be drunk. It was only when I got out of the car that I saw all the blood.'

'You got out of the car?' Cormac asked. 'You got close?'

Emma just nodded, her eyes hooded, and put trembling fingers to her mouth. 'Her poor face. Jesus.'

Cormac cursed inwardly. The fact that she'd gotten close to the body meant that her involvement in the case, at least to some degree, was now inevitable. To a different person a couple of police interviews, necessary to rule her out as a suspect, would be no big deal. For Emma it might bring back memories that were better forgotten.

'You didn't see anyone else?' Cormac asked. 'A car? Any pedestrians?'

Emma shook her head, looked around the car park. 'It's so quiet. Much quieter than usual. The library should be open. It's open twenty-four hours at this time of year. Why are all the lights off? Where is everyone?'

The faint sound of a siren came to them, far away but coming closer. Cormac walked back in Carrie's direction, drawing Emma with him. The taxi was gone, Carrie must have gotten rid of it. Carrie had finished with her phone, was tucking it back in her pocket.

'What have we got?' she asked.

'A hit-and-run,' Cormac said. 'Victim is a young woman.'

'Dead?' Carrie asked. Cormac nodded.

Carrie gestured to the empty car park 'The place is deserted,' she said. 'Where are all the students?'

Cormac shook his head, and as the siren grew louder they turned and watched the ambulance pull into the street. Carrie raised a hand in greeting. The driver parked and two paramedics got out, moving quickly.

'The poor girl doesn't need an ambulance,' Emma said. 'There's nothing they can do for her.'

Carrie was walking towards the paramedics. Cormac squeezed Emma's shoulder, followed Carrie, overtook her. She'd said that as far as Murphy was concerned, he was back on active duty. Fine. He would take this case on and make sure that Emma didn't get too badly knocked around in the process.

He spoke to the paramedics. 'It's looking like a hit-and-run. A woman. I couldn't find a pulse. I'll ask you to do formal confirmation, but please try to disturb her as little as possible, all right? And watch where you step.'

The paramedics exchanged glances.

'I'll do it.' The older man sent his partner, defeated looking, back to the ambulance, then nodded his readiness to Cormac, who led the way past Emma's car to the body.

'You're police?'

Cormac nodded. 'DS Cormac Reilly. Mill Street.'

They approached the body. Cormac waited on the footpath while the paramedic stepped forward, moving gingerly. He took a flashlight from his cargo pants pocket, turned it on, then reached down and placed one gloved hand against the woman's bloody neck. 'No pulse,' he said. Without moving it, he held one of the outstretched hands in his, then held the wrist. 'She's still warm, but she's apneic and I see brain matter.' He allowed his torch to play over the woman's body again, then abruptly switched it off. 'I can't officially pronounce her dead, as I'm sure you know, but it's my recommendation that no treatment is provided.'

Cormac nodded. 'We'll call in the medical examiner. Will you wait? To take her when she's released?

The paramedic shook his head. 'They'll be at it for a few hours. The hospital's only around the corner. Have someone call us when you want us, all right?'

Cormac borrowed the torch from him and let him go. The paramedic made his way to the footpath and walked away without another word.

Cormac turned the torch back on, and let the light play over the victim. She was wearing fitted blue jeans, ankle boots. The open cardigan was lined with a turquoise fabric that looked like silk. It gleamed dully where it wasn't dark with blood. He leaned down, looked more closely at the skin of her hands and wrists, which was firm, and unmarked except for blood spatter. If he had to guess he would have said she'd been young, maybe in her twenties. The torch was a powerful one. Cormac shone the light on the road – there were bloodstains and tyre tracks in both directions.

Cormac walked back towards the women. As he approached, Carrie turned to Emma with a question.

'The whole place seems to be on lockdown,' she said, with a nod towards the university buildings, which were in darkness. 'But you were going to the laboratory, you said?'

'Yes,' said Emma.

'Is there anyone else there this evening?'

'I … don't think so. I haven't been in yet, so I can't be sure, but there isn't usually, not this late.'

Carrie nodded, glanced around her again, asked her next question casually. 'She couldn't have been going there to meet you then? You didn't have an arrangement with anyone?'

'No. God no. No arrangements.' Emma's voice was sharp, stressed.

Carrie nodded. 'Could she have come along just in the hope of bumping into you there? If you're a regular late worker, she might have thought she'd find you.'

Cormac glanced at Carrie sharply. She'd asked the question with the mild, guileless tone of voice that Cormac himself put to good use himself on a regular basis.

Emma flinched She opened her mouth to speak, hesitated. She was about to lie, Cormac could tell. He started to interject but Emma was already speaking. 'There'd be no reason for her to think that … I … I don't work late often.'

Shite. Emma avoided eye contact. They both knew she had just lied, and, though Emma didn't know it, Carrie did too. He'd certainly mentioned Emma's penchant for late-night work at least once in the past. Cormac knew that people lied to the police all the time, for the stupidest of reasons and for no reason at all. Because they were nervous or stressed. Because they wanted to hide something immaterial that they were embarrassed about, or conversely because they liked the attention and would say whatever would draw more of it. Emma had lied because she was tired and upset, and because she was gun-shy from hours and hours of police interviews. She would have recognised the false casualness of Carrie's tone. She'd reacted by shutting down, pulling back. By lying. He wished she hadn't. It was pointless and dangerous, and likely to draw exactly the kind of attention she was trying to discourage.

Carrie gave a wide, involuntary yawn.

'The scene of crime lads shouldn't be long,' she said, all relaxed unconcern. 'I asked for four uniforms, two to secure the site, two to start the door to door.' She yawned again. 'Christ. I feel like I haven't slept in a month.'

'You should go home, Carrie,' Cormac said abruptly. 'Only one of us can run the case. Leave it to me. Go home to your family.'

Carrie looked at her watch. 'It's eleven-fifteen,' she said. 'If I go home this early Ciarán might get a shock.' A tight smile. 'I'll stay and help out.'

'That's not necessary, Carrie,' Cormac said. 'You can leave this one with me.'

They locked eyes. Cormac could hear a siren approaching.

'The lads are nearly here,' he said, keeping his eyes on her. 'Once scene of crime have checked Emma over, maybe you'd be good enough to make sure she gets home all right?'

Carrie glanced at Emma. The tight smile relaxed into something more genuine. 'Of course,' she said. 'Pleasure.'

Cormac was conscious of Emma, very quiet at his side. He turned to her. 'Em, the scene guys will need to check you over when they arrive. Because you got so close to the body. Just to deal with any contamination issues.' And to make damn sure that no one could suggest anything had been covered up here.

The first squad car pulled up, light flashing, siren muted.

'There's no need to wait for the specialists,' Carrie said. 'I can take an evidence kit from the squad car, and take care of it right now, if that's okay with you, Emma?'

Emma shrugged. She glanced back towards the body.

'Em, I'd bring you home myself but ...' Cormac started to say.

'It's fine.' She cut him off. 'Of course you should stay.'

'I'll give you a minute,' Carrie said. She waved to the uniforms who were out of the car and approaching, walked to meet them.

'Cormac,' Emma said. 'Did you notice the girl's cardigan? It's very distinctive. I thought I recognised it, but I've just remembered where I saw it before. I think I saw a student wearing it.' She hesitated, glanced towards Carrie and the uniforms, then back to him. 'Cormac, it was Carline Darcy.'

Cormac froze. 'Are you sure?'

'No.' Emma shook her head firmly. 'There's no way to be sure, with her injuries ...' She let her voice trail off, swallowed, then continued. 'But her hair is the right colour. Maybe she's the right height, I don't know. And that cardigan she's wearing is last season's Stella McCartney. I don't think there are many students here who are spending three thousand euro on something like that.'

Christ. The powers that be would be all over this case like a bad rash. If he wanted to keep it, he would need to nail his name to it good and hard, before the word got out. As Cormac thought it through, two marked police cars pulled into the car park.

'Right,' Cormac said. 'Leave it with me, okay? I'll get one of the lads to bring you home. Promise me you'll look after yourself. Eat something.' Cormac felt like an asshole. He *should* be bringing her home himself.

Carrie came back, evidence bag now in hand. She waved it at them. 'If you can give me your cardigan now, Emma, I can take your other clothes at the house, before I head back to the station. I'll need to get a saliva and hair sample too.'

Cormac tamped down his irritation. It was what he had asked for, after all. Emma stared for a moment, then nodded numbly. She didn't say anything, but she didn't seem upset at the idea of the evidence collection, or of going home alone. Maybe it was the prospect of getting away from the gruesome scene, or maybe she just wasn't going to cry in front of a bunch of young fellas he had to work with. She gave him a quick hug, then turned and walked to the squad car without looking back. Carrie looked at him.

'You're sure about this, Cormac?' she asked.

'Very sure.' He half expected her to object, was relieved when she didn't.

She nodded. 'Okay. Look, there's an interview scheduled with Lucy Henderson tomorrow at eleven-thirty. Give me a call in the morning. I won't come in. I'm desperate for a day at home to be honest with you, and it's not worth the trek in if it's not my interview. But you call me and I'll talk you through what's happened so far. All the statements are on the system if you have time to scan them beforehand.'

Cormac nodded but his attention was on the case at hand. 'Emma thinks she might know the victim.'

'What?'

Cormac lowered his voice. 'She recognised the cardigan the victim is wearing. It's designer, not something someone else is likely to have. The girl also has the same build, same hair. Emma thinks the girl is Carline Darcy.'

Carrie stared up at him. It was as well he was taking the case and she was going home. In the thin light of the street lamp her mouth was like a bruise, her dark curls matched by the circles under her eyes.

'Darcy. Is that who I think it is?'

Cormac nodded. 'This case is going to blow up.'

'Right.' Carrie nodded. 'You're sure then, that you should take it?'

She let her eyes drift back towards Emma.

'Very sure,' said Cormac. His tone did not invite a rejoinder. As far as he was concerned, the conversation was at an end.

CHAPTER THREE

When Emma and Carrie had gone, Cormac put the uniforms to work taping off the scene while they waited for the garda technical bureau to arrive. One of the squad cars had a decent set of lights, and he had them set up in the car park, overlooking the scene.

Uniformed officers stood about, waiting. One of them, an older man with a bald patch, and a beer belly that must make the annual physical a challenge, pulled a packet of cigarettes from his jacket pocket, offered it around.

'No smoking,' Cormac said. 'You're not on a break.' He got an eye-roll for his trouble, but the packet was put away. Cormac decided to call in Peter Fisher. He wanted someone of his own on the ground. Someone he could trust. Fisher was the closest thing he had to that in Galway.

He arrived twenty minutes later, five minutes after the technical bureau had arrived and started to set up shop. Fisher was in jeans, boots, a T-shirt. He pulled a jumper over his head as he approached.

'Did I pull you away from a date?' Cormac asked.

'Only with my PlayStation,' Fisher said. He tried to flatten hair that was two inches longer than it needed to be, then gave it up. 'What have we got?'

They both turned in the direction of the taped-off scene, where technicians were setting up bigger and brighter lights, and camera flashes were already going off. In a couple of minutes they would position a tent over the body, but first came the photographs. Dr Yvonne Connolly, the assistant state pathologist, was standing off to the side.

'A young woman, a hit-and-run, but based on the tyre tracks it's murder,' Cormac said. 'They hit her once, took her down, then turned their vehicle and ran her over, made sure of her. Severe injuries. Facial disfigurement.'

They took a couple of steps closer to the scene. Fisher looked it over, his face tight.

'No handbag,' he said.

Cormac nodded. 'No sign of a handbag, or laptop bag, or book bag. If she's a student you'd expect her to have something with her.'

'Do we think she's a student?'

Cormac hesitated. 'The witness who found the body thought she recognised the cardigan the girl is wearing. It's designer, apparently. Expensive.'

Fisher shrugged. 'Okay. Who are we talking about?'

'Carline Darcy.'

Fisher looked back at him, face blank.

'Granddaughter of John Darcy.'

Fisher shook his head.

Cormac blew out a breath. 'Jesus, read a newspaper once in a while, will you Fisher? Darcy Therapeutics started here, on campus, sixty-odd years ago. John Darcy was a student when he came up with some compound or other that he sold for a fortune. After that he started his own company, built it up so that it's the seventh largest pharma company in the world. More than seven thousand employees worldwide. John Darcy's worth billions.'

'Shite,' Fisher said. He nodded towards the body. 'And you reckon that she's his granddaughter?'

'It's looking likely,' was all Cormac said.

Fisher nodded. His eyes went back to the body. 'The witness will be a good place to start, at least,' he said. 'She just stumbled on the body and happened to recognise a piece of clothing? Sounds dodgy.'

Cormac grimaced. 'Not this time,' he said. 'The witness is my partner. Dr Emma Sweeney. She was here to work at one of the labs. Called me when she found the body.'

There was an infinitesimal delay. Then Fisher said, 'Right.' Another pause. 'And she knew the Darcy girl?'

'Emma works at a Darcy Therapeutics laboratory,' Cormac said shortly. He pointed back up the road. 'The lab is down beside the river. They sponsor her research. She was introduced to Carline Darcy. Saw her in the labs from time to time, but didn't know her well.'

'Right,' said Fisher again, nodding.

They fell silent for a long moment. Cormac was conscious that he had sounded defensive. The sooner he could move the case forward, the better. Forensics would confirm that Emma's car was clean. A little bit of short-term awkwardness was a small price to pay to keep the case.

'I need to get back to the station,' Cormac said. 'I want you to stay here and manage the scene. As soon as Connolly gives the okay I want the girl's pockets checked. She might have been carrying a phone. If the killer was in a hurry he could have missed it.'

Fisher nodded his agreement. He cast a glance towards the library, then around the near-empty car park. 'Is it me or is it weirdly quiet here tonight?'

Cormac nodded. 'The whole place seems shut down. We'll need to find out why.'

Cormac took his leave of Fisher, commandeered the keys to one of the squad cars from a uniform, and set out. He was intent on getting to the station but at the last minute found himself taking the turn for Canal Road and pulling in outside the little house he shared with Emma.

The house was in darkness. Cormac looked at his watch. He'd lost track of time somewhere, it was after midnight. Emma must be in bed. She hadn't called anyone for company, but then, who could she call? Her family were in Dublin, the few friends she had in Galway were work colleagues, not the people you lean on in times of trouble. Cormac sat for a moment, drummed his fingers on the steering wheel. Emma was probably already asleep, or trying to get there. He'd nothing new to tell her. Christ. Why did this have to happen now? Why did it have to be Emma who stumbled across the body? She'd put her life back together after all she'd been through, but it hadn't been an easy journey, and her nightmares, a constant presence in the early days of their relationship, had only recently fallen away.

But Emma being at the lab so late was nothing new. She'd always worked long hours, always been dedicated to her job, and their move to Galway the year before had done nothing to change that. They'd moved for Emma's job. She'd been headhunted by John Darcy himself. He was familiar with her work – she was a research scientist, a designer specialising in cutting-edge biotechnology – and he'd argued that only Darcy Therapeutics could offer her the environment she needed to make the kind of breakthrough she was capable of. Other pharma companies were either too small to carry the cost, or so big that corporate processes would slow her down.

Emma had wanted it badly, had been ecstatic when Cormac said he would support her, move with her, but he'd always wondered how much of her enthusiasm was rooted in a wish to get away from Dublin, to get away from everything that had happened there. Cormac had played down to Emma the degree to which he'd been sidelined in Mill Street over the past year. He hadn't wanted her to worry, hadn't wanted to disturb the stability they'd managed to establish in Galway. And now here she was, smack in the middle of another trauma. If they were lucky this case would pass over quickly, at least as far as Emma was concerned. He found himself hoping that the dead girl wasn't Carline Darcy, that she was instead a stranger with no connection to Emma's lab. Emma could give her statement about finding the body and that would be the end of her involvement.

Cormac had just about decided not to wake her, to continue on into the station, when his phone rang. Fisher's name flashed up on the screen, and Cormac answered it.

'It's Darcy all right,' Fisher said. 'The pathologist had a quick look at her, then they turned her, checked her pockets. No phone, no wallet, but she had an ID tucked deep into her back pocket. Some sort of security swipe with her photo and her name. The killer must have missed it. It's a small card.'

Christ. He'd have to call Murphy at home.

'Is there an address?' Cormac asked.

'Not on the ID,' Fisher said. 'But I ran a search. She lived at 1 Harbour View, Dock Road, Galway.'

Dock Road was city centre, a few minutes' drive from the station. Cormac pulled away from the kerb and headed that way. He called Murphy on his way. Cormac didn't like him, was all but convinced that Murphy was corrupt. There had been hints, suggestions that Murphy might be dirty when Cormac had first arrived at the station, but in the year since Cormac hadn't seen him put a foot wrong. He was political, sure, and he kept Cormac on way too tight a leash, but he seemed to run a clean station.

Murphy was at home when Cormac rang, had obviously been asleep, and asked only a few questions. He said nothing about Cormac being on the case. His only concern was notifying the Darcy family, before the media started circling and Twitter made the notification for them.

'I'm heading to the girl's apartment now, sir,' Cormac said. 'Possibly there's someone there who'll be able to identify her body, though her face was badly disfigured. I don't know if she had any distinguishing marks. We might have to wait on dental records, possibly even DNA.'

'Do what you can as quickly as possible,' Murphy said. 'If it has to be DNA it will be fast-tracked. I want a call from you the moment you have confirmation.' Murphy hung up without another word, and Cormac drove on.

It was nearly one a.m. but it might as well have been early morning; any tiredness had been burned off by the adrenaline rush of having a live case again. He dialled Fisher's number, waited for him to answer.

'I want you back at the station,' Cormac said. 'Get the case room set up. We're not likely to get much done tonight, but I want it ready to go for the morning. Grab a few bodies if you need help. I'm going to the address now, to see if there's someone there who can confirm the ID so we can notify the family.'

'Yeah, no problem. On the way.'

'And Fisher? See if you can track down whoever's been working with Carrie O'Halloran on the Henderson case. I'm taking it over and I want a briefing on that too, first thing.'

Cormac got off the call quickly, focused on what he might find at Carline's home. He was hoping for at least one roommate. If she'd lived alone he would need her family's permission to enter the property. A roommate would have information, could consent to him looking around, maybe picking up a toothbrush or hairbrush for DNA. If he was exceptionally lucky, said roommate would be able to describe a birthmark or tattoo that could identify the body. Murphy wasn't likely to wait on DNA before getting the news out to John Darcy.

CHAPTER FOUR

Cormac pulled up outside the apartment block. Harbour View. He didn't recall seeing the structure before, had a vague memory that 1950s terraces had once occupied the space to the right of the Dockgate building. They were gone now, replaced by an ultramodern apartment building, all oversized glass windows and wood-look composite panelling. Cormac parked directly outside, noting the clearway sign that wouldn't be in force for another few hours. There were two young fellas smoking outside. They looked up at his approach but didn't break from their conversation, which seemed to involve a considered, if drunken, discussion about whether the taller of them should try his luck with some girl named Rebecca, or settle for Ailbhe, who was more of a sure thing. The main door to the apartment building, an impressive-looking creation that stood a good four feet higher than Cormac's own six feet three inches, had been wedged open with a hurley; the smokers, probably, holding the door open so they could return to the ever fortunate Ailbhe.

Cormac entered the hall and went straight to the lift. The button for each floor had a little brass plaque off to the side, listing the apartment numbers. Apartment 1 was the only apartment listed for the fourth floor. He pressed the button, and the lift started its ascent. Cormac ran through possible approaches to the conversation ahead as the lift climbed. Notifying family members and close friends of the death of loved ones was never easy, but he had become removed from the process as the years had gone by. More than once he had watched a family member fall into believable paroxysms of grief, only to find some days later that the grieving sister, or brother, or parent was the one who had wielded the axe. Cormac understood the importance of holding on to his humanity in this job that could so easily burn it out of you, but he approached notifications now with his compassion tightly zipped and antennae raised.

The apartment door was directly opposite the lift. Cormac knocked, and waited, then knocked again. After a delay of some minutes, the door was opened by one of the most beautiful girls he had ever seen. She looked like someone who had just come in from an evening out – her face was still made up and she was wearing fitted jeans with a black silk shirt. She didn't look Irish – maybe Italian, South-American? Her skin was light brown, her hair very dark. When she spoke it was with a south county Dublin, private school accent.

'What?' she said. As she took Cormac in her initial irritation gave way to interest. 'Oh. I thought you were those guys from downstairs. They're having another party.'

'Detective Inspector Cormac Reilly,' said Cormac, holding out his ID and giving the girl time to look it over before he put it back in his pocket. 'I'm afraid I have some bad news.' He paused to give her a moment to take in his presence and what it might mean. 'May I come in?'

She hesitated, then stepped back, opening the door wide and leading him into an unexpectedly large open-plan space, with floor to ceiling windows that looked out over the harbour. It was still dark, so he could see little of the sail boats that he knew were moored directly below, but the working lights at the coal yard on the north-eastern boundary of the docks were lit up, so that there was a distant view of a coal barge unloading its cargo. The apartment looked nothing like any student digs he had ever seen. Everywhere he looked, from the polished concrete floor to the designer light fittings, he saw money.

The girl stood a little awkwardly in the centre of the room. She tucked her fingers into the pockets of her jeans. 'Sorry,' she said. 'What can I do for you? I'm Valentina by the way. Vee.'

'I understand this is Carline Darcy's apartment?'

'Yes.' A lightly furrowed brow.

'I'm sorry to have to inform you that a girl carrying Carline's identification was involved in an accident this evening.' He paused, giving her a moment before he continued. 'Her injuries were very severe, and she did not survive.' It was brutal. Every time it was brutal. Delivering those words felt more like an assault than if he'd reached out and punched the girl.

'What?' The furrowed brow deepened to a frown.

'We need someone to help us identify the body. To confirm that it was Carline who died.' Cormac kept his voice gentle. 'You, or perhaps a boyfriend, someone who knew Carline very well. If there's someone who could describe any birthmarks she may have had, or provide us with her hairbrush or toothbrush. Anything you could do to help us confirm identification.'

The girl looked back at him blankly, obviously not taking it in.

'Is there someone I can call for you, Valentina? Someone who can be with you through this?' Cormac asked.

The girl paused for a long moment, then held up one finger in a *wait please* gesture, and turned on her heel. She walked barefoot to another door at the far end of the room, knocked and entered without waiting. The door swung shut behind her. Cormac heard the faintest murmur of voices from the other room, before Valentina reappeared.

'You've made a mistake,' she said. A second girl emerged from the room behind her. About the same age, twenty or so, but blonde this time, and blue-eyed. She wore a silk dressing gown, which she belted as she entered the room.

A second before she spoke, Cormac realised what was coming.

'I'm Carline Darcy,' she said. 'Can I help you?'

The tension Cormac was carrying between his shoulder blades ratcheted up another notch. He looked from the blonde to Valentina and back again, but it was evident that she was telling the truth.

'Miss Darcy,' he said, 'I'm Detective Sergeant Cormac Reilly. Earlier tonight a young woman was killed in what appears to have been a hit-and-run. She was carrying an ID with your name in her back pocket. It seemed that the young woman might have been you. I came here to try to find someone to confirm the identification. I'm very glad to find you alive and well.' Cormac let his voice trail off.

Carline exchanged glances with Valentina. 'I don't understand. You thought it was me?'

'Yes.' Cormac hesitated. 'The young woman's injuries made her difficult to identify.' He was choosing his words carefully, but Carline paled. She knotted her fingers in the drawstrings of her dressing gown.

'Did you give your student ID to another student for any reason?' Cormac asked.

Carline opened her mouth to answer but turned at the sound of a mobile phone ringtone coming from her bedroom. Without explanation or excuse, Carline disappeared into her room, closing her door behind her. Cormac waited in silence, and heard the ringtone stop and the sound of Carline's voice from within.

'What did she look like? The girl who died?' Valentina asked.

Carline's door opened again before he could respond.

'Yes, Mother. The police are here now. I told you, a detective. No, I don't know his name.' She looked straight at Cormac. 'Yes, I'll call him.' A pause. 'I said I'll call him, okay? Yes, tonight.'

She hung up. 'Someone called my grandfather. Was it you?' There was irritation in her voice, but distress too.

'I'd imagine it was the superintendent,' Cormac said.

'I don't understand how this could happen. Don't you have procedures for this sort of thing? How can you ... how can you notify family of someone's death before you're even sure who has died?'

Cormac silently cursed Murphy for his busy phone calls.

'I understand that this is very upsetting. But in cases where there is significant disfigurement we are obliged to contact family members, to ask their help so that we can identify the body. We might need a DNA sample, for example, to rule a missing person in or out of our inquiry.'

'I'm not a missing person,' she said, her voice sharp.

'Did you give your ID to a friend? To another student?' He'd already asked the question, and hadn't missed the fact that she hadn't answered it.

Carline shook her head. 'No. Though I lost an ID at the beginning of the academic year. Some time around October I think.'

He paused. 'And you reported it missing?'

'To the gardaí you mean? I would have been laughed out of the station. I'd imagine twenty a week go missing.'

Carline had regained her composure. She was still pale, but looked more sure of her ground.

'Okay,' he said. 'You'll understand that we need to identify this girl as quickly as possible. If there's anything you know that is relevant, either of you, now is the time to tell me.'

'I'm not in the habit of lying to the police, detective. I didn't give my student ID to anyone, and I have no idea who that girl may have been.' Carline hesitated. 'Didn't she have anything else with her? A phone or a bag, a computer or something? Something that would help you identify her?'

'I'm afraid not,' Cormac said. He made a show of taking out his notebook, opening it, and reading from his notes. 'Do you own a long blue cardigan, lined with purple silk, made by Stella McCartney?' He didn't miss the quick look of surprise Valentina shot at Carline, though she tried to hide it a moment later with a theatrical yawn.

'I don't believe so,' said Carline.

He waited, allowing the silence to spin out, waiting for her to backtrack, to elaborate, to stumble. But she compressed her lips in an unconscious manifestation of her internal self-control and said nothing. At the same moment, a door on the other side of the kitchen opened and a young man came out. He was pulling a T-shirt on over his head, looked half-asleep. He came to a standstill in the middle of the kitchen, only belatedly realising that Cormac was there. He stood, bemused, looking back and forth between Cormac and Carline.

'What's going on?' he asked.

Valentina turned to him. 'There's been an accident. A girl died.' Then, to Cormac, 'This is Mark Wardle, our other roommate.'

'It's nothing to do with us,' Carline said quickly. 'No one we know.'

'An accident?' Mark said. 'What sort of accident?' He took a couple of steps in Carline's direction, positioned himself to the front and slightly to the side of her. The boyfriend, maybe? He was a good-looking guy, tall, in good shape, but with a weak chin. Carline shifted slightly away, a suggestion of irritation in her expression. Not the boyfriend then.

Cormac turned to Valentina. 'What about you? Do you own a cardigan that fits that description?'

44

'Stella's not really my style,' she said. 'I'm more into Adam Selman. I like a bit of edge to my clothes, you know?' Another look at Carline. 'If the drama's over for tonight, I'm going to bed. Things to do in the morning.'

Cormac made no objection. Now was not the time to press her. He was going to talk to Valentina again, but next time without Carline in the room.

'You're sure? About the cardigan?' he said to Carline.

'What accident, Carline?' Mark said again. He crossed his arms and looked like he expected an answer. Carline ignored him, addressed herself to Cormac.

'I'm sure,' she said. She looked at her watch then – discreet, gold faced, leather strap, it had probably cost more than his yearly salary. 'I'm very sorry to hear about the accident, detective, but if you have any other questions perhaps they can wait until tomorrow? Valentina's right, it's late, and I have an early commitment.'

Cormac thought about pushing her further. Then about the shit that would undoubtedly hit the fan when this evening's mess came to light. He was on the back foot because of the screw up with the ID. If Carline knew something about the dead girl, and he thought she did, he wouldn't get it out of her without some leverage. It was time to retreat and regroup.

CHAPTER FIVE

Carline shut the door on the detective, and turned to face Mark. Valentina emerged from her bedroom, eyes sparking. 'Shiiit.' Valentina drew the word out. 'What a screw-up. Your grandfather is going to lose it.'

Mark was still standing in the middle of the room, arms crossed, disapproval all over his face.

Carline turned and went to the kitchen, took a cup from the cupboard and flicked the kettle on. 'Please,' she said. There was no shake in her voice. She concentrated on that, and on keeping her face smooth and unconcerned. This was just someone's administrative screw-up. Nothing to do with her.

'What's going on?' Mark asked.

'You don't think he's upset? Someone just called him to tell him his granddaughter is dead, and you think he's going to be completely chill?' Valentina said.

Carline shook her head, took a lemon from the fridge and sliced it neatly. Valentina sat on the arm of the couch, letting her pedicured toes brush lightly on the floor. Her toenails were painted scarlet, the polish shining as if still wet.

'What's going on?' Mark asked again. 'Carline?'

'It's nothing. There was an accident. A girl died, and she had my ID in her pocket. The police thought it might be me, and somebody called my grandfather.'

'Jesus,' Mark said. 'Who was it? Who had your ID?'

Carline didn't look at him. She refused to catch his eye, looked at Valentina instead. 'Can we not make a thing of this? Please? It's bad enough that my grandfather heard about it without you two making a drama as well.'

Valentina's eyes were bright as she watched Carline move around the kitchen. She knew Carline had lied about the cardigan and she would want to know why.

'Any news on your big night out? Isn't it next Thursday? Have you decided where you are going for dinner?' Carline asked.

Valentina's eyes narrowed. 'Did you know her?' she asked.

'Who?' Carline sipped from her cup. Her hand was completely steady.

'The girl who died, obviously. She was wearing your cardigan – you have a Stella one just like that, don't you? Who is she? Did you give her your ID?'

'Please. It wasn't my cardigan, or if it was I must have off-loaded it at some stage. A charity shop maybe. Actually, that probably explains the ID. I might have left it in a pocket.' Valentina didn't look convinced and it dawned on Carline that she'd already told the detective that she'd lost the ID at the beginning of the year. Valentina would have seen her wear the cardigan in the last few weeks. Christ, she was tying herself up into knots. She needed a minute to herself to get her head straight.

'People do, you know. Lend their IDs I mean. To a friend not in college who wants to use the computer labs. Or to an underage friend who wants to get into a club.' Valentina was watching her so carefully. Mark was just standing there like a great lump. She should never have agreed to him moving into the apartment.

Carline let out a small laugh. 'My ID has an electronic key to the labs. I'm hardly going to hand that around to just anyone.'

'Was it that ID then?' Valentina asked. 'I didn't think he'd said. I thought he just meant your standard University ID. The same one issued to the rest of us plebs.'

'I suppose it might have been,' Carline said. Jesus. She took another sip from her tea, then made a face. 'Yuck,' she said. 'This is off.' She dumped the rest of the cup into the sink, then turned to walk towards her bedroom. 'I'm going back to bed,' she said. 'Exams next week.'

Valentina's voice followed her. 'As if you need to worry about that.'

Carline laughed as if Valentina's words had been intended as a compliment and waved over her shoulder as she disappeared into her room, horribly conscious of her roommates' eyes on her, every step of the way.

Saturday 26 April 2014

CHAPTER SIX

It was very late by the time Cormac finally found his way to bed and although his mind was busy with plans for the following day he fell asleep as soon as his head hit the pillow. He'd always found sleep easy to come by. The same, unfortunately, could not be said for Emma. He woke with a sinking feeling just after 3 a.m., his subconscious recognising what was happening before he was fully awake. Emma was tossing and turning, murmuring distressed snatches of a one-sided conversation. Cormac sat up in the bed. He hated seeing her like this. She was sleeping, but she was afraid. He thought about waking her, knew that he shouldn't – if he did she wouldn't sleep again for the rest of the night. Instead he did what he always did, just stayed awake, watched over her, put his hand on her shoulder and kept it there. Eventually she fell into a more restful sleep.

Cormac leaned back against the headboard, looked at Emma in the dull light of the streetlamps that crept in between the curtains, and struggled with a sudden and unexpected resentment. He had thought this was behind them. He wanted to throw himself heart and soul into his work, and not be distracted by other responsibilities. Emma murmured again, but softly this time as she turned and reached for him, even in her sleep. Cormac closed his eyes. Christ. He was a shit.

It may have been guilt, or it may have been thoughts of the case, but something kept him awake until just before dawn when, predictably, he fell into a deep sleep. The sound of the hairdryer coming from the next room woke him just after eight. Cormac got out of bed, used the loo and went looking for Emma. He found her in the kitchen, pouring a coffee into a go-cup.

'You're heading out?' He leaned against the door jam, yawned.

Emma looked a little guilty. 'I figured you'd be working. With what happened last night, and everything. My article was due yesterday, so I thought I'd go into the lab and finish it off.'

'You're not tired?' Cormac asked.

She grabbed her coat from the back of the kitchen chair, kissed him and kept moving. 'Not a bit,' she said. 'If you finish by lunchtime will you give me a call?

'Emma,' he said.

'Yes?' She'd turned in the doorway, stood looking back at him.

'You sure you're all right?'

She hesitated. 'I'm trying not to think about it. I just … want to get on with things, you know?'

Cormac nodded. She smiled at him as she left, and he felt a bit easier about things. He showered, ate toast and drank coffee standing up in the kitchen. He decided to walk to the station. He could pick up a marked car when he got there, and the walk would give him time to work through the events of the night before.

Fisher either had excellent timing or he'd been keeping an eye out of the window for Cormac's arrival. He met Cormac on the stairs.

'The case room's all sorted. I took the room upstairs, the big one. It's booked for the next few weeks. I also got the files for the cases you're taking over. Durkan, Henderson, Nesbitt.'

'Right,' Cormac nodded.

'The super's aide had all the information. I just asked her.'

Cormac started towards the squad room.

'All right,' he said. 'Get Ceri Walsh on the Durkan and Nesbitt files. Tell her I want her to brief me as soon as she gets through them. There's an interview on the Henderson case today so I'll concentrate on getting up to speed on that. But other than that, our first priority is to identify the victim of last night's hit-and-run.'

'Is there any chance I can get the Henderson case?' Fisher asked.

Cormac gave him a look. Fisher wasn't asking to play a bit part; he wanted a leading role. 'Who was DS O'Halloran's second on it before now?'

Fisher grimaced. 'Moira Hanley.'

'Right. Well if she's available, I'll be taking Hanley. It's nothing personal, Fisher, but Hanley's been on it from the beginning. Another change in personnel would be too high risk at this stage.'

Fisher nodded, said nothing. Another few steps and he'd perked up. 'What's the next step on the hit-and-run? Did you find someone to confirm the ID, or are we looking for dental records?'

'It wasn't the Darcy girl. I met her myself last night, alive and well. She claims she never gave her ID to anyone, but she did lose one at the beginning of the year. She says she knows nothing about the victim.'

'Right,' said Fisher. 'That must have been a bit of a shocker. You think she's lying?'

'Maybe. Maybe not. I didn't spend enough time with her to get a read either way. For now, I just want to get the team up and running. I'll want five. You're my second. Moira Hanley can join the team for this one too, I think, in a supportive role. I'll talk to her now and see. I'll take McCarthy if I can get him.' Dave McCarthy was older. Had fifteen years on Cormac. He could be a grumpy fucker but he knew his way around a case.

'For the other two I'll take your recommendation. I want people who'll work the hours and not worry about overtime. But I want workers, all right? I don't want any politicians. Nobody trying to prove themselves or just make it up another rung on the ladder, do you get me?'

Fisher nodded, slowly. Cormac could tell that he was wondering if the last was a jibe aimed at him. Fisher had a bit of a reputation for ambition.

'Look, I need people with judgement on this case. No one who's going to do something rash just to get their name up on the board,' Cormac said.

Fisher nodded again, this time with a little more confidence.

'When the team's in place send one of them to relieve the lads who are guarding the scene. Once I've spoken to Hanley I'll want you two out knocking on doors.' Cormac checked his watch. It was just after nine. 'Get the door to door started, but don't take Hanley. I'll need her for the Henderson interview. That's at eleven-thirty – we'll do a case briefing immediately after. Got it?'

Fisher nodded.

'Start at the entrance to Distillery Road,' Cormac said. 'I don't know if any of those houses are still occupied, now I think of it. They might all be taken over by the college.'

'We'll check,' said Fisher. 'And after that we'll do Newcastle Road, door to door.'

'All right. Any problems, I'll want to know.'

Five minutes after Cormac left Fisher he was standing in Murphy's office, called there by an aide. The Superintendent eyed him from behind his desk, then, belatedly, nodded towards one of the seats opposite. Cormac sat. It was harder to take Murphy seriously in lycra shorts and top emblazoned with purple and yellow stripes and numerous screaming brand names, as if he were an in-his-cheating-prime Lance Armstrong, rather than a middle-aged, pasty-legged Irishman. Not that he was in bad shape. The guy was obsessed with what he ate, obsessed with the hours he logged every day, measuring and recording every heartbeat, every calorie consumed. Cormac, on the other hand, was vaguely aware that his waistbands had grown a little tighter since his arrival in Galway. He was pretty sure he could blame it on the weather. When it rained constantly, comfort food and a pint in a warm pub were infinitely more inviting than a run.

'Going for a cycle, sir?'

Murphy couldn't help himself. 'Galway to Spiddal by way of Moycullen,' he said.

Cormac sometimes wondered if Murphy exaggerated the whole fitness-fanatic persona so that people would underestimate him. It was so over the top. He had a signed picture of Stephen Roche winning the Tour de France on the wall, for fuck's sake. A bunch of others showing Murphy himself crossing various finishing lines. Nobody liked a self-promoter; it wasn't the Irish way. But while people were busy sniggering and exchanging glances, Murphy could watch and observe and take note of the shifting alliances in his squad room.

'Good route,' Cormac said, nodding.

'Cycled it, have you?'

'Not yet.' And never would.

'Talk to me about the interview with the Darcy girl. What's your read on her?'

'She said she lost an ID at the beginning of the school year, had to have it replaced. Said she had no idea who the girl was. But the witness who found the body thought she recognised the cardigan the girl was wearing. Apparently it's designer, very expensive, and not something you'd pick up on the high street. Not many Galway students would be able to afford it. Witness said she thought she saw Carline Darcy wearing it.' He'd made the decision not to mention Emma at the last minute. He didn't want her anywhere on Murphy's radar.

Murphy was watching and listening in a way that Cormac found disconcerting, if only because it was so different from his usual lack of attention during Cormac's bi-weekly cold case updates. At those meetings he was treated to a range to keyboard tapping, pencil rolling, and unconnected document examination, designed, Cormac thought, to let him know in what low regard he was held. Now Murphy hung on his every word.

'Darcy could have donated the cardigan, or given it to a friend. Girl that wealthy wouldn't consider the cost of the thing,' said Murphy.

Cormac nodded. It was a reasonable suggestion.

'If Darcy lost her ID at the beginning of the year, the suggestion is what? That this girl found it and has been carrying it around ever since? What for?'

'I don't know yet, sir. You need an ID to access certain parts of campus. Possibly you may be able to use them to access computer time, or pay for photocopying. Carline Darcy may not be the type to notice small debits on her college account. Or it might be as simple as an underage girl coming across the ID, or stealing it, and using it to get into bars and clubs.'

'You felt the Darcy girl was cooperative?'

'Yes sir. No issues there,' said Cormac. He didn't blink, made sure his tone conveyed absolute sincerity. He'd been around long enough to know that Murphy would be keen to avoid any tension with a family as powerful and connected as the Darcys.

Murphy drummed his fingers on the table for the first time. 'What are your next steps?'

'Identify the body. I have some uniforms checking the missing persons registers. I want some door-stepping in

Newcastle – the houses on Distillery Road are unoccupied, they've been taken over by the college, but there are homes on the Lower Newcastle Road and someone might have seen or heard something. I'll need to talk to the university president too. Find out exactly why the university was closed last night, if there was anything on that the girl could have been coming to or going from.'

Murphy's nod of dismissal was clear enough. As Cormac stood, he spoke. 'You won't need to see the Darcy girl again?' He threw the question out like an afterthought, but Cormac knew that this question was the point of the meeting. If Murphy thought for a second that Cormac had Carline Darcy in his sights, he'd whip the case out from under him.

'No sir.' Cormac's answer was delivered in precisely the same offhand manner.

Murphy didn't acknowledge the answer, but it was certainly noted. 'I'm told your girlfriend found the body.'

'Yes.' Shit. Cormac's mouth felt dry. Which of his team had come running with the news? Not Fisher. And Carrie had her hands full at home. Beyond that it could have been anyone. There wasn't a uniform in the place that owed him any loyalty – a year spent generating paperwork on cold-case files hadn't given him much opportunity to earn that yet – and Emma's presence hadn't been a secret.

Murphy was watching him with those dead eyes of his, giving nothing away. 'Forensics also tell me that her car was clean. No damage, no traces of blood. It seems she was in the wrong place at the wrong time. Unfortunate. I'm sure the experience was upsetting.'

'Yes, sir.' As always, Cormac was left wondering exactly what Murphy knew.

'Keep me informed,' Murphy said.

'Of course, sir,' Cormac said. He nodded once and took his leave.

CHAPTER SEVEN

The Henderson case had been talked about enough around the station that Cormac had picked up the basics. Rob Henderson was a married father of three children, the oldest a fifteen-year-old boy, the youngest still a baby. Rob was a bank clerk, his wife Lucy a nurse. The trouble started with the fifteen-year-old at school. A quiet child and a good student, he'd suddenly started acting up, and at a level the school had trouble dealing with. After a day on which he'd picked a fight with two older boys, and been found stealing from the school canteen, the guidance counsellor had called him in for a meeting and the boy had broken down. He'd confessed to being afraid of his father, and worried for his mother and sisters. After that he'd clammed up.

The guidance counsellor had been concerned enough that she'd called it in to the police. Moira Hanley was on duty. She took a drive out to the house, where she found Rob Henderson climbing about on the roof. When Hanley called him, he didn't come down. He claimed to be making repairs but to Hanley he seemed nervous, agitated. When Henderson refused her second request to come down and talk, she walked to the back of the house, where she saw a set of industrial gas canisters stacked against the wall, rigged up to what looked like a DIY piping system. Further examination found that the ground floor vents had been blocked with expandable insulating foam. The canisters were clearly marked – the gas was carbon monoxide. Hanley called in back-up, and when Henderson was eventually persuaded off the roof, he was arrested and charged with attempted murder.

Cormac worked his way through the file, reading every witness statement, every interview transcript. It took time. The case was only a couple of weeks old but Carrie was nothing if not thorough. Her notes told Cormac that Henderson had been denied bail, and was decompressing entirely while in custody. The speed of his disintegration was such that it was hard to believe he'd been functioning normally or even quasi-normally before his arrest. Which raised an obvious question – had Lucy Henderson known of his plan? Had she been complicit? If it had been some sort of murder–suicide pact, the children could still be at risk.

'Sir? You asked for me?'

Cormac looked up to see Moira Hanley standing beside his desk. They were in the squad room. Everyone worked open plan in Galway, only the Superintendent had a private office. Cormac had no problem with it. The layout worked well enough, encouraged communication, even if the relatively close proximity of thirty other gardaí got old from time to time. On that particular day the coffee machine was working overtime, and the smell of coffee almost overwhelmed the ever-present odour of stale gym gear.

'Moira.' Cormac gestured to her to take the empty chair to his right. She sat, her eyes on the file in his hands. Hanley was in her late forties, heavy-set with a face that gave nothing away.

'You know I've taken over the Henderson case?'

'Carrie called me. I mean, DS O'Halloran. Sir, Lucy Henderson just phoned the station. She said she's not going to make it in for her interview today. Claims she has food poisoning.'

Cormac blew out a breath. 'Does she?'

'Hard to know. She didn't sound great on the phone, but that's an easy fake.'

Putting the interview off for a day or two shouldn't be the end of the world – it would give him a bit more time to prepare. The problem was, he wasn't sure of the degree to which he should be worried about the kids. Lucy Henderson had been no assistance to the inquiry so far. Based on the interview transcripts she was in complete denial about her husband's actions. But what if it wasn't just a bad case of denial? If Lucy Henderson had had some sort of murder–suicide pact with her husband, it would explain her silence.

'Where are the kids?' Cormac asked. 'Are they with their mother?'

'The Henderson kids?' If Moira was surprised by the question it didn't show on her face. 'They're at home.'

'Still living with their mother?'

Moira grimaced. 'DS O'Halloran wasn't keen on the idea. She wanted them taken into care until we could get to the bottom of things. But Tusla didn't agree. They said there was no evidence that Lucy presented a risk to the children. In the end Lucy's sister moved into the house to keep an eye on things. That was the compromise. And social workers are going in every day.' Tusla was the Child and Family Agency. Newly formed out of an amalgamation of the old Children and Family Services, the Family Support Agency and the National Educational Welfare Board, it remained to be seen if it was any less dysfunctional.

'Right.' He didn't like the sound of the arrangement, but there wasn't a lot he could do, and he needed to get moving on the hit-and-run case. 'We won't call her in for another formal interview. We'll go to the house first thing Monday instead. Take her by surprise. Get her just after she's dropped the older kids at school. Come with coffee in hand – we're just here for a chat. Thought we'd save you the bother of the drive. Sit in the living room with the baby playing on the floor. Get her on her own ground and she might be a bit more relaxed. I take it the gas has been disconnected?'

Moira nodded. 'An engineer went out with forensics and took the whole thing apart so it couldn't be used. Henderson had been working on it for weeks. Jesus, can you imagine what was going on in his mind? Sick bastard. His own kids.' She curled her lip.

'What does Lucy have to say about it? What did she think he was doing?' Cormac knew the answer the file would give him, but he wanted to hear it from Moira Hanley.

'He told her he was putting in a gas connection for a new fireplace. Showed her the model he supposedly ordered on the internet and everything. She says she was surprised, he wasn't usually handy. But she claims to have believed him.'

'What about the boy?'

'His name's Fearghal. We haven't been able to interview him yet. He's had a Guardian ad Litem appointed by the court, and the guardian says he's too distressed to be interviewed. But she also told me, off the record, that Fearghal figured out what his father was planning, saw the canisters and Googled the label, realised what was in them. Now he feels guilty that his father might spend the rest of his life in prison because of him.'

'Christ. Poor kid. We'll need to get him in though.'

Moira shrugged, as if the issue were out of her hands. It irritated Cormac, that passivity.

'I'd like to keep you on the case, Hanley. I know you work closely with DS O'Halloran as a general rule, and I don't want to take you from that work, but I need someone who's been on this case from the beginning.'

She nodded, a little warily. 'Yes sir. I'd like to see it through.'

'Excellent. I'll talk to Carrie, make sure there's no problem there. You working anything else right now?'

She shook her head. 'Nothing that needs ongoing attention.'

'Right. I've a fresh case, a deliberate hit-and-run. I'm putting a small team around it and I'd like you on that too, if you want it.'

She nodded again, a bit dubiously, and he thought about the clock-watching, but he wanted to know if she was any good, and the best way to find that out with anyone was to pile on a bit of pressure and see how they responded.

'Right, case conference as soon as possible so. Fisher is my second on it, talk to him and get up to speed.'

CHAPTER EIGHT

The case room was on the third floor of the building. The four windows along the western wall gave a less than spectacular view of grey skies and sodden car park. The floor was faded blue industrial carpet. There was an old-fashioned whiteboard, and several noticeboards were nailed to the walls, the boards scarred from a thousand pins. Despite the general shabbiness there was a sense of privilege in the room, the excitement that was common to every major case room Cormac had ever run. This was what it was all about. Every cop in the building, whether they'd admit it or not, wanted to work the big cases, the ones that mattered.

The meeting had been called for noon and the last of the uniforms arrived as Cormac took his place at the top of the room.

'Right,' said Cormac. 'We don't have a lot of time so let's get going. We'll do a brief run-through of what we have. We won't have time to explain anything twice so pay attention and take notes.' He paused. 'That being said, if you do miss something or don't understand it, don't for God's sake leave this room without talking to Fisher first.'

Fisher muttered something that caused a ripple of humour through the room. Cormac ignored it. He pointed David McCarthy towards a stack of photographs sitting on one of the desks.

'Dave – let's get those up while we talk.' McCarthy took the photographs and handed them off to a much younger uniform, who stood immediately and started pinning them up. All eyes turned to watch as first one, then a second, then multiple crime scene photographs were separated from the bundle and pinned. Seeing the photographs in this context, pinned to a noticeboard in a case room, took some of the horror from them. It was easier to focus on what they were there to do, rather than the brutality of what had been done to the victim. Nevertheless, the mood in the room settled down as the photographs went up.

Cormac nodded to Fisher who stood and spoke. 'Victim is unidentified. The autopsy will be carried out on Monday by Dr Connolly. In the meantime, we know that she was aged between eighteen and twenty-five. That hair is dyed, by the way. Natural colour is brown. Cause of death is not yet confirmed, and we'll keep an open mind until it is, but it's almost certainly the case that she was killed due to the impact of the vehicle that ran her over. Time of death is estimated to be between 9 and 10 p.m.'

Cormac stepped forward and pinned up a large diagram showing Distillery Road. 'This is where the body was found,' he said, indicating a point on the sheet. 'Scene of Crime have confirmed that the vehicle entered Distillery Road, took the corner, then accelerated on its approach to the victim. It hit her hard, causing multiple injuries and throwing her into the air. Based on the markings on the ground the thinking is that the car continued on before turning and coming back to hit her again. You can see the extent of her injuries.'

'There were no witnesses to the incident itself, that we know of,' continued Cormac. Then, to Peter Fisher, 'What's the latest on the door to door?'

'Not much. All of the buildings bordering Distillery Road are university owned now. Some of them look like homes, but they're all converted inside, and used as offices or tutorial spaces. We tried the houses on Newcastle Road, but it was too far away. No one heard or saw anything of interest.'

'What about CCTV?' Cormac asked.

'No good. The only cameras in the vicinity are one outside the Centra shop, and one outside the AIB cash machine. I know from a previous case that the Centra camera only picks up activity directly outside the store – it doesn't capture any of the road – and all the cash machine cameras are the same. Straight down views only.'

'I want those followed up on anyway – let's get the footage and review everything.'

'Already requested. Centra will have everything on USB for us to collect this afternoon. The bank won't release the footage without a warrant, but we're working on that.'

'Okay,' said Cormac. 'Moving on then. The body was found by Dr Emma Sweeney at ten-forty p.m. The university was closed last night for reasons yet unknown and the place was much quieter than usual. But Dr Sweeney was going to work at one of the private labs hosted by the university – they have their own security arrangements.' Cormac was conscious of the shift of mood in the room when he mentioned Emma's name. He allowed his eyes to rest briefly on the face of every man and woman in the room as he continued.

'As you're no doubt aware, Dr Sweeney is my girlfriend. There is no suspicion that she is involved in any way, but Fisher will take her statement later today, and Dr Sweeney will be treated as we would treat any other witness. Is that understood?'

Cormac's question provoked a mumbled agreement and another round of exchanged glances. He moved on. 'We'll need to interview everyone who had access to the private labs, to see if the girl had planned to meet someone there.'

'She was carrying an ID,' Fisher volunteered. 'But it wasn't hers.' He handed Cormac a photograph of the white plastic card. 'The original is with scene of crime for testing.'

Cormac took the photograph, examined it. The photograph showed a plain white card, with no date of birth, just a name and a smudged photograph of Carline Darcy on one side. 'This isn't a college ID,' Cormac said. He was aware of sudden tension in his shoulders. 'This is a swipe card, an access card,' he continued. 'Probably for the private lab.' It was exactly the same as Emma's, down to the shitty quality photograph.

'Her bag was gone, her phone, assuming she had one. That was tucked deep into her back pocket. It could have been missed.

'If she had a handbag with her, or a backpack, that's an easy grab and run. Harder to turn a body and search the pockets. It might not have occurred to him. Or he might have been worried about picking up trace,' Cormac said absently, his mind still snagged on the thought that this girl, whoever she had been, had a connection to the place where Emma spent most of each day. Cormac shook his head, forced himself to focus on the task at hand. 'This ID belonged to Carline Darcy. I've interviewed Darcy and she claims to have lost an ID at the beginning of the academic year. She got a replacement and thought no more about it. She also claims to have no knowledge of who the victim might be. Identifying the victim is our first order of business. McCarthy and Hanley, I want you on the missing persons registers. Fisher and the rest of you get working on body shops, just in case the driver is stupid enough to bring the car in for repair.' He paused, glanced around the room. 'Any questions? Anything to add?'

A tentative hand went up at the back of the room. A young garda Cormac didn't recognise, hair cut very tight, the sleeves of his uniform shirt a little too short for his arms.

'I heard there was some kind of asbestos scare at the college. That's why it was closed.'

'Right.' Cormac nodded. The kid looked young enough to be in college himself; he probably had friends who were. 'Your name?'

A flush. 'Rory. Rory Mulcair.'

That brought the meeting to a close, and Cormac gave Fisher a nod to follow before walking out of the case room, down three flights of stairs – the lift in the building was old and painfully slow – and out into the car park.

'Emma said she should be free sometime this afternoon. You'll get her on her mobile if you try her now. She's expecting your call.' He tried to read Fisher's face, wanted to take his temperature.

'Yes sir.' Fisher avoided his gaze. 'Happy for me to go to the house?'

'I think that's best,' said Cormac. 'But see what she says. She might be happy to come in, or might ask you to go to the lab.'

'No bother either way,' said Fisher. And Cormac told himself that this sort of consideration would be extended to any witness. Fisher was still standing there, waiting for further instruction. Was he expecting Cormac to send him down a particular path?

'Look, Fisher, Emma's had a rough couple of years, and this thing might be affecting her more than it should. I'm not suggesting you give her special treatment – I want to you deal with Emma as you would any other witness, all right?' Christ, it was becoming a catch phrase already. *Like any other witness*. Which of course she wasn't. No amount of saying the right thing would change that. 'No special treatment in the interview, ask whatever questions you feel it necessary to ask. But just, let me know if you think she struggles at all, if she gets upset. I'll want to get home and keep an eye on her.'

'No bother, sir,' Fisher said, easy-breezy. 'I'll keep you posted.'

Christ.

Moira Hanley pounced as soon as Fisher got back to the case room. She had been sitting at one of the desks but she swivelled the chair around and sat looking up at him, heavy eyebrows drawn together.

'What's all this stuff doing on the case file?' she asked. She held out a thin bundle of paper and Fisher took them from her automatically, glanced at the top page.

'It's nothing,' he said.

'What's it doing on the case file then?' she asked again, and despite himself Fisher felt his irritation rise.

'It's just background on Carline Darcy. I sent it to the printer from my phone from the scene, before we found out she was still alive.' That was sort of bullshit. He hadn't sent it from the scene, had looked it up afterwards. The bit he'd learnt about her from Reilly had made him curious, that was all. He wasn't going to explain that to Moira Hanley. She was a pain in the arse. Always spoke to him as if he was an idiot. Her problem was that they were the same rank, even though she had twenty years' experience on him. As for that, she only had herself to blame, didn't she?

Hanley gave a minute shake of her head, as if she wasn't fully convinced by the explanation. 'Right, well, you can shred it now, can't you?'

Fisher looked down at the papers in his hand, then turned back to his desk. He'd have to hold on to them now, whether he wanted to or not. It wouldn't do to let Hanley think she could order him about. He'd only gone a few steps when she spoke again.

'What did he say to you?' she asked. 'Reilly, I mean. When he spoke to you outside just now.'

Fisher didn't turn around. 'If he'd wanted to say it to the squad room, he'd have said it to the squad room.' He kept going, returned to his desk, and logged into his screen. He quickly flicked through the forensics evidence that had come through, then found Emma Sweeney's number, and dialled. She sounded happy enough to meet him, but wasn't available until after 5 p.m., so he made arrangements to see her at her home. Only after he'd hung up did it occur to him that there was a solid chance Reilly would walk in the front door before he'd finished the interview. Shite. That would be bloody awkward. The sooner the whole Emma Sweeney thing was put to bed the better. In the meantime he'd better get on with the job. Being Reilly's second meant he had more responsibility, did a bit of extra running, but he didn't get to offload any of the routine stuff. Like every other garda on the team, Fisher had been assigned a list of body shops and garages to work his way through. He made a few calls, got nowhere, and wasn't surprised. The car that hit the girl would be found abandoned and burnt out within the next twenty-four hours, he was ninety per cent sure. Chances were all these phone calls were a waste of time, but then that was the nature of police work. The devil was in all those boring little details. If he'd learned anything from Cormac Reilly, he'd learned that you dot those i's and cross those t's and follow every open lead to see where it might bring you.

Whether due to his feeling that it was all a waste of time, or his tension over the upcoming interview, Fisher was distracted. His attention kept wandering back to the papers he'd taken from Moira Hanley. His research on Carline Darcy. There was always something morbidly fascinating about the super-rich. It was like sniffing at a piece of meat that had been hung a bit too long, that had a taint of rot about it. The Darcy family had billions. It was unnatural, that money like that should be held by just a handful of people when there were people starving, or sleeping on the streets. And Fisher could tell that Reilly didn't think that ID had been a coincidence. If he'd had to bet on it, Fisher would have said that the Darcy girl knew exactly who the victim was, and knew exactly what she was doing at the college last night. He wouldn't go so far as to say that Carline Darcy was the murderer, at least not yet, but he wouldn't rule it out either. Reilly might not have said it out loud, but he had to be thinking the same thing. Peter Fisher put aside his list of body shop phone numbers, pulled his Carline Darcy research closer, and started to read.

CHAPTER NINE

Cormac called the university from the car. He expected to have some difficulty tracking down the president – it was Saturday after all – but instead had the distinct impression that his call was expected. He was told the university president would be happy to meet with him within the hour.

The university campus was a hodgepodge of architectural styles, from the beautiful limestone quadrangle that had opened its doors in 1849 and still featured in college brochures, to the extraordinarily ugly concourse (built in the 1970s and inexplicably backing onto the beautiful River Corrib rather than facing it), to the modern installations. Cormac parked his car in a reserved spot and placed a police sign conspicuously on the dashboard. He took a moment to look around. The campus was going through major renovation, but the area around the quadrangle was peaceful and undisturbed.

Nathan Egan's outer office contained a desk, probably usually occupied by a secretary. When he arrived it was vacant, and the door to his office was ajar. Cormac knocked briefly, and entered. Egan was sitting at his desk, mouse under hand. Two over-sized flatscreen monitors held his attention but he looked up on Cormac's entry.

'Detective Reilly?' he said.

'Thank you for meeting me this afternoon, Professor Egan. I'm sorry to drag you in on a Saturday afternoon.'

'Nathan, please. And you've given me the excuse I needed, I'm afraid.' He smiled with practised charm. 'I need to work today, and weekend disappearances are never very popular at home.'

The man was younger than Cormac had expected, channelling not so much the grizzled academic as the Silicon Valley up-and-comer. He wore a grey blazer over a black button-down shirt and dark jeans.

'I have just a few questions for you, and then I'll let you get on with your day.'

Egan spread his hands in an expansive gesture. 'I'm happy to help, detective. Your superintendent happens to be a friend. He gave me a call and asked me to do what I could to help with what is obviously a priority investigation. Not that I wouldn't have helped without the call, of course.'

Cormac nodded as if he'd known that Murphy had made the call, as if it was par for the course, rather than out of left field. It was rapidly becoming clear that Murphy wouldn't take his eye off this case for a minute.

'Let's start with the closure of the University,' Cormac said. 'How did that come about?'

Egan nodded enthusiastically. 'We're renovating, as I'm sure you know,' he said. 'Well, we're expanding, but the renovation is part of that. Major works on the concourse, but work all over campus. A lot of landscaping work.'

'I was told asbestos was found. Was that in the concourse?'

'I wish. That would have been relatively easy to deal with. No, it was in the landscaping. Wherever the landscaping contractor picked up his mulch – that we are still looking into – it was full of waste material, including small lumps of concrete that apparently contain asbestos. And that mulch has already been spread across half the campus.'

Christ. Cormac thought about the men and women he'd had stationed outside on the other side of campus all night. 'All right,' said Cormac, his tone cool. 'I've got two uniforms who spent the night out there. And two more who've been out there for the past couple of hours. Are you telling me that it's not safe?'

Egan held up his hands in a calming gesture. 'No, detective, sorry, I should have been clear. I understand that the asbestos is completely stable and cannot get airborne. There's no risk to anyone's health.'

'Well that raises an obvious question, doesn't it?'

Egan grimaced. 'Yes, we clearly didn't need to shut the campus down at all. And of course the contractor maintained it was safe from the start. Once he admitted it was there, which took longer than it should have. But the insurers insisted on taking the precaution until testing had been carried out. So we closed the campus for a day, had the testing done, and thankfully confirmed what we expected – there is no trace of asbestos in the air. We're still having the whole lot dug out and removed, which will take about a week.' Egan eyes had glazed over, his mind had gone down a rabbit hole of university planning. 'A major hit for the contractor, but that's what he gets for taking a short cut. And of course we made sure he was well insured and solvent, before we appointed him.' He looked back at Cormac, and spoke more briskly. 'Which isn't always guaranteed, particularly these days.'

'When did you make the decision to close the campus, and how and when did you notify the students?'

'It all happened on Thursday afternoon. The decision was taken by close of business, and an e-bulletin was sent to the students that evening, and again early the following morning.'

'An e-bulletin.' It wasn't exactly a question.

'Yes. An email, basically, to their student email accounts. We also posted a notice on all student electronic noticeboards, and paper copies around campus of course.'

Cormac was taking notes. 'What time did the email go out?'

Egan tapped at his keyboard, clicked something. Cormac couldn't see the screen from where he was sitting, but Egan was able to give him the times – just after 5 p.m. on the Thursday and again at 7 a.m. the following morning – and offered to forward the original email to Cormac.

'I can't give you student email addresses, of course, but you won't expect that.'

Cormac didn't comment. Data protection legislation might be good for human rights, but it was a bastard for police work.

'And just like that, it was enough? Not a student out of how many thousand showed up?'

'Four thousand, six hundred and thirty-four, give or take a recent dropout,' Egan said promptly. 'But yes. It's the emails that do it. Every student has a student email account, and every student has a phone. We manage virtually all the university communication online these days. And I think most of them took it as an excuse for a mini-Rag Week. I'm told many of the off-campus bars and half of the pubs in the city were full by the afternoon. We had people at the campus entrances all day, to keep visitors from straying inside, but I understand that very few students showed up. And once the results came in we took security down too.'

'What time was that at?' Cormac asked.

Egan glanced towards his screens. 'I'll have to check exactly what time they stood down. I know I gave the order around 5 p.m.'

'So some time after security stood down, people could come and go on campus without being challenged. What about college buildings. Did you open those?'

Egan shook his head. 'The concourse would usually have been open until nine, the library twenty-four hours at this time of year, and some of the computer labs until nine p.m., or later by special arrangement of the relevant head of faculty. But the security staff we usually have on to manage the buildings worked extra shifts to manage the crisis. I wasn't willing to ask people to work late that day, so we kept everything shut down until this morning at the usual times.'

'So no one could enter or leave a university building last night? They were completely locked down?'

Egan stood up, pointed to an expensive-looking coffee machine at the side of the room. 'Coffee?' he asked. When Cormac declined Egan made a cup for himself, talking all the time. 'We host a couple of private labs on campus. I understand some of the researchers can access those out of hours. But otherwise, yes, the buildings were completely locked down.'

'The woman who died last night, our initial impression is that she was young – probably late teens or early twenties. There's a strong possibility that she was a student here. She was carrying another student's ID.'

Egan nodded seriously. 'Carline Darcy's.'

Cormac raised an eyebrow. 'Who gave you that information?' he asked baldly. Not Murphy – Cormac was certain he would want to keep talk of a Darcy connection to a minimum.

Egan leaned forward, adopted the mien of someone passing on a confidence to a trusted friend. 'I had a call last night from an associate of John Darcy's. Understandably upset about last night's misunderstanding.' The barest suggestion of irritation from Egan, well hidden. 'Wanted to read me the riot act, I'm afraid. Concerned about campus security. Reasonable, really, given the circumstances.'

Cormac wanted to ask more about the university's relationship with John Darcy and his company, but he didn't want to get sidetracked.

'Our priority now is to identify the girl. Would you know if a student was missing?'

Egan shrugged. 'There's no way to tell, unless someone reports it. We take attendance for tutorials, but not for lectures, and even tutorial attendance is not recorded centrally. If an undergrad misses more than five tutorials their tutor is supposed to notify their lecturer, and the student is given a warning but it's not a process that is strictly followed. And post-grads and PhD students aren't monitored at all.' He paused, glanced again towards his computer screen. 'We have twelve hundred students living in residence at the university, but we don't monitor their comings and goings.'

Something about Egan was irritating Cormac. For all his superficial concern, it was clear that Egan cared only about one thing.

'I'm going to need you to send out another email,' Cormac said. 'Can you ask every student to check on their flatmates, and if someone is missing from last night, to email your office, or this address?' Cormac took a card from his wallet with his email address and number and handed it over. Egan took the card and examined it. 'It really is urgent, Professor Egan. The sooner you send the message the better.' And it was Cormac's turn to glance towards the keyboard.

'I'll send the message, detective, but you do realise last night was Friday night? You're going to get a bunch of emails about friends who will turn out to have gotten lucky at a bar.'

'Tell them to call the friend first then, but if the call isn't answered straight away, I want to know. Tell them not to delay.'

Without further comment Egan pulled the keyboard towards him and started to type. When he'd finished the email he turned a screen so that Cormac could read and approve the wording. That done, he pressed send.

'Thank you for your help,' Cormac said. 'We'll be on campus throughout the day doing local door-to-door, and we may put up some posters. I'll need the names of the researchers who have access to the private labs, by the way. Do you have that information?'

For the first time, Egan hesitated. 'I have … or at least I have the names of those who are employed by the university and also have a relationship with Darcy Therapeutics. But that list is not complete. Darcy Therapeutics employs many staff members who are not on the faculty. Like your Emma, for example. I'd be happy to provide you with the list I have, but I'm afraid I will have to see a warrant first.'

Cormac's shoulders tensed but Egan's body language was relaxed, conversational. There was no reason for him to know that Emma was his partner. That information had to have come from Brian Murphy. But why? To smooth Cormac's path into the university? Maybe. But hearing her name in this room, in this conversation, felt like a threat.

Egan stood. 'You have my number. Call me if and when you need anything else.'

Cormac was almost at the door when Egan spoke again. 'Detective? I presume it won't be necessary to involve Carline Darcy any further in this matter?'

'Excuse me?'

'It's not my place to tell you how to do your job, of course, but it seems that she was brought into this matter due to an unfortunate misunderstanding, and it shouldn't be necessary to interview her again. As I said, I'm more than happy to assist in any way I can.'

Cormac looked at him for a long moment, long enough to embarrass the man if he could be embarrassed. If he was, he didn't show it, just waited.

'Quite right, Professor,' Cormac said. He watched a hint of relief creep into Egan's face. 'It's not your place.'

CHAPTER TEN

Emma opened the door to Fisher's knock almost immediately, a mug of coffee in her hand. She looked behind him, as if expecting to see Reilly, then paused.

'Just you?' she asked.

'Just me.'

She stepped back and led Fisher into the kitchen. He had to remind himself, firmly, to keep his eyes off her arse and to take in the house instead. Emma Sweeney was gorgeous. Distractingly gorgeous. He'd seen her, what, three times now? Each time she'd come across as low key, casual, not particularly keen to draw attention to herself. Today she wore jeans, a white shirt with its sleeves rolled up. No makeup, or not much of it anyway. But she had a body that was pretty much perfect. Curves in all the right places.

'Coffee?' she asked.

'Please. Milk and one sugar if you have it.'

Emma flipped the switch on the kettle, then put two slices of bread in the toaster. 'Have you eaten anything? I'm starving. I've been at the lab all day, so nothing since lunch.' She moved what must be her coat – it was green wool, not exactly Reilly's style – off a chair for him and indicated that he should sit.

Fisher settled in, put all thoughts of her looks firmly out of mind.

'What are you working on?' he asked.

Emma took a mug from a cupboard and milk from the fridge as she answered. 'I work in biotechnology. Medical devices. We're running tests at the moment.'

'Sounds interesting.'

Emma laughed, shook her head. 'Everyone says that, before they change the subject.' She made the coffee and handed him the cup, pulled a stool around so that she could sit opposite him. This close, he could see a silvery scar that ran along her jaw-line, another at her temple.

'I'm interested, really. The DS says you're doing really high-tech stuff.'

She took a sip of coffee. 'It is interesting, actually, to me at least, and to quite a few others if we're successful. Essentially, we're working on something that would be a bit like an artificial kidney, using silicon nanotechnology. It uses the same processes that were developed by the microelectronics industry for computers.'

'An artificial kidney. To replace dialysis?'

'Exactly.'

'And you've made one?'

'We're getting closer. My team has designed the little chip that forms the basis of the technology, but there are still some challenges. That's why we're in Galway. My colleague Alessandro – he's our biomedical engineer – Alessandro is working with me, using computer programs to study the prototype's fluid dynamics and further refine the channels for maximum blood flow efficiency. Getting blood flow right is essential if we're going to make this thing work, and it's incredibly challenging. The other challenge is that we need to layer the device with living kidney cells, that can distinguish between toxins that need to be flushed from the body, and nutrients that should be absorbed.'

She was more animated when she talked about her work, sitting up straighter. She held her hands up and layered one on top of the other to demonstrate their work with kidney cells. Her enthusiasm was contagious – Fisher found that he'd sat up straighter, that he was leaning forward in his seat as he listened.

'That bit is really challenging,' she continued. 'We can grow kidney cells in the lab easily enough, but the process after that – layering the cells on the device, and building a membrane – it's never been done in the way we want to do it. And then we have to permeate the whole device with a drug that has to be released slowly, slowly, slowly into the blood stream. So very difficult to get right. Fortunately we have a bit of a head start with that.' Emma stood up and left the room without explanation, returning a moment later with a copy of a technical magazine in her hand, put it in front of him.

'There's an article in there about our device,' Emma said. 'If you'd asked me to explain our research a month ago I couldn't have, not really, but patent applications have been updated and we're going public with some of our progress, so it's not so very hush hush.'

Fisher pulled the magazine a little closer, looked it over. There was a photograph of an older man in a lab coat on the front cover.

'That's James Murtagh,' Emma said, pointing to the picture. 'He's head of the lab I work out of, and James did all the early work on the slow-release drug, years ago really.'

Fisher nodded, turned a page, then asked, 'You work late a lot then?' It wasn't subtle, but he had a job to do.

Emma curled her hands around her coffee cup, took a breath. 'Yes. When we're testing I need to be there at odd hours sometimes.'

'Can you tell me about last night?'

'I went in pretty late. I was working at home most of the day, writing an article that we're planning on submitting to *The Lancet*. I was pretty close to finishing up but I needed something from the lab to complete the section I was working on, and I didn't want to leave it until the following day. I wanted to get it down on paper while the logic of it was fresh in my mind.'

Fisher nodded. 'Why don't you start from when you arrived at the college. What you saw, what you did.'

Emma took a deep breath. Her expression tightened into one of concentration, like someone about to take an important exam, determined not to miss a single question.

'I always go by Newcastle Street, and turn into the campus by the Distillery Road entrance. You know the way?'

Fisher nodded again. He had seen it all the night before.

'So Distillery Road splits into two. One fork continues down to the laboratory, and the other turns right and leads down towards the library and the chapel car park. I took the right turn.'

'You didn't go directly to the lab?'

Emma shook her head. 'There's no parking down there. We always park in the chapel car park. So I took the turn, and was just about to take the entrance to the car park when I saw her, just lying there.'

'You didn't realise that the university was closed?'

'No. The university sent out an email alert ... you heard about the asbestos scare?' She waited for his nod, then continued. 'Well, the university sent out more than one alert, actually, but I didn't see them until this morning because I had my email turned off yesterday. I often turn it off when I'm working on something that requires a lot of focus. So I never got the message that the campus had been closed. Even if I had, it wouldn't have stopped me going to the labs, probably. I have a swipe key for access after hours.' Emma's voice grew quieter as she spoke.

'Finding the body must have been very traumatic for you,' Fisher said.

She was silent for a moment. 'I thought it was a student who had had too much to drink. It wouldn't be the first time some kid drank too much and fell asleep on the side of the road. Did you hear about that first year in UCC last year? Died from exposure after a Christmas party?'

Fisher shook his head.

'Well, I thought it might be something like that.' Her expression darkened. 'Or, you know, the victim of a rape. I stopped the car, then I got out to check. When I got closer I saw how … twisted she was. So unnatural. And then I saw her poor face.' Emma shook her head, blinked back sudden tears.

'And that's when you called Sergeant Reilly?' Fisher asked.

'I thought I should check to make sure that there was no pulse. Thought maybe I should do CPR, you know? So I went right up close, put my fingers to her neck.'

'Did you do CPR?'

'No. It was obvious it was too late. There was no pulse. And her injuries seemed far too serious.'

Fisher nodded. 'After you confirmed that the victim was deceased, what did you do then?'

'I called Cormac. Straight away. Then I got back into my car and sort of reversed it, put it in the centre of the road and turned on my hazard lights.'

'You moved your car?' Fisher was thinking about the forensics. There had been no trace of the victim's blood on the car. Emma must have stopped far enough back that she hadn't driven over any trace evidence. She had been lucky.

Emma nodded. 'I wanted to stop anyone else from driving down. What if they hit her again? It was pretty dark. I thought it would have been easy to miss her until it was too late. And I couldn't bear that to happen. So I drove back out onto the road and parked in the middle, put my lights on.' Emma's eyes were on his face. 'What is it?' she asked. 'Did I do something wrong?' Her face creased in distress. 'Did I mess up some evidence?'

Fisher shook his head. 'No, no, you're grand.' He repressed the urge to reassure her further. Her face had lost colour. She looked shaken, like she might be about to cry in earnest.

'Did you see anyone else at all?'

Emma shook her head. 'No one.'

'You thought you recognised the victim as Carline, is that right?'

'Not straight away. But when I was sitting in my car, waiting for Cormac, I couldn't get her out of my mind. All that blonde hair. That cardigan with the purple lining. I realised I recognised the cardigan.'

Fisher nodded. 'Right. Do you know her well, the Darcy girl?'

'James introduced me to her when I started at the lab. She's a second-year student. Brilliant, by all accounts, and a research assistant, but she works out of James's lab, not mine.'

'Must have been a bit awkward, was it? She's your boss's granddaughter.' He gave a laugh. 'Might even *be* your boss someday, right?'

See, this was the thing. You couldn't shut off being a policeman, even if you wanted to, and he didn't. He liked Emma Sweeney, for herself, not just her looks. She struck him as a good person. But first impressions were wrong as often as they were right and good people did bad things all the time, they were just a bit more inventive at finding justification for it than the average gouger. Fisher didn't need anyone in his ear to remind him that he was there to do a job and do it well. He thought Reilly would understand that. If he didn't, would that change anything? Fisher told himself that it wouldn't. And so he needled Emma the way he would any other witness. To provoke a reaction.

'It doesn't really work like that,' Emma said. 'John Darcy owns the company, yes, but he's not my boss.' She was relaxed. No sign of a nettled ego.

'You don't have to report to him? Discuss progress or anything?'

'Well, yes. We have quarterly meetings where we discuss progress and agree project target dates. But I'm not an employee, exactly. I'm a contractor. I'll stay with Darcy Therapeutics until this project is completed, then I'll move on. And I have part ownership of the intellectual property. I developed the nanotechnology with my team. So I suppose I see it as more of a partnership, really.'

Fisher wondered if Darcy saw it the same way. He tapped the magazine.

'And this guy?'

Emma shrugged. 'James has worked with John forever, and the lab is his really, to run. We don't see a great deal of each other, day to day. James is the one who introduced me to Carline Darcy, soon after I came to Galway. After that I ran into her a few times around the labs, but I've never gotten to know her. We nod and smile, you know the way.'

'Right. But you would have seen her fairly regularly, if she worked in the same lab?'

Emma shook her head. 'My lab can only be accessed by me and my researchers. Only those who need to know – those working directly on the project – get swipe cards. Even James doesn't have one. Carline worked on her stuff in James's lab, in the work spaces he makes available to students.' She looked at him curiously. 'It wasn't Carline anyway, was it? It was another girl who died.'

Fisher decided to change direction. 'Is there anyone else you can think of who would fit the description? Someone with a connection to the Darcy lab? With the campus shut down it's hard to see why anyone would have been hanging around, unless they had a swipe to the labs, like you.'

'I'm not sure that's right,' Emma said. Her voice was firm but she was still pale, looked tired. 'She could easily have been a student walking through campus from town on her way to the student residence. If she came out of town by University Road she would have seen that security had been lifted and she could easily have walked through.' She looked at her watch.

'I'm sure you're right,' Fisher said, and he stood, closed his notebook. 'I've taken up enough of your time.'

'It's not a problem,' Emma said, but there was little animation in her voice.

'What did you need?' Fisher asked, his tone conversational.

'Sorry?'

'You said you needed something from the lab, to finish your article. I'm just wondering what it was.'

'Oh.' Emma put her head to one side. 'I'm not sure I remember exactly. Let me see if I made a note.' She pulled a battered but expensive looking leather handbag to her and started to rummage through it. How much did researchers earn, exactly? More than Fisher had assumed, obviously, given the bag, and the small but fashionable and extremely well-located house they were sitting in. Not the kind of place a detective sergeant normally lived in. Well, rumour at the station was that she came from money. Emma found what she was looking for – a palm-sized notebook with a virulent orange cover. She leafed through the pages, her brow a little furrowed. 'Yes,' she said. 'I remember now. I didn't have a data set I needed to refer to for my article – some of the data is too sensitive, too valuable to be removed from the lab, even on an encrypted laptop. I'm afraid I can't tell you the details, not without clearing it first with the company lawyers. It's all subject to a non-disclosure agreement. Does it matter?'

'I'm sure it doesn't,' said Fisher. But he wondered.

CHAPTER ELEVEN

Cormac didn't get in that night until after nine. It had been a long and frustrating day. Professor Egan's email had received only two responses, which his office had forwarded, along with each girl's college photograph. They had been young, both blonde, interchangeably pretty. The team had tracked the first girl down within the hour. The second girl had taken a little longer. They'd spoken to every family member, every friend by the end of the second hour. By the end of the third, with the girl not found and the feeling they were on to something, they'd brought in CCTV footage captured in the area of her last known movements and started exhaustive analysis. The girl's mother, terrified, distraught, had agreed to provide a DNA sample. And then, just after 7 p.m., the girl herself had sheepishly phoned the station.

'I bumped into my old boyfriend in the pub,' she said. 'We ended up going back to his place and just, you know, hanging out. My phone died, and he's not in college so we didn't hear about all the fuss, you know? Sorry. Like, I'm really sorry. But was it completely necessary to call my mum?'

The missing persons files had proven equally unrewarding. A day down, and no real progress made.

Emma's car was sitting in the driveway when he got home – he'd made arrangements for it to be dropped back that afternoon, when forensics finished with it. He was pleased they'd brought it back quickly, less pleased to see that there was a crack in one of the brake lights that he hadn't noticed before. He looked the car over, then went inside. The house was quiet except for the intermittent sound of canned laughter from the TV in the living room. He went in, but the room was empty, felt empty. He tried the kitchen but it was similarly deserted, everything as it had been when he left that morning, except that two additional dirty coffee cups had joined his in the sink.

He went upstairs in search of Emma, found their bedroom empty, and the door to the en suite closed. He heard the unmistakable sound of someone being sick.

'Em?' He knocked on the door. 'You okay?'

The sound of the toilet flushing, then Emma's voice. 'Give me a minute.' She turned on the tap at the sink – he could hear the water running.

Cormac retreated a few steps and sat on the end of the bed to wait for her. It crossed his mind that she might be pregnant, and he didn't know whether he was delighted or terrified at the possibility. When she emerged she was pale, harried-looking. She held up one hand.

'Don't come near me,' she said. 'It's probably just something I ate, but just in case it's probably better to keep your distance.' Thoughts of fatherhood died a swift death.

Cormac stood up, put his hand to her forehead, gave her the gentlest hug he could manage. She didn't feel feverish. He let her go so she could make her away around to the bed. She climbed under the covers and leaned back on the pillows, looking up at him.

'The timing is rubbish,' she said. 'I really need to be at work tomorrow. I can't afford to miss a day right now.'

'See how you feel tomorrow,' Cormac said. 'It might have run its course by then.'

She half-smiled at that. 'You sound like my mother,' she said. 'When we were kids, whatever was wrong with us, she'd tell us to take a disprin and wait for it to run its course.'

'Your mother's a doctor.'

'Well, shoemakers' kids and all that.'

Her voice was dry and tired. He wanted to lie down beside her but if she was feeling rubbish his presence might not be welcome.

'Your left brake light's had a bit of a bang,' he said. 'Did you know? Was that you or do I need to have words at the station?'

'Gawd,' she said. 'Men and cars, you're all the same. Fisher noticed too, on his way out. Pointed it out to me and even recommended somewhere I can get it fixed. I was hoping I'd get it done before you noticed. I dinged it when I went to the shops. Parking, if you can believe that. And no comments about women drivers, please.' She was trying to force a lightness of tone, not quite making it.

For a moment there was silence. 'I'm sorry that you had to deal with Fisher today,' Cormac said quietly. 'If you're feeling sick I'm sure it's the last thing you wanted to do.'

'It was fine,' Emma said, but she didn't meet his eye. 'He was fine.'

'Emma.' Cormac waited for her to look at him. 'I'm sorry too that I wasn't here with you. Last night. I know it was a shock.'

'It would have been a shock for anyone,' she said, chin coming up.

'Yes. But particularly given everything you've been through. I feel like a dick for not getting home.'

'You were doing your job,' she said.

He opened his mouth to speak again but she cut him off. 'It's fine, Cormac, honestly. I called Rachel but she was at a wedding. She couldn't come over, but we talked for ages before I went to sleep. She was so good. I must have totally screwed up her night. We talked until I was so tired I just fell asleep.'

'Well,' he said, feeling completely inadequate, 'I'm sorry.' He was conscious that he felt irritated, tried not to show it.

He wanted to do it all, that was the problem. Be there for her, always, but he had to do his job.

'He wasn't too hard on you, was he?'

'Who, Peter? He was just doing his job.'

'Em, come on.' He wanted her to talk to him.

In a burst of obvious exasperation Emma sat up for long enough to rearrange her pillow, then lay down again and pulled her blanket determinedly up over her shoulder. She paused before she spoke. 'Cormac, I'm not going to fight with you. I'm really tired, and I don't know what you want me to say, okay?'

At that he did go to her, lay down beside her on the bed, took her hand in silent apology, and she curled into him. They lay there for a time, not speaking, until he thought she had fallen asleep. When she spoke her voice was quiet, sleepy.

'I'm sorry I got it so wrong,' Emma murmured.

'Sorry?'

'I was so sure that was her cardigan. I'm sure I saw her wearing it.'

She sounded exhausted. Not really awake.

'Go to sleep, Em,' Cormac said. 'We'll talk in the morning.'

She was out in moments, and he stayed where he was, initially because he was unwilling to risk waking her. Then, as time passed, because he hoped to fall asleep himself. And eventually he just lay there and thought about Carline Darcy, tried to convince himself that she wasn't involved. No connection to Darcy meant no connection to the lab, which meant he would be able to keep this case where it belonged – at the station, far away from his home, far away from Emma.

Monday 28 April 2014

CHAPTER TWELVE

Cormac and Moira Hanley left the station for the Henderson interview at 8.30 a.m. on Monday morning. The drive was accomplished mainly in silence. Moira gave directions as they drove up into the hills, but she didn't seem to feel the need to fill the silence with an unnecessary briefing or anxious questions. Cormac was glad of it. He had read the Henderson file cover to cover for a second time the night before. He felt he knew where they were with the case, and the quiet drive to the house gave him an opportunity to clear his mind so that he could form his own first impressions of the woman who may or may not have conspired with her husband to murder their three children.

Lucy Henderson opened the door to them with a baby in her arms and milk stains on her shoulder. She was a bird-like little woman. Petite and fine-boned and with a definite air of abstraction. She stood looking from Cormac to Moira, as if uncertain what came next. A second woman appeared from further down the hall. The second woman looked very like Lucy, but sharper somehow, more robust, as if Lucy was an artist's rough pencil sketch, and the second woman was the finished picture.

'For goodness sake, Lucy, would you bring them in out of the cold?' The woman introduced herself as Susan Armstrong, Lucy's sister, as she took the baby from Lucy's arms and led the way into a comfortable living room. The room was furnished with a couch and matching armchairs that had seen better days. A white IKEA storage unit housed an oversized TV, and the hearth was dark with old ash and half-burnt embers.

Lucy Henderson took a seat in the corner of the couch, and her sister placed the baby in her lap.

'I hope you're feeling better now, Mrs Henderson?' Cormac asked as he sat in the armchair opposite her.

'She is,' Susan Armstrong said firmly. 'And she's ready to answer any question you need to ask her. Isn't that right, Lucy?'

Lucy nodded slowly.

Susan Armstrong was clearly reluctant to leave. She hovered over her sister until she realised that nothing of substance would be said in her presence. 'I'll be in the kitchen if you need anything,' she said eventually, as she retreated towards the door. 'The older children are at school so you've no need to worry about being overheard or anything like that.' A last look at Lucy and she disappeared.

'I think it's all just a big mistake,' Lucy said. Her voice was hoarse, her stare unfocused. 'Rob would never hurt the children. Could it just be a mistake?' Her eyes found Cormac's.

'You know it isn't a mistake, Lucy,' Moira said, before Cormac could reply. 'All the windows were sealed. Your husband blocked the ventilation shafts. He bought eight canisters of carbon dioxide – and built the pipe system into the house. He knew exactly what he was doing and his intention was to kill you and the children.' Moira was leaning forward in her chair, her voice low and intense. She was trying to make a connection but she was moving too fast, giving Lucy nowhere to go.

Lucy shook her head, blinked, shook her head again. 'I know I've neglected him,' she said. 'Our marriage, I mean. It's just, the baby's so small. There's always so much to do.'

'He didn't do this because you haven't been paying enough attention to him, Lucy. This is about much more than that,' said Moira.

'Has Rob ever been diagnosed with a mental illness?' Cormac cut in, keeping his tone conversational. 'Ever suffered a brain injury?'

'What?' Lucy looked at him, met his eyes for the first time. 'No. Never. He's always been well.'

Cormac worked at keeping warmth in his eyes. 'Rob hasn't been well since he's been in custody.' Which was the understatement of the year. According to Carrie O'Halloran's meticulous file notes, Rob Henderson was catatonic, would lie for hours in whatever position the nurses placed him. He was doubly incontinent, which would have been a bigger problem except that he hadn't eaten anything for three days. The doctors had him on an IV for electrolytes, and might soon have to introduce a feeding tube. They were talking about electroshock therapy. All of which sounded very much like a man who wasn't going to trial.

Lucy Henderson's anxious eyes held his.

'He's not physically unwell, Lucy, at least not yet. But he seems to be mentally unwell, not able to engage with anyone, to speak, or react in any way. I wondered if this was something Rob had experienced before, or if you'd ever seen any signs.'

'No. Nothing like that. Rob's never been sick in that way. Never sick at all really. He has a good job, you know? He's a programmer. He just got a big promotion. That's why he was off work, having a little holiday before he took on all the extra responsibility. He got paid a big bonus too. We were all going to go to Euro Disney for my birthday.' She looked back and forth between Cormac and Moira. The baby squirmed on her lap and Moira put her on the floor, where she sat for a moment before moving to all fours and crawling clumsily in Cormac's direction.

'He was fired,' Moira said bluntly. 'There was no bonus, no holiday. He lost his job because he was surfing porn on the bank's computers and he didn't stop even after two warnings.'

Lucy shook her head. Her eyes wandered and rested on a framed wedding photograph that sat on the bookshelf. 'We have a happy marriage. We don't even fight, not like Susan and John. They fight all the time. Rob says Susan just likes to row. Not me though. I like everything to be peaceful.' She smiled in a distracted way, eyes wandering. Christ. She'd gone from anxious to soporific in less than two minutes. She was definitely medicated.

'That may be, Mrs Henderson,' said Moira. 'But if your boy hadn't let his teacher know that something wasn't right, that he was afraid, your husband would have killed you and your children, including that baby at your feet. You owe Fearghal your life. And you owe him the truth. You keep denying it and where does that leave him? He sent his dad to jail for the rest of his life and it was all a big mistake? Because Rob is going to prison. And you can either be a support to your boy or you can bury your head in the sand.'

Lucy squeezed her eyes shut, rubbed at her forehead with both hands. The baby had made her way across the room and was sitting at Cormac's feet, pulling at his shoe laces.

Cormac stood, picked up the little girl, who looked surprised but not wholly dissatisfied with the turn of events.

'You're not quite well, Lucy,' he said gently. 'I'll say goodbye to your sister, and then we'll head away, okay? We'll come back and finish our chat another day.'

He handed the baby to Moira Hanley, who looked at him as if he'd asked her to hold his dirty gym gear. Cormac indicated with a nod that Moira should stay with Lucy, then he headed off to the kitchen. He found Susan Armstrong in the process of bleach-cleaning the kitchen sink. Every other surface gleamed. She must have been here for a couple of weeks, if she'd come shortly after Rob Henderson's arrest. It looked like she'd spent her time cleaning and scrubbing. Maybe she thought that with enough elbow grease she could rid the house of the stain of what had almost happened here.

She turned at his greeting, looked unsurprised to see him, offered him a cup of tea which he accepted. He took a seat at the table at her invitation. She leaned on the back of a kitchen chair and looked down at him. The skin on her hands was dry and reddened.

'She wasn't much good to you, was she? Lucy never could see what Robert was really like.'

'Has the doctor been to see her? Did he give her some tranquillisers? Valium, or something?'

Susan looked taken aback for a moment, then resigned. 'Not since I've been here. Did she tell you he'd been?'

Cormac shook his head. 'She didn't tell me, and I didn't ask. But she's taken something.'

Susan nodded grimly. 'I should have thought ... I knew she wasn't right but I thought maybe it was the shock of everything. A long time ago she mentioned something about Rob taking her to the doctor, to get something to help with her anxiety, she said. I didn't point out that she'd never suffered from anxiety before she met him, and that the best cure for what was wrong with her might be a Rob-ectomy.'

'You don't like him,' Cormac said, stating the obvious in the hope that it would draw her out.

'I think he's the worst kind of shite. Rob wouldn't be satisfied with you just running around after him, picking up his mess and shining his halo for him. He's the type who'd expect you to thank him for the opportunity.'

'I can't interview her when she's under the influence,' Cormac said. 'Do you think we could work something out where you keep an eye on her before the next appointment, make sure she doesn't take anything?'

Susan's eyes darkened, and her face closed off. Her hands gripped the back of the chair. 'Tell me something, detective. Are you shaping up to make my sister a suspect?'

Cormac wasn't sure of anything yet. Lucy Henderson had a neon sign with the word 'victim' flashing over her head, but underneath that beaten, fractured exterior there was another Lucy, and who that person was remained to be seen. Susan Armstrong was watching him, trying to read him. She struck him as bright, honest, tough. Better to have her as an ally than as an enemy.

'What I know is that two weeks ago Rob Henderson set about killing his three children, probably Lucy, maybe himself. Lucy says she knew nothing about it, but she also claims that Rob is innocent, so her word isn't that reliable right now. My job is to keep those children safe, and to do that I need to get to the truth.'

'That's not your job though, is it? Your job is to get Rob put away for a long time. It's my job to keep the children safe. Isn't that what I'm doing here, day and night, while my own children sit at home without me?'

'Do you want him to come home?' Cormac kept his voice low, calm. 'Do you want Rob Henderson back in this house?'

Face frozen, she shook her head. 'That would never happen.'

'If Rob is found to be mentally ill and incompetent to stand trial, he won't go to prison, he'll stay at the Central Mental Hospital in Dublin, where he'll be treated. Treated, in the hope that that treatment will make him well. And if he's well he'll be released. What do you think are the chances that after a year, maybe a little longer, Rob Henderson will make a full recovery? And if that were to happen, if Rob were to knock on the front door a year from now, do you think Lucy would turn him away?'

Susan's hands had dropped from her hips, the fight went out of her shoulders.

'I need your help to make sure that never happens.'

Her chin came up. 'I'm not going to help you build a case against my sister.'

'I'm not asking you to. The best outcome would be for the children to be with Lucy, if she's well enough to care for them. If it's safe.'

She nodded once, reluctantly.

'I'll arrange for another time to meet Lucy. Keep her off the tranquillisers the day we meet her. I can't question her if she's on something, and I can't make her see the truth if she's drugged up to her eyeballs either, all right?'

Another nod, and Cormac decided to leave it at that for the time being. He said his goodbyes to Susan, gathered a resentful Moira Hanley from the living room, and left the house more aware than ever that this case wouldn't wait for him to have time. It would have to be the priority investigation, whatever the political or personal pressure he felt to put the hit-and-run case to bed. Deeply occupied with his thoughts, he didn't notice that Moira Hanley stayed silent all the way to the station.

CHAPTER THIRTEEN

Carrie had spent the entire weekend at home, the first time she'd managed that in something approaching two months. Ciarán had gotten up on Saturday morning and had left straight away for the golf course, barely waiting long enough to confirm that she would be home for the day. When she'd wandered downstairs herself half an hour later, it had come as a shock to realise what a state the house was in. Oh the basics were done all right, the dishwasher was clean, the counters more or less tidied off, but the whole place felt ... unloved. Uncomfortable. The hall table was cluttered with old post, bits of toys, the girls' school cardigans. The bread bin was empty, except for a mouldy croissant and a heel of bread. The laundry baskets were full. The house smelled stale.

The girls had been delighted to see her, but their excitement just underlined how shit she'd been lately. They were so young still, only ten and five. Having their mother home on a Saturday morning should be the norm, not a treat. They had cereal for breakfast – there wasn't much else in the cupboard – and then she brought them swimming. Miriam's togs were frayed, she was overdue a new pair. All Carrie could think about, as the girls swam up and down in their roped off lanes, was how badly she was letting them down. She kept up a cheery chatter all the way home, then hid in her room for ten minutes and cried until it was out of her system.

After that the weekend got a bit better. Her mind drifted to work more than once, bouncing back and forth between the Henderson case and the hit-and-run. Despite what she'd said to Reilly, it would be hard to let the Henderson case go, and the hit-and-run bothered her. If she hadn't been so tired on Friday night, so worried about home and so pissed off with Brian Murphy, she might have pushed back harder when Cormac moved to stamp his authority all over the case. Emma Sweeney had lied about her working hours at the lab. It was possible that the lie meant nothing – the kind of stupid, reflexive lie many people told when they were questioned by the police – but equally it might mean that Emma had something to hide. In which case Cormac was surely the wrong person to be leading the investigation. She half-expected to get a call at any time – Brian Murphy would almost certainly pull Reilly off the case as soon as he heard the story. More than once Carrie thought about taking a drive into the station, to suss out progress, to try to step in if she was needed. But she was on such thin ice with Ciarán as it was. She knew she needed to sort her shit out, make a decision about her career, and have an honest conversation with him about where they were going. She settled for getting in a food shop, cleaning the bathrooms, cleaning the girls' rooms with their almost enthusiastic assistance and cooking two decent family meals.

When she pulled on her jacket and kissed the girls goodbye at 7 a.m. on Monday morning, she still hadn't had the conversation, and Ciarán barely looked up to see her leave. The last thing she saw as she pulled the door closed behind her was the hall table, Friday's clutter still intact, joined now by a half-drunk cup of tea she'd abandoned the day before.

She made it to the station for 8.30. The first thing she did was check the preliminary forensics reports on the hit-and-run, on Emma Sweeney's car and clothing. Nothing suspicious had been found and Carrie breathed a sigh of relief. She settled down to her own paperwork, and was interrupted by a call from the desk officer at 9 a.m.

'I've a boy here. Name's Paul. Says his sister's missing.'

'What age?' Carrie asked.

'Uh ... I've not asked him. Maybe fourteen, fifteen like?'

'I meant the sister.' *Gobshite.*

'Oh right, yeah. She's eighteen, he says.'

She told him to pass it to Cormac Reilly, then hung up. Tried to concentrate on her paperwork backlog, and not let her mind wander back to Reilly or his cases. Her conscience nagged at her. She turned the page on the statement transcript in front of her, tried to make herself give a shit about a string of burglaries on Circular Road.

The phone rang again.

'Can't reach him. Just getting voicemail. Is there any chance you could ... only the young fella's getting a bit upset here.'

'Right,' Carrie said, swallowing her irritation. 'I'll be down.'

She went first to the case room on the top floor, stuck her head in the door. Fisher and a few other uniforms were hard at work. Dave McCarthy was working on a cuppa and a crossword.

'Where is he?' she asked.

Dave didn't look up. 'Haven't seen him yet today,' he said.

'He's out,' Fisher offered. 'Interview on the Henderson case.'

Carrie thought briefly of the pile of paperwork that awaited her, suppressed a flare of irritation that Reilly was out on her case while she was picking up his bits and pieces. 'There's a kid downstairs, wants to report his sister missing.' Every head in the room went up. Irritated, she chose the least experienced of them. 'Mulcair, you're with me.' She didn't wait for him to follow, just took the stairs down to the waiting area, where the boy was waiting. He was sitting on the plastic waiting room chair, wearing tracksuit bottoms, a pair of seen-better-days runners, and a fleece jumper. He had dark hair, and a thin, clever face, pale-skinned and freckled. His hands were tightly clasped in his lap, and one foot bounced continuously with nervous tension.

'Paul?'

He looked up, and the fear in his face was unmissable.

Carrie introduced herself, finding that her irritation was melting away. Whatever else this boy was, he wasn't a time waster. She led him down the corridor to a family room, had him take a seat, offered him something to drink, which he refused. When she sat, Mulcair took the seat to her left. The family meeting room was an interview room, tarted up in what was presumably an attempt to make it feel a bit friendlier, a bit less intimidating. It had an ageing couch and two armchairs. There was a sad-looking box of toys in the corner, suitable for a toddler, half of them broken.

'Paul, you may not be aware that it is against the law for gardaí to interview a minor – that means anyone under the age of eighteen – without a parent or guardian being present. Is there someone we can call for you?'

He shook his head. 'But I'm not in trouble. I'm not a suspect for anything. I just want to report my sister missing.' He looked from Carrie to the uniform and back, settled on Carrie. 'I haven't heard from her in a few days. Her phone's turned off. She's not answering emails. I went to her work, but she wasn't there.' He was flushed, holding back tears. 'I'm nearly eighteen, okay? You can just talk to me.'

He had a nice face, this boy. Honest. But he was nowhere near eighteen.

'Tell me about your sister,' Carrie said. She didn't open a notebook, folded her hands in her lap.

'My sister – her name's Della – she lives in Galway. Has done for the last two years. She's just normal, you know? Like, just a normal girl.'

'Does she go to the university?' ask Mulcair.

Paul shook his head. 'She's a waitress.' Confusion crossed his face. 'I mean, but I went to the place she works, and they said they don't know her. That she doesn't work there.' He looked from Carrie, to Fisher, and back, as if hoping that they had an explanation.

'How long has Della been missing?' Mulcair asked. 'When was the last time you were in touch?' Carrie could almost feel his nervousness as he asked the question, and she tried to remember if Mulcair had ever sat in on an interview before.

'On Friday,' Paul said promptly. He pulled a smartphone from his pocket. It was a new model, expensive. He woke the screen, turned it to them so they could see. 'We use this app to talk, every day. The last time we talked was Friday. She was thinking about coming out for a visit on Saturday. And then that's it, nothing.'

'Friday to Monday is not a very long time really,' Carrie said. 'If Della's only eighteen, you know, eighteen-year-old girls, they sometimes like to go a bit off-radar, get a bit of space.'

Paul shook his head vehemently. 'Della's not like that. I know you're not supposed to get on with your sister, but Della and I do. She's my … she's my best friend,' he blurted, immediately looking mortified, but he kept talking, determination that they should hear him battling embarrassment and winning. 'Della and I talk almost every day, and I've tried and tried calling her, texting her. She would never leave me to worry for no reason. Besides, I've been to her apartment.'

'This morning?'

The boy's flush deepened. 'I went yesterday evening. She wasn't there, so I sat outside and waited for her. She didn't come home, all night.'

'You sat outside Della's apartment all night?' Carrie asked. 'What about your mum and dad?'

Paul looked at his hands, said nothing.

'Okay, Paul,' Carrie said. 'Tell us again about going to Della's work. You said they hadn't seen her?'

'They said she'd never worked there.' The boy was blinking back tears, fear and confusion written all over his face. 'But I know she did. She's been working there for two years, she *told me that*. But she said never to go there or I'd get her in trouble. Said that because they serve alcohol if she was seen talking to someone under age on the premises her boss would get really angry and she'd be in trouble. She must have been lying, right?' He looked so betrayed at the idea. His breathing came harder, all the fear he'd suppressed for the last few days let loose and running him ragged. 'But I believed her. I didn't want to get her in trouble, even when she stopped messaging I waited days and days. But in the end I had to go, didn't I? And they said they'd never heard of a Della Lambert. I made them get the manager. They didn't want to, but they did in the end. I even showed them all a picture of Della, but they all looked at me like I was crazy.'

'Do you have a picture with you?' Carrie asked.

Paul flicked on the phone again, found a picture, showed it to Carrie. Della Lambert, sitting beside her brother on a dry-stone wall, matching goofy grins on their faces. She had a nice face, mousy brown hair to her shoulders; her smile said *this is cheesy but I don't care*.

'What about your parents, Paul?' Carrie asked. 'They're not worried?'

The boy opened his mouth, then stopped. 'My mother said she might just need some space, that she can't keep in touch with me all the time. Said something about Della growing up.'

'You're sure that Della hasn't been in touch with anyone else in the family this week?'

He shook his head vigorously. 'No. We've got a little sister, Geraldine, but she's got Down's Syndrome, and she doesn't like talking on the phone. So Della sees her just when she comes home.'

'She doesn't call your mum or dad? They don't call her?'

The answer was obviously no. He shrugged uncomfortably.

That something wasn't right at home was obvious. Carrie had worked enough domestic violence cases to see the signs of neglect in Paul's clothes, which were too small and looked like they had had been put on dirty. Besides, you didn't have to be a garda to know that if parents don't react when a boy this young spends a night away without notice – despite Paul's bravado he couldn't be much more than fifteen – there's a problem at home. She had Mulcair take Paul's details, his home address, Della's apartment.

'Okay,' Carrie said. 'Rory here is going to drive you home now, and he'll speak to your mum and dad.' Paul shook his head immediately, opening his mouth to object, but Carrie spoke over him. 'I will send someone to Della's apartment right away. If she's there I'll get a call and I'll be able to let you know, all right? But if she's not there we can talk to your mum and dad about making a formal report. Confirm that Della hasn't been in touch with them, so that I can get this moving officially. Do you understand?'

'But I'm telling you, amn't I? Della hasn't called our parents. If she had I'd know about it.' His face was miserable. Tearful. He looked very tired and very young.

Carrie stood up. 'Come on, Paul. Let us get you home.'

He looked at her for a long moment. Finally he scrubbed the tears from his face with the sleeves of his jumper, then stood, looking away from her and shoving his hands deep into his trouser pockets.

Carrie opened the door and let Paul out, then turned back to Mulcair and spoke urgently. 'Bring him home to his mother. Make sure he gets inside the door, and that there is a responsible adult to supervise him before you leave. Make sure you get the transcript of the interview and the address of the apartment to DS Reilly as soon as possible.'

Mulcair nodded in a determined-to-do-well manner that made her feel older than her thirty-five years. She left him to it, feeling that she had done what she could. She returned to her desk and descended again into her paperwork.

CHAPTER FOURTEEN

Carline had slept late on Saturday morning, and again on Sunday. Sleep seemed to be her body's way of dealing with the situation. Instead of lying awake all night, her mind run ragged with anxiety, she fell asleep the moment her head hit the pillow, woke late and went through the days in a kind of stupor. She had an exam on Monday morning, should have been awake and frantically revising from the early hours. Instead she slept through her alarm and woke to the ringing of her phone just after 9 a.m.

It was her grandfather. Carline sat up in bed and stared at the phone for a long moment before answering. It was three days since he'd received a phone call telling him that she was dead, and only now was he calling her. That really told Carline all she needed to know about where she stood in John Darcy's affections, not that she'd needed the reminder. John had waited three days, but the company publicist, Anna Sheldon, had called her at 10 a.m. on Saturday morning, anxious to *get ahead of the story*. It was all so very predictable. If John thought of her at all it was as a source of embarrassment. Unfortunately, Anna's efforts had come too late. By Saturday afternoon she'd emailed Carline to tell her that at least one article would appear, and an hour later Anna sent the link to Carline's inbox.

The article was mean-minded and snarky. She'd expected something small in one of the local papers, but it was a lengthy piece that took up half a page of one of the tabloids, in between an ad for botox and an article about Kate Middleton looking tired. *Poor little rich girl Carline Darcy caught up in college death*. The article was largely a copy and paste job. The hack who had written it had had plenty of material to work with.

The piece dealt briefly and brutally with Carline's early life – Carline was the product of a one-night stand between her late father, Eoghan Darcy, going through some sort of playboy rebellious stage, and Evangeline Grace, a part-time model, part-time escort, who had slept her way around the kind of European cities that attracted Russian oligarchs and British drug dealers. As an infant, Carline had been the subject of a hard-fought custody battle, which had played itself out in the newspapers, despite the fact that family law matters were supposed to remain confidential. (Carline was fairly sure that Evangeline had fed details to the tabloids in exchange for payment.) And then years later she'd been the subject of another flurry of negative publicity, when an in-depth exposé on some of John Darcy's more aggressive business dealings also mentioned that his granddaughter Carline had been permitted to live with Evangeline after the death of her father. By then Evangeline had a sort of Z-list profile as an aging party girl. She was regularly photographed staggering out of some club or other. Given that and the character assassination the Darcy publicity machine had very effectively carried out during the original custody battle, she was widely understood to be an unsuitable parent. The journalists had come late to the story. Carline had only lived with her mother for three years. By the time she was fifteen Evangeline had grown bored with the arrangement, realised that she'd extracted as much money as she was ever going to get from the Darcys, and shipped Carline off to boarding school.

All this old ground was rehashed in the latest piece. The only new material was a final paragraph explaining that Carline's ID had been found on the body of a young woman, killed in a hit-and-run. *To date gardaí have not been able to confirm Ms Darcy's presence at the scene.* The piece ended with a snide comment about how Carline's version of student digs was a penthouse apartment overlooking the docks.

Carline had deleted the article, the link and the email, then put her phone into her drawer and closed it. She went to the shower and spent a long, long time under the hot water. All of that was supposed to be in her past. Her mother, all that mess. That wasn't who she was. She was the girl who worked hard. She was a Darcy, not her mother's daughter, and she was earning a place in the Darcy world. She was so close, so very close, if she could only manage to hold on to what she'd already won, if she could cobble together a new pattern from the remnants of her perfectly woven plan. She'd tested the ground with Anna Sheldon, mooted the idea of joining the company early, and hadn't been shot down. There was hope.

Her phone kept ringing. She toyed with the idea of letting it go to voicemail, then forced herself to answer.

'John,' she said. 'How are you?' She'd never called him grandfather.

'Carline, I've been meaning to call you. I hear there's been some … difficulty on campus.' His tone was relaxed. Carline drew her knees to her chest, pulled her duvet to her body. She was home, she was safe. Why did she feel afraid? She worked hard at keeping her tone light, amused.

'I'm so sorry you were bothered with it. What a mess. I still can't quite believe that they started making phone calls before they even identified the girl.' She paused long enough to be sure he didn't want to respond, then rushed on. 'I wish you could have seen the guard's face when Valentina introduced me. Honestly. It almost made the whole thing worthwhile.' Her voice sounded tinkly, vapid. Unlike herself. A wave of heat swept over her.

'You didn't know the girl?'

'As far as I know she hasn't been identified yet, so I can't be sure, but I don't believe so. None of my friends are missing.' Her first lie.

'I'm told she had your ID.'

Carline closed her eyes, clenched her right fist around her duvet. How much did he know?

'I lost one, or had it stolen. At the beginning of the year.' Her second lie.

'College ID? Or a lab swipe card?' He still sounded relaxed, but she doubted very much that he was.

'College ID. If I'd lost a swipe I would have let security know.' A third lie, and this one was stupid, so easily disproved. For a moment she hated him. Hated the way he made her feel, hated the way she answered him, as if she were a little girl, scared and guilty.

'Of course you would.' He was silent for a moment, or perhaps he had just held the phone away from his mouth. She could hear voices speaking in the background, then he returned to the call. 'Carline, I have to go, but Anna mentioned you had asked about joining the company after your summer exams. That's not a good idea. I'm sure I don't need to remind you that pharma is not Silicon Valley. You need your doctorate if you ever expect to be taken seriously.'

'Of course, I never meant …'

He cut her off. 'I'm sure you didn't.' His tone was dry. 'Why don't you just concentrate on your thesis? If you finish early, perhaps we can look at it again.' Message delivered, he ended the call. Carline lay in bed and nausea pooled and curled in her stomach. What the hell was she going to do now?

CHAPTER FIFTEEN

Cormac returned to the case room after the Henderson interview at 10 a.m to get an update from the team. There'd been nothing yet from the coroner. Fisher had called the morgue and had been told that Dr Connolly was just starting the autopsy. Dave McCarthy had organised a shortlist of possible matches from the missing persons list. None of them seemed likely candidates but until the autopsy was complete they couldn't rule any of them out.

Cormac sat in silence for a moment, considering his directionless team. They were doing good work with what they had, which wasn't much.

'Moira, I want you to start the door to door again. You might get people we missed on the last go around.' Moira Hanley barely looked up from her work. 'Dave, I want you here keeping an eye on things. Keep track of comms, and let me know when Dr Connolly finally calls in.'

'Not a problem,' said Dave. His eyes went to Moira. Dave could be relied on to get her moving.

'Fisher, you're with me,' Cormac said. Peter didn't need to be asked twice. They were out of the door moments later. 'I want to walk the scene,' Cormac said. 'And I want to check out those labs.'

Fisher nodded. 'That ID in her pocket. She had it for a reason, didn't she? Any chance of grabbing some food on the way? I'm bloody starving.'

They picked up a couple of sausage rolls at the Centra store opposite the campus, washed them down with coffee.

'I've been reading about Carline Darcy,' Fisher said. He looked out of the window as he spoke, had a sip of coffee.

'Yes?' Cormac said.

'That ID. It's hard to believe the girl just picked it up. And I don't think Emma was wrong about that cardigan. I think Carline Darcy knows who our victim is.' There was tension in Fisher's voice, as if he wasn't sure how Cormac would react to the idea.

Cormac nodded. 'Let's not broadcast that too early, all right, Fisher? Someone like Darcy, there's political pressure to stay away from her. We're going to need a lot more before we take her on directly.'

'Right. Okay.'

'What did you learn from your research?' Cormac asked.

Fisher shook his head. 'Well, if she was involved in the murder, she wasn't motivated by money. If the articles I read were accurate, her father left her somewhere north of forty million when he died, and she came into that money the day she turned eighteen.'

'That's a lot of money for an eighteen-year-old. I wonder how the rest of the family felt about the inheritance.'

Fisher gave him a look. 'According to the articles Darcy Therapeutics is worth somewhere in the region of eight billion euros, and John Darcy owns fifty-one per cent of that company. In comparison to that sort of money, it's a drop in the ocean.'

'Presumably she'll come into some of that too, in due course,' Cormac said.

'I wouldn't count on it,' Fisher said. 'It seems like she's the black sheep of the family. Her mother is a good-time girl her father picked up for a one-nighter. If you believe the tabloids she was a model who was available for a lot more than modelling for the right man at the right price. Carline's father sued for sole custody and won, but when he died the

113

family didn't seem to have much of a problem letting her go back to her mother. John Darcy had two children. His son, Eoghan, Carline's father, and a daughter, Melanie. Melanie's married with two kids.' Fisher took a last sip from his coffee, waved his right hand in the air. 'The family owns this huge luxury ski chalet in Switzerland and the entire Darcy clan spend Christmas there every year, including Melanie and her two daughters. There are loads of photos online – *Hello!* magazine seems to do an article every year. Carline Darcy has never been part of it.'

Cormac nodded slowly, thinking it through. 'And yet she's here, in Galway, working out of a Darcy laboratory. And the story going around is that she's something special. That maybe she's the one who inherited her grandfather's brilliance, if not his money.'

Fisher shrugged.

'I'd imagine that might be galling for John Darcy. If he all but froze her out, only to find that she has that sort of talent.'

Fisher was silent for a moment. 'So this guy, Darcy. He started out here? As a student?'

'So I'm told,' Cormac said.

'D'you think that's why he came back? Set up the labs here I mean, rather than somewhere a bit, you know, sexier?'

'Somewhere warmer than the rainy west, you mean? My guess is that setting up here had more to do with government grants and tax incentives than loyalty to his alma mater. I don't think Darcy spends much time here.'

Cormac got out of the car long enough to bin the remains of their meal, then pulled out of the car park back into traffic, and took the turn down Distillery Road.

His first visit to the Darcy lab had been with Emma. On their first weekend in Galway, she'd wanted to check out the place where she would be spending most of her time for the next five years. It had been a grey February day, rain spitting down intermittently and the temperature never quite making it over five degrees. The sort of day, in other words, that might have sent them running for Dublin. The labs looked like nothing much – a low concrete building with white plaster, and few windows. Emma told him later that the lab offices, on the other side of the building, had windows that overlooked the river, but he hadn't known that at the time and if he had he wouldn't have been particularly impressed. The water that day had been grey and hostile, uninviting and uninspiring. He'd half-expected Emma to change her mind about the whole move. But she'd turned to him with shining eyes and professed that this was the place where she could do her best work.

'The labs are at the back of the concourse,' Cormac said to Fisher. 'There's no parking back there so we'll have to find a place here and walk over.'

The scene was very much as they had left it on Friday night, except that now the sun was shining. Crime scene tape was up, the scene guarded by a single garda, who brightened up when she saw them, and resumed her slumped stance when Cormac gave her a nod but didn't stop to chat. A few students walked the path towards the library, slowing, but not stopping, as they passed.

Cormac could see the girl in his mind's eye. A dark night, the car barrelling towards her. How afraid she must have been. Had she tried to run? He didn't think so, not given her position on the road. If she had run, if fear hadn't frozen her in place, she might have had a small chance. The footpath was the only barrier between the road and the car park. It wouldn't have stopped a determined driver, but it might have slowed him down a little. She might have made it behind one of the parked cars, made a well-timed dash to the other side of the car park, over the low wall of the chapel and out and down the lane to the busy road beyond. But no. She had turned at the sound of the car engine, she had seen death in the approaching headlights, and fear had frozen her in place.

It took only a few minutes to make their way down towards the river. Today, the lab looked less bunker-like. The sun had broken through and was reflecting off the bright, white plaster. The river beyond was blue and deceptively inviting. The water would be bloody cold, if you were stupid enough to take a dip. Many had, and quite a few hadn't survived to tell the tale. On a calm day the Corrib looked meek and unthreatening, but lethal currents lurked under the surface.

'So what's the plan?' Fisher asked.

'I want to talk to James Murtagh. He's been the lead for this place for years. Carline Darcy works for him. If the girl spent time at the lab Murtagh should know about it.'

CHAPTER SIXTEEN

There were no windows at the front of the lab building, just an entrance with a narrow porch to offer shelter from the weather. The building had no signage of any kind, and the entrance door was dark, opaque glass. There was no doorbell either, just a sensor for security swipes fixed to the wall. Fisher tried the door but it was locked. Cormac nodded to the camera fixed to the wall above their heads.

'The security guard will have seen us,' he said. 'If we wait I presume he or she will come to the door eventually.' He leaned forward and rapped on the door with his knuckles, just in case. The sound was dull rather than sharp, as if the noise had been sucked into the building and absorbed by it.

'Emma works here?' Fisher asked. The expression on his face said that he didn't see the appeal.

'She says it's better inside,' Cormac said.

Eventually the door was opened by a sandy-haired man in a security guard uniform. 'Can I help?' he asked. He spoke with an accent, had those high, Eastern European cheekbones. Polish probably.

Cormac showed him his ID. 'We'd like to speak with James Murtagh,' he said.

The security guard stepped back and held the door for them. The entrance foyer was more welcoming than the outside of the building, but it was still very functional. The floor was polished concrete. There was a single desk and chair – for the security guard presumably. The desk held a monitor, a phone and a paperback copy of Adrian McKinty's

The Cold Cold Ground, the same book that sat on Cormac's bedside table. The walls of the foyer were largely taken up with lockers.

Cormac offered his hand for a shake. 'Cormac Reilly,' he said.

'Josep Zabielski.' The security guard shook with a cautious smile. 'Everyone calls me Joe.'

'You're from Poland, Joe?' Cormac asked.

The security guard nodded. 'From Zamość' He looked from Cormac to Fisher, as if hoping for a nod of recognition. 'It's a small city, very beautiful, little bit smaller than Galway. It's south of Lublin.'

'Lublin,' Fisher repeated, nodding.

'You know Lublin?' Joe asked, brightening.

Fisher shook his head.

'Joe,' Cormac said. 'Talk to me about your security cameras. What can you see?' He gestured towards the monitor.

Joe hesitated, glanced towards the door that led into the lab, as if he expected someone to come out. He turned the monitor a little way towards them, so they could see the screen. 'I just see the entrance, that's it. No other cameras.'

'No cameras inside the facility? Nothing around back?'

'Nothing inside. That would be a security risk. The feed could be hacked and a competitor might see the very private work. That is a very real risk, you know. The work here, it is worth many millions. And at the other side of the building there is only the river. No door leading inside.' His accent was strong but his English was excellent.

'Okay,' Cormac said. 'What about video?'

Joe furrowed his brow. 'Video?'

'Recordings, taken from your camera at the front. How long do you keep them for?'

The furrow disappeared, eyes widened. 'No video. We record nothing. The camera, it just helps me to see who is outside before I open the outside door.' He gestured to the interior door behind him. 'Only employees come here usually. They have security passes that permit them entry to this room. It is my job to make sure that they leave all their technology here. They are permitted no phones, no tablets or outside computers in the lab.' He gestured to the lockers. 'They leave everything here, then go inside. That's my job.' He looked from Cormac to Fisher and back.

'Okay,' said Cormac. 'That's fine, thank you Joe.' The guy was a bit nervous. Worried that he'd screwed up somewhere along the line maybe. 'But we'll need to see Professor Murtagh, and I'm afraid we can't leave our phones out here. We can't leave garda property out of our view in that way.'

Cormac had expected an objection, but Joe nodded seriously. 'It's not a problem. I do not think police could be security risk. I will show you to his office now, if you would like to meet with him?'

Joe led them through the interior door, and down a narrow corridor which had a bare concrete wall on the right – the outer skin of the building – and an internal wall on their left, broken up with multiple doors. The doors were anonymous, identical, with no signage to distinguish one from another. As they walked Fisher asked if someone was on duty at the front desk twenty-four hours, and Joe shook his head.

'It's Monday to Friday, nine to six only,' he said, and kept walking. Joe chose the fourth door and led them down another short corridor, before finally pausing in front of yet another anonymous door, knocking, and entering. James Murtagh sat behind a polished oak desk. He had a pen in one hand and appeared to have been marking up a paper. Joe made hurried introductions and excused himself at Murtagh's nod.

Murtagh stood and held out his hand. 'Professor James Murtagh,' he said. 'James.' The hand was thin, with long, elegant fingers. His clothing was simple – trousers and an open necked shirt – but the fabric looked expensive and as if it had been tailored to fit. His hair was grey and cut very close to the scalp.

Murtagh gestured to two seats in front of his desk and took a seat himself. The office was a decent size, with room for the large oak desk, a beautiful piece of furniture very obviously not standard issue, and a small round meeting table, currently overloaded with stacks of papers and scientific journals. One wall was largely taken up with bookshelves, which were packed two deep and overflowing. Against another wall Murtagh had placed a narrow oak table – a companion piece for his desk – on which he kept a number of silver-framed photographs. There was also a window, finally – a fantastic floor-to-ceiling number that looked out over the river. The view was striking; all the more startling for the austerity of the building up until that point.

'How can I help you, detectives? I presume you are here to speak to me about that terrible accident. Nathan Egan did mention that you may have some questions. He has asked me to give you every cooperation, though, I hasten to add, I would have been happy to help in any way I can, regardless. I have the greatest respect for the work you do.'

'You're aware that the body of a young woman was found on campus on Friday night?'

'Yes, the victim of a hit-and-run, I understand.' Murtagh looked genuinely distressed. 'I hadn't heard that she was young. I don't know why but that somehow makes it worse, doesn't it?'

Cormac thought about all the houses he'd visited where Mummy or Daddy, or on one awful occasion both, hadn't come home, and felt he couldn't agree.

'I understand that the university was entirely shut down, that the buildings were in lockdown and couldn't be accessed,' he said. Out of the corner of his eye, Cormac could see that

Fisher had taken out his notebook and was sitting with an attentive look on his face, pen at the ready, for all the world like an eager young uniform at his first interview.

'So I'm told,' said Murtagh. 'I wasn't here on Friday. I went away for the weekend actually, with my wife. It was our wedding anniversary.' Murtagh nodded in the direction of the photographs. One of the photographs appeared to be recent – in it Murtagh looked much as he did now. He had his arm around a woman who was presumably his wife. She smiled gently at the camera but her face, which was beautiful, was tired and too thin, and her head was wrapped in a silk scarf.

'My wife is recovering from cancer. It's been a difficult time,' Murtagh said. 'But she's been feeling better lately, so we took the opportunity to get away for a few days.' He frowned. 'I can't see how my being here that night would have saved that girl, but you can't help but think about it, can you?' His eyes went from Cormac to Fisher then back. 'If I'd been driving down the street at a particular time would my being there have stopped the accident?'

'Would you have been there?' Cormac asked. 'If you hadn't been away for the weekend, is it likely you would have been in the lab on Friday night?'

Murtagh gave a slight shake of his head. 'I suppose not. I do often come to the lab at odd hours. We all do, those of us who have the security clearance, if there is work that needs monitoring. But we finished up a long-running series of experiments last week, and we're reviewing results before we start working on the next run. I can check the logs, people do come and work in the evenings sometimes, but there's no guarantee that anyone was actually here when the young woman was killed. What time was the accident?'

Cormac's eyes were beginning to water. The sun had made its way through the window at just the wrong angle for his comfort. He tried to shift his position to avoid it, but failed.

'How is your work going, Dr Murtagh?' he asked.

Murtagh smiled. 'Very well, thank you, detective. Better since the arrival of your lovely partner Dr Sweeney, as I'm sure she's told you. I asked John to find us the best, and he certainly did that.'

Cormac was slightly taken aback by the mention of Emma – he hadn't expected Murtagh to realise the relationship, though of course there were any number of ways he could have come across that information, including, and perhaps most likely, from Emma herself. How absolutely natural it would be for Emma to tell her colleagues that her partner was a police detective, to mention him by name, though coming so soon after Nathan Egan waving her name around like a threat, it was disconcerting.

'Your security man tells us that there are no internal security cameras. Does he have that right?' Fisher asked.

'He does. There are no cameras inside this facility.'

'The system relies on employees swiping themselves in and out, is that correct?' Cormac asked. Murtagh nodded and Cormac continued, 'Each employee has a unique identification that permits them access?'

'Yes, that's correct,' said Murtagh. He narrowed his eyes.

'In that case you must have a record of when people swipe in and out,' Fisher said. 'For health and safety reasons if nothing else.'

'I'm not sure why you're asking about our security arrangements. The young woman who was killed had no connection to this laboratory, surely?'

Cormac held Murtagh's gaze, said nothing. After a moment Murtagh looked away.

'I see,' he said. 'This wasn't just a hit-and-run, was it detective? You don't think it was an accident.' He waited, but seemed to accept that he wouldn't get a direct answer. 'Well, Joe will be able to help you with the details, but I believe that there is an electronic log that tracks our comings and goings.' Murtagh paused. 'Should I be concerned for our staff here? We have a number of young women working here you know, some of them students who are very young indeed.'

'There's no need for concern, Mr Murtagh,' Fisher said. He handed Murtagh a card. 'If you can have someone email the electronic log to me at that address as soon as possible, that would be very helpful.'

Fisher delivered the request in just the right manner – casual, but with an assumption of cooperation, and it seemed to work. Murtagh made an expansive gesture. 'Anything I can do to help.'

'You mentioned students,' Cormac said. 'Carline Darcy is one of those students, is that correct?'

'Yes,' Murtagh said. 'Carline does some research work with us.' He looked from Cormac to Fisher, waiting for the next question.

Cormac was conscious of stepping onto dangerous ground. Murphy clearly wanted him to give the Darcy family a wide berth. But Carline Darcy was hiding something. The dead girl had had Carline's ID for a reason, the obvious one being to access these laboratories. He couldn't avoid the obvious questions that led to Carline and therefore the laboratory, even if he wanted to. And he shouldn't want to.

'Is she a good student?'

Murtagh answered the question with some enthusiasm. 'Carline Darcy is far more than a good student. She's exceptional. Truly exceptional. She's about to complete a four-year degree in two years and has had early acceptance for her doctorate. Her topic for her doctoral thesis is incredibly ambitious – I cautioned her against it frankly – but she's already proving me wrong.' He paused, then finished his sentence in the tone of one making a pronouncement. 'Carline Darcy is exactly like John Darcy was at her age. She has a genius for compound design. A natural instinct that is quite exceptional.'

'Is it awkward? Supervising the work of your boss's granddaughter?' Fisher asked, his tone sympathetic.

Murtagh laughed. 'I wouldn't call John my boss. I'm sure he wouldn't either. We've known each other since we were undergrads.'

Neither Fisher nor Cormac responded, and after a moment Murtagh filled the silence.

'Obviously John has had significant commercial success, though I'd like to think I contributed to that at a few pivotal moments along the way.' He held Fisher's gaze, then looked at Cormac. His manner said that he knew those words sounded self-aggrandising but he was sticking to them all the same. There was a self-respect in that that was admirable.

'Did you ever see Carline Darcy with a blonde friend?' Cormac asked. 'Around the same height? Either at the lab or at any other location?'

'I'm sure I have. Not at the lab, but I've seen Carline from time to time around the campus. She tends to be surrounded by a group.'

'No particular friend?' Cormac asked.

Murtagh thought for a moment. 'Not that I have noticed, but I wouldn't have, really. I don't see Carline outside the lab. I don't socialise on campus, certainly not with students, and when I'm here I'm usually in my office. Forgive me. I suspect you won't answer but I find it difficult not to ask the question. Do you suspect Carline Darcy of some involvement in this girl's death?'

'Not at all, Professor Murtagh,' Cormac said smoothly. 'We are merely trying to identify people who had access to Carline's identification card.'

Murtagh nodded with a concerned frown. 'Well, as I've said, anything we can do.'

Cormac wrapped up the interview, taking the name of the hotel Murtagh had stayed in for his weekend away, and confirming a few other details. Then Murtagh called Joe Zabielski to escort them back through the lab. Fisher took the opportunity to request again the access log for the lab.

'Professor Murtagh said that you'd know where to get it,' Fisher said. 'If you can send it through to the station as soon as possible, that would be very helpful. Or I can wait and take it with me now, if that works.'

Joe shook his head. 'I would like to be helpful, but all of the records are held centrally, at the company headquarters in Berlin. I only see the records from the same day, you understand? Nothing historical.'

Fisher and Cormac exchanged a glance. 'Please put through a request for the records to your headquarters immediately,' Cormac said. 'It's essential that they are provided to us without delay.' Their best chance of getting the records was if security personnel processed their request without referring it up through the ranks. If a company lawyer got wind of it there was a chance the request would be nixed or delayed on privacy or data protection grounds, and as they were held overseas, accessing them would be a challenge if the company chose not to cooperate. Joe looked doubtful, but agreed to make the request. He showed them out into the afternoon sunshine, and the door shut firmly behind them.

'Why do I feel like we're not getting anywhere, Fisher?' Cormac asked.

Fisher grimaced. 'I have a feeling we won't be getting those records.'

Cormac blew out a breath. 'We need to find the car,' Cormac said. 'it has to be somewhere. Even burnt out it would tell us something. Let's get back to the case room. See what progress has been made in our absence.'

CHAPTER SEVENTEEN

As a police officer, Moira Hanley had a lot of flaws. She was lazy, for one thing. She worked, with no extraordinary degree of effort, up to the hour exactly and not a minute beyond, and deeply resented anyone who either drew attention to that fact or asked more of her. She was also prone to taking a sudden and intense dislike to one individual or another, often for spurious reasons. Peter Fisher was right to suppose that she disliked him. Fisher's obvious ambition, his drive, and the hours he put in at his desk offended her. Despite all this, she did care deeply about the victims she encountered in her job, and when not blinded by one of her irrational dislikes, she was capable of moments of great insight into other people's behaviour. With the Henderson case, she had known that something was very wrong from the moment she saw Rob Henderson, hunched and wary on the roof of his house. She was also capable, when she had decided on a course of action, of dogged pursuit of that course. Carrie O'Halloran, who had worked Galway stations in Hanley's company for years, knew her strengths and weaknesses, and exactly how to make the best of the former and avoid the latter. Cormac Reilly had no such advantage.

Cormac had therefore made the dual mistakes of assigning more work to Moira than could easily be achieved in a seven-hour day with a break for a lengthy lunch, and sending her a follow-up email regarding an unanswered query on Sunday afternoon. Moira hadn't approved of the transfer of the Henderson case from Carrie O'Halloran to Cormac Reilly, and she approved even less of the resulting changes to her comfortable work environment. A great deal of her energy, that Monday morning, was taken up therefore with stoking her growing dislike of Cormac. She wasn't the type to admit to herself that her dislike of him was due almost entirely to the fact that he was asking of her more than she wanted to give, so she cast about to find a more palatable explanation. She found that justification in his running of the Henderson case.

She had raged internally as she drove him back to the station, as she climbed the stairs to the case room, as she sat and stared blankly at her computer screen. He didn't care about the case. Clearly, he couldn't care less that Rob Henderson had tried to murder his kids. Three innocent children, and Cormac Reilly couldn't even be arsed interviewing the star witness properly because he was too busy ... what? Covering up for his girlfriend? He'd asked Lucy Henderson a total of two, three questions? And they were all gentle little lobs, he might as well have sat in behind her and given her a back massage. *And* he'd interrupted her, Moira, every time she'd found her flow and started to push Lucy Henderson as she should be pushed.

Well, she wouldn't stand for it. It was as simple as that. Moira glanced around the room, at all the gardaí with their heads down over their computers or huddled together running through transcripts. Making phone calls, checking and cross-checking statements. And not one of them pursuing what should really be pursued, which was Emma Sweeney's connection with this case. There had been a rumour about Cormac Reilly and his girlfriend, back when all that drama had been going on. Moira had only ever heard bits of it, suggestions, but she had a fair idea who would be able to fill in the missing gaps.

She meandered over to Dave McCarthy. He had a missing persons listing open in front of him, but she doubted he was doing much reading.

'Do you fancy a coffee?' Moira asked.

McCarthy turned to her, looked her over. There was a knowing look in his eye that Moira didn't like.

'I've had one, thanks Moira,' McCarthy said. He waited, eyebrow raised for her to say whatever it was she had come to say. He wasn't going to make it easy. Fine. She wasn't the one who had something to be ashamed of, after all.

'What do you know about Emma Sweeney?' Moira asked. 'Should we be worried?'

'Worried?' The eyebrow went higher still. 'About what, exactly?'

The fucker. He knew exactly what she was talking about, but he'd obviously figured out which side his bread was buttered on. Moira felt the expression on her face tighten despite her best intentions.

'I just don't think it's appropriate that DS Reilly is running a case where his girlfriend is the prime witness,' she said.

McCarthy actually made a flapping gesture with his hand, as if she were a small annoying child he could usher away. 'Give it a rest, Moira,' he said. 'The forensics are clear. Her statement's been taken, she was just in the wrong place at the wrong time. It's grand.'

Moira retreated. She had been planning to ask him about the rumours that had gone around gone round about Reilly and his penchant for beautiful witnesses, before the shooting. She was sure that Dave McCarthy, who was the king of gossips despite his sudden holier than thou stance, would have heard all the juicy details. Well, fuck him. For whatever reason, he'd obviously decided Reilly was his new best friend. Moira sniffed. Never mind. There were other sources in the station, people who wouldn't hesitate to share a bit of inside information with a colleague. She would just have to go about this a little more carefully.

CHAPTER EIGHTEEN

Carrie had found it difficult to focus on the minutiae of her work after she sent Rory Mulcair to bring Paul Lambert home. The young boy's sincerity, his obvious distress, was difficult to shrug off. His was a story that needed further inquiry and she had second thoughts about Mulcair's ability to shepherd things to the next stage. She told herself that Cormac Reilly could manage his own team and forced her attention back to her own work. By eleven she'd worked her way through some long overdue witness statements. At eleven-fifteen she was interrupted by Moira Hanley delivering a coffee and a sandwich to her desk, *ulterior motive* written all over her face.

'What's this?' Carrie asked.

'I wanted five minutes. Figured if I brought lunch I'd have a better chance of getting it.' The expression on Moira's face told Carrie she didn't want to have the conversation in the open squad room. They went to a meeting room, shut the door. Carrie unwrapped the sandwich. Egg salad on granary, it didn't appeal. She sipped the coffee and listened.

Immediately after her conversation with Moira, Carrie went looking for Cormac Reilly. She found him at the university. She had just parked when she caught sight of Reilly and Fisher walking back towards the car park. Carrie got out, leaned against the car, and waited.

Whatever else you could say about Cormac Reilly, and right now she felt like she could say plenty, he wasn't stupid. He knew she wasn't there for a social chat as soon as he saw her. He exchanged a few words with Fisher, then sent him on his way, walked in her direction.

'Carrie,' Cormac said, as he reached her. 'To what do I owe the pleasure?' It pissed her off that he looked good, that he looked rested.

'We need to talk,' she said. It came out sharper than she'd intended, and her irritation rose. She'd wanted to be cool, calm, just as in control as he always seemed to be, but she was worried now, and her frustration was boiling over.

'Grand,' Cormac said. 'I've sent Fisher back to the station. Do you want to get coffee, or …'

'No coffee,' she said. 'This won't take long. I want to know why you're not pushing the Henderson case.'

He gazed back at her, an unreadable expression on his face. She wanted him to be angry, to have a go, because then she could have a go too, and a good row might lance the festering boil of anger and frustration in her belly. Instead the bastard just stared her down.

'There are three kids at risk in that house, Cormac. Rob Henderson is making solid progress towards an unfit to stand trial plea, and you're out here messing around doing interviews that Fisher could be handling alone.'

'Moira Hanley talked to you.'

'She did.'

'And she told you that I cut the interview with Lucy short.'

'You weren't even there ten minutes. You basically awarded her Mother of the Year and walked out the door. Are you distracted? Is it the hit-and-run? Is it Emma?' She glanced in the direction of the road, where they'd stood together over a body only a few days before.

Cormac's steady eyes were on her. There was no anger in his voice when he answered. 'Did Moira Hanley also tell you that Lucy was on tranquillisers? That she was high as a kite when we arrived and getting worse by the minute?'

Carrie opened her mouth to reply but nothing came out. Tranquillisers? She tried to think back to her own interview with Lucy, the slow speech, the abstraction. She'd thought Lucy had been in shock, in denial.

'Did she also tell you that I spent time talking to the sister, working to get her on board? We're going to need her help to get Lucy sober enough to talk to us. Sober enough to realise what's going on under her own roof.'

Christ. Suddenly Carrie felt an overwhelming and unfamiliar urge to cry. She swallowed it. She was fucking things up but that was no reason to make things worse. She felt a spatter of raindrops, looked up at the clouds gathering overhead. 'You need to get her in. You need to get her talking,' she said, uselessly.

'I know that, Carrie. I'm working on it.'

She nodded, glanced away, swallowed again. 'Right.'

The rain started to fall in earnest. He was still taking her measure. Christ, was that sympathy in his eyes?

'I've sent Fisher off,' Cormac said. 'Give me a lift back to the station?'

She drove for the first few moments with only the sound of the windscreen wipers breaking the silence.

Eventually, he said, 'Things aren't so great at home?'

She didn't answer. Had absolutely no urge to discuss her home life with him or anyone at the station. She just shook her head and they lapsed into silence again.

'We went to the lab,' Cormac said eventually. Maybe he felt sorry for her, wanted to shift the focus of the conversation. 'I'm not sure that we're focusing on the right things,' he went on. 'I don't know if the lab connection is going to get us anywhere.'

Carrie nodded. The car was idling at the lights on University Road. 'I heard Fisher interviewed Emma,' she said. 'How did that go?'

Cormac turned to look at her. She said nothing, kept her eyes on the road.

'Is there something else you want to ask me, Carrie?'

Carrie hesitated. She'd been way off on the Henderson thing, which made it much harder to open her mouth about something this sensitive. But she didn't have a choice. This was too important. 'Emma found the body. She works at the lab, and it's clear that there's a connection there. She lied when I asked her if the girl could have come looking for her on Friday night. People are asking if you're the right person to lead the case, that's all. It's not personal.'

It was a moment before Cormac responded, and when he did the edge to his voice let her know that this time, his self-control had taken effort. 'Are you volunteering to take over, Carrie? Because my memory of the thing is that you're not really in a position to do that right now.'

Carrie said nothing. What was she doing? Testing him? Helping him? The lights turned green and she was finally able to inch out, but the traffic was brutal, had slowed to a crawl as the rain came down.

'I'm going to say this once, and only once,' Cormac said. 'Emma had nothing to do with this.'

'I never said she did.'

Cormac gave her a sideways look. 'No bullshit between us, all right? You've already said that everything about this points to the labs. I'm not blind to the connection. The university was closed, so there were very few places she could have been going. It's looking like she wasn't a student, and she had an ID in her back pocket that belonged to Carline Darcy. Not just an ID, a security swipe for the lab. And the first witness at the scene was Emma, who works there. I understand what that might look like to the wrong eyes, but I'm telling you that wherever we end up, it won't be with Emma in our cross hairs, so don't waste time and energy working up a theory involving her.'

Carrie looked out through the windscreen at the falling rain. It was almost hypnotic, sitting there in the car, only the quiet sound of her own breathing in her ears, the rain a soft counterpoint, conscious of Cormac as a silent presence beside her. She replayed his words in her mind. Why did it feel like he was trying to convince himself, rather than her?

'That rumour, about Emma, last year,' she said in the end.

'Yes.'

'I never asked you about it then.'

Cormac shifted in the passenger seat beside her, suddenly seemed much too big for the small space.

'I'm asking you about it now.'

Carrie learned something about Cormac Reilly that day. That cool, calm exterior was not impenetrable. She asked her question, and as he turned his head in her direction, his body suddenly tense with unmistakable fury, she was abruptly aware of the vast physical differences between them. Carrie never let herself be intimidated. She was the kind of woman who stepped up to every challenge. Got in its face and stared it down. But every now and again she was confronted by realities that no amount of chutzpah and confidence could overcome, and this was one of those moments. He was so much bigger than her, so much stronger. She told herself that she wasn't afraid of him.

He jabbed a finger across her field of vision.

'Turn down there,' he said.

'What?'

'There,' he said, impatiently, and if she'd been a second later responding she knew he would have reached for the steering wheel himself.

She turned down Canal Road and pulled in. He didn't speak until she turned to look at him.

'You've met Emma. You know her. Are you seriously asking me if she's a murderer?'

Carrie said nothing. She wasn't willing to say out loud what she was thinking, which was that making polite chitchat with the partner of a colleague on a handful of occasions did not equate to knowing someone.

Cormac's mouth was set in a grim line. 'Because that was the story, wasn't it? That Emma murdered someone and I helped cover it up. Christ, Carrie, you're not stupid. How the hell do you think I would have pulled that off?'

Carrie shook her head, her tired brain failing to provide her with something sensible to say. 'There are rumours …'

'There are always fucking rumours, Carrie. What's different is that this is the first time that I'm aware of that you've listened to them.'

Carrie looked out at the grey day through the rainwater running in little rivulets down the windscreen. She drew in a long breath and let it out. 'The story I've been told is that Emma killed someone. In Dublin. She met you when you were investigating the case. You got involved and pulled strings to make the case go away.'

'Jesus.' He sounded horrified.

She turned to him. 'I ran a search on PULSE, Cormac. All I managed to find was a case reference number. Everything else has been expunged somehow, almost as if it was never there. There are just traces, a few hints left behind. But there's enough so that I know there was a case. And Emma was involved.'

The expression on his face was a combination of fury and disgust. Involuntarily, she dropped her eyes to his hands and saw that his fists were clenched so tightly that his knuckles were whitening. But his gaze followed hers. With an obvious and deliberate effort, he relaxed his fists, shifted his position so that he was facing away from her and out of the window, and drew in a long breath. Let it out. A moment passed, and he started to speak.

CHAPTER NINETEEN

'The first time I saw Emma, she was unconscious on an ambulance gurney,' he said. 'She was battered and bruised. Her right hand and sleeve were covered in blood. They wheeled her past me outside the house and she never opened her eyes.'

Carrie stayed very still. The rain was falling gently, silently around them. The road was quiet. The car felt like a cocoon, a confessional, as he told the story. It came in fits and starts, as if he'd never spoken about it before.

The beginning was that Emma came from money. Her father, Richard, had been an investment banker. He made his fortune in London, in the City. A talented investor, he made his millions, made his tens of millions, and got out while he was still in his forties. The family left London, moved back to Dublin, where Emma's mother Caroline returned to college to finish her medical studies and qualify as a GP. They built a beautiful house in Dalkey, overlooking the ocean. The girls went to private school. Richard did a bit of day trading. Life was good.

A few years passed. It was 1995 and the Irish property market had put on cleats and taken off at a promising pace. Richard, bored with his day trading, set up a property investment company with friends. It did well. Better than well. For eight years the investment company made Madoff-level returns, and Richard, who really didn't need the money to fund his modest (relatively speaking, at least) lifestyle, was quietly satisfied that he still had it. But in time he had seen the complete absence of regulation, the bankers only too eager to offer one hundred and twenty percent finance on any deal going, the unsophisticated investors piling into the market with equity borrowed on family homes and credit cards, and he wanted out. By 2003 he was shedding investments as fast as possible. Some of his partners in the fund, grown too used to thirty per cent plus returns year on year, objected. They didn't want out. They were sure there was more on the table. A deal was struck. Richard sold his stake in the firm to his partners. He retreated back to his quiet family life, fortune comfortably expanded and intact.

In Richard's absence, his partners looked around at an overheated, under-regulated market, and saw opportunity. For opportunity, they needed capital. They opened the partnership up to people who had no business in that sort of high-octane, highly leveraged environment. They invested and re-invested. When the subprime crisis hit America in 2007, liquidity froze, Irish property prices fell by fifty per cent or more, and the fund was suddenly and irrevocably insolvent. Some of the original partners went broke. Some of them were wealthy enough that they were able to wash their hands of it, move on to their other investments with nothing more than a backward glance and a lesson learned.

But those little investors, those eager men and women who read the fine print without understanding it and signed on the bottom line, they lost everything. The banks came for their investment properties, then their family homes. If they held on to their jobs the banks garnished their incomes. The Irish government, which had pledged the credit of every Irish man and woman to pay back German bankers, imposed budget repair levies and cut human services to the bone.

Carrie listened to him talk. She didn't need Cormac to tell her how the country had suffered after the bust, but better to let him tell it his way.

'You know all this about Richard Sweeney, or this is what you were told?' Carrie asked.

'Emma told me a lot but I confirmed most of it through the investigation, directly or indirectly. Richard definitely sold out of the fund. By 2004 all the paperwork was done and dusted and the money paid over. After that he had no business relationship with his former partners. If he saw them at all it was for the occasional round of golf.'

'Then what happened?'

'Some hack did a hatchet job on the family in the *Herald*. Big splash about how Richard had made a fortune and sold his part to the little guys just before the shit hit the fan. Big photo of the family home in Dalkey. A photo of Emma's little sister getting out of a limo. It was her bloody debs night, by the way, and a friend had rented the car.'

Carrie was conscious of the time ticking by, conscious of the work waiting for her attention at her desk, conscious that her children would soon be boarding school buses and heading home. She wanted to get going but she needed to hear this too, and Cormac needed to tell it.

'More than one investor blamed everything on Richard, after the *Herald* was done with him. But there was one guy who made it personal. Padraig Flynn. Flynn had invested a quarter of a million in the fund. He'd pulled the money together from a range of sources, some of them more legitimate than others. He re-mortgaged the family home, forged his wife's name on the paperwork. Flynn lost his job in the crash, then the fund went under, and he couldn't make the repayments on the second mortgage. His wife left him. The bank came calling. He fought the bank in the courts and lost. He fought his wife for custody of the kids and lost. Look, there's no doubt Flynn had a tough run, but he was a dirty bastard. Loads of priors for assault, including domestic violence. When the dust settled and Flynn was left with nothing, he looked around for someone to blame and decided to focus on Richard. He started with a bit of social media ranting, and then he escalated. Flynn played dirty. Dog shit through the letterbox. Threatening letters. Some petty vandalism. Then he escalated again. Started following the girls home from school. Showed up at Emma's mum's medical practice, pretending to be a patient.' Cormac twisted his face in disgust. 'He said he had an infection on his penis, and when she was bent over examining him he told her the truth.'

'Christ,' Carrie said.

The next bit came out in a rush. 'One day Emma was at home alone, and the guy broke into the house. She was in the kitchen, with music playing.' Cormac's voice thickened. 'Emma loves music, you know?' He didn't turn to look at her, and Carrie looked straight ahead, out through the windscreen.

'He hurt her, badly. Beat her. He had a baseball bat. She had three broken ribs, a fractured arm. Her jaw was broken. She had internal bruising. She tried to fight back, but she hadn't a chance. Tried to get away, but she couldn't. And then her little sister came home.'

Oh shit.

'Roisín was only seventeen at the time. She opened the door and saw him. She could have run but Emma was unconscious on the floor and she didn't want to go without her sister.'

There was nothing objective about Cormac's retelling of this story. He wasn't a cop recounting witness statements. He was intimately involved. He told it as if he had been present.

'When Emma woke up Flynn was on top of Roisín. He had his hands around her throat. By then Emma's left arm was broken but her right arm was working fine. She pulled herself up off the floor, took a kitchen knife, came up behind him, and slit his throat.'

'Jesus Christ,' Carrie said. She felt the shock of it. Thought of that beautiful girl. The scientist with the manicured nails and expensive clothes. Carrie wouldn't have thought her capable.

'Afterwards she went into shock. Roisín was the one who called 999. Emma fainted again. She was hospitalised. She was badly injured, of course. She was also in a profound state of shock. Just withdrew completely. It took days for her to recover enough to be able to tell the whole story. And that's the only reason she was ever technically a suspect, when it was clear to even the dumbest fucker on the scene that it was a self-defence situation.'

There was silence for a moment in the car. 'And the records?' Carrie asked.

Cormac shook his head. 'I worked for the anti-terrorist squad. You know that. Long after the case was put to bed, when Emma and I started our relationship, I reported it up the line. After that everything on PULSE about Emma and her family became need-to-know.'

Almost every member of the Garda Síochána had some level of access to PULSE, and quite a few civilian officers too. Access to some information – particularly personal information regarding serving members of the anti-terrorism unit – was therefore restricted, for obvious reasons. Cormac didn't say it, but his tone made it clear that she should have thought of that, and he was right.

He finally turned to her. 'Who told you, Carrie?'

'What?'

'I want to know who it is who's spreading the rumour. I think you owe it to me to tell me.'

She felt pinned under his gaze. She looked back into his green eyes. She trusted him. She didn't know why. What was it about Cormac Reilly? Was she fooling herself? What did she really know about him?

'I already know it was Moira Hanley. She was pissed off, she went looking for dirt and she found it. I'm not worried about Hanley but I want to know her source.'

Carrie shook her head. 'I don't know. She didn't tell me, but it probably doesn't take much imagination to figure it out. It will be the usual suspects. The no hopers who sit in the corner bitching and moaning about ...' Carrie paused, shook her head, angry with herself that she hadn't stopped to properly consider the source of the information before coming to Cormac all guns blazing. 'Do you want me to find out?'

He brushed her off, made his excuses. He clearly didn't trust her, and could she really object? She hadn't exactly covered herself in glory over the past twenty minutes.

They sat in silence for another moment. Then Carrie put the car into gear, turned it, and headed back towards the city. The story about Emma was too much to take in ... she needed time to think it through. On the one hand, Emma's injuries and the fact that she was at home minding her own business when the attack took place made it fairly clear that it had been a legitimate case of self-defence. On the other hand, not many people would have the balls to cut a man's throat. It was so brutal, so final. There was no getting away from the fact that she had actually killed someone. Taken as a whole, did the story really make Emma less of a suspect in the hit-and-run case?

'Cormac,' said Carrie. She spoke in a clear, steady voice, wanting him to hear her. 'You need to think about whether you running this case is the right thing for you, or for Emma.' Carrie knew that she had some blame in this too. She'd been too tired and too pissed off to do what she should have done on Friday night. She should never have gone along with Cormac running this case. 'Maybe you should step back. Hand the case over to someone else.'

'I'm not going to do that, Carrie. There's no conflict here. Emma is nothing more than a witness to the aftermath of a crime, and I'm not going to give credibility to a bunch of bullshit by stepping back now.'

There was no point in arguing with him. He wasn't going to move.

Was he blinkered, blind to the possibilities because he loved the girl? A stray thought crossed her mind … what would it be like to be loved by a man like that, to be supported by him? She slammed the door on the thought.

'If the Lambert lead works out then the case may not be connected to the lab after all, of course,' she heard herself say.

There was a pause.

'What Lambert lead?' Cormac said.

CHAPTER TWENTY

Cormac picked up a squad car at the station and drove straight to the Lambert house. He switched on the lights and siren to expedite his drive through Galway traffic, switching them off again once he made it out of the city. He called the station on the way, got Fisher who was full of apologies. He'd thought the lead had been tied off, or he would of course have mentioned it. More voices in the background as clarification was sought. Eventually Fisher came back on the line.

'Sorry sir. The report came in first when you were at the Henderson interview. Then Rory dropped the boy – the brother that is – home and when he came back to the office he reported that it was a false alarm. I'm afraid I didn't ask any follow ups. It seems that Rory spoke to the mother who assured him that her daughter was not missing, and Rory took her at her word.'

Cormac made not much more by way of comment. He had work to do and there was no time to waste on recrimination. He drove on and fifteen minutes later he pulled in outside a nice-looking semi-d in Athenry, a small commuter town. There was a car parked in the driveway, boot open, groceries half unloaded. As Cormac watched, a middle-aged woman emerged from the house and gathered bags of shopping from the boot of the car.

'Mrs Lambert?' Cormac approached, ID out. 'DS Cormac Reilly, Mill Street. I'd like to talk to you about your daughter Della, if you have a moment.'

'This again. Look, whatever Della's done has nothing to do with us. She doesn't live here anymore. Barely bothers to call home even.' She straightened and looked at him with a sour expression on her face, plastic shopping bags digging into her fingers.

'Right,' Cormac said. He looked behind her to the house. The curtains in the upstairs windows were closed, and there were no signs of life. 'I'm not here about anything Della might have done. I'm here to speak to you because your son Paul has reported Della missing.'

She looked at him with narrowed eyes, like someone waiting on the punchline for a joke that she so far found distasteful. 'What, because she didn't call him for a couple of days? A teenage boy has a tantrum and you lot jump. What is it, a slow month?'

'Could we speak inside, Mrs Lambert? It would be better if we could speak inside.'

She rolled her eyes, shifted the weight of her shopping bags in her hands. 'It's Eileen,' she said. 'You'd better come in.'

He followed her through and into the kitchen. A little girl with the distinct almond-shaped eyes of a child with Down's Syndrome was methodically unpacking each shopping bag, putting everything neatly away in cupboards and shelves. Eileen put the last of her bags on the floor beside her daughter, and turned to Cormac, hands on hips.

'When was the last time you saw Della?' Cormac asked, and leaned down to roll a tin of peas that had escaped the little girl back towards her. He smiled at her and got a careful smile in return.

'I don't know.' Eileen paused. 'I suppose she was here for Geraldine's birthday in February. For lunch. Probably not since then, but Della never does make much of an effort to stay in touch with her family.'

'Let's sit, will we, Eileen?' Cormac stepped forward smoothly, moved a stack of laundry to one side, then took a seat at the kitchen table. The gesture was deliberately familiar, as if he were a regular visitor to the house. Eileen Lambert hesitated, then moved to take a seat.

'Will I make tea, Mama?' Geraldine asked.

'Go and watch TV, Geraldine,' Eileen Lambert said, her voice tight. The little girl looked at her mother, then disappeared from the room without another word. A moment later and they heard the theme tune for *Dora the Explorer* coming from the living room.

'Nice kid,' Cormac said.

'Looking after Geraldine is a full-time job,' Eileen said, her voice sharp. 'I haven't worked outside the house since she was born. If I wasn't here, playing with her, working with her, giving her day structure, what do you think would happen to her?' Her tone was more than defensive; it was almost an attack, as if she and Cormac had been engaged in a long and bitter argument about Geraldine's fate and Eileen's choices.

Cormac didn't react. 'Paul is very concerned about Della, Eileen. He says that they are usually in contact every day, or every second day. But he hasn't heard from Della since Friday, and she's not answering her phone.'

'For God's sake. She's probably gone off with friends for a few days. Della's eighteen years old. She never comes home, never telephones her own mother. What eighteen-year-old keeps her teenage brother informed about her every movement?'

'Did you know that Paul went to Della's apartment? That he waited for her there, alone, overnight? He didn't have a key so he just sat in the hall.' Cormac's tone was measured. He was careful to ensure that the question did not sound like an accusation. He didn't want Eileen Lambert to shut down,

144

and she was very obviously the type who wouldn't take criticism lying down.

'What are you talking about?' Eileen asked.

'Paul went to Della's apartment yesterday. He stayed there all night.'

'No, he didn't. Paul was at home all day yesterday. And he slept in his own bed.' The words were flat, absolute.

'You saw him?'

Eileen compressed her lips. She wore a slash of deep red lipstick, and it had bled into the corners of her mouth.

'Paul told us that he got the train to Galway after school. He took a bus and then walked to Della's apartment. Someone let him in the main security door. He was there all night.'

Eileen Lambert shook her head, face grim, lips thin.

'You didn't put your head in the door at bedtime, check up on him?'

'He's fifteen years old. More than old enough to put himself to bed. I have a child with real needs to take care of. Forgive me if I get a little distracted.'

'Tell me about Della, Mrs Lambert,' Cormac said. 'Does she often go away for a few days without telling you?'

'I wouldn't know. Della is an adult. She makes her own money, pays her own way. I don't look over her shoulder.' She looked at Cormac, read something into his steady gaze. 'Della and Paul know that in this house Geraldine comes first. That's the way it should be and that's the way it is.'

'Paul mentioned that Della moved to Galway just over two years ago, when she was, what, sixteen? Was that for work?'

'College. Della was accepted early at the university, to study chemistry. She would have gone the year before but her father said no.' Eileen delivered this as if the idea of a fifteen-year-old studying university level chemistry was completely run of the mill.

'She must be a very bright student.'

Eileen shrugged. 'It didn't suit her in the end.'

A noise from the hallway distracted Cormac for a moment – then he returned his attention to Eileen. 'You were saying it didn't suit her ...'

Eileen was looking down at her wedding ring. 'Della lost interest. She always did get bored easily. She dropped out of college and got a job. I think it suited her better.'

The kitchen door opened then and Paul came in, his face flushed. His eyes went straight to his mother. 'Mum,' he started.

'Is what he said true?' Eileen asked, voice tight. 'Did you go to see Della without telling me? Spend the night sitting outside her apartment in Galway?'

Paul hesitated then nodded his head once.

'If you thought there was something wrong with Della you should have come to me. I am her mother. If there was reason to be concerned, of course I would be, more than anyone. If I'm not worried about her why should you be?'

Paul was facing his mother but his eyes were slightly averted. He didn't say anything.

Cormac cleared his throat. 'I'd like to look at Della's apartment,' he said. 'I'm sure you're right, Mrs Lambert, that Della is just busy. But given that she hasn't been in touch, and that no one seems to know quite where she is ... I think it would be no harm to make a few preliminary inquiries.'

Eileen Lambert wanted to object, that was written all over her face. But how could she? What sort of mother tells the police not to look for a daughter who may be missing? She was trying to frame a counter-argument and coming up with nothing. Paul took advantage of the distraction to slip quietly from the room.

'Do you have a key to her place?' Cormac asked.

Eileen didn't, but she made no argument against Cormac's proposal that he seek out Della's landlord and request access that way. She walked him to the door, opened it for him, then held it, half-leaning against it, and spoke again as he left. 'Della's fine, you know,' she said. 'She doesn't care about this family, that's all it is. She thinks she's better than us. That's why she never comes home. Paul always thought he was different. I told him and told him, Della doesn't care about you. But he wouldn't listen, he thought she loved him. This is just Paul waking up and realising that he's just the same as the rest of us.'

Christ. 'We'll be in touch Mrs Lambert,' Cormac said.

'Whatever Della's been doing, it's her business, you understand me?' she called after him as he walked away down the path. 'She's an adult. She's living her own life. It's got nothing to do with me. Did you hear me?' He kept walking.

CHAPTER TWENTY-ONE

Cormac rang the station and had Fisher call the letting agent – a quick online search for Della's address had disclosed the historical rental listing and the name and phone number of the agent. By the time he reached the outskirts of Galway, Fisher called back to confirm that the young woman who had leased the property was willing to open the place up for them.

'She's coming now,' Fisher said. 'By the time you get back in she should be there.'

'She didn't ask for a warrant?'

'Didn't seem to occur to her. She met Della Lambert herself and was worried to hear she was missing. Said she'd always thought Della was too young to be living alone.'

Fisher suggested that he park at the station. The apartment was less than five minutes away and it would be easier to walk over than drive and look for a place to leave the car. Fisher was waiting at the station gates when Cormac pulled in.

'Rory's very aware that he fucked up, and so am I,' Fisher said a bit grimly. 'He let the mother give him the bum's rush, and then I compounded the error by not asking for a detailed report. Sorry sir.'

Cormac nodded, chose not to pursue it. 'I just met Eileen Lambert. She wasn't particularly interested in the fact that her daughter is missing, and we're on her doorstep asking questions. For whatever reason, she's working hard to distance herself from her older daughter.'

'Did you meet the brother?' Fisher said.

Cormac shook his head. 'He came in briefly, but his mother didn't give him much of an opportunity to speak.'

'You think she's involved in some way?'

'I think she's afraid of something. Not that her daughter is dead, I don't think. Something else.'

They walked in the direction of the city. Cormac cast a dubious eye at the darkening sky, but they'd only been walking for a minute when Fisher turned down Dominick Street and led the way across the road to a narrow alleyway.

'The apartment building is accessed this way,' Fisher said. 'It's infill development. It used to be all storage yards for old mills, backing up to the river bank. They knocked them all down, built forty or fifty apartments back there. It's a nice building.'

'You've been here before?' Cormac asked.

Fisher shrugged. 'Not inside, like. But I walk up this way to the station. I walked past every day when all the work was going on.'

They turned down the alley. It was just wide enough to allow the passage of a small car, assuming the wing mirrors were tucked in.

'What's this place like?' Cormac asked. 'The kind of place students would rent?'

'I wouldn't think so. I'd say it would be too pricey.'

Cormac thought of Carline Darcy's designer digs but said nothing.

'I called the café Della was supposed to be working at,' Fisher said. 'The manager had never heard of her but he'd only been working there a year. I get the impression they have pretty high staff turnover.'

They turned the corner and found the apartment building. It was nice-looking, if a bit twee, with cut-stone walls at the ground-floor level, and wooden window frames painted red.

Despite the olde-worlde look the front door had an electronic lock, accessible by pass card.

They waited for the estate agent for another five minutes or so, were alerted to her arrival by the sound of a pair of heels hurrying down the cobble-stoned alleyway in their direction.

'Sorry. Sorry.' A young woman appeared around the corner, arrived in a flurry of explanations and too much perfume. 'I got here as fast as I could. But I can't get the car down the alley, so I had to find parking, and it's a nightmare at this time of day.'

'You have the keys?' Cormac asked.

She poked about in her shoulder bag and pulled out a heavy keyring. 'We manage the place. I mean my agency, Donnellan & Molloy, manage it.' She pressed a key pass to the pad and the lock buzzed and released. 'It's 4B, right? That's the fourth floor.' A nervous laugh. 'I hope she's okay. She seemed like a nice girl. A bit young to sign a lease for a place like this in her own name, but she was happy to pay the equivalent of six months' rent in as security deposit, so I thought it would be okay.'

The estate agent subsided into a nervous silence as they rode the lift to the fourth floor. She led the way down the wide, tiled corridor. The lock on the apartment door was a standard Chubb lock, not electronic, and she fumbled with the key before she got it right. Cormac asked her to wait outside for them, then he opened the door and entered, Fisher on his heels. They found themselves in a small hall, which had four doors leading from it. Only one was ajar, and through it they could see a kitchen, a dining table, and a large window looking out onto the dashing water of the river below. The room looked empty.

'Check the kitchen,' Cormac said and Fisher nodded and moved off. Cormac opened the door to his right. A bathroom, very clean, white fluffy towels placed strategically, like a show home. The next door led into what must be the master bedroom. A double bed, neatly made, bright white linen, a thick-knit throw that looked expensive on the end of the bed. A curved window offered a second view of the river. The room had a fresh smell, like clean laundry brought in from the line. Nothing personal on show, no photographs, but there was a stack of paperback books on the bedside table, more on the floor beside the bed. There were a couple of prints on the wall – anonymous splotches of abstract colour that left Cormac cold – and a white phone charger cable snaked out from behind the bed and onto the bedside table. There was an en suite bathroom, smaller than the bathroom he'd already seen, and this one had shampoo and conditioner bottles, one of each, a toothbrush and a toilet bag on a single glass shelf. He returned to the bedroom as Fisher entered.

'Living room's unremarkable,' Fisher said. 'The second bedroom's been used as a study. Empty.'

Cormac went to the living area next. It was one decent-sized open-space area, segmented by a breakfast bar into kitchen and living area. There was a small glass circular dining table with four chairs, a dark blue velvet couch and two striped armchairs. More books on the coffee table. Two large windows – one was really a door leading to a Juliet balcony – overlooked the river, which boiled darkly below, white tipped waves frothing. It was slightly surreal, looking over that rushing water and hearing nothing. The room was eerily quiet. Triple glazing.

'It doesn't feel like she was working out of here,' Cormac said.

'You're thinking she might have been a prostitute?' Fisher asked.

Cormac grimaced, shook his head.

Fisher nodded. 'I thought she might be on the game, when you said she was living here. I mean, because of the expense. But you're right, it doesn't have that sort of feel.'

Cormac opened the fridge. A pint of milk, open. Jars of this and that, orange juice, a few sausages in an opened pack, their skin pink and drying. 'She could have been working out of another place.' He closed the fridge and walked out of the room again, past Fisher and into the second bedroom. No bed this time, just a packed bookshelf, and one large desk installed against the wall, not looking out over the water as it might have been. There was a large, expensive-looking computer screen on the desk, and a keyboard. No hard drive, but there were unplugged cables on the desk.

'She must have used a laptop,' Fisher said, from behind him. 'Plugged it in when working from home, taken it with her when she left.'

Cormac was looking at the books. Novels, some of them, but mostly textbooks. Textbooks with obscure titles. According to her brother, Della Lambert had dropped out of college by the end of her first semester. He would have to check with Emma, but he felt sure that most of these books would be beyond first year undergraduate chemistry. He took *Structure and Mechanism in Protein Science* from the shelf. The spine was well cracked, and it fell open at a page titled *Transition States in Protein Folding*. There were handwritten notes in the margin, in a scrawl he couldn't quite make out. He put the book back. They had no warrant to search the place.

'It's very clean, isn't it?' Fisher said. 'The whole place I mean, not just this room. Almost as if she was preparing for visitors.'

Cormac shrugged. He looked over the desk. There was a small stack of expensive looking notebooks, still wrapped in cellophane, the brand name Clairefontaine embossed on the front of each one. Nothing else. No unwrapped notebooks, no scrap paper, no print outs. He turned to the wardrobe, flicked through the rack of clothes. High street brand names, some of them still with tags attached. No Stella McCartney here.

'Okaaaay,' Fisher said.

Cormac turned. Fisher had opened a desk drawer and was staring down at the content. Cormac crossed to him and found himself looking down at neat stacks of fifty-euro notes, still bound in a bank's sticky white labels.

'She didn't earn that as a prostitute,' Fisher said. He reached out to one of the bundles.

'Gloves,' Cormac said sharply.

Fisher pulled his hand back, flushed.

'Get her dental records in straight away, all right? Call her mother and don't take no for an answer. If Della Lambert is our victim I want ID confirmed before the end of the day and a team back here with a search warrant.' Cormac thought about Paul Lambert, waiting for news in that oppressive house in Athenry, and his stomach sank. Whatever Della Lambert had been up to it wasn't waitressing, and it was looking very much like it might have gotten her killed.

Tuesday 29 April 2014

CHAPTER TWENTY-TWO

Valentina was awake when the knock came at six o'clock in the morning. She ran in the mornings, a nice six-kilometre round trip that took her down the Dock Road and over the bridge, out through the Claddagh and along the sea front. But six was early for her, and she was lying in bed, debating whether to make an early start or turn over for another hour's sleep, when she heard someone at the door. Valentina sat up in bed and looked around for clothes. She pulled on the previous day's T-shirt and jeans over the singlet and shorts she wore to bed, feeling a sense of dread and not entirely understanding why. Except that ever since that sexy policeman came to the door, Carline had been jittery, maintaining a brittle good humour that was unnerving.

She opened the door to a stranger. An old man, in his late seventies maybe, very thin, with his hair cut short and wearing a dark suit with a white shirt open at the neck. He looked through her in a way that made her uncomfortable.

'Yes?' Valentina said. She wanted to pull the door across her body but he'd already taken a half-step forward, almost into the room.

He didn't answer, just waited with a bored expression, as if he was dealing with a particularly slow waitress. It took her another moment to twig. She had seen him before, if only in photographs. Carline's grandfather. John Darcy, the Grand Poobah himself. He read the dawning recognition in her face, stepped forward into the room without waiting for an invitation, took the door from her, and closed it behind him.

'Get her for me, would you?' John Darcy said.

Valentina wanted to refuse. Wanted to take the last moment back and pretend she didn't recognise him, demand of him the mean politeness of a basic introduction, but instead she found herself walking – trotting damnit – over to Carline's room and knocking on the door.

When Carline didn't immediately respond, she opened the door to a dark room, a room with a faint scent of illness about it, the hint of stale sweat.

'Carline.' She whispered the name. Stupid. Valentina reached for the light switch and turned it on. The light was too bright, she had to blink against it.

'Carline,' Valentina said again, louder this time, and took a few steps towards the bed. The other girl lay tangled and hot in her bedclothes. She woke slowly, turned a tired, puffy face in Valentina's direction.

'Vee?'

Carline was disoriented, still half-asleep. As she came to full wakefulness what stole into her expression was not understanding, or wakefulness, but fear.

'Carline, what's going on?' Valentina asked impulsively. She didn't get an answer. Carline's eyes went to something behind her and Valentina turned to see that John Darcy had followed her into the bedroom.

'Thank you. Carline and I will speak in here.'

Darcy stood, taking in his granddaughter's bedroom in an unimpressed manner, before allowing his gaze to fall dispassionately on Carline. She sat up and straightened her blankets so they covered more of her body. Her expression, as she came fully awake, was one of mortification. One bare foot still protruded from under her blankets, and she drew it back, curling in on herself protectively.

'John,' she said, her voice rough with sleep. 'I'm so sorry, I wasn't expecting you.'

'Evidently.' John Darcy turned to Valentina with an expression that told her she was intruding in a private conversation.

Jesus, what a wanker. Valentina rolled her eyes at Carline but was met with such a look of terror that she retreated from the bedroom at once, closing the door quietly behind her. She hesitated, heard a low murmur of voices. Maybe she should make an excuse to go back in. Darcy was a shit. Carline was so clever. Why couldn't she see how manipulative he was? She came back reeling from every conversation she'd ever had with him. He'd never once paid her a compliment without undermining her with his next breath. But talking to Carline about her grandfather had always been a waste of time. Valentina disappeared into her bedroom, feeling disloyal, and shrugging her shoulders against the creeping discomfort that followed her.

As soon as Valentina had left the room, John Darcy took a seat in the chair that faced Carline's desk and started to leaf absently through the loose papers that were there. He laid a hand on her closed laptop, drummed his fingers lightly.

'You're unwell?' he said.

'I ... a little. My stomach.'

A slow nod. 'It is important to take care of your health. You've worked hard this year. If you feel a break is needed, certainly, you should take it.'

The words were conciliatory, supportive even, but John Darcy was looking at her with blue eyes as cold at the Atlantic on a winter's day, and just as comforting.

'I'll be better soon.' Her eyes strayed to her computer, where his hand still rested. 'I'll get up, get some work done.'

John nodded again. The worst of it was that he reminded her so strongly of her father. She wondered, not for the first time, if that was something she had constructed in her head.

Her father had died when he was thirty-five. John Darcy was seventy-two. What similarity could there really be between them? And yet she felt it, that pull towards him, so strongly.

'James has been telling me about your thesis proposal. I'm impressed Carline. Very impressed.'

Carline felt a rush of heat to her cheeks, a mix of happiness and dread.

'I ... thank you,' she said.

'When do you expect to complete the paper?'

Still sitting on her bed, Carline drew her knees to her chest, wrapped her arms around them. It felt like a childish pose, but she held it. 'It's not ready. It has potential, but it's not there yet.'

'It's important, I think, that nothing distracts you from completing the work. You feel confident that you will finish? Notwithstanding recent ... events?'

She nodded slowly. What did he know? Nothing surely, he couldn't know anything or he wouldn't be sitting calmly in her room, talking to her as if she still had some value, as if she was worthy of his attention.

'We spoke about your exams the other day. James tells me that you have sufficient credits to graduate without them. If your work on your doctoral thesis requires all of your attention, I have no objection if you choose not to sit the exams.'

Carline felt a flare of hope, which she quickly quenched. What did this mean? She wasn't naive enough to believe that there was love behind her grandfather's sudden gesture of support. She knew he didn't care about her, at least not yet, and she didn't resent that. Because John Darcy wasn't like other people. He was better. He didn't bestow love like beads at Mardi Gras, handed out lightly to a pretty smile and just as quickly forgotten. No, his love had to be earned, through a slow accumulation of achievement. And she'd never been afraid of hard work.

Carline hadn't always understood her grandfather. She'd felt his rejection hard as a child. When she turned eighteen and inherited her father's shares in the Darcy companies, and her grandfather had chosen to exercise his option to buy them back, that had been a blow. The lawyer her mother hired had hastened to assure her that the purchase price was market rate, more than fair, and that if she spent responsibly – this with a judicious look at Evangeline – she would never have to worry about money again. He'd expected her to be happy, but money wasn't enough. How could it be? Money didn't keep you safe, she'd known that since she was a little girl. Without position, status, power, protection, what was she but just another pretty girl, floating around Cannes or Marbella?

When she finished school and her grandfather wrote to her, advising her not to attend Trinity College as she'd planned, but suggesting Galway as an alternative, she'd finally understood. He promised to arrange a research position for her in the Darcy laboratory on campus, and Carline realised that he was offering her a test. If she could perform well enough, really impress him, then he would take her in and raise her up, and she would be a true Darcy. Untouchable.

With a prize like that she'd had no choice, no choice at all, but to take drastic action.

'It can't have been easy for you this week. The death of a young woman your age. The confusion over her identity. To have the police show up at your door like that must have been very unsettling.' His words were kind but the look in his eyes was dispassionate. He was so hard to read.

'Do you need help? Why don't you send me your current draft? I'd be happy to give you some notes.'

'I … I would rather wait until it is more advanced. I think it would be better if you saw my best work.'

Carline felt pinned under his gaze.

'It's not a weakness to ask for help when you need it, Carline,' he said.

Before she could speak, the door opened behind him and Valentina came in. She was wearing a very small pair of lime green running shorts and a sports bra. Her dark hair was pulled back from her face. She was angry. Carline could see it in the curve of her back, the cock of her hip, the challenge in her eye as she looked straight at John Darcy but spoke to Carline.

'I'm going for a run, Carline. Do you want to come? I'm sure your grandfather won't mind, seeing as he didn't tell you he was coming.'

John Darcy took his time standing up, as if to make it clear to Valentina that her presence and her words had no influence on him. 'I'll be in touch,' he said, and he turned a stiff shoulder to her and left.

CHAPTER TWENTY-THREE

Eileen Lambert wasn't able to give them contact details for Della's dentist. She claimed the girl had never seen one. Instead the team managed to track him down the old-fashioned way – they broke down the list of dentists in the Galway metropolitan area and kept phoning until they found the right guy. Della had gone to him for a filling six months before, and had been up-sold a comprehensive, and according to the dentist, overdue treatment plan. As a result, the dentist had a complete set of X-rays and identification could be confirmed. The dead girl was Della Lambert.

'Why do you think Eileen Lambert lied?' Fisher asked, when he delivered the news to Cormac. 'Do you think she's expecting this and she just doesn't want it confirmed?' Fisher was bright-eyed, despite the gravity of the news he carried. He was buzzing with the excitement of a good catch.

Cormac shook his head. 'Might not have been a lie, this time. I don't think Della kept her mother informed about her day to day movements.'

Fisher nodded, hesitated. 'I'd like to come with you, help with the notification,' he said.

They drove out in silence, neither of them speaking until they reached the bridge on the outskirts of Athenry. It was a bright and sunny day. As they drove up Court Lane they passed a group of school kids eating ice-cream cones. Cormac looked them over carefully, realised he was checking to see if Paul Lambert was among them, and looked away.

Paul Lambert was not the type to be walking along on a Wednesday morning, eating ice-cream and flirting with girls.

'They should be in school,' Fisher said, nodding in the direction of the small group.

Cormac shrugged and Fisher kept driving. They turned off Court Lane and onto the Caheroyan Road.

'Make sure you watch the family,' Cormac said. 'Get the best read you can. Watch for any reaction that feels off. It's better not to try to analyse it in the moment, just catalogue it and consider it afterwards. Have you done many of these?'

'A few,' Fisher said.

'Any murders?'

'No.'

'Ever tell a mother her child is dead?'

Fisher's face was stiff. 'Once. A three-year-old wandered off, fell into a slurry pit.'

Cormac nodded, looked out of the window. 'You'll have something to compare to then,' he said.

They pulled into the driveway of the house. The curtains in the front room were drawn. Something about the Lambert house was unfriendly. It wasn't the neglected, scrubby plants in the garden bed, or the too-long grass of the front lawn. It wasn't the absence of a kid's bike discarded on the drive, or that all the windows were closed on one of the warmest days of the year so far. It was a combination of all of these things perhaps, and something else. An atmosphere.

Cormac rang the doorbell, and a minute or so later it was opened by Geraldine, balanced on a box placed, it seemed, for that purpose inside the front door.

'My mama's busy,' she said, almond eyes staring unblinking at Cormac. Before he could answer, the kitchen door opened at the other end of the hall, and Eileen appeared, wiping her hands on a tea towel. She took in Fisher's uniform, turned to Cormac.

'Well?' she said. She put one hand on a thin hip, gestured with the other to Geraldine, telling her to get inside. The little girl disappeared back into the kitchen.

'Eileen,' Cormac said. 'There's something we need to talk about. Can we come in?'

She made an impatient gesture. 'I've children to feed, and a husband who'll be in the door for lunch any minute.'

'It's about Della.' Cormac held her gaze. Did she know what he was about to tell her? He thought perhaps she did. She hesitated for one moment longer, then turned back to the kitchen, leaving them to follow.

The kitchen was a little too warm. A radiator pumped out unnecessary heat in the corner, and onions sizzled on a frying pan that had been left on the hob. Three raw beef burgers sat on a cutting board on the counter top, ready to fry. Eileen Lambert switched off the heat under the frying pan, and turned to them.

'Well?' she said again.

'Is your husband here, Eileen? It might be better to speak to you both together.'

She shook her head impatiently. 'Just tell me, for God's sake.'

Geraldine was sitting at the kitchen table. It was already set for lunch, but the little girl had created a small space for herself, and she was slowly and meticulously colouring in a picture of Elsa and Anna, from the Disney movie. Cormac thought about suggesting that Fisher take Geraldine out of the room, opened his mouth, but Eileen cut across him.

'She might as well hear it,' she said. 'Whatever it is you've come to tell us, she'll have to deal with it soon enough.'

Cormac nodded, his eyes on the little girl. Geraldine didn't look up, seemed to be completely absorbed in her work.

'I'm very sorry to tell you that Della was hit by a car on Friday night,' Cormac said. 'Her injuries were severe and she passed away at the scene. I'm so very sorry for your loss.' His voice was as gentle as he could make it. He hated to do this. Hated to steal away hope and love. Eileen Lambert was not a good person, had certainly not had an easy relationship with her daughter. But some part of her, at least, must have loved her daughter.

At first, the expression on Eileen Lambert's face didn't change. Then she spoke. 'You knew this, didn't you? When you came here the other day.' Eileen twisted her face into a grimace, and her voice, though still quiet, was vicious. 'Della was already dead, wasn't she? And you knew it. You kept it from me on purpose.'

As the tone of Eileen's voice changed, Geraldine picked up her colouring page, curled her hand around three or four crayons, and silently left the room. She didn't look at her mother, or Cormac or Fisher. Just left. Fisher caught Cormac's eye, waited a moment, then followed.

'Della's injuries made it difficult to identify her,' Cormac said, when the door closed behind them. 'When we were here last we knew it was a possibility that Della was the victim we were trying to identify, but at that stage it was only one of a number of possibilities. That's why we asked you to sign the release for Della's dental records. The confirmation of Della's identity came in less than an hour ago, and our first action was to come and tell you what we had found out.'

'I suppose you want me to thank you, do you? For telling me that my daughter is dead.' Eileen held the tea towel in one hand; she pressed it to her eyes, her breathing ragged.

Cormac pulled a seat out from the table. 'You should sit, Eileen. I know this must be a terrible shock.' She allowed him to lead her to the chair, her body rigid. Her eyes when she let the tea towel fall away were painfully dry. She sat and stared into space, and Cormac sat too, waiting. A minute passed and she said nothing, asked no questions.

'Della was at the university when she died. It was Friday night, not too late. We think around 10 p.m. Do you have any idea what she would have been doing at the university at that time?'

'What?' Eileen looked at him, and there was confusion in her eyes – genuine, if he had to call it. 'At the college?'

'Yes. On the road just beside the university chapel. Do you know of any reason why she would have gone there?'

Eileen shook her head. 'Della didn't go to university. She was a waitress.'

'You told me before that she did attend once, a couple of years back. She couldn't have gone back to study?'

'She didn't like it. Della dropped out just after Christmas her first year. Didn't even tell her father or me. She got a job without telling us, got a flat, then moved out. She told Paul what she was doing, and we had to hear it from him. She didn't want to study anymore, she told him. Wanted a job so she could have her independence.'

Fisher had gone looking for Geraldine. He didn't find her in the small, cluttered living room, so he turned and went up the stairs. The carpet felt sticky underfoot. As he reached the top of the stairs he found himself locking eyes with Paul Lambert. The boy was sitting on the edge of his bed, his bedroom door wide open. His face was very pale, his shoulders rigid with tension.

'Della's dead, isn't she?' The boy's voice was tight, rasping.

'I came to look for Geraldine,' Fisher said. 'Make sure she's okay.'

'She'll be in her room. Ger knows to get out of the way when trouble's brewing. Della's dead, isn't she?'

Fisher hesitated. He should leave notification to Reilly, but there was no point in denying the truth now, when the boy had obviously either overheard or figured it out. 'I'm very sorry,' Fisher said.

Paul nodded once, grimly. He blinked hard, but tears escaped and slipped down his face. 'That was Della's body you found on Friday night, wasn't it? I read about it online. About you not being able to identify her. Because of her injuries.' Paul bent over double at the last, the pain of his grief suddenly and violently contracting his body. He sobbed and sobbed again, then straightened himself. He tried to pull himself together, gasping in a deep breath and shuddering, scrubbing tears from his face with the sleeve of his jumper. After a few moments his breathing slowed to a more normal rhythm, but his tears kept coming.

Fisher shook his head slowly. 'I'm sorry it took us so long. If you hadn't come forward it would have taken longer. I'm so sorry for your loss, Paul.'

'It's so shit,' Paul said. 'She'd only just got out of here, and then this happens.' He pulled in another deep breath, forced himself to sit upright.

Fisher let his eyes wander around the bedroom. It was very clean, very tidy. The walls were painted a grubby magnolia, but the bed was neatly made. There was a desk in the corner. Lots of books on the desk, on the bookshelves. Tattered copies of Isaac Asimov, Arthur C. Clarke, Ursula Le Guin. A neat stack of books too on the desk, though these were textbooks.

'I'm very sorry, Paul. It seems like you and Della were close.'

Paul scrubbed again roughly at tears that kept coming. 'She was my sister.' His tone said of course, as if there was no question, as if all siblings were close. Fisher was an only child, but he had plenty of friends from big families, and besides that had been a cop long enough to have seen sibling rivalry taken to the extreme.

'Where's your dad?' Fisher asked. 'Can I call him, get him home for you?'

'He's gone for a walk. That's all he ever does since he lost the shop, just goes walking for hours and hours. He never takes a phone, so you can't call him. He doesn't want to be here. None of us do.'

'I'm very sorry, Paul,' Fisher said again, after a pause. He shifted his weight, wished for a moment that Reilly had come up here with him, or maybe Carrie O'Halloran. She was good with the younger ones. The ones that got under your skin. He wanted to ask Paul why he wasn't in school, but it wasn't the time. Paul looked up at him. 'She was so smart, you know? Della was so good, and so smart. You'd think if anyone would be safe out in the world it would have been Della. But if you're a good person, it's like you're a magnet for the shitheads.'

Fisher blinked. He leaned against the door jamb, looked the boy over carefully. 'Were there bad people in Della's life?'

Paul stared at him, eyes raw and red-rimmed, for what felt like a long time. 'I don't know,' he said in the end. 'Della doesn't … didn't have friends, not really. She wasn't lonely or anything. She just … liked different stuff. She wasn't the same as everyone else …'

'If there's anything you want to tell me,' Fisher said carefully. 'Anything at all. I'd like to hear it.'

A spasm of frustration and grief crossed Paul's face. 'I don't know anything,' he said. 'That's why I came to you, wasn't it?' He screwed his eyes shut in an effort to stop the tears, but they kept coming, a raw, hard manifestation of his grief. 'Can you just go?' he asked. 'Please?'

Fisher wanted to stay, offer the lad a bit of comfort. But there was nothing he could say that would make things better. And he was here as a policeman, not as a friend. He couldn't switch that part of his brain off. If he stayed to talk he'd be watching, analysing everything Paul Lambert said, and right now, in this moment, something about that felt dirty.

'I'm sorry, Paul,' Fisher said. He pulled a card from his pocket and gave it to the boy. 'Some people will come and talk to you in the next few days. It might be me, it might be someone else. But if you need to speak to me at any time, you'll get me on that number, all right?' The boy took the card without looking at it, and Fisher retreated quietly, pulling the door closed behind him.

He opened the door to the second bedroom as quietly as he could. Geraldine was there all right, playing with dolls, her back to the door. Her room was very different from Paul's. The bed could barely be seen under the weight of soft toys. An empty packet of Jacob's cream crackers stuck out from under the bed. She must have felt the weight of his presence. She turned and looked at him seriously.

'Do you want to play?' she asked. 'You can have a turn of my best Barbie.'

Fisher took a seat beside her on the carpet.

Downstairs Eileen Lambert had started to clean the kitchen. She clattered the dishes in jerky movements, but her eyes were dry.

'Where was Della working?' Cormac asked.

'At that coffee place, off Shop Street. The Long Bean. Something like that.'

'You've never been there?' Cormac asked.

She shook her head, looked away.

'We spoke to the manager,' Cormac said. 'He said he's worked there for over a year himself, and he had no memory at all of Della.'

Eileen shook her head again, her mouth set in a grim line.

'Della didn't tell you about a change of job? Didn't say anything in passing?'

'Della never told me anything. Why would she? I was only her mother.' Distress in her voice, getting louder.

'When did you last speak to her?' Cormac asked.

'January,' Eileen said stiffly. 'Or it might have been February.'

Cormac was silent for a long moment, waited for the tension to ebb a little before he spoke again. 'Can I call your husband for you? Or a friend?'

She looked towards the front door. 'He'll be walking,' she said. 'He'll be home soon enough.' She looked down at her hands, then stood abruptly, pushed her chair back under the table, and turned to Cormac, the expression on her face tight and closed.

Cormac stood too. 'Della was living in an expensive apartment. The rent would have been more than she could have afforded on a waitress's salary. Did you or your husband support her at all? Or did she have other money, independently?'

'We didn't give Della any money. She was old enough to support herself. She could have lived here, could have kept going to college, but she chose to leave and the first thing she did was get her own place. After that she was on her own.' Eileen looked towards the door. Her face twisted in sudden, furious anger. 'Get out of my house,' she said, her voice low and vicious. 'I've answered your questions, as best I can. Have some decency and leave us alone to grieve.'

'The key to it has to be the money, doesn't it?' said Fisher, as they made their way back to the station. 'Chances are it was something illegal, whatever she did that got her paid.'

Cormac nodded, but said nothing. His mind was occupied with sorting through his impressions of the house, of the family.

'But what, like?' Fisher asked. 'D'you think it might be drugs? The books in her room, they were all about chemistry, weren't they? Do you think it could be a meth thing?'

'It's an idea,' Cormac said, half-listening.

Fisher cast him a sideways glance. 'An idea, but not a very good one?'

'I'm not saying it's impossible.' Cormac gave up on the introspection, came back to the conversation. 'But I keep going back to the ID in her back pocket.'

'You think her death is connected to the Darcy girl?'

'I think the money and the ID make it a strong possibility. I want to find a connection between those girls. I think Carline has been lying to us, and if she has we need to prove it.'

'So where do we go from here?'

'Start with the financials,' Cormac said. 'Get bank statements for Della Lambert, see if there's any unusual activity on her account. If we're very lucky something will show up there.'

'And the Darcy girl?'

Cormac shook his head. 'No basis for a warrant, and we have to step carefully with her.' He left out the fact that Murphy had warned him off. Fisher had been around long enough to read the lay of the land. They pulled into the station.

'I've somewhere I need to be. Get started on the warrant for the financials. If you need help McCarthy will walk you through it.'

'Before you go …' Fisher said.

'Yes?'

'Paul Lambert was upstairs. I spoke to him in his room. He'd either overheard or figured out that Della was dead. He was upset, understandably.' Fisher looked a little tense, as if expecting a bollocking.

'Right,' Cormac said. 'Why wasn't he at school?' He would have preferred to tell the boy himself, if the opportunity was there, but there wasn't much Fisher could have done about that.

'I didn't ask him,' Fisher said. 'He didn't look sick, just, you know … he was obviously upset. He was crying.'

'Right.' Cormac asked Fisher to run through his impressions of Paul, everything the boy had said and how he'd looked when he'd said it, but he was listening with only half an ear. His mind was elsewhere.

CHAPTER TWENTY-FOUR

Cormac got home after seven, and Emma was there before him. She was in the living room, curled up on the couch in pyjamas and one of his old jumpers, watching television. She turned to smile at him as he entered, but the smile fell away as she took in his appearance.

'You look awful,' she said. 'Did something happen?'

'It's just been a long one.'

He sat beside her, she pushed her feet under his leg, wriggled her toes against him.

'Tell me,' she said.

He put a hand on her leg, let his head drop back against the couch. 'Let's talk about something else. How's everything at work?' He spoke without thinking. The last thing he wanted to do was interrogate her. But he felt like the words hung in the air between them, and when he turned to look at her he was struck by the weariness in her face. She wasn't sleeping – the last few nights the nightmares had been as bad as they'd ever been. She didn't say anything for a long moment.

'This whole Galway thing, it's been a disaster for you, hasn't it? This move,' Emma asked. She'd picked up on his mood, maybe misinterpreted the reason for it.

Cormac paused. Emma knew that things at the station had been challenging. They'd spoken about it, more than once, but he'd kept the full truth from her. She didn't realise how unusual it was that he'd been kept to working cold cases for a full year. She didn't realise how strained his relationship with Murphy had become. In Galway he had the constant sense that things were not exactly right, that everything was slightly off kilter. A year had passed and he still didn't know his team well enough to trust them. Murphy may finally have given him a live case but he'd given it reluctantly and he was looking over Cormac's shoulder. It might be paranoia, but Cormac wondered if he was being set up to fail. Or did the problem lie with him? After what had happened the previous year he found it harder to trust anyone in the station. But he didn't want to share any of that with Emma. He wanted her to feel that she could rely on him. Besides which, he wanted to stay positive. He was sure that with enough time, he could get things on the right track.

'Emma.' He waited until she looked at him properly. 'Moving to Galway was my decision as much as yours.'

'I know, yeah. I know it was.'

'I was ready to leave the special detectives unit. I'd been working out of the same office, with essentially the same bunch of people, for over twelve years.'

Something in his tone had caught her attention. She was really listening now.

'We were getting bogged down in process. Every operation was the same as the last one. Systems of cross-checking information back and forth before we take an action. We'd turned into a bunch of statisticians, doing … what did you call it? Backstrapping?'

She smiled. 'Bootstrapping the data.'

'Exactly. There was very little room for intuition. For following your instinct and an unlikely lead. I'm not saying it wasn't work worth doing, but there was no challenge in it for me anymore. No satisfaction.' He'd started talking to try to cheer her up. But as he spoke he realised there was truth in his words. It wasn't all bullshit, he had been ready to leave. And one year down the line, even with everything that had happened, wasn't he doing more actual police work than he had in years?

'Why haven't you said any of this before?' Emma asked, looking at him steadily. 'About Dublin, I mean. I've thought you must be missing it.'

He shrugged. 'I've missed having live cases. I'm not going to pretend working thirty-year-old cold cases is where I want my career to be. But I don't miss the SDU. I don't miss Dublin Castle. And now I'm running cases again, things are good. There's real talent on the team. Fisher, for starters, but some of the younger ones too.'

He wrapped his arms around her, pulled her closer, but she leaned back, keeping a bit of distance between them. Her eyes searched his face.

'You wouldn't go back to Dublin, if you could? If we both went, I mean. Or somewhere else, abroad even.'

Cormac shook his head. 'Galway is home now,' he said. 'Whatever comes our way, we'll sort it. There're bound to be … challenges. We just have to give it time to work itself out.'

She looked at him for another long moment, as if trying to assess whether or not he was telling the truth, then she kissed him briefly, and relaxed against him, laying her head on his chest.

'We should talk more,' she said. 'Life gets so busy, and sometimes I look up and days have gone by since we've really talked to each other.'

Emma's eyes were closed but there was a trace of tension in her face. Cormac felt disconcerted. Had he read her right? Something was bothering her. Maybe it was something more than just the Galway move. Before he could say anything she'd given him a final hug, then sat back, putting distance again between them.

'I can't face cooking, can you?' She picked up her phone. 'Let's just order in.'

'Is everything all right?' he asked.

She didn't answer, flicked through screens on her phone as if she were absorbed in choosing takeaway, but he could still see the tension in the set of her neck.

'Earlier, when I came in, I thought you looked very tired. Are you sleeping?'

She put the phone down for a moment, held it between her hands. 'I'm fine,' she said. 'Work is hard. We've run into some problems I didn't anticipate, we're having some problems duplicating results.' She held up a hand to forestall questions. 'You know this is just par for the course. It's the nature of the work, there are good days and bad days. We'll get there. In the meantime ...' She lifted the phone to her ear with a sideways smile. 'Pizza okay?'

He nodded, and she ordered. She read the look on his face and saw that he wasn't going to let it go. When she hung up she came back to him, kissed him deeply. 'Sometimes we need to talk, and sometimes there are better options.' She kissed him again. 'Pizza's going to take at least half an hour. Let's not talk for a while, all right?'

He had no argument with that.

CHAPTER TWENTY-FIVE

Carline waited until the apartment was very quiet, waited for Valentina to turn off her music, and for the light under Mark's door to go out, then waited for another hour. When she was sure, she locked her bedroom door and dressed in clothes she had bought earlier in the day. A pair of boy's black jeans, her size, but cheaply made and straight legged. A black hoodie. They were both second-hand, the hoodie greying a little with age. She dressed quickly, put on her own runners, tied her hair back and pulled the hood up. She glanced at the mirror, then stopped, arrested. She looked so different. So anonymous. That had been the point, of course, but wearing it, being it, was stranger than she had expected. She shifted her weight so that it fell evenly on both feet, let her shoulders droop and her head drop forward a little. So different. There was nothing to see in that person before her. Nothing to assess or judge. Her face was in shadow. Her small breasts were enveloped by the jumper, her slight curves overwhelmed by the heaviness of the fabric. She felt – oddly, given what she was about to do – a little bit safer. Was this what it was like to be a man? She made a face at herself in the mirror, then turned away, picking up a plain navy backpack and slinging it over her shoulder.

Taking the car would be a bad idea. There were at least three cameras between the apartment and the college that she knew of, and God knows how many others. Walking felt dangerous too. It would take too long for her to get there, too long to get away. The apartment was in darkness, but she used the light of her phone to find Mark's keys were he had left them, as always, on the kitchen counter. He cycled to college sometimes. That way he could have a drink or three in the afternoon and cycle home. He stored the bike in the basement of the apartment building, but he was obsessive about locking the thing up, so she would need his keys.

It was strange, cycling through the quiet streets. It had rained in the afternoon and evening, but the clouds had cleared to reveal a starry sky, and the air was fresh and clean. Maybe it was the air, maybe the clothes, but she had a sense of being newborn. Of being free.

She cut down by St Joseph's college, and around by the cathedral. She kept her head ducked low as she entered the campus. There were cameras for sure by the new engineering buildings, and near the library and the main concourse entrance, but she'd walked the route and was sure there were none on the little access route that ran under the concourse. The lane wasn't secret. During the day it was used a bit – there were bike racks under there, and doors that you could use to reach the ground floor classrooms. But it wasn't a popular place – it was creepy and dark, even during the day. Keeping her head low, she cycled around and under, then dismounted, and locked the bike to one of the bike stands. For the first time that evening, Carline felt a tangle of unease. It was freaky under here at night. Shabby. Old looking. An old crisp packet blew along the ground. Broken glass crunched under her feet; the noise too loud in the quiet. Carline kept walking.

If she'd screwed up and missed a camera it shouldn't matter. If her theory about what had happened was wrong, then what she was about to do would cause a great deal of fuss, police would be called in and tapes would be reviewed. If she was right, then it would be kept very, very quiet. She didn't know which outcome she was hoping for, but she was prepared regardless. If a camera did catch her she shouldn't look anything like Carline Darcy. She adopted a slouched adolescent gait, exaggerated it to the point of caricature, then abandoned it with a hysterical giggle.

She left the road long before she reached the laboratory, finding the water's edge and walking by the riverbank until she reached the lab building. The water was black, silent. Carline knew the window she was looking for. It was a locked office, one to which her swipe card would not grant access. She would have to be very quick. Campus security weren't completely useless, and they might do a drive-by. She had a brick in her backpack. She hefted its weight in one gloved hand, and threw it as hard as she could, heard herself gasp involuntarily as the glass shattered loudly. She reached a shaking hand through the broken pane, unlocked the window, and climbed inside.

She turned on a light, worrying less about being seen now than about finding what she thought might be there and getting out quickly. She searched frantically, overturning papers and emptying cupboards as fast as possible. There was a locked cupboard to the left of the desk. She hadn't brought any tools, felt a moment's apprehension. Carline wedged her fingers into the small gap at the top of the cupboard door and pulled hard. The lock gave. The cupboard was stuffed with old papers, notebooks, copies of scientific journals. She rifled through it, pulling papers out onto the floor. For a moment she didn't see it and relief swelled within her. Then she shifted another bundle of notebooks, and there it was. Plain, black, a little scratched and completely innocuous looking. She could have cried then, felt tears threaten, but she blinked them back, lifted the computer out and slid it quickly into her backpack. There was a charger and she took that too, then stood, climbed back out through the window and started retracing her steps.

So now she knew. Della had been murdered and she had a choice to make. Between justice and her own future. The tree branches moving in the breeze were suddenly threatening. The access road where Mark's bike was waiting was like a black maw under the concourse, waiting to swallow her whole. Della had died very close to here, only a few nights ago. Died on the street. Died alone. Carline pressed on. She had started crying, somewhere between the lab and Mark's bike. Why hadn't Della left everything as it was? Everything had been perfect. Everyone had been happy.

Carline wiped her nose on her sleeve, unlocked the bike, and settled the bag on her back before cycling silently off through the campus. The wind dried the remaining tears from her cheeks.

Wednesday 30 April 2014

CHAPTER TWENTY-SIX

At ten o'clock on Wednesday morning Fisher came to Cormac's desk, a stack of bank statements in his hands. Cormac saw the Bank of Ireland logo straight away.

'Already?'

'The warrant came through this morning and Dave McCarthy walked it straight over to the bank himself. His brother used to play Gaelic football with the assistant manager. Gave Dave a cup of coffee and had the statements printed out there and then.'

'Good work,' Cormac said. 'Run them through the copier. We'll talk when we've both been through them.'

'What are we looking for?' Fisher asked.

'Everything and nothing,' Cormac said. He stood up, empty coffee cup in one hand. 'We don't know anything about this girl. Let's start filling in that picture.'

Minutes later Cormac was back at his desk, pen in hand, working his way through the stack of paper. The first statements, from Della's few months as a student, held no surprises. She hadn't been a spender, Della Lambert, no five-euro coffees for her. No spending sprees in Brown Thomas. There were small fortnightly electronic deposits to her account – probably her waitressing salary. The charges to her card were for cheap, subsidised meals in the college canteen, was his best guess. No pub charges, no major cash withdrawals. She charged forty euro a month to Iarnród Éireann. About the cost of a monthly pass for the train from Athenry to Galway. So Della was living at home, going to college, and working part-time as a waitress to cover her fees, her books, and her food. Based on the bank statements, she hadn't had a social life. All that changed in January 2013.

For two weeks over Christmas the electronic deposits increased back to four hundred a week but in the second week of January, the deposits stopped abruptly. No action for the next two weeks, no deposits, no withdrawals. Then on 28 January 2013, a cash deposit of just over eighteen thousand euro was lodged to her account. A week later, a direct debit for rent came out, paid to the estate agent, nineteen hundred euro. That withdrawal came out like clockwork on the first of the month thereafter. But if the rent payments were like clockwork, so too were the deposits. First Friday of every month, Della Lambert went to the Bank of Ireland branch on Mainguard Street and made a cash lodgement. Every month for the past fifteen months Della had made a lodgement of eighteen thousand euro to her bank account.

After that first January deposit there was a sudden flurry of spending, charges to clothes shops, to bookshops and restaurants. And exactly four weeks later, there was an electronic transfer of five thousand euro to another Bank of Ireland account, this one in the name of Eileen Lambert. That transfer had also been repeated every month since. However Della Lambert was getting her money, she was using it to support her family.

A shadow loomed over the pages. Fisher, eagerness all over his face.

'Did you see it?' he said. 'Cash lodgements, all under twenty thousand euros. Bank of Ireland prompts its tellers to ask questions about any lodgement in excess of twenty thousand. Do you think she knew?'

'Probably,' said Cormac. Almost certainly. 'It would explain the cash in her apartment. Maybe she got all of the money in one cash payment, wanted it in her bank account but realised she'd have to break it up into smaller lodgements to avoid difficult questions.'

'She was supporting her parents. She paid utilities from the account, and a weekly food shop at Tesco. Went a bit mad at the shops for a few weeks, although she knocked that on the head fairly quickly, did you see?' Fisher asked. 'Where was she getting it?'

Cormac shook his head slowly. Fisher sat against the next desk, eyes on Cormac's face.

'There's nothing in there to connect her or the money to Carline Darcy,' Fisher said.

'No.'

'And no chance of getting a warrant on Carline's accounts, not with what we have.'

Cormac leaned back in his chair, looked at the statements and other paperwork spread out on his desk. 'We don't know this girl,' he said. 'We don't know who she was, what she liked, what she disliked, who she spent time with apart from her little brother. The mother told me she had no close friends from school, no particular hobbies or interests.'

'Yeah, but I don't know that she's the most reliable source. She must have known Della wasn't working as a waitress. There's no waitress job would let her pay her mother five grand a month, plus the rent on the apartment. Eileen Lambert has to be lying.'

'She knew that Della wasn't working as a waitress,' Cormac said. 'That doesn't necessarily mean that she knew the truth of what was going on. She might not have asked the question, might have been happy to keep the money and keep her mouth shut. Particularly if she thought she already knew.'

Fisher thought it through for a moment. 'She thought Della was working as a prostitute?'

'That was our first assumption. Maybe it was her mother's too,' Cormac said. He thought of Eileen going on about Della being an adult, about Della making her own decisions.

'Christ,' Fisher said. 'And she was happy to live off it.'

'We need to know more about her,' Cormac said. 'We need to get back to the college, find people who knew her when she was there.'

Nathan Egan was happy to meet but had meetings in the morning and plans for the afternoon – a conference in Manchester – which required him to leave the university by 3 p.m. He agreed to see Cormac at 2 p.m. and this time when Cormac arrived the academic looked genuinely pleased to see him. He shook Cormac's hand, invited him to take a seat.

'I understand you identified the poor dead girl,' Egan said. 'A waitress, I understand. Tragic, tragic.'

Cormac hid his irritation, unimpressed by more evidence of the speed and efficiency of the Galway grapevine, but unwilling to display his frustration in front of Egan.

'We've identified the victim as Della Lambert. She was eighteen years old. I'm told she was enrolled here, from September 2012, but that she dropped out after her first semester. Can you confirm those details?'

Egan's face fell. 'But … I was told that you had identified the victim, and that she had no connection with the university.'

'I'm not sure who could have told you that, Professor. No one connected to the investigation, I'm sure.'

Egan flushed. 'Who told you she was enrolled here?' he asked.

'Her bank statements,' Cormac said baldly, and waited.

Egan, who had been hovering beside his chair, finally sat, and put his right hand on his mouse. 'I should be able to confirm enrolment,' he said slowly. Cormac hoped he wasn't about to invoke data protection legislation. But Egan's mouse hand moved and clicked, clicked again, and a few moments later he nodded his head.

'Yes,' he said. 'I have her here. Della Lambert. Date of birth third of March, 1996. Yes?' He looked up at Cormac and waited for his nod before continuing. 'Yes, she was enrolled. Bio-Pharmaceutical Chemistry. But as you say, she never returned for the second semester.'

'Do you know why?' Cormac asked.

Egan spread his arms in a helpless gesture. 'It's not unheard of. At NUIG we have a nine per cent dropout rate. That's vastly better than the Institute of Technology, which last year was running at almost twenty-five per cent. It's not something we're proud of, and we're always working to bring the number down, but it's inevitable, to some degree.' He paused, but when Cormac didn't speak he continued. 'People think that there's a correlation between the points you need to do a course and the difficulty of the subject matter, but that's not always the case. Points are a function of popularity and supply. Points for Medicine are among the highest, because it's a prestige course, and there are limited places. Medicine is demanding, of course, but so are some of our science courses that have admission points in the low three hundreds. We have young people going into these courses woefully under-prepared for what lies ahead of them.'

It felt like a speech Egan had delivered many times before.

'And that's what happened to Della Lambert?' Cormac asked. He felt sure that it wasn't. Something else had prevented Della from returning to college, something that had also delivered hundreds of thousands of euros into her hands.

'Possibly. Most of the time it comes down to the fact that the student just doesn't have the ability to keep up with the work. They realise that for themselves and drop out. Sometimes the kid has the academic ability but not the psycho-social nous to get by. They're the ones who come from an over-protected, structured childhood where parents did everything for them, up to and including filling in their university application form. Most of them struggle to some degree at university, but they'll often turn it around in second year, if we can get them that far. But there are kids who should never have been admitted, and for those we can do very little.'

Cormac glanced at Egan's computer. 'Do you have Della's academic record? Any way to determine if she was one of those kids who was just out of her depth?'

Egan pulled the keyboard towards him, re-entered his password, and clicked his mouse. 'Right,' he said. He read for a moment, then turned the screen a little in Cormac's direction. 'Well, she wasn't failing out. She sat her Christmas exams, got solid 2:1s across the board, except in Chemistry where she managed a low first. Quite good results. Really, very good.' He sounded surprised.

'Good, but not brilliant.'

Egan grimaced. 'Not everyone aspires to brilliance, detective. For most people it's enough to be able to get a job.'

'And then there are those who don't need to work at all.'

Egan compressed his lips into a thin line.

'Carline Darcy studies Bio-Pharmaceutical Chemistry,' Cormac said. He said it as if he already knew, though it wasn't more than a solid guess – until Egan's reluctant nod confirmed it. 'I'm told she works hard. Surprised me. Attractive girl, with her kind of money. Her father was something of a playboy.'

Egan leaned forward across his desk. 'Whatever her father might have been, Ms Darcy is exceptional. Don't misunderstand me, detective. I'm not saying that she's a bright girl, or even that she's gifted. I'm telling you that she has the kind of mind that comes along once in a generation.

Like her grandfather. Carline will do great things. We are privileged to have her at this university.' Egan's lips were dry and chapped, and there were little white flecks in the corners of his mouth.

'But Della Lambert, as a student, wasn't particularly memorable?'

As intended, the change in direction put Egan off balance. His eyes narrowed for an instant before his face reassumed its guileless, sincere expression. It was clear that Egan wasn't sure how to take the question. Wasn't sure if it was intended as an accusation, or just a simple statement of fact.

'I'm sure to her friends and classmates Della was very memorable,' said Egan.

'I'd like to speak with Della's teachers. Anyone who knew her well, who had direct interaction with her.'

Egan frowned. 'You'd almost certainly be wasting your time with her lecturers. In first year the Biopharma students have their lectures with the Chemistry and Biology students. There would have been about a hundred students in every lecture, and virtually no one-on-one interaction. Her tutors would be a better bet, if they're still at the university.'

Tracking down the information took a couple of phone calls, which Egan made right in front of him. He had perked up, confirming Cormac's first impression – that he would go to a great deal of effort to help the investigation, as long as that help pointed in a direction other than Carline Darcy.

CHAPTER TWENTY-EIGHT

Cormac left the office with the mobile phone numbers of two former tutors. According to Egan, one of the two had completed his PhD and now lectured at the university, the other had just handed in her thesis but should still be in Galway and available for a call. Cormac tried the woman first. She answered the phone, but sounded harried, said she didn't remember Della and she was on the way to the airport so did he mind? The second was much more promising. Graham Nicholls, former tutor, now biochemistry lecturer, was having coffee not far from the campus. He was distressed to hear that Della had been killed, and eager to talk.

It was a five-minute walk to the café. Nicholls was keeping an eye out for him – he was sitting at a table towards the back, but half-stood and waved when Cormac opened the door. Cormac made his way through the tables. The place was full, but the murmur of conversation was quieter than might have been expected. Half the tables were occupied by students with a laptop or iPad open in front of them, earphones in ears and heads bowed.

'Detective Reilly?' Nicholls said, as he held out a hand to Cormac.

Nicholls had obviously been working. There were a few printed journal articles on the table, and an open notebook with some scrawled notes, mostly drawings of chemical structures that meant nothing to Cormac. A waitress looked their way, and Cormac said to Nicholls, 'I think I'll grab something, if you don't mind. I haven't had an opportunity until now.' Nicholls indicated he was in no rush. He ordered another coffee, though he hadn't finished the cappuccino sitting in front of him, and Cormac ordered a sandwich and coffee.

Cormac sat back, glanced around the café, adopted a casual tone. 'I haven't been here before. Must be handy for the college.'

'Food's better than the canteen,' said Nicholls. 'Quieter too.' He looked expectantly at Cormac, waiting for Cormac to get to the point.

Cormac took the cue. 'Thanks for the chat. I want to speak to anyone who knew Della Lambert during her time at college. I'm not looking for anything specifically. Just to get a feel for the kind of girl she was.'

'Her family couldn't help with that? Friends?'

'We haven't managed to track down any friends yet. I'm hoping you might be able to help with that. And its seems like she wasn't that close to her family, other than a younger brother, who probably only knew a younger brother's version of her.'

'I can't help you with her friends I'm afraid. I only saw Della at tutorials, and she didn't seem to be particularly friendly with anyone.' Nicholls sat back, rubbed the palm of his left hand against his jaw. He had a full beard that was well trimmed. Brown eyes, dark brown skin, the hint of a Scottish accent.

'You must see a lot of students, and it's been, what, fifteen months? Since you saw Della. But you remember her. Why?'

Nicholls grimaced. 'Della was impossible to forget, if you got her talking. It's devastating that she's died. A bloody tragedy.'

'In what way, impossible to forget?' Before Nicholls had a chance to answer the waitress arrived with Cormac's sandwich and both coffees. The food smelled good. Cormac took a bite of his sandwich, added milk to his coffee, and listened.

'Della had an incredible mind,' Nicholls said. 'She was a genius, without a doubt. The kind of thinker who comes along once in a generation.'

Cormac shook his head as he chewed and swallowed. 'I saw her Christmas exam results. They were solid. Better than solid, maybe, but not spectacular.'

Nicholl's face darkened. 'Those results were bullshit,' he said. 'There must have been some sort of mix-up with exam numbers. I looked at the results of all of the students who were in my tutorial groups. I couldn't believe it when I saw Della's. I went to look for her, more than once, to talk to her about it. I would have told her to appeal the results.'

'But she dropped out, never came back.'

Nicholls nodded. 'Exactly.' He took a sip from his coffee. 'By the time I saw her again she'd moved on.'

'You saw her again? On the campus?'

'Just once. I bumped into her outside the library. She'd come in to meet a friend. She said she'd had to do it – drop out, I mean. Her parents had some sort of small shop. They lost money in the crash, the business staggered on for a couple of years, then fell over. She needed to work to help support them.'

Cormac finished his sandwich and wiped his fingers on the napkin as he thought. 'What led you to believe that Della was a genius?'

Nicholls pushed one hand back through his hair, then shook his head. 'It was just the way she was. What she talked about. Look, all the kids in that class are very bright. Every kid in there got pretty much all As in their Leaving. But they're still kids. Bright enough to be able to understand the material, but they need plenty explained to them. Della wasn't a show-off. She kept herself to herself and let the others answer the questions.' Nichols paused. 'This is hard to explain.' He fooled with his pen for a moment, doodled something on the notebook, as if working something out, then replaced the pen on the table. 'This is what it is. If we were working our way through a basic concept, Della would wait until the end, until everyone else had had their time, and then she would ask a question. And the question would demonstrate that not only had she understood the concept perfectly, but that she had followed that concept all the way through the most complex iterations. Her questions were the sort of thing that might be raised by a very talented PhD candidate, or an expert in the field, not a first-year student at her intro to basics tutorials.'

'Could she have just read ahead?'

'No way. Or rather, yes, but it was her ability to understand and break down what she was reading that was exceptional. I consider myself a pretty smart guy, but I struggled with her. She needed more than I could give her.'

'A statistical improbability,' Cormac murmured.

'Sorry?'

'It just occurs to me. You tell me that Della Lambert was the kind of mind that comes along once in a generation. Egan tells me that Carline Darcy was another. And both of these young women end up in – forgive me – a small university in the West of Ireland. In the same class.'

'Yes.' Nicholls looked down at his coffee cup.

'And both of them in your tutorial.'

'I know.' Nicholls looked back at him. 'But Carline Darcy has every advantage, doesn't she? And less than two years later Della Lambert has dropped out – sorry, I still can't get my head around the fact that she's dead – whereas Carline Darcy is this close to her degree.' There was something in Nicholls' face, the slightest curl of his lip when he said Carline's name.

'You don't think it's deserved?'

Nicholls hesitated. 'I'm not saying that. I'm just pointing out that Carline Darcy has everything going for her, including the support of her grandfather. Della Lambert had nothing but a brilliant mind, and she's dead on the street.'

'What did you think of Carline, when you taught her?'

'I only had her for that first semester. She was quite … intense. Very focused. Aloof, I suppose. She kept herself to herself, didn't talk much, didn't really contribute.'

'And after that?'

Another shrug. 'I should have had her for the following semester too, but she didn't show up. Fair enough. By then she was accelerating. After her Christmas exams the faculty agreed she could complete the four-years honours programme in two years. I was teaching first-year Chemistry and by that January she was beyond it.'

'They weren't friends then, Della and Carline? I would have thought … kindred spirits.'

'Not that I saw. Maybe they would have been, if they had had more time.'

CHAPTER TWENTY-NINE

Cormac returned to the station. The team had pored over everything they could find about Della Lambert, which was little enough. She had no social media presence at all. A warrant for her calls and texts was working its way through the system at her phone company. The company had prioritised the request to track her phone, but the last signal they'd received had been a ping to the tower closest to the campus on the night that Della had died. Nothing more. Whoever had killed her had been smart enough to destroy the phone straight away.

McCarthy suggested accessing the Bio-Pharmaceutical Chemistry class list. With only twenty-five students some at least would remember Della, and it was possible she'd been on campus to visit one of them. It was a good idea, but a call to Nathan Egan found that he had already left campus and his mobile was diverting to voice mail. The university's administrative staff wouldn't release any student information without a warrant.

'What's happening with the swipe records?' Cormac asked. 'The records from the lab. Murtagh said they kept a record of everyone swiping in and out of the building. Had to for health and safety reasons, right? Have they sent that on?'

Fisher grimaced. 'We got it, after a bit of pushing on our part and a bit of delay on theirs. He leaned over to his desk, pulled a thick bundle of printed A4 pages, stapled together, towards him. 'This is the record for the last six months.

The highlighted lines show when the ID Della Lambert was carrying accessed the building. And yes, it was used right up to the day before her death, but not on the Friday night.'

'Carline told us she lost that ID at the beginning of the year,' Cormac said. 'She's either lying about when she lost it, or Della was using it herself.'

'Yeah, but why?' Fisher said. 'Why would she want to access the lab? And why so often? Unless it was some sort of like, industrial espionage.' The look on Fisher's face said he thought the idea was ridiculous. 'But if it was, then why would she go so often or for so long, and why wouldn't anyone ask her what she was doing there?'

'Look at the records again. Did anyone swipe in at the same time as her? We need to correlate the records, see whose visits consistently overlapped with hers,' Cormac said. He took the print out, found himself looking at an anonymous list of ID numbers and dates. He looked back at Fisher.

'Yeah,' said Fisher. 'We don't have the names to go with the ID numbers, and Darcy Therapeutics has refused to hand them over. Said it would be a breach of their privacy policy in the absence of a warrant.'

'We don't have enough for a warrant,' Dave McCarthy said. 'Judges will be careful with this one.' Dave was right. No judge liked to have their decisions overturned by a higher court, so they were likely to tread very carefully when it came to a company like Darcy Therapeutics, with its near endless resources, which could if it chose fund near endless litigation.

'We need a connection,' Cormac said. 'Something other than the ID to link Della Lambert to that lab, or to Carline Darcy.' He looked at his team and was met by a sea of blank faces. 'Right,' said Cormac. 'I have an interview now. Keep on it, update me when I get back.' He left the case room with a sense of foreboding. He had a theory that seemed to fit, but there were undercurrents in this case, little hints and pressure points that told him he had missed something. He worried that time was a factor. Whatever had set these events in motion hadn't yet fully played out.

CHAPTER THIRTY

The interview with Lucy Henderson and her son had been scheduled for 4.30 p.m., after school hours. When Cormac got to the family room Lucy and Fearghal were already there, waiting for him, with Moira Hanley for company. No one looked comfortable. The family room was supposed to be friendlier than a formal interview room. Cormac decided that it was poorly named. Nine times out of ten the room was used to interview victims of domestic abuse, or sexual assault. The place was depressing, carried the imprint of too many broken families. He made a mental note to see if something could be done to take the taint of failure from the place.

Cormac tried to catch Moira's eye but she looked away. He hadn't had an opportunity to speak to her about her misunderstanding of what had happened at the Henderson house, but judging by her stiffness and the colour in her cheeks, he thought that Carrie might have done it for him.

Lucy Henderson looked more alert, but it would be hard to argue that she looked better. She was jittery. The fingers of her right hand twisted the wedding ring on her left, around and around. She looked from her son, to the ratty couch, to the box of toys in the corner and back again with quick, jerky glances. Absent the numbing effect of the tranquillisers, she appeared to be a woman worn thin with nervous tension.

Fearghal Henderson sat on the couch beside his mother. The boy was fifteen years old according to the file, the same age as Paul Lambert, but that was where the similarities ended. Cormac wouldn't have given Fearghal Henderson a day more than thirteen. He was slight, thin and hunched. He sat turned slightly away from his mother, averting his gaze as if he could remove himself from the scene just by wishing. Cormac took a seat in one of the armchairs. He sat forward, made eye contact.

'Thank you for coming Fearghal, Lucy,' Cormac said. He walked them through the process, explained to the boy that he had some questions he needed to ask him about his father, and that his mother would stay in the room at all times. If he needed a break, for the bathroom or just to think, he should let Cormac know at any time. 'All right, Fearghal?' Cormac didn't wait for a nod.

'You told your guidance counsellor … Mrs Fitzgibbon, isn't it? You told Mrs Fitzgibbon that you were worried about your family. That you were worried about your mother and your sisters. Is that right?'

A shrug, a slight shake of the head.

'You did, Fearghal,' Cormac's voice was gentle. 'Tell me why you told her that. What had you worried?'

'I don't know,' Fearghal's voice was rough. He had been crying. Lucy's hand fluttered in his direction for a moment, then she returned the hand to her lap.

'He's told you he doesn't know,' she said. 'You're harassing him.' Her fingers still worried at her ring, twisting and twisting.

Moira sat forward in her chair. 'You have nothing to be afraid of, Fearghal,' she said. 'And nothing to be ashamed of. When you spoke to your teacher you saved your own life. Saved the lives of your mother and your sisters. That makes you a hero.'

Fearghal's face twisted at the word, nose wrinkled as if he had caught a bad smell. Moira Hanley looked in Cormac's direction and with a slight shake of the head he warned her not to push. They sat in silence for a long moment.

'I have a sister,' Cormac said at last. His tone was conversational. It took some of the tension from the air. 'She's younger than me. Rebecca. Becca and me were always good friends. We had to be, because of our dad.'

Fearghal Henderson was very still.

'Our dad wasn't the worst. Like, on the face of it, some of our friends were way worse off. He never hit us, wasn't really much of a drinker. But I still hated being around him. He didn't like us. I dunno if he ever wanted kids. Dunno if he wanted to get married even.' Cormac sniffed. 'I wish he'd made his mind up about that before he landed himself on my mother.'

And the boy finally looked up. Everything Cormac had been hoping for was there in his eyes – Fearghal Henderson wanted a connection. He was smart enough, or damaged enough, to suspect that Cormac might not be telling him the whole truth, but he was still drawn to the story. Cormac had met a lot of abused kids over the years. He knew what they felt – that the stain of their background was indelible, that it marked them as different. Cormac could guess that for Fearghal, meeting someone who'd lived through something similar would feel like making a friend.

'When I was about ten Dad started keeping all the money. They both worked, my parents, but Dad insisted on *managing the money*.' Cormac let his voice drip with sarcasm. 'Except he didn't really manage anything, just pissed it away on anything that took his fancy. One year he bought himself this really fancy bike for his birthday. It was five hundred pounds or something like that. The next day he screamed at my mother because she bought herself a cup of coffee at the place down the road for what, like, two quid? I don't think he ever rode that bike once.'

Lucy Henderson was watching him now too. As if he were fascinating. As if he were dangerous.

'Living with Dad was awful,' Cormac said. 'We never knew when he was going to blow up about something. He used to unplug the phone from the wall – this was before we had mobile phones, you know? Anyway, he'd put it away somewhere, said if we really needed to make a call we could ask his permission. The few times we asked he said no, of course. And getting rid of the phone made my mother more isolated. She couldn't call a friend. Couldn't call her sister.'

Fearghal turned to look at his mother. Lucy Henderson didn't react. Her pale blue eyes were locked on Cormac. The sleeves of her cardigan were pulled down and tucked protectively inside each tightly clenched fist. Cormac kept his attention on Fearghal.

'He never hit us, and there really wasn't that much shouting in the house, but we didn't have a very happy home. I never wanted to be there. If I had a choice I would have stayed on at training after school every day, but I had to go home, because of Becca.'

Fearghal gave the smallest of involuntary nods.

'Does your dad hit you, Fearghal?' The question so matter of fact it felt like conversation.

Fearghal shook his head.

'Yeah,' Cormac said. He paused, put his head to one side. 'But it's weird, isn't it? I hated being at home but I couldn't have explained why. My dad just ... scared us, I suppose. He had a heart attack when I was about the same age you are now, and he died in hospital the next day. It was an awful shock. My mother cried at the funeral. But honestly, we were so much happier after that. Everything was easier. And afterwards, if you'd asked me why we were so unhappy when my dad was alive, I really wouldn't have known how to explain it.'

Lucy Henderson was very pale. She was so thin. Her skin stretched over her cheekbones, her lips were so dry they had cracked.

'It was the small things,' she said. 'He made you feel like you couldn't do anything right.'

Cormac nodded, very slowly, holding her gaze. He waited.

'Rob had so many rules. He wasn't like that when we married first, he really wasn't. But after, there were so many rules.'

'Did he hurt you, Lucy?' Cormac asked.

'He never hit me. Never hit the kids. But … he made it very hard.'

'He did hit you, Mum,' Fearghal said quietly. 'At Christmas. He hit you because you made the brussels sprouts wrong. He said you got the wrong variety. He said he'd wanted local. He hit you so hard he broke your glasses.'

Lucy Henderson looked at her son as if she had never seen him before. 'I'd forgotten,' she said. 'How could I have forgotten something like that?'

Fearghal shook his head.

'But that was the only time. The only time he hit me.' Lucy looked from Cormac to Fearghal and back, as if asking them to confirm it.

Eventually Fearghal shrugged. 'I don't know,' he said again. 'I think so.'

Cormac let the silence sit for a moment. Moira Hanley hadn't said a word since he'd started telling his story.

'Were you afraid of him, Lucy?'

For a moment he thought he had pushed too fast. He could see the fear, the self-protective mask slipping back over her face.

'Mum,' Fearghal said.

It was enough. Lucy blinked, then turn a helpless gaze in Cormac's direction.

'There were so many rules,' she said. 'What to use to wash the floor, and only wash it from left to right. How to wrap the cheese in the fridge. The right way to make the beds in the morning. And he wouldn't let the kids breathe. He told Gracie that she would never have a boyfriend. She could get that idea out of her head right now. She's only seven.' Lucy started to cry, dropped her head into her hands.

Fearghal turned to her, patted her ineffectually on the shoulder. 'Don't cry, Mum,' he said. 'Please don't cry.' But Lucy didn't stop, couldn't stop it seemed. She wept into her hands as if her heart was broken.

After that it was easier. It took time, but they drew the story from Lucy Henderson, and it was an old pattern. Her relationship with Rob started with ostentatious romantic gestures from him, over-the-top birthday and Valentine's Day presents. A holiday abroad for her first Christmas present from him – a holiday that happened to overlap with Lucy's parents' fortieth anniversary celebrations. A mistake, he'd told her, head hung low, but he'd gotten a deal on the holiday. It couldn't be cancelled, couldn't be postponed. And Lucy, not wanting to ruin the joy of the moment, had agreed to go. He'd proposed to her on that holiday. She'd accepted. And they'd married three months later, eloping at his insistence.

She told them that he wanted her to stay at home with the children and she hadn't minded that at all, not at the beginning. Over time his mania for control of the minutiae of their household got worse and worse. There were chore lists, with allocated timings, that he posted for her on their bedroom door. He set impossible budgets and monitored them religiously. She told them about the cleaning checks. The homework checks. The rituals.

'When did he decide to do it?' Cormac asked in the end. 'Can you think of anything in particular that might have set him off?'

Lucy and Fearghal were holding hands now. It was hard to tell who was providing the support, and who was receiving it.

Lucy shook her head. 'I still can't believe it. Can't believe that he would try to do that. Kill the children. There's no reason in the world ...'

'It was because he was fired from his job, Mum,' Fearghal said, cutting across her. 'He would have hated you going back to work, even if you gave him all the money. He couldn't have handled it.' He glanced in Cormac's direction. 'Michael Hutchinson told everyone at school. His dad works for the same bank. Michael's a ... he's not a friend like, but I knew he wasn't lying. And there was another thing.' Another pause. A longer hesitation. Then he squeezed his mum's hand and looked straight at her.

'He knew that you'd stopped taking the pills.'

'What?'

'The pills he gave you. You stopped taking them and he knew it. You thought he didn't know. But you were different, Mum. I could see it, and so could he. He watched you.'

Cormac stayed in the interview until it was done, but he stepped back from the questioning bit by bit, letting Moira Hanley step forward. She needed to have her own relationship with the family, would need to work with them as they prepared for trial. She found her rhythm after a little while, did a good job. He told her that afterwards, in a brief exchange outside the room. She looked mortified, avoided his eye.

'What you said in there. I didn't know you had such a difficult childhood. I'm sorry you went through that.'

Cormac debated with himself for a moment. He recognised that she was the type who might react badly to what he was about to say, if only because she would feel exposed and taken in, but he couldn't maintain the fiction with a colleague.

'Moira. My father's alive and well and living happily with my mother in West Cork. They go on cruises. Play cards with their friends. He's a good man, a good father, and my mother wouldn't put up for half an hour with the sort of bullshit Henderson got up to.'

Moira stared up at him, lips parted, looking like he had slapped her. For Christ's sake. She'd been a cop long enough. How many interviews had she been part of? None of this should be a surprise.

'All that stuff about routine and chore lists was on the file.' She'd probably gathered half the evidence herself. 'You use what you have to use, Moira. You find common ground and you lead them to it until they start talking.' But there was a flash of fury in her eyes, quickly hidden under hooded eyes, and Cormac ran out of patience.

'Let's move on. Talk to the social workers and make sure that a counsellor goes by the Henderson house today.' He asked her to get the interview recordings to the typists and have the transcripts typed up as soon as possible. 'You do the first pass on them, and then I'll have a check. And let's set up a meeting with the DPP for next week, all right?'

By the time Cormac got home that night, Emma was already in bed. He looked in on her. She was sleeping deeply but not well, murmuring in her sleep and tossing and turning. He lay down beside her for a few minutes, held her hand, felt his usual sense of helplessness. She didn't wake, but seemed to settle into a deeper sleep. He returned to the living room, turned on the gas fire, and went in search of food. He spread the Lambert file out on the coffee table and ate reheated takeaway Indian he found at the back of the fridge, washed it down with beer. Eventually the words started to blur. He sat back on the couch, a photograph of Della Lambert in his hand. It wasn't good quality – just a black and white print out of a photo

Paul Lambert had sent them – but it was the best he had. Della Lambert looked back at him, a laugh in her eyes. She looked very young. He fell asleep and dreamt that he met her by the river on a sunny day. She had a chemistry textbook on her lap and tried to explain the same concept to him again and again, but he couldn't understand.

He woke, confused, to find Emma standing over him. It was dark, the room lit only by the flickering flames of the fire. Emma was in her pyjamas. Her hair was tousled, loose around her shoulders. She was holding Della's photograph in one hand.

'Em?' he said. He blinked himself awake, swallowed against the sour taste in his mouth.

'I know this girl,' she said, her voice a little hoarse with sleep.

'What?'

'I think I know this girl. I've seen her.'

It took him a moment to make sense of what she was saying. 'Where?' Cormac asked.

'In the lab. I'm sure of it. I saw her with Carline Darcy, more than once.'

Cormac sat up straighter. 'Emma, are you sure?'

'Yes. I remember thinking how young she looked, for a student. Is this her? Is this the girl?' Emma turned to him, held out the sheet of paper.

Cormac sat up, ran his hand through his hair. 'Her name's Della Lambert. She's ... we've identified her as the victim of the hit-and-run.'

Emma's eyes dropped to the photograph. 'But ... she has dark hair in the picture.'

'She dyed it.'

'So she was a student?'

'She used to be. But she dropped out a year and a half ago, after her first semester. Her family thought she was working as a waitress.'

'And she had Carline Darcy's ID in her pocket,' Emma said. It wasn't a question.

Cormac shook his head slowly. He wanted to talk about the case, but he should stop this conversation now. Emma would need to give a statement, and it couldn't be to him. He felt a creeping sense of dread. He would have to give a statement too, as to exactly how it had come about that she had seen the photograph, and exactly what they had each said after that.

'We can't talk about this anymore, Em,' Cormac said. 'You'll have to give a statement about what you saw. If it ends up being relevant you'll have to give evidence. Better that we don't discuss it further. I'll ask Fisher to come over in the morning.'

'If that's what you want.' She sat down on the edge of the chair opposite him. 'There's something else. Did you hear that someone broke into the lab last night?'

'What?'

'Nothing was taken, they just trashed one of the offices. It's just … I don't think it was reported, and given everything that's going on, I thought you should know.'

He had so many follow-up questions, and every one of them related in some way to a case he couldn't discuss with her. He stood up, took her hand. 'Let's go to bed,' he said. 'It will wait until morning.'

Thursday 1 May 2014

CHAPTER THIRTY-ONE

Carline was awake when Mark knocked on her bedroom door. She hadn't closed her curtains properly the night before, and early morning light streamed in between them. She lay, cheek against her pillow, and watched the dust motes dance in the air. She was conscious that the laptop was lying on her desk, out in the open, and couldn't bring herself to care.

The knock came again, and this time Mark opened the door without waiting for her to respond.

'Carls? Do you fancy a coffee? I'm making breakfast if you want to eat.' He took in her appearance and his brow creased. He looked at his watch. 'It's after eight you know. Exams start in an hour and a half.'

Carline's eyes felt gummy, her face hot and flushed. There was a strand of hair stuck to one cheek. Conscious of Mark's eyes on her, she sat up in bed, started to tidy her hair with her hands then felt a wave of fury so powerful and so unexpected that it made her dizzy. She dropped her hands.

'What do you want, Mark?' she said.

'Aren't you feeling well?' His gaze travelled behind her to her desk, taking in the used tissues scattered about, the mess of papers.

'I'm fine,' she said. 'I mean, no, I'm feeling sick. I'm not sure that I'll make it to my last exam. It's not a big deal.'

'Right,' Mark said. He looked confused. 'Well, can I get you anything? I'm making breakfast ...' His concern was so obviously insincere that it only fanned the flames of her anger. Once she'd been stupid enough to think he liked her for herself.

Until Valentina had pointed out that Mark's sporadic and half-hearted efforts to bring his relationship with Carline to another level were always preceded by a phone call from his father.

'I'm not hungry,' Carline said. Mark didn't move, and she felt a sudden urgent need to get him out of her room. She stood and pulled on her dressing-gown, walked to the door.

'I'll have coffee while you're eating.'

Carline took a seat on one of the barstools, watched him make toast and eggs, turned a cup of coffee in her hands but didn't drink it. She felt unsettled and jittery and coffee wouldn't help.

'Did I hear you on the phone last night?' she asked.

He grimaced. 'Dad,' he said. 'Wanting to know how I'm going with the exams. Went on and on about how well Sinéad is doing at Trinity. I don't know why he thinks that would motivate me.' A quick flick of his eyes in her direction. 'He's got this really amazing development on the go. Sort of mixed-use light industrial on the outskirts of Dublin. Actually, he thinks it could be a great location for Darcy Therapeutics if you're going to expand.'

'Right,' she said.

'He's happy to show it to you, next time you're down. He was wondering if we want to go down after the exams, take a weekend off, go sailing or whatever. Sinéad will be home too, before she goes to the States. He thought we might like to have a party at the house.'

Carline closed her eyes, passed her hand across her forehead. 'It's not my decision. Whether or not the company expands or where. That has nothing to do with me.' Her tone was sharper than she'd intended, exasperation leaking through.

'Yeah, of course,' Mark said. He took a bite of toast as a flush stained his cheeks. 'Dad just thought you might like a party, before you go to France.'

'France?'

'I thought you were going to spend the summer with your mother.'

'I don't think so,' Carline said. The thought of living with her mother again made her stomach clench. 'I'm going to stay here and work on my thesis.'

'Your mother won't be disappointed?'

Carline almost laughed, except that a laugh right now would almost certainly turn into a sob. Evangeline had never minded her absence, preferred it really, as long as the cheques kept coming. She took a sip from her coffee, put it down. 'I think I'll go back to bed for a while. Good luck with your exam.'

His eyes were on her as she stood. 'You're not coming to the dinner tonight?'

'Vee's thing? No. Have fun though.'

'Carline.' His voice was quiet. 'Carls.' He waited for her to look at him. 'You know that it was Della who died. The story's all over college.'

Despite herself, Carline stiffened. 'I know,' she said. She tried to sound natural.

'When are you going to tell the police about her?'

Carline stiffened. 'I'm not,' she said. 'I mean, there's nothing to tell.'

'You told them you didn't know her. That she was a stranger.'

'God, Mark. They're a bunch of bloody clodhoppers. They called my grandfather, for God's sake. You can imagine how that went down.'

'Right ... but ...'

'And I didn't tell them I didn't know her. When that detective came here he didn't mention Della's name once. No one knew that it was Della who had died at that stage, and no one's asked me about her since. If they did then of course

I'd tell them the truth. But I don't see why I should seek the police out, just because Della and I were classmates once. '

He fell silent, and there was something ugly, something knowing in his expression. 'A bit more than classmates, Carline,' he said.

She hesitated for a second, her mind flick-flicking through what he might know. Almost nothing, surely. She could call his bluff, but the look in his eyes held her back. He was waiting to pounce.

Carline reached for whatever bit of fight was left in her. 'I'm going to do some work,' she said. She gave him her best and brightest smile. 'Have I told you that I'm nearly finished with my thesis? Nobody knows ... they think I'm just getting started but it's nearly ready. I'm going to submit it early. Two thousand words and the thing is done. Would I be the youngest PhD in Ireland, do you think? Or did someone get there before me?' She paused, then turned towards her bedroom with a girlish, theatrical twirl.

'Carline,' he said again.

Carline opened her door. She leaned against it as she turned a smiling face in his direction.

'Oh, and Mark? Do you think your dad would invite me to his party, if you asked him nicely? I'm going to be working very hard, and it would be good to have something lovely like that before I really get into it.'

A range of emotions passed over his face then, in the space of a few seconds. She watched them war with each other – relief, frustration, anger and a few others she couldn't put a name to. Then he gave her a sour smile, and nodded, and turned away.

CHAPTER THIRTY-TWO

For two long days Paul Lambert had hidden in his room, pulled the blankets up over his head and ignored the disrupted rhythms of the house outside his closed bedroom door. He knew that his mother was angry, his father worried, and Geraldine likely suffering the results of both, but he turned away from that knowledge. He couldn't stop thinking about Della. When had she stopped trusting him? And how could he have been so stupid? How could he have thought she paid for that flat working as a waitress? She'd bought his phone for him, given him her barely touched laptop when she'd upgraded. She'd been giving their parents money too – their mother had been talking of sending Geraldine to a state home, then Della had dropped out of college and all that talk stopped and suddenly there was steak every Friday and a new telly in the living room. Paul went over it again and again in his mind. All the mistakes he'd made, all the signs he'd missed.

On Thursday afternoon his mother entered the room and opened the curtains. She pulled his covers from him, and he sat up, slowly blinking his dry, sore eyes against the light.

'Get up,' she said. Her voice was flat. 'You're needed downstairs.'

She turned and trudged down the stairs. He followed a minute later, like a puppet on long string, pausing only at the bathroom to unload a bladder that was suddenly achingly full. He tried to remember when he had last pissed, when he had last eaten something, and couldn't.

She was waiting in the kitchen. Her good coat, a sickly pale pink wool thing she'd had for years, was buttoned to her neck. She had her car keys in one hand. His father sat at the kitchen table, finishing a cup of coffee, eyes, as always, averted.

'You're needed to look after your sister.' Her voice was clipped, angry.

'Where are you going?' His own voice was hoarse from disuse.

'It's nothing to do with you,' she snapped. She nodded at his father, who stood on cue and made for the door, then she turned back to Paul. 'You've no appreciation for anyone else's feelings. Lying in bed all day as if you were the only one who suffered a loss. I've lost my daughter. My first born. You don't see me lying around and crying. Someone has to think about our future.' She gave him a hard, eager stare, but he knew better than to respond. Giving his mother what she wanted – whether it was an argument or anything else – never made anything better. A moment later, a grunt, and she was gone.

He found Geraldine in the living room. She was watching TV, rocking herself gently, forward and back.

'Ger,' he said.

She didn't respond. He waited a second, tried again. 'Ger.'

She flicked her eyes towards him. 'I'm watching Peppa,' she said. Her hair was greasy, there was dirt under her fingernails, and she didn't look well. Paul felt a sudden pang of guilt.

'I'll make you a sandwich, will I?' he said.

'I want a treat,' Geraldine said, her eyes still on the television.

'I'll have a look,' he said. He made the sandwich, and one for himself too while he was at it, the smell of fresh bread and cheese awakening his hunger. He cut up some fruit, and put that on the side of the plate, then found a packet of biscuits at the top of the long cupboard. They weren't allowed to eat in the living room but fuck it. Paul brought the plates along with two glasses of milk to the living room, then sat cross-legged on the floor beside his little sister. They ate together, quietly watching Peppa, and when she'd finished eating Geraldine sighed, then reached out and took his hand.

'My tummy feels better,' she said.

'Mine too,' he said.

He stayed with her for another few minutes, then got up to run her a bath. He used the last of the bubble bath he'd bought her for Christmas, and she didn't object too much to the plan. She splashed around for a while, he washed her hair a bit awkwardly – he'd never been much good at that – then got her out and dressed again in clean clothes. He sat on the end of her bed and watched her play with her dolls. He couldn't bring himself to join in, but she seemed happy enough. He thought about Della.

Paul was absolutely sure that she had done something that had gotten her killed. It hadn't been an accident, and it hadn't been a random act of violence. Something had been going on in her life for months, something that had allowed Della to give up her job as a waitress and still pay her rent. He was so stupid. So fucking stupid.

Time went by. Paul heard movement downstairs and was tempted to retreat back into his room. His parents were in the kitchen, talking. Their words drifted out through the door that had been left slightly ajar, and he sat at the top of the stairs and listened.

His mother's tone of voice registered first. She was tense still, but there was an eagerness in her voice that disturbed him.

'It might take months, Michael,' she said. 'We can't get carried away.'

'No, Eileen,' he said.

'And we don't know how much there is, of course. There might not be as much as we think.'

'But the money, Eileen. If Della got it from something illegal, wouldn't there be a problem ...'

His mother's voice came again, tight, and fast and angry. 'There's nothing to say it was anything but legitimately earned. Jesus, Michael. You're like a child with your questions. You nearly said it to the lawyer, didn't you? And then how would we have looked?'

There was silence for a moment from the kitchen. In his mind's eye Paul could see his father's head drop, as it always did. Could see his mother lean over him, hawk-like, looking for the smallest sign of disagreement.

Paul stood and went back to his room, shut the door quietly behind him and leaned on it. Tears welled and fell. He walked to his desk and took up his laptop and hugged it to him, retreated again to his bed. He climbed under the covers, still holding the computer, the last thing he had of his sister.

Everyone seemed to know more than he did. That was almost the worst part. He knew there was no point talking to his mother. She would tell him nothing. No point talking to the gardaí, they thought he was a kid. Paul opened his laptop and ran a search for Della's name. There had been a newspaper article, hadn't there? About another girl. There had been some sort of mix-up because Della had been carrying the girl's ID when she died. Paul found the article, re-read it. There wasn't much in it, not really, but he should be able to find this Carline Darcy, and at least ask her a few questions. If Della had been carrying her ID then they must have known each other, must have been friends. Maybe Carline Darcy had some answers.

CHAPTER THIRTY-THREE

Cormac called the station first thing on Thursday morning while Emma was in the shower. It took a couple of minutes to confirm no report had been made of a break-in at the lab. He sat on the bed for a moment longer, phone in hand. Carrie might have been right. Maybe he shouldn't have taken the case. The smart thing to do would be to find her now and tell her that, swap cases around so that he took on some of her workload and she took the hit-and-run. He already knew he wouldn't do it. This case was his. He didn't trust anyone else, not even Carrie, to see it through.

He got to the lab at 9 a.m., allowing enough time for Emma to go ahead of him, for her to get through security and into her own workspace. Josep the security guard let Cormac into the foyer, where he had to wait while arriving employees divested themselves of coats and bags and swiped their way in to work. He could see the corner of Emma's coat – bright green – poking out of one of the lockers. As the last employee disappeared through the staff door with a curious glance in Cormac's direction, Josep turned to him with a smile.

'What can I do for you today, detective?' he asked.

Cormac took the photograph of Della Lambert from his pocket, unfolded it, and put in on the desk in front of him. 'Do you recognise this girl?' he asked.

Josep barely looked at it. 'I don't think so,' he said. 'But I see many young people at the college. I do not remember them all.'

'Not at the college, Joe,' Cormac said. 'Here at the lab. Have you ever seen this girl at this laboratory? Ever signed her in to work?'

The security guard glanced at the photograph again. 'I don't believe so,' he said. He shifted his weight on his feet, all hint of a smile gone.

Cormac let the silence sit, let Josep's obvious discomfort grow. He was clearly lying. But he couldn't have thought things through. If the girl had been here, and here many times according to Emma, many of the other employees would have seen her. They would hardly all be willing to lie about it.

'She has been here, Joe. She's been here many times. It's hard to believe that you don't remember her.'

'I just … I'm not sure,' Josep said. 'She may have been here. But, you know, there are many employees of the laboratory. I do not know all of them well.'

More bullshit. The lab was too small to employ more than thirty or forty people. Not difficult to get to know the faces if you saw them at least twice a day. But if Josep had been allowing her in as a favour to Carline Darcy, despite knowing she didn't belong, he wouldn't be in a rush to confess it now.

The door behind him opened, and another two employees entered the room, greeting Josep loudly and continuing their conversation as they opened lockers, hung up coats and bags.

'I'm told there was a break-in here on Tuesday night,' Cormac said, making no effort to keep his voice down.

'Oh yes,' said Josep, eyes flicking to the left. 'A very little one, and they took nothing. Professor Murtagh thinks it was probably students. Drinking too much and doing stupid things.'

'You didn't report it?' Cormac asked.

'It did not seem important,' Josep said, his eyes wide and guileless. 'It was not my decision of course. The professor did not think it was necessary.'

Cormac asked to see James Murtagh, and Josep's relief that his questioning was at an end was all too obvious. He escorted Cormac back to the office, handed Cormac off to the professor without a backward glance.

Murtagh was buried in some paperwork, an empty coffee cup beside him. 'Sit down, detective,' he said, gesturing to the chair opposite him. 'How can I help you?'

'Have you seen Carline Darcy today?' Cormac asked. 'Is she working?'

Murtagh shook his head. 'Exam season,' he said. 'Not that she needs to worry, of course, but even Carline would surely take the time to look over a few notes.'

Cormac caught a note in Murtagh's voice, a hint of resentment, and he looked at him sharply. Murtagh was sensitive enough to notice. He waved a hand in front of his face.

'It's been a long week, detective,' he said. 'I think perhaps I'm feeling my age.'

'You had a break-in, Professor. That may have added to the stress.'

Murtagh betrayed no surprise at Cormac's knowledge. He sat back in his chair, glanced over his shoulder to the vast window behind him. 'They came through there. I've always said that those windows are very impractical from a security point of view. No one can see what's happening on this side of the building, unless they just happen to be boating down the river. Whoever it was just threw a rock through the window, messed some papers around a bit, and wandered off home. Almost certainly an idiotic student who drank too much Buckfast Tonic Wine. I can't quite believe they drink that stuff. A university tradition, I'm told.'

'You didn't report it,' Cormac said.

Murtagh widened his eyes. 'Didn't seem much point. Nothing was taken. We had something similar happen a few years back. We did report it that time and to be candid, detective, your colleagues didn't seem particularly interested. So, I just called and had the window repaired. Got the cleaners in to get rid of the broken glass and give the place a proper spruce up, then got back to work.'

It was all very reasonable, but there was a discordant note in Murtagh's response. It was too glib. Murtagh spoke as if tidying up after a break-in were a standard part of his day, as unremarkable as picking up his morning coffee. Cormac took the photograph of Della from his pocket for a second time that day, placed it on the table.

'Have you seen this girl?'

Murtagh picked up the paper, examined it carefully, put it down. 'It's not a great photograph,' he said. 'But I don't believe so. She doesn't look familiar, but I don't pay a great deal of attention to the students, to tell you the truth. Who is she?'

'Her name is Della Lambert. She was a student at the university at one time, though not recently. She's also the young woman who was killed last Friday night, and she died with an access card for this laboratory in her pocket.'

Murtagh looked at the photograph again, studied it more carefully, then shook his head. 'She must have picked it up from somewhere.' Then realisation dawned. 'It was Carline's card, wasn't it? That's why there was a mix up in identification. This young girl was carrying Carline's access card.'

Cormac took the photograph back, put it away. 'If Della had been in the laboratory, if she had spent time here, would you have known it?'

Murtagh thought for a moment. 'I'd certainly like to think so. But really, I'm holed away in my little cave for much of the day. If I do venture into the lab it's into what I like to call the inner sanctum. The internal laboratory that the students are not permitted to enter.'

'Not even Carline?'

Murtagh smiled. 'Not even Miss Darcy. There is valuable intellectual property on these premises.'

Cormac paused, decided to take the conversation in another direction. 'Tell me, professor, what's it like, teaching a genius?'

Murtagh's expression settled back into tired patience. 'I'm not precisely her teacher, you know. Carline Darcy has worked as a research assistant in the outer lab from time to time during the year, when her timetable allows. But I have very little to do with the students. My own work demands too much of me.'

'But you're her supervisor too, aren't you? For her thesis.'

When Murtagh's face wasn't animated by speech or a particular expression, his mouth fell into a downward turn, deep grooved lines either side of his mouth emphasising the downward curve. Resting old-and-pissed-off face. 'I was a member of the panel that assessed Carline's thesis proposal. That is not quite the same as a teacher-student relationship. Assuming her proposal is accepted, I will be her supervisor and we will likely spend more time together as the work progresses.'

'There's a possibility her proposal won't be accepted?' Cormac didn't try to hide his scepticism; he wanted to see if a light needling would provoke some honesty. With the amount of money Darcy had donated to this university, if Carline Darcy wanted to do a degree in knitting they would have created one for her.

Murtagh sighed, shook his head. 'The early work is very exciting, detective. If Carline wants to continue her studies here then I'm sure that's what she'll do. She does, however, have undergraduate exams to complete. Even Carline Darcy has to graduate first.'

The interview went downhill from there. Murtagh didn't move from his position that he had never seen Della Lambert, and Cormac didn't have much more to ask him. They would need to interview every employee of the lab, find out who remembered seeing Della and where, then confront Carline with that evidence. Confront Murtagh too, and Josep Zabielski. Josep was clearly lying. Murtagh was harder to read but it felt like he was holding something back. Josep's motivation for lying seemed obvious – if he'd allowed Della to access the lab knowing she didn't belong there, his job would be at risk. Murtagh's motivation was less clear. Was he trying to protect Carline? Protect the Darcy name, the Darcy money? It was all possible.

CHAPTER THIRTY-FOUR

Cormac left the lab and walked to the concourse. He wanted coffee before he went back to the station to pick up the threads of the investigation. He found his way to the coffee shop, ordered it black, added two sugars. The place was packed, students loading up on caffeine. They looked very young to him, despite their air of serious endeavour, like children playing shop. He took his coffee and left the building. The day was warming up, and Cormac shrugged off his jacket as he went down the steps outside the library. Some of the students had taken their books and tablets and set up in a small park between the library and the engineering building. They were lying in the grass. Not a smart move, there was no way in hell that it had dried since the rain the day before. The influence of American movies. They all thought they were going to Yale or Harvard and studying in the sun-dappled shade of east coast North America. Cormac watched, amused, as students arrived, sat, checked out the talent around them, realised the damp was rapidly seeping through the arse of their jeans, and stood again, trying to look like that had always been their plan.

Cormac walked past the little park and on towards the chapel car park. He'd parked the squad car midway between the library and the chapel, and as he drew closer he saw a young man loitering on the footpath near the car. He'd clearly noticed the marked car. As Cormac drew nearer the loiterer turned in his direction, and he realised it was Mark Wardle, Carline Darcy's roommate. Mark froze when he saw Cormac approaching, looked for a moment as if he might make a bolt for it, then stood his ground.

'Detective?' he said, as Cormac drew near. 'Were you … you were looking for me?'

There was anticipation in Mark's eyes. Nervousness too. He had something he wanted to share but he was conflicted about it.

'I wasn't,' Cormac said. 'Were you for me?'

'Oh God. No,' said Mark. He shook his head, raised his hands in a mock warding off gesture, and Cormac suppressed a sigh of exasperation. Mark wanted to talk all right, but he was the type who wanted a push first.

'Walk with me, Mark,' Cormac said, and he turned in the direction of the car park. Mark fell into step beside him, and they walked in silence. Cormac stopped at the spot where a week earlier he had first seen Della Lambert's broken body. The crime scene tape was gone, whatever blood had been left after the scene of crime lads had done their job now washed away by the rain. It was as if it had never happened. As if she had never died.

'When did you meet Della, Mark? For the first time I mean.'

He kept his eyes on the road, until he heard Mark speak, a stuttered 'Sorry?' Then he turned his gaze to the younger man and his eyes said *don't bullshit me* and *I know so much more than you think I do* and *you are a boy and I am a man, and that you don't know the difference proves it.* Mark held his gaze for a minute, then looked away.

'I don't know. I mean, we were introduced, I suppose, in like, first year?' Mark pushed both hands back through his hair. He was flushed now, and his eyes darted one direction, then another, as if looking for an audience, or a saviour or both.

'But you saw her more than once, Mark, didn't you?'

'I might have seen her around the campus, sure,' Mark said. 'I mean, we weren't friends or anything. She was just a girl, you know?'

'Just a girl.'

Mark shrugged. He must have been aware of seeming callous, because he spoke again quickly. 'It's shit that she died. She was only twenty, right? Same age as us. But it was an accident. A shitty accident. Whoever hit her, I'm sure they're scared. It's probably a fucking lecturer who had a few too many and was too fucking scared to own up to it.' He said *fucking* in a south Dublin accent – *focking* – and looked a little more confident.

'She wasn't the same age as you, Mark. She was sixteen when she started college, and eighteen when she died. And it wasn't an accident. You know that. Someone hit Della so hard that she bounced off the front bonnet of their car. Her head hit the ground so hard that her skull fractured in fourteen places. That first impact would almost certainly have killed her, but it wasn't enough for whoever was behind the wheel.' Cormac turned and nodded back in the direction they had come. 'First they drove straight over Della where she lay on the road, crushing her pelvis. Then they drove to the other end of the road, turned their car, and drove over her for a second time. That time the car crushed her nose, broke a cheek bone, an eye socket, ripped the skin from her face.'

Mark grimaced. He swallowed once, then again. His hands were buried deep in his pockets but Cormac could see his fists clench through the fabric. 'If you think I had something to do with it, you're wrong,' he said. 'I never touched Della. Never would have. And not like that. Jesus.'

'Della and Carline were friends, weren't they, Mark? You saw them together. At the apartment, around college?'

'You can't seriously think Carline had something to do with this?'

'I'm not suggesting that Carline killed Della, or even that she knows anything about her death.' And if Mark believed that, it would surely be the worst possible case of wishful thinking. 'But we know that Carline knew Della. She knew her well. She gave Della her ID. An ID that allowed Della to access the Darcy labs, where extremely valuable and secret research was stored. Why did she do that, Mark? If there's a reasonable explanation, I need to hear it.'

'For God's sake. You think Carline could kill a girl she knew, a girl she befriended? Run her over with a car? That's just sick.'

'You might be right, Mark. Maybe I have Carline all wrong. But I've met a lot of murderers. A couple of them were even good-looking blondes from nice families.'

Mark looked at him as if he were pleading for Cormac to take it back. When Cormac said nothing. Mark pushed his hands deeper into his pockets, face set.

'Rich people commit murder too, Mark,' Cormac said. 'They have a couple of things in common, these people who have everything and still feel the need to take a life. The first is that, more often than not, when they finally confess, they give us some convoluted story. They want their reasons to be heard. That's because deep down, right down to their core, rich people believe that they are different, that they are special. So even when they're snivelling, having a good cry and telling us all about it, telling us how sorry they are, how much they regret it – even then they really believe that they had the right to do it. Your average gouger, he'll keep his mouth shut, because he knows what he did was wrong, and that no amount of explanation will change that. The wealthy though, they're convinced that they have the right to kill, and that if they can just get us to listen, we'll understand.'

Mark was staring back at him now, hypnotised and horrified by his words.

'They have one other thing in common, Mark, and I mean this sincerely. Every single time I arrest someone with money, there'll be some fucking sacrificial lamb standing in the wings, all prepped and ready to take the fall. Sometimes they'll even volunteer for it. Is that you, Mark? Tell me you're not going to be that idiot. Tell me you're not willing to lie for Carline Darcy, when there's so much evidence her story is bullshit that we're knee deep in it.'

There were tears in Mark's eyes as he slowly shook his head.

CHAPTER THIRTY-FIVE

Cormac brought Mark to the station, where he took his statement. They sat in a grey interview room with the recorder running and Rory Mulcair quietly taking notes, while Mark told them everything he knew.

'Carline introduced us. To Della, I mean. She brought her around and introduced her to everyone.'

'When was this?'

'Maybe back in first year. Early on.' Mark was sitting upright in his chair, his hands clasped in front of him on the table. He picked at a hangnail on his left thumb. 'It was weird. It wasn't like Carline, to just rock up with someone new. Vee, yes, all the time, but Carline didn't make friends with new people.'

'Tell me about Della,' Cormac said. 'Did you like her?'

'She was all right. Quiet. Didn't seem very interested in us.' Mark clasped and unclasped his hands. 'Look, I'm not being harsh. We only met her I think twice. She dropped out of college, and we never saw her again.'

'You never saw Della after she left college? Never saw her with Carline?'

Mark swallowed. 'Not ... officially. I bumped into her coming out of our building one night. She said they'd been hanging out but when I got upstairs Carline said she'd been alone all evening.'

'Did you tell Carline that you'd met Della? Confront the fact that she'd lied to you?'

Another swallow. A shake of the head.

'Why not?'

'Just, there didn't seem to be much point. I mean, Carline was entitled to see who she wanted. She didn't answer to me. And if she wanted to keep her thing with Della a secret, that was up to her.'

'Her thing? Are you suggesting that Della and Carline were in a romantic relationship?'

He offered them a shrug, looked down at his hands.

'Mark?'

'I don't know.'

Cormac nodded, decided to back off for the time being. 'Why did Della drop out? Did you ever talk about it?'

'Carline told me her parents were wiped out in the crash. Lost the family business or something, so Della had to work. Couldn't afford the fees, or her rent, and she didn't want to move home. I got the impression that her mother was a nightmare.'

'Carline told you a lot,' Cormac said.

Mark shook his head. 'No. She didn't, actually. Once Della dropped out of college Carline never spoke about her, never mentioned her.'

Cormac said nothing for a moment, let the silence sit until it thickened into pressure.

'But Carline continued to see Della,' he said.

'Yes.'

'And she hid this from you, and from your other roommate.'

'Yes.'

'If Carline hid the relationship from you, how did you know they were still seeing each other?'

Mark's picking at his hangnail intensified. 'Carline ... she's sort of self-contained. She's not really interested in other people's lives. So if she starts asking you what your plans are for the evening, it's pretty obvious she wants to know where you'll be for reasons of her own.'

'You followed her,' said Cormac.

A nod. Very little embarrassment in Mark's face, a hint of self-righteousness if anything. 'She went to Della's apartment. Stayed there for a few hours, then went home. And that wasn't the only time.'

Cormac let the silence draw out again, waited until Mark shifted uncomfortably in his chair. 'Why do you think they kept their meetings secret, Mark?'

Mark rolled his eyes, shook his head.

'You think they were in a relationship, but they weren't willing to go public.'.

The corners of Mark's mouth went down. 'What other reason could there be?'

'Is Carline a lesbian?'

Mark let out a breath, making a show of reluctance, but he was more relaxed now. They had come to the point of the interview, as far as he was concerned. He spread his hands, telling this story, getting into the flow of it. He had very little self-awareness, didn't seem to realise that he was unzipping his own bitterness, leaving it on show. 'Before Della, I never saw Carline in a relationship with anyone. Nothing. Not even a snog or a one-night stand. She just had zero interest. Before Della I figured maybe she was asexual, or just playing the virgin to keep her grandfather happy. Then after she met Della I figured she was just gay, and afraid to tell her grandfather.'

'Her grandfather? You mean John Darcy?'

A nod.

'You think Della kept her sex life secret to try to please her grandfather?'

'I'm not saying he would have cared one way or the other,' Mark said. 'I mean it's not like I know him *personally*. I'm just saying that Carline lives her life to try to impress him. And her mother's a complete slapper. She was basically a high-end

hooker when she met Carline's father – you know that, right?'
He waited for nods of acknowledgement. Cormac kept his
face impassive, but it didn't knock Mark off his stride. 'So I
think maybe the whole sex thing, maybe she was just trying to
differentiate herself from her mother. Like, show Darcy, I'm
not like my mother, you know? Either that or maybe she saw
shit when she was younger that fucked her up. She lived with
her mother for a few years when she was a kid.'

It occurred to Cormac that this sneering twerp sitting
across from him was one of Carline Darcy's two best friends
in the world. Despite himself, Cormac felt a pang of pity for
her.

'But you're suggesting all that changed when she met
Della.'

Mark shrugged. 'I mean, I don't know for sure. But why
else would they keep it secret? Why spend hours holed up in
Della's apartment?'

Cormac let nothing of what he was feeling colour his tone.
He kept his voice neutral, showed no judgement. 'Friendship?'
he suggested.

Mark grimaced, a twist of the mouth. 'They had nothing in
common. Della's parents had nothing. She was just a country
girl. Carline has so much. Even to see them together. I mean,
Della was such a mouse. I couldn't believe that Carline would
choose to be with her, but I suppose that was the appeal. She
probably thought she could control Della. You know, maybe
have her as a quiet bit on the side.'

Cormac sat back in his chair, looked over the younger man.
'They were in the same class,' he said in the end. 'Studying
the same subject. I'm told Carline is a dedicated student, that
she's talented. If Della Lambert had the same interest, had
similar ability, isn't that the basis for a friendship?'

Mark was sceptical and didn't try to hide it. Something
in him couldn't imagine a friendship between two people

who weren't equals in wealth or social status. Which said something about his own relationship with Carline Darcy. How much of that was based on mutual convenience, mutual advantage? Carline's position in the world, or rather her possible future, was clearly of great importance to Mark. Did he look at Carline and see only the advantages a friendship with her could bring his way? And if so, why was he in such a rush to give away all her secrets?

'But you never asked Carline about her relationship with Della?'

Mark shook his head. 'Not then. I figured it was her business, and if she ever wanted to talk about it she would.'

Relationships could be complicated, Cormac knew. It was possible to hold a range of contradictory emotions towards those you were close to. It was certainly conceivable that somewhere inside him, Mark held a true affection for his friend and roommate, but what came across most clearly in that interview room was that whatever his more positive emotions might be, Mark also carried an undiluted streak of resentment towards the blonde girl. He wanted to have her, and failing that, he wanted to hurt her.

'But you did speak to Carline about it at some point,' Cormac said.

'It was after you guys had been around. After it got out at college that you'd identified the body. That it was Della. And we didn't talk about their relationship exactly. I just asked Carline if she was going to tell you lot that she'd known her.'

'And?'

'And nothing. Carline has no intention of telling you the truth about knowing Della. She said that she had no idea what had happened to Della, had no idea who had killed her, and she didn't intend to do anything to draw you on her again.'

Cormac drummed his fingers on the table again. 'Maybe that's not unreasonable,' he said. 'She's sitting exams. Most people aren't that comfortable with police coming around, asking questions. Isn't it perfectly possible that she knew Della, had a friendship with her, but feels she knows nothing that would assist police in figuring out who killed her?'

That was Mark's cue to agree. He could salvage his position as a friend of Carline's, assuage any guilt he might feel about what he'd said, backtrack on his insinuations. Or he could double-down.

Mark pursed his lips.

'It seems to me that you're worried about something, Mark. I think there's something on your mind.'

'I don't know. Maybe. I just can't help but wonder, if Carline wanted to keep their relationship quiet ... but Della didn't?'

Christ, he was a contemptible little shit. Cormac would also have bet money on him being wrong. This wasn't about a romantic relationship turned to bitterness. That was all a creation of Mark's sad little mind. But something had been going on between Della and Carline, and that something had led to Della's death. Cormac drummed his fingers on the table, and Mark flinched at the sudden noise.

'Where were you last Friday night from nine o'clock?' Cormac asked.

Another flinch. 'What?'

'It's a simple question Mark.'

'I ... I went to dinner with friends, and then I went home. I'm not sure what time exactly.'

'What about Carline? Were you with her?'

'Carline stayed at home. She was at home when I got in.' He might have been telling the truth, he might have been lying. Something lurked in his eyes that was difficult to read.

'What time do you think you got home?'

A shrug. 'Look, I don't know. I'd say it was before ten. We had a seven o'clock booking at Ard Bia. We took our time. When we'd finished I walked home. I don't remember checking the time or anything.'

There were cameras at the Spanish Arch. They could check to see what time Mark had left the restaurant, assuming that he was telling the truth. 'But Carline was there when you got home?'

'Yes. Definitely.'

'You saw her?'

Mark hesitated. 'Yes ... no, I saw her. She was definitely home. She was studying. I made her a cup of tea.'

'And your other roommate, Valentina. She can confirm this?' Cormac asked.

'Valentina was out. She didn't come home until much later.'

'I see.'

The interview went downhill after that. It was difficult to tell if Mark was lying. He might have been telling the truth, or it might have occurred to him that providing Carline Darcy with an alibi for a murder could be a valuable proposition. He had laid the trail of a theory – Carline and Della in a secret sexual relationship, Della wants to come clean or blackmail Carline, Carline kills her to keep her quiet – then balked at the finish. Cormac couldn't tell if Mark really hadn't seen the obvious conclusion to the story he was telling, or if he had rushed up on it in a fit of pique, and only when he was staring it in the face realised what he had done, and the price he would possibly pay. He backtracked where he could, obfuscated where he couldn't, and resorted to tears when he had no other option. Cormac let him go after an hour. They weren't going to get much more of use from him. Carline Darcy was the one they needed sitting in that chair. She was the one with the answers.

CHAPTER THIRTY-SIX

While Rory walked Mark out, Cormac returned to the case room. The room was unusually quiet, he picked that up from metres away, and when he reached the door he saw why. Brian Murphy was there, leaning against a desk and having a quiet word with Dave McCarthy. It was all very casual, but he'd no doubt picked up a fair bit just by being in the room. Dave looked up at Cormac's arrival, acknowledged him with a nod. Murphy took his time finishing his conversation, then stood, and finally looked Cormac's way.

'A word in my office, detective, if you have a moment,' he said.

Cormac followed him downstairs, took a seat. Murphy looked him over, his grey eyes unreadable. For once the pristine white desk was less than immaculate. There was a case file open on the table; notes, reports, photographs spread out in no apparent order.

'Tell me where you are on the Lambert case,' Murphy said.

Cormac held his gaze. 'I want to bring Carline Darcy in,' he said. 'I have a statement from her roommate that she was friends with Della Lambert, may have been in a relationship with her, and that she deliberately misled us about that relationship.'

Murphy didn't bat an eyelid. 'You think Carline Darcy killed the girl?'

'I think it's possible she was involved,' Cormac said slowly. 'She certainly knows more than she's telling. At the very least, if someone else killed Della Lambert, I believe that Carline Darcy knows why.'

Murphy nodded slowly. He held a pen in his right hand and turned it intermittently as he stared Cormac down. 'What have you got?' he asked. 'Other than the roommate's statement, that is.'

Cormac didn't have much choice but to walk him through it. He started with the evidence connecting Della with Carline. There was the ID. The fact that Della and Carline had been in the same class in college for a few months. That they had been friends and had taken the trouble to hide their relationship. He talked about the money found in Della's apartment, the deposits to her bank account. Carline the likely source for both. He acknowledged Mark Wardle's theory that Carline and Della's relationship had been a romantic one, the possibility that blackmail had been the motive for murder, though that theory didn't ring true to him. The next step was obviously to question Carline Darcy. Presumably she would continue to deny her connection with Della. That denial, in the face of Mark Wardle's evidence to the contrary, would give them the basis for a warrant for her bank accounts, and with those they should be able to prove that she had paid Della. Murphy said nothing as Cormac recited the facts, but the pen in his hand stilled. The job wasn't finished, not by a long shot, but Cormac had too much now for Murphy to persist in holding the investigation back from the Darcy family.

'I need a few more bodies, if you can spare them,' Cormac said. 'We have to interview the lab employees, and it would be better to get through them all on the same day.'

There was a short pause before Murphy spoke. 'It goes without saying, detective, that I rely on your judgement. I don't second guess my senior officers' investigative decisions.'

'Sir.' Cormac said the word automatically. Murphy was rolling over. He had seen that he couldn't hold the investigation back, and that Cormac's next steps would almost certainly provoke a response from the Darcy family, so he'd quickly defaulted to a bit of arse-covering. So far, so predictable.

'I can't give you more resources. We are overloaded at the moment, and you have plenty of people. Set up your interviews and keep me informed as you see fit.'

Cormac left Murphy's office a few minutes later, feeling more unsettled than satisfied. Why did he feel like Murphy had just laid a trap and was sitting back to watch him spring it?

CHAPTER THIRTY-SEVEN

Cormac took the time to grab lunch before he drove to Carline Darcy's apartment building. He felt like he needed a moment to gather his thoughts before he spoke to her, but he hit the café in the middle of the lunchtime rush. It was noisy and chaotic. The tables were all taken, the few that looked close to finishing up had already attracted a number of impatient hoverers, ready to pounce the moment a chair was pushed back. Cormac settled for a pre-made sandwich from the fridge, took it with him and ate it on the riverside walk beside the Corrib, leaning on the railing and looking down into the water. He thought over the day so far, tried to put a finger on why he felt so unsettled. The meeting with Murphy had thrown him. It had felt as if Murphy had already known every detail of what Cormac had reported to him. Disconcertingly, it had felt as if Murphy knew more.

When he was finished, Cormac picked up a car from the station and made the short drive over to Carline Darcy's apartment. He was still deep in his own thoughts, so when he passed Paul Lambert just as Paul took the corner at the Dock Road, it took him a moment to recognise the boy. Cormac looked in his rear-view mirror, in his wing mirror, but Paul had already disappeared around the corner. Cormac pulled in outside the apartment building and thought about turning the car and going in search of Della Lambert's little brother. But the Dock Road was one way. He would have to drive around the block and by then Paul would have taken one of the many narrow roads or laneways that led into the centre of the city. What had brought the boy here? It had to be Carline.

Cormac parked and made his way to the apartment building. This time the door was shut and the lock engaged. Cormac pressed the intercom. Carline Darcy answered, listened to him give his name and the reason he was there, then buzzed him through without comment. When he reached the fourth floor she opened the door to him before he knocked, then held it wide and gestured for him to walk straight through.

'I can offer you water, detective, or tea, coffee?' She stood beside the breakfast bar, the window behind her perfectly framing the view of the docks and the moored boats beyond.

'Thank you, no,' Cormac said.

Carline was dressed simply. A pair of skinny jeans, a fitted white T-shirt that looked brand new, boots that looked like they'd never walked a Galway street. She wasn't wearing makeup and she was clearly tired, but she looked like a girl who had pulled herself together. It would have been easy to miss the very slight tremor in her hands.

'Shall we sit?' Cormac asked. He gestured towards the table.

Carline didn't move. 'Could we … I'd be grateful if we could make this quick. It's been a busy week.'

Cormac nodded slowly. He pulled out one of the breakfast bar stools, leaned against it as he flipped through a notebook. 'We first spoke on the night of Friday the twenty-fifth of April,' he said.

'The night you came to notify my friends of my death.' She interrupted him. The words were confident, sparring even, but there was a tired rasp in her voice.

'Exactly that,' Cormac said. He tried to hold her gaze. 'When I spoke to you on that night you denied all knowledge of Della Lambert.'

'No,' she said, shaking her head. 'I didn't. How could I have known that Della was the girl who had died? You didn't know yourself, no one did. You just asked me if I knew who the victim was and I told you the truth.'

Cormac nodded slowly. 'That's true, Carline. Are you telling me now that you did know Della?' He waited for her nod. 'How did you meet her?'

'We were in the same tutorial group in the first few months of first year. I wouldn't say we were friends, but we were friendly acquaintances for a time.' Her arms were tightly folded across her chest, those betraying hands tucked into her armpits.

'When was the last time you saw her?'

A hint of tension in her face. She wasn't sure how much he knew. 'I … can't recall,' she said. 'Or at least I can't be sure.'

Cormac waited for her to elaborate but she was being oh-so careful now. No rushing in with explanations to smooth out an awkward silence.

'Did Della ever come here? Spend time in your apartment?'

Carline shrugged lightly. 'I'm sure she did. All of my classmates spent time here at one time or another. I have parties, occasionally. More last year than this.'

'And did you ever visit Della's apartment?'

She made a show of thinking about it, tilting her head to one side. 'Where did she live, the Cornstore? I may have. In fact, I think I did. Della borrowed some of my books, I called by to collect them, went in for tea.' And just like that she'd explained away any DNA evidence they might find in the apartment. Not that they had a sample for comparison's sake, not that they were ever likely to get it unless he got black and white proof of her guilt. The Darcy family attorneys would be all over him like a bad rash if he even suggested it. Carline was watching him, with a hint of frustration in that perfect face. She couldn't read what he was thinking.

'Did you stay in touch with Della after she left college?'

'For a time. Della would come along to college gatherings. She was lonely, I think. Sometimes I felt she regretted leaving college as she did.'

'Why did she leave, Carline? She must have spoken to you about it. It seems like such a drastic decision, for a girl with so much potential.'

Carline swallowed, blinked. 'I don't know why she left. Whatever the reason, Della must have thought it was worthwhile.'

'Della came to the Darcy laboratories. She spent time with you there.'

Another head tilt. 'I don't think so.'

'You never saw her at the lab?'

'No. Security is very tight. Della wasn't a student, and she wasn't working there. She wouldn't have been permitted access.'

Cormac held her gaze. 'I have a witness who says she did visit you there. That she did more than visit. That she worked alongside you for hours at a time, and very frequently.'

Carline shook her head but she was paler now. 'That's not true,' she said. 'Who told you that?'

'You're telling me that if I speak to the lab employees, not one of them will tell me that they saw Della with you?'

Carline took a breath, gathered herself. 'I'm telling you that I never spent time with Della in the laboratory. I … I think I would be surprised if any of the employees at the lab would say otherwise. Partly because it's not true, and also because they're not supposed to talk to anyone about the work carried out in the laboratory. It's all highly confidential. Everyone signs a non-disclosure agreement. I expect that if you were to question Darcy employees in relation to their work in the lab, the company would have to call in our lawyers.' She paused, permitted a crease in her perfect brow. 'Perhaps I should ask a lawyer to be present for this discussion. Do you think that would be appropriate?'

'This is a murder investigation, Carline,' Cormac said. His tone was gentle, but his words were clear. 'We will question the employees, and they will speak to us. And if you feel you need to speak with a lawyer, you shouldn't hesitate to make a call.' He gestured to where a mobile phone was sitting on the kitchen counter. She looked towards it, hesitated. He wondered if calling a lawyer would mean calling her grandfather. If it would, that might explain her hesitation. He pressed on.

'You say that you can't remember when you last saw Della Lambert. Have you seen her since Christmas?'

'I can't recall.'

'I think you did. I think you saw Della, and you gave her a gift of a very expensive cardigan, the one she wore on the night she died.'

Carline stayed silent for a long moment, and when she spoke her voice was steady. She had found a reserve of strength from somewhere. 'I may have, if I saw Della and she admired it. As I've said, I really don't recall. Or possibly she picked it up at a charity shop. Every so often my wardrobe gets excessive, I suppose, so I clear it out.'

'Did you pay Della Lambert? Give her money, a salary, or a gift?'

A pause. Then, 'No.'

'You didn't give Della Lambert half a million euro, in exchange for her assistance?'

'What sort of assistance?'

'Helping you in the laboratory.'

She laughed, but it was brittle. She hadn't expected him to get so close to the truth.

'Please. I don't like to toot my own horn, but I don't need anyone's help.' She shook her hair back from her face, chin high. 'Least of all Della Lambert's.' She looked at her watch. 'I have work to do, detective. I'll have to ask you to excuse me.'

Cormac nodded. 'I hear you're sitting your finals. A four-year degree in only two years. Must be a lot of pressure. How disappointing it would be, if your results didn't quite meet expectations.'

Her lips compressed, but she said nothing, just showed him silently to the door. He paused in the threshold.

'Why did Paul Lambert come to see you, Carline?'

The self-possessed, self-contained young woman of a week ago was unravelling. Now he could read every thought that crossed her mind. There was shock first – she hadn't expected the question – and then she thought about lying, and finally decided to tell the truth, or at least a version of it.

'He thought I knew what had happened to his sister.'

'And why did he think that?' Cormac asked.

'You'd have to ask him.'

The obfuscation was so clumsy, so obvious. He should bring her in now, really, shouldn't he? She was on the point of breaking – one firm push would send her over the edge and start her talking. Why was he hesitating? Was he afraid of what he might find? Or was it the meeting with Murphy that held him back, his feeling that he might have missed something there? As he stood there, undecided, Carline Darcy, pleading eyes holding his gaze all the while, slowly closed the door.

CHAPTER THIRTY-EIGHT

Cormac second-guessed his decision not to bring Carline in all the way down in the lift. When he reached the street he found that the decision had been taken out of his hands. A man and a woman waited for him there, leaning conspicuously against an unmarked car parked just outside the apartment building. They were young, maybe mid-twenties, and dressed alike in neatly pressed slacks, collared T-shirts and jackets, as if they would really have preferred the uniform, and had opted for the next best thing. They weren't subtle. Cormac didn't need car or the clothing to figure out that they were police, and that they were there for him.

'To what do I owe the pleasure?' Cormac said.

They exchanged a glance, then reached for badges and briefly flashed them.

'Detective Garda Michael Moltoni, and this is my colleague, Katherine Naude.'

'Kat,' the woman said, interrupting her colleague and offering her hand for a shake.

'We're with Internal Affairs,' Moltoni continued. 'Can we have a word? We can drive you back to the station now, if you prefer.'

Moltoni and Naude. Not exactly Irish names. Was that why they'd chosen IA? Once an outsider, always an outsider?

Cormac put his hands in his pockets. 'Oh, I don't think there's any need for that.' He glanced both directions. The street was deserted. The sun was setting, the streetlights had come on, and night was beckoning. 'I think we can get it done here, don't you?'

Another exchanged glance and again Moltoni took the lead. 'If that's your preference.' He leaned back against the car again, working too hard at looking confident and casual. 'Do you know why we want to talk to you?'

Cormac snorted, shook his head. 'I'd say I've a fair idea, but I'm not about to do your job for you, so why don't you just spit it out, all right?'

'We've been informed that you are investigating the death of Della Lambert, who was killed in a vehicular collision on the night of Friday twenty-fifth of April,' Moltoni said. 'We've also been told that your partner, Dr Emma Sweeney, found Ms Lambert's body, and that Dr Sweeney is also a witness to your investigation. That she has given evidence. Is that correct?'

Cormac blew out a long breath. 'It is,' he said.

Moltoni nodded. There was a suggestion of relief in his face. Maybe glad to avoid a confrontation? But Cormac wouldn't argue what could be so easily proven. He needed to choose his battles more carefully.

'I think you know the rules as well as I do, DS Reilly. You should have handed the case off to your colleague from the get-go, but certainly from the moment you became aware that your partner had not only found the body but was also a witness in the case.'

Cormac nodded. Looked past them and out across the water beyond. 'Is it to be a suspension?' he asked.

Moltoni hesitated. He seemed thrown by the direction the conversation had taken. He had expected more of an argument. 'Not a suspension,' Moltoni said. 'Nothing so formal.' Then he added, as Cormac laughed, 'At least not for now. You're off the case, and we'll have to look into the work you've done on it so far. Make sure you haven't breached procedure any more than we have identified so far. But it's been strongly recommended that you take some leave.'

'I see.' Take some time off, long enough for the case to run its course. See how it all turned out. He told himself that he should be relieved. It could have been worse. It seemed there wasn't an appetite to go after him, if that could be avoided. And maybe that made sense. The previous April, when the media pack had gathered and howled, they'd had to build Cormac up as the model officer, hadn't they? What complications would it cause if it were publicly known that he had been put on suspension just over a year later?

'Who's going to take over the case?' Cormac asked. It would have to be O'Halloran. Hackett wasn't due back from holidays for another few days.

'It will be looked after,' was all Moltoni said.

Cormac laughed again, shook his head. He wondered who had set them on him. It could have been Moira Hanley, it might have been Murphy. Hanley's motivations were easy enough to discern – that would be plain old-fashioned resentment and revenge. Murphy was harder to figure out. A favour to John Darcy? Or did he just see Cormac as a threat, and this case as an opportunity to take him out?

'We do have questions for you,' Naude piped up.

Cormac looked at his watch. 'I'm on leave. If you want to talk to me, why don't you make an appointment?' He was almost at his car when he turned back to them. 'Carline Darcy is waist-deep in this thing,' he said. 'Waist-deep.' They looked back at him dumbly. Cormac got into his car and drove away.

CHAPTER THIRTY-NINE

When Cormac Reilly left her apartment, Carline sat for a while, eyes closed tight and fingers pressed to her ears. The apartment was very quiet, but his questions lingered, echoed and refused to leave her in peace. She'd wanted to tell him the truth, had come so close when he'd asked about Della, but then she'd opened her mouth and the lies had come pouring out. Carline's fists pummelled her legs, once, then again. She'd lied because that was what it took to preserve her chance at a future. Selfish, selfish bitch that she was. But she'd lied too because she couldn't bring herself to tell him what she had done. His questions had forced her to realise, for the first time, how utterly wrong she had been. She should have told him but guilt and self-disgust and an absolute conviction that he would never understand had stopped her. How could she explain that she had never seen Della as vulnerable? Carline had had money and a powerful family, but Della had been the strong one all along.

Carline looked towards the closed door to the outer hall. Maybe she should follow him. She could go after him now, try to reach him before he got to his car, tell him everything. Carline sank her head back into her hands. She couldn't do it. Not yet. Not until she'd thought it all through, and she was at least in the right place to do that. The apartment was so quiet. Mark and Valentina wouldn't be back. They would go straight to the college bar after their last exam, then on to their end of exams dinner. For once Mark hadn't pressed her to join them. In a few hours it would grow dark. And she felt safe here. She should be able to think clearly, if only her head would stop aching.

It was early Friday evening when Della had arrived at the apartment unannounced. The building's main entrance was supposed to be a security door, accessible only to those with an electronic key, or to those who were buzzed through by an apartment owner. More often than not on a Friday night, that front door was propped open by some student hosting a party. Della had made her own way through and up in the lift, and her knock on the door had taken Carline by surprise. She'd been alone that night too, studying, trying to force her mind to understand concepts that were becoming more and more complex, spiralling beyond her ability to grasp. Carline had been almost relieved to see Della at first, despite the fact that they had agreed that Della would never come to the apartment.

'I've made my decision.' Della's cheeks were flushed from the cold. She was breathing quickly, as if she'd been rushing. 'We can't keep this secret any more, it's too important.'

Carline felt only sinking dread, but she stepped back and opened the door wide in an unspoken invitation for Della to enter.

'Would you like tea?' she asked.

'God no,' said Della, shaking her long hair back from her face with her right hand. It was blonde again, dyed for the exam season. She had sat five exams for Carline over the past two weeks, only two exams left to go. She put her backpack on the table, pulled her slim laptop out from between the miscellaneous papers and notebooks that filled the bag.

'I'm so close to finishing,' she said. The laptop stayed closed. Della lay her hand palm down on top of the computer. 'Did I tell you? It's nearly there, and it's so good, Carline. I really think you're going to get your money's worth.'

Carline felt a rush of anger. What good would the thesis be to her if Della went ahead with her plan?

'It's a mistake, Della,' said Carline. Her voice shook a little. 'It's dangerous. You want a career. I know you do. This isn't the way to make a name for yourself. You're talking about destroying someone's professional reputation, taking away their position, the respect that they've earned. If you talk to James Murtagh, he's going to slap you down, hard, and everything we've worked for will have been wasted.' Carline knew she had lost before she finished speaking. This was not the first time they had had this argument.

'I'm not going to speak to Murtagh,' Della said. 'I'm going to speak to Emma Sweeney.'

Oh God. It made sense. Of course it made sense. Emma Sweeney, who could be trusted. Emma Sweeney, who would know just what to do. No wonder Della was sparking with confidence. There would be no stopping her now.

'You can't go today,' Carline said. 'Campus is closed because of the asbestos thing.'

Della waved a hand in the air. 'The lab will be open. It's always open. And if it isn't, I'll try again tomorrow.'

There was a long pause when neither girl said anything.

'No matter what happens, I'm still going to give you the thesis,' said Della. 'A deal is a deal after all.'

Carline wanted to hit her. Two years of planning, trying, striving to be something. To become something. Every day wasted. It had been wrong, of course it had been wrong, but it had been so easy to justify in the context of a world so rife with corruption that every second headline brought some new scandal. It had been easy to tell herself that this small lie was a white one. Della had needed their arrangement just as much as she had, maybe more. She'd taken the money, happily. She'd taken everything Carline had to offer: her friendship, all her secrets. And then, like everyone else, she'd looked for more. She'd wanted Darcy Laboratories. The only difference between Della Lambert and Mark Wardle was that Mark wanted money and power, and Della wanted knowledge and position. Looking at Della, Carline felt both a sense of recognition and a profound weariness.

'Okay,' she said.

'Okay?'

'You're going to do what you're going to do, Della. We both know that. You've already made your mind up.'

The other girl flushed. She didn't want to be the bad guy in this little farce, resented the suggestion that she was doing something unfair. She pushed her laptop back into her bag, then slung it over her left shoulder.

'I'll call you,' she said. 'And I'll send you the thesis when it's finished.'

Carline didn't say anything. They both knew that the thesis would be useless to her, but there was no point in saying it again. Della had convinced herself that delivering the thesis meant she had satisfied her side of the deal, the letter of it at least, even as she tore the spirit of it to shreds.

Della stopped and stared out of the window. 'It's freezing out there, you know? It feels almost like winter.' Della rested her hand on Carline's cardigan, which was hanging over the back of the chair. She closed her hand over it, plunged her fingers into the soft wool. 'This is lovely,' she said. 'Is it warm?'

Carline looked back at her steadily but the other girl's expression was guileless – she had been admiring, not asking. Her version of an olive branch.

'Take it,' Carline said. 'It's cold today. You can bring it back next time you come.'

Della hesitated. 'Thank you,' she said. She took the cardigan, slid her arms into the sleeves a little awkwardly and buttoned it closed.

'Carline,' she said. 'You know this wasn't the way, right? It wouldn't have worked, not in the long run. You have other options, you know? Lots of choices. This …' She shook her head. 'This was just a bad idea.' She ran her hand down the soft wool of the cardigan, said a final, quiet, 'Thank you.' And then she left, bag still slung over her shoulder, without a backwards glance.

Now was the time. She needed to make a decision. She had the laptop. She could take the thesis, try to move ahead with her plan, one way or the other. Or she could go to the police with what she knew and then try to start again. She could leave this place. Go to another college town, where no one knew her. Buy another apartment just like this one and do it all straight this time. She could change her name, be an anonymous girl in the crowd. Was she ready to give up on the dream of becoming a Darcy in more than name? She thought of her grandfather's cold blue eyes, and wondered why she'd ever thought she had a chance.

CHAPTER FORTY

Cormac went home. It was a short drive. He was angry, furious with himself for screwing things up so badly. Guilt gnawed at him too. The case would now be shunted on to Carrie O'Halloran and suffer the inevitable difficulties of a case in full forward motion suddenly left with a new pair of hands at the wheel. He parked and went inside. The house was empty and felt unloved. They had spent so little time there over the past weeks. He tried calling Emma's mobile, twice, but it rang out. More of the bullshit Darcy security measures. Ridiculous that she couldn't keep her phone at her desk.

Cormac turned to the desk pushed up against the far wall of the living room. It was an unruly mess of old newspapers, junk mail, leftover bits and pieces of work that each of them had brought home and left there. She'd given him the number for the direct line at her desk. He riffled through the mess, trying to find the post-it note she'd written it on, but failed. Frustrated, he sat on the couch, contemplated the six-pack of beer in the fridge, thought better of it. If he sat there drinking, waiting for her and thinking about how much he'd fucked it all up, he'd be climbing the walls by the time she got home. He forced himself up off the couch, up the stairs to their room, and into his running gear.

The first ten minutes were enough to remind him that he'd spent too much time lately sitting at a desk. His legs ached and he was heaving air into his lungs like an old man. He pushed harder, pushed through it. He found his anger and his stride at the same time. He ran for almost an hour, pushing himself harder and faster than he had in months, welcoming the pain.

When he got home the house was still empty. He hit the shower, took his time, and an hour later when there was still no Emma he opened a beer, turned on the fire and the TV and stared vacantly at one or the other until he nodded off.

Emma came home at ten. He woke as she opened the front door, turned to see her through the open doorway, taking her green wool coat off in the hall and hanging it at the bottom of the stairs.

'Em?'

She leaned in the doorway. Her hair was wet from the rain. She looked very tired and her eyes were red-rimmed. Had she been crying? Cormac sat up straighter.

'Are you okay?' he asked.

She rubbed at her cheek, looking distracted. 'I'm all right.' She sat on the arm of the armchair opposite him. 'Have you been home long?'

'A few hours I suppose,' Cormac said, sitting forward in his chair. He pushed the heels of his hands into his eyes, blinked a few times, trying to wake up fully. Neither of them spoke for a few moments. They sat in silence and listened to the rain falling outside.

'You look like you've been crying,' Cormac said.

'Crying? No.' She shook her head. 'I'm sure I look rubbish. I'm frustrated. I've been poring over the same question again and again for the last couple of days and I just can't make this thing I'm working on link up. I can't make sense of it.'

'What's the problem?' Cormac asked. He sat back again in his chair, knowing that if she told him he probably wouldn't understand, but it would be a relief to listen to an ordinary, everyday problem for once. Something that had nothing to do with murder, or suspensions.

'It doesn't matter,' Emma said. 'Or rather, it does matter, but I think maybe I'm too close to it. I just need to step back, maybe get some sleep, and look at things from a different angle.' She was silent for a few seconds. 'Do you know what, I'm bloody starving. Are you hungry? It's late, I know.'

'I'll make something,' he said. 'Go and shower. When you come down we can talk.'

She kissed him and disappeared upstairs. He made for the kitchen, put together sandwiches out of what was left in the fridge, decided that toasting them might make them more palatable, and turned on the sandwich maker. He opened another bottle of beer for himself, took one out for her. She wasn't long, returned in pyjamas, hair still damp, the day's clothes bundled under one arm. She put them in the washing machine, turned on a cycle, and there was something comforting about the simple domesticity of the moment.

'You're a star,' she said, taking in the food and nodding a yes to the beer. They sat and ate in companionable silence. She did look better after her shower, Cormac decided, but still very tired. She was paler than usual, and the shadows had deepened under her eyes.

'Do you want to talk about it?' he asked. 'Might help to get it off your chest.'

She looked at him. 'I was about to ask you the same question. You look like you've had a bit of a day.'

He'd have to tell her. There was no way of avoiding it. 'I'm off the case, Em. Not officially suspended, or anything like that. But it's been recommended to me that I take a bit of leave. Stay home and stay out of the way until the dust clears.'

She stared at him, eyes wide. 'But ... why? What's happened?'

'It's nothing too serious. I don't want you worrying about it. Internal Affairs aren't happy that I'm running a case when my partner found the victim, that's all. It's a technicality. No one is suggesting that I – or you for that matter – did anything wrong.'

Emma knew him too well. 'Tell me the truth, Cormac,' she said, quietly. 'How much trouble are you in?'

Cormac got up to get another couple of beers from the fridge. 'Not much,' he said. 'At least not yet.'

'Is someone looking to change that?'

Cormac thought about it. 'Maybe,' he said. 'But they won't succeed. I haven't done anything wrong, and neither have you, Emma. I don't want you worrying about this, all right? It's just political bullshit. Game-playing.'

Emma took the beer he offered her, opened it and drank. 'Is your job at risk?' she asked.

'I don't think so,' Cormac said. 'They will look at the case closely, see if I did anything I shouldn't have. There's nothing to find.'

They fell silent for a while. He wondered if she was thinking about the conversation they'd had the other day, about whether or not to stay in Galway. He wondered what he would say if she asked the question again.

'I shouldn't have called you,' Emma said eventually. 'If I had just called 999 on Friday night, instead of calling your mobile, this wouldn't have happened.'

'It would, Emma,' Cormac said. 'Murphy had just agreed to put me back on rotation. The case would have fallen to me either way. And what's going on here has nothing to do with you, and everything to do with the bullshit that goes on in every police station. I'm going to ask you to trust me to handle it, all right? I've been handling it for twenty years, and I've done all right, haven't I?' He took her hand. 'This isn't something for you to worry about.'

She squeezed his hand, lifted it and pressed her lips to his skin, her eyes on him. 'All right,' she said. 'But I'm sorry that you lost the case.'

'Yeah.'

Emma started to clear away the dishes, and Cormac let his mind wander back over the case, back over his conversation with Nicholls, with Carline. He should talk to Carrie O'Halloran, if she ended up running the case. They might bring someone down from Dublin, in which case it could end up being anyone.

'Someone will have to interview you,' Cormac said. 'Maybe Fisher again, maybe someone else. They're going to want to take your statement about having seen Della in the lab.' He hesitated. 'You should probably have a think about who else might have useful information. Is there anyone they should speak to? Anyone else who would have seen Della inside the lab?'

Emma sat back down, made a face at her half-drunk beer, and went to get a bottle of wine instead. She opened it and poured a glass for herself, then one for Cormac when he nodded at her unspoken question. 'Alessandro works out of the same lab, and has done all year. Emily Houghton too. And there's the student, a third year, I think her name's Alison. They would all have seen Della, more than once. They must have met her.'

'Will any of them talk to us without a Darcy lawyer being present?'

'I ... don't know. Not if they've been told not to. John Darcy has a reputation for being litigious. We've all signed NDAs. If he's worried about the nature of the questions, concerned that they might stray into areas of proprietary information, then he might send in the lawyers. But he has no reason to think that, so maybe it'll be okay.'

Strictly speaking, he shouldn't discuss any garda business with her. But that was a stricture followed only loosely – there weren't very many garda spouses who hadn't heard a few stories over the years – and now the case was no longer his. And she knew the academic world far better than he did. He wanted to hear her take.

'Graham Nicholls told me that Della was a genius. A once in a generation mind, he said. Which is exactly what Egan said about Carline Darcy. Except that Della's results at the Christmas exams were middle of the road. Carline's were stellar, so good that the college bent over backwards to accelerate her through her degree programme.'

Emma nodded. 'She really is exceptional though, Corm. Her work in the lab – she's worked closely with James on finessing the drug design, you know that?'

That wasn't how Murtagh had described Carline's involvement but Cormac nodded. He wanted her to continue.

'I haven't worked with her directly, but word around the lab is that the work she's producing is something very special.'

'Tell me about exams,' he said. 'Where do they take place, and who supervises them?'

Emma shrugged, sipped her wine. 'I didn't study in Galway, so I don't know that much about it. I think the exams are held all over the campus. Some of the sports halls are used for bigger ones – you see the signs going up at this time of year. I'd imagine the university hires in invigilators to supervise.'

'I know the exams are supposed to be marked anonymously. How does that work?'

'If it's the same as Trinity, each student would be given an exam number, and each number is allocated to a desk. When you arrive you go to your allocated desk, and when you fill in your answer sheet you write your student number on the top.'

'But each student knows their own number, right?'

'Right.'

'So what's to stop that student paying someone to take their place in an exam? Say I've got a brother or cousin, and they just happen to be brilliant at maths, or physics, or whatever exam I have this week. What's to stop my brother taking my place in the exam, writing my number on the answer sheet and working away?' Cormac asked.

Emma frowned. 'Well, the invigilators have a list of exam numbers and names. They go along the rows of desks before the exams start, and check everyone's ID to make sure that they are sitting at the right desk. And then when they collect exam papers at the end they check the number on the exam paper against the one on the desk, to make sure that no one has substituted someone else's number.'

Cormac turned his wine glass on the table, drank. 'Do you know how high the error rate is in photograph recognition, even among professionals? Passport officers have an error rate that lies somewhere between fifteen and twenty per cent, and that's with passport quality photographs and training. I've seen those student IDs the college issues. The quality is shite.'

Cormac stood up, walked to the desk in the living room and found his laptop bag. He looked through the papers inside until he found what he was looking for. He put it on the table in front of Emma. 'That's a colour copy of the ID that Della was carrying. That's supposed to be a photograph of Carline Darcy. If it is I doubt her own mother would recognise her.' The girl in the photograph had moved as it was taken, and the portrait was blurred. Her face was also tilted forward and downwards, so that her hair obscured part of her face.

Cormac pointed at the photograph. 'That's not her college ID, it's a copy of an access card she was given for the lab, but what are the chances she used the same photo for her other ID?' Cormac didn't wait for an answer. 'Della Lambert dyed her hair blonde,' he said. 'She was a similar height to Carline, similar weight. Examiners ... what did you call them? Invigilators? If they have two to three hundred IDs to check and they're in a hurry, they're not going to do much more than glance at them.'

'What are you suggesting? That Della Lambert sat Carline's exams for her? Why?'

'Just think about it for a moment. Carline Darcy must be very bright. Has to have been. She got a great leaving, got into her course at the university. But everyone keeps telling me that there is a difference between very bright and extraordinary. And when you get to the sort of level Carline was aiming for, the level John Darcy operates at, what you need is genius.'

Emma, who had had her name on two major patents by the time she was twenty-five, nodded slowly.

'Imagine that Carline is bright and works hard. She got through her leaving cert with all A's or close to it. Then she gets to university. A selective programme. Bio-Pharmaceutical Chemistry. Only twenty-five students, all of them bright, a few of them more than that. And then there was Della. A bright, shining light. Something special. And Carline can see it. She can see the gap between what she can do with hard work and perfectionism, and what Della just is, naturally. How does someone like Carline react to that?'

Emma shook her head. 'Tell me what you're thinking.'

'I think she saw an opportunity. I think she saw Della Lambert, a genius, but naive, broke, living at home with a mother who hated her and an absent father. She paid Della a ton of money – something close to half a million euro – and in return Della agreed to do her work for two years. To sit her exams for her, write her papers, her thesis for her PhD. Solidify Carline's reputation as the next John Darcy. I think Carline Darcy wanted to show she wasn't like her playboy father – bright, charming, but a lightweight. Certainly not like her mother. No. Carline wanted to be like her grandfather.

A heavyweight intellectual who could be, should be, heir to the throne of Darcy Therapeutics.'

'But what would she do then? What's the point of it all? Once she finished the PhD and went to work in the lab, she would be exposed.'

'But would she have worked in a lab? Once her reputation was in place, couldn't she have chosen to work in other areas of the business, areas where she didn't need to be as hands on with the technical work? And come to think of it, why not hire Della? I wouldn't be surprised if the plan was for Della to re-enrol, at Galway or better yet some other university. Della could blast through another four-year degree program in two, or even shorter. Carline hires her for a high-level technical position somewhere within the company, keeps her close. Della gets money and a fast-tracked career, Carline has her go-to girl for anything that she can't grasp without help.'

Emma was quiet for a long time. Something about the set of her shoulders told Cormac that her earlier tension had returned. Her brow was deeply furrowed when she spoke again. 'I still don't see why she would do that. Carline, I mean. She has money. Her father had shares in the company, and she got them when he died. She has access to plenty of money. Why would Carline go to all that trouble?'

'I think only Carline can tell us that.' He had his own ideas about what had motivated her to take such risks, what might have motivated her ultimately to murder, but he was distracted by the cloud in Emma's eyes.

'What's wrong?' Cormac asked.

Emma shook her head. 'Nothing,' she said. Then, when he wouldn't let it go, she answered, without looking at him, 'I just can't help but wonder. If what you say is true – who else at the lab knows?'

Friday 2 May 2014

CHAPTER FORTY-ONE

Carrie O'Halloran took Friday off work and it felt good. The girls' school was closed for a teacher training day, would be closed on Monday for the public holiday, and Ciarán had even started making noises, late on Thursday night, about possibly heading away for the weekend to West Cork, as a family. Carrie had been awake since six, and that was actually okay. More than okay. She'd been woken by chilly little five-year-old fingers, lifting one eye-lid then the other, followed a hoarse whisper of, 'Mum. You awake?' It was after ten now. Ciarán was still asleep upstairs, and she was in the kitchen with the girls, messily making pancakes. She felt absurdly happy. The web of responsibilities she wove every day had for once settled into a harmonious pattern, instead of the usual tangled mess. The girls had dawdled off in the direction of the TV after early morning toast, which had given her time to sort out the kitchen, put on some washing, and even a glorious five minutes alone with a cup of tea and a magazine. She hadn't even minded the inevitable call of 'Mum, I'm staaaarving' when it started again ten minutes later.

So now she was making pancakes. Lainey was still plonked in front of *Inspector Gadget* and Miriam was hanging out with her in the kitchen, glancing at her from time to time from the corner of her eye in a way that let Carrie know she had something she wanted to ask her mother. There was something lovely about that, about her daughter lingering in her presence, handing her flour and eggs, debating the wisdom of adding leftover chocolate chips to pancake batter, all the while sneaking looks at her mother's face, building up the confidence to ask whatever was on her mind. Carrie smiled at her daughter, reached out and smoothed back her hair, then moved to the hob and the waiting frying pan. Ciarán arrived just as Carrie poured the first pancake into the pan.

'Hey,' he said. He was leaning against the kitchen door jamb, watching her.

'We're making pancakes,' Miriam said, smiling at him. 'Mum's added chocolate chips.'

'Wow.' He smiled at Carrie, a slow smile she hadn't seen in a while. It tugged at her, somewhere deep inside.

'It's not in the recipe, but we said we'd risk it.' Carrie looked down at the pancake, watched the chocolate chips disappear from view to the bottom of the pan. She loved Ciarán really, sometimes could even believe that he loved her. He was a decent man, a good dad, and he deserved to be happy. She believed that. She just wished he didn't see it as her responsibility to deliver that happiness, preferably wrapped up in a bow and delivered by a smiling 1950s housewife along with a 1950s dinner on the table. But all that was for another day.

Ciarán started the coffee machine. Miriam was looking at the pancake, a doubtful expression on her face. 'Mum ...' she said.

The doorbell rang. Miriam looked at her. Carrie's stomach tensed.

'Will you get it, love?'

Ciarán left the room and Miriam followed him. Little bubbles expanded in the pancake, the batter solidified at the outer ring. Carrie waited for it to cook through, listened to the voices at the front door. Her phone was sitting on the counter, switched off. Maybe it wasn't for her. She tried to turn the pancake, but the chocolate chips had melted and were sticking to the bottom of the pan. The whole thing creased and stuck together in a half-cooked mess. Shite.

'Carrie,' Ciarán said. He nodded towards the front door. 'You need to go out there.'

Carrie turned the heat off, pushed the pan aside, went to the door. Put her hand on Miriam's shoulder. The little girl was standing in the doorway, stance wide, arms crossed. Moira Hanley stood at the threshold.

'Go in Mir, love. Help Daddy with the pancakes.' Miriam left, dragging her feet and looking over her shoulder, a ten-year-old's protest.

'Moira,' Carrie said.

'I'm sorry,' Moira said. 'Cormac Reilly's been taken off the Lambert case. Someone else needs to run it and Murphy says it has to be you.'

For a moment Carrie hated her. Moira who had no kids, and had once confessed to Carrie that she didn't particularly like them.

'What are you talking about, he's off the case?'

Moira sniffed. 'Internal Affairs got wind of what he's been up to. Running the case when his girlfriend is a possible suspect. They stepped in.' There was a lurking triumph at the back of Moira's eyes.

'What do you mean, suspect? Emma Sweeney's not a suspect.'

A shrug. 'Maybe she should be.'

Carrie felt a flare of anger, and she didn't bother to mute it. 'This is your doing, isn't it, Moira? You've decided that you don't like Reilly, for whatever reason, and you're determined that he's going to pay a price for that, aren't you? What did he do to piss you off?'

Moira's face reddened, and she started to splutter a reply.

'Don't bother,' Carrie said. 'I have a fair idea.' She paused. 'You should choose your enemies more carefully. Reilly's no fool. He's survived much worse than you, and the last man to take him on is dead and buried. You might want to give that some thought. Now, it's going to take me a few minutes to get ready. You can wait in the car.'

She shut the door on Moira Hanley's red face, and headed up the stairs, swallowing back tears of anger and disappointment. It took her ten minutes to find clothes, throw some water on her face, tie up her hair. By the time she came down again Ciarán was in the kitchen, had scraped clean the mess in the pan, was starting again with the pancakes. Both girls were watching television now. She went to kiss their heads, got a cuddle from Lainey, averted eyes from Miriam. Ciarán was watching. He came forward, gave her a one-armed hug.

'Never mind it,' he said quietly. 'I heard her boasting to her friends the other day about her mum who catches the bad guys.'

And Carrie had to blink her eyes against sudden tears at the unexpected support. Christ. She was getting soft. She hugged him back, grabbed her jacket, and made for the door.

Moira drove the car in resentful silence. Carrie stared out of the window, in no mood for conversation or conciliation. They were at the lights at Doughiska when she finally spoke.

'What's the urgency about?'

'Sorry?' said Moira.

'The urgency,' Carrie said. 'So I'm taking over the case. Why does it have to be right now, on my day off?'

'There's been a development,' Moira said, sulkily.

'Well?' Carrie asked. She resisted the urge to reach out and smack the other woman.

'There's been a death.'

'Who died?'

'Sorry?' Moira said. She shifted gears, badly.

'Who died, Moira?' Carrie's tone was ice-cold.

'Carline Darcy,' said Moira. The lights turned green, and she put her foot on the accelerator.

It took twenty minutes to drive into the city, and a couple more to get to the docks. There were three marked cars parked outside the modern-looking apartment building, an ambulance alongside them. Moira Hanley and Carrie O'Halloran rode the lift in silence. The apartment door opened to a scene of some distress. Carrie stood in the doorway and took it all in.

A beautiful dark-haired girl sat shivering on the couch. She was wearing pyjama shorts and a T-shirt, and as Carrie watched a young man came from a room behind her, carrying a quilt, which he spread over the girl's shoulders and tucked around her. There were two uniforms in the room, hovering uselessly, their attention focused on an open door at the other end of the room. One of them turned and caught sight of Carrie.

'Sergeant …'

'Let's hear it,' Carrie said.

'Uh … we received a report of a death by suicide.' He jerked his head in the direction of the open door. 'Paramedics have been and gone. There was nothing they could do. We're just waiting on the scene of crime lads. They're running a bit late.'

'Suicide?' Carrie asked.

The uniform glanced towards the pair on the couch, and shook his head. He lowered his voice. 'Paramedic didn't think so, and I don't either.'

'Why not?' Carrie asked.

'Because she's got a bloody great lump on the back of her head,' the garda said. 'Blood all down the back of her neck.'

'You've been in there?' Carrie asked.

He shook his head. 'Paramedic told me. We've stayed out here. Preserved the scene, like.'

Christ. 'This place is all scene, you great, gormless eejit,' Carrie said. She ignored his flush of embarrassment and nodded towards the couch. 'Get her roommates out of here. There must be a neighbour who can take them in for a few hours.'

The dark-haired girl looked up. 'We have names you know.' She jerked her thumb towards herself. 'Valentina.' To the young man. 'Mark.' Valentina stood up and dropped the quilt on the couch behind her. 'I want to see her,' she said. She started towards the open door.

'Stop.' Carrie's voice was sharp and the girl – Valentina – stopped. There was a faint smear of something dark on the pale limed floorboards beside her right foot.

'What is that?' Valentina asked, her voice rasping. 'Is that her blood? How …?'

'You need to leave. Right now,' said Carrie. 'You too.' Mark stood up from the couch, was staring at the stain now too. Carrie nodded to the uniforms who finally stepped forward and started to usher the two roommates from the room. To Moira Hanley she said, 'Make sure that scene of crime are on the way. Keep everyone else outside – they can wait downstairs in the foyer if need be.'

Carrie walked towards the bedroom. She didn't enter, just stood on the outside and tried, as she always did, to shut down her emotional response to what she was seeing, to consider the scene with a dispassionate and professional eye. It wasn't easy. The body of a young woman sat, hunched over, at the foot of the bed. She would have slumped to the floor, if it weren't for the fact that someone had tied her by the neck to the bedpost, using what looked like a dressing gown belt. Carline's blonde hair was loose and had fallen forward, obscuring her face a little, but not enough to spare Carrie the sight of her bloodied, swollen mouth, and an open, staring eye. She was fully dressed except for her feet, which were bare, and her white T-shirt was stained red with blood. Nothing about the scene suggested suicide to Carrie. There was more blood inside the room – not a great deal, but there were spots on the quilt that had half-fallen to the floor, more on the floor between the bed and the door, a smear where someone had stepped on it.

Carrie retraced her steps as carefully as possible away from the bedroom, then from the apartment. The lift opened and she saw the first white-shod foot of a scene guy step out. Scene of crime, with Yvonne Connolly, the pathologist, hot on their heels.

Carrie shook the pathologist's hand, gave a nod to the officers with her. 'She's inside,' Carrie said. 'The middle bedroom. There's a smear in the living room that looks like blood.'

Connolly nodded. 'We were delayed,' she said. 'Three car pile-up on the M6.' She was pulling on gloves, then a hair cover handed to her by one of the men. 'Much contamination of the scene?' she asked.

'Inside the bedroom we're talking one paramedic, and the roommate who found her. The living room had both roommates, myself, and three other gardaí.'

Connolly rolled her eyes but chose not to say anything. She snapped on her second glove, gave Carrie a nod, and walked past her towards the apartment.

'Dr Connolly,' said Carrie.

The pathologist turned.

'I know you don't like to be prejudiced before you view a scene, and I'm not trying to do that, but … you know who it is you're going to find in there.'

'I got a phone call,' said the doctor, her tone very dry.

'Look, you'll make your own mind up. It was called in as a suicide, but to my view it's definitely not that.'

Connolly had drawn her eyebrows together and was looking at Carrie as if reassessing her formerly positive opinion of her.

'The politics of this thing are all over the place. If you are satisfied that it's not a suicide, if you could call that in sooner rather than later, it could make this day easier for everyone.'

Connolly snapped the elastic at the wrist of one of her gloves in an unnecessary adjustment. 'I'm not here to make the lives of the gardaí easier, sergeant. And I'm certainly not here to concern myself with politics, no matter who the victim is. That's a policy you may wish to adopt for yourself.' She gave Carrie a last cold look, then turned to the apartment.

Carrie stood still for a moment, then raised a finger at Connolly's departing back.

CHAPTER FORTY-TWO

Carrie made for the lifts again, checking her watch on the way. It was 11.30 a.m. She couldn't let time get away from her. She wondered briefly where Cormac Reilly might be, and if the news had reached him yet. Carrie took the lift to the ground floor, was redirected to the second by a uniform waiting for her below. Mark and Valentina had gone to Apartment 22B. They were waiting for her there. Carrie found the apartment and knocked. Mark opened the door wordlessly and stepped back to allow her to enter.

God, what a contrast between this place and the *Grand Designs* nirvana on the top floor. For starters, the kitchen-living area was about a quarter the size. Same view, if from a lower vantage point, but here obscured by the grubby guard wall of a small balcony. The room was cluttered too; a pile of laundry sat on one arm of the couch and the sink was filled with dirty dishes and more than your average number of empty beer cans.

Mark took a seat on the couch, turned anxious eyes to a pacing Valentina. A gangly-looking youth, wearing boxers and a T-shirt, hovered anxiously in the kitchen.

'I can make tea,' he said. Carrie got the impression it wasn't the first time he'd offered. 'I'm sorry about the gaff. We had a party last night ... weren't expecting ...'

'You're always having bloody parties,' Valentina snarled at him. Then she turned on Carrie. 'Someone killed her,' she said. 'They must have done. There's no way Carline would kill herself. She isn't the type.'

'Did you see her? This morning I mean?' asked Gangly from the kitchen. Carrie heard only concern in his voice, but it might as well have been ghoulish interest, for the look that Valentina turned on him.

'Of course she didn't,' Mark said. 'I went in to wake Carline. When I saw her … I knew straight away she was dead. The way she … Christ. I'll never forget it for as long as I live. I wasn't going to let Vee in there to see it too.'

'It was you who reported her death as a suicide?' Carrie asked.

Valentina turned on him. 'You are so wrong, Mark. If you think for a second she would have done that … you must never have known her at all.'

Mark shook his head, said with a paternalistic weariness that made Valentina bridle, 'People have their reasons, Vee. Maybe she had her reasons.'

Gangly-boy started to speak but Carrie cut across him. 'I need to bring you both to the station. We'll need to take your statements, and the sooner we do that the better, all right? Before you start to forget the details.' And before they had the opportunity to settle their nerves or marry their stories, if that was what was going on here.

Mark looked like he might argue, but Valentina nodded, looking almost relieved. She was aching for something to do. Gangly-boy looked at Valentina in her little pyjamas, then out at the rain that pulsed against the windows. He hurried forward, grabbed a jumper that looked like it had seen better days from the back of a chair.

'Here, you can borrow this.'

'Christ,' Valentina gave the jumper a look that should have shrivelled the thing in his hands. 'I wouldn't be seen dead.' She blanched, closed her eyes. A moment passed before she scrubbed away tears with the back of each hand, she lifted her chin and walked past Carrie out of the door and into the corridor beyond, Mark hurrying after her.

Carrie had a uniform drive the roommates to the station. She commandeered a squad car and drove herself, taking a detour to the house beside the canal. It was noon when she knocked on Cormac Reilly's door. He opened it a moment later and didn't seem entirely surprised to see her.

'Carrie,' he said. He stood back and held the door open for her. 'Come in.'

He was barefoot, which felt weird, was wearing old jeans and a T-shirt. She was distracted by the thought that Cormac Reilly was a very attractive man, when he wasn't shouting at you in a small car.

'Is Emma here?' Carrie asked.

'She's gone to the lab,' Cormac said. 'Did you want to speak to her?' He led the way into a messy living room. There was a half-empty coffee cup on the coffee table, along with a stack of old newspapers. There were more stacks of paper on a desk at the other end of the room. Cormac leaned down and picked up the cup. 'I'm trying to sort this place out, but it's a waste of bloody time. If I stack it together it only goes and breeds.' He gestured with his cup in her direction. 'Coffee?'

Carrie nodded. 'I will, yeah.'

He asked her how she liked it, and disappeared into the kitchen. Carrie sat on the couch. She looked around the room while she waited, comparing it to the house she had left a couple of hours before. There was no kids' stuff here. No Saturday morning cartoons, no Lego half under the couch, no scooters in the hall. It was nearly as messy as her place, though, in its own way, and she felt a little better.

He came back with the coffee, placed it in front of her, and sat. He'd taken the time to put some shoes on.

'Right, Carrie,' he said. 'I'm sure you'd like to discuss the case. I want to start by saying I'm sorry that it's fallen on your shoulders. I should have seen there was a strong chance things would end up as they have, and I should have taken steps to make sure there was someone else who could take it on.' His brown eyes were serious, but he didn't seem quite his usual coolly confident self.

'Cormac,' she said. 'Carline Darcy is dead.'

He looked at her so blankly that for a moment she thought he hadn't heard her. Then he swallowed and put down his coffee cup.

'Tell me,' he said.

'It was reported as a suicide,' she said. 'But it definitely wasn't. There might be mixed messages for a while. I came here myself to tell you that Carline did not kill herself.'

Cormac rubbed a hand across his mouth. 'Christ, Carrie. I interviewed her yesterday afternoon. I didn't go easy.'

Carrie nodded. 'I don't expect you did,' she said. 'And I'm telling you that nothing you said killed her – she didn't kill herself. Dr Connolly hasn't made it official yet, but there's no doubt in my mind that Carline Darcy was murdered.'

Cormac stood up, agitated, and walked to the other side of the room. He looked out through the window in the direction of the city, as if he could see through the buildings, right across town to the apartment on the water.

'Cormac, I'm new to this case as of a couple of hours ago. What can you tell me? Do you have any idea who might have done this?'

He turned back to her, his face pale. 'I don't,' he said. 'I believed … I thought that Carline Darcy was responsible for the death of Della Lambert. My theory was that Carline had been paying Della for help with her academic work, and something went wrong. I thought that Carline had killed her, or arranged to have her killed to keep her quiet. But I've missed something. If Carline Darcy has been murdered, then I've missed something.'

Carrie stood slowly. She couldn't discuss the case with him, that wouldn't help anyone. 'I'd better go,' she said. 'I need to get to the case room. It's going to take a little time to familiarise myself with everything, start the ball rolling again.'

He nodded and she moved towards the door.

'Look after yourself, Cormac,' she said. 'You'll be back on the job soon enough.'

'When did she die?' Cormac asked. 'Was it last night or this morning?'

'It's not official. We don't have anything from the pathologist but my best guess would be sometime last night. What time did you leave her?'

'Just after six,' Cormac said. 'No one saw her this morning?'

Carrie shook her head. 'Her roommates haven't seen her since yesterday afternoon. From what I know so far, other than the killer, you may be the last person to have seen her alive.'

CHAPTER FORTY-THREE

After Carrie left, Cormac sat on the stairs of the small house on Canal Road, head in his hands, for a long time. He thought about Carline Darcy, that beautiful, frightened girl whose life had had now been taken from her. He had missed something. Somewhere along the way he had missed the thing on which the whole case turned. This was a death that could have been prevented. All he could think about were those pleading eyes that had held his as she'd closed the door on him. If only he'd brought her in, she would surely be alive today. Cormac took a breath and reminded himself that he wouldn't have gotten as far as the car with her, not with Internal Affairs waiting downstairs. He took the emotion, the guilt, and set it very deliberately to one side. He had no time to waste berating himself for his failure. Cormac sank his head onto his hands so he could close out the world, close himself off from all distraction, and work through the case from beginning to end.

He found nothing. He had no answers, just a loose end he hadn't yet followed up. He stood, grabbed his jacket and car keys, and left the house.

It took him half an hour to reach Athenry, another couple of minutes to wind through the narrow medieval streets and out the other side to where the Lambert house was located. There was no car parked in the driveway, but Cormac got out anyway and went to the front door. He rang the bell, waited for a couple of minutes, and rang it again. A moment passed and he heard footsteps on the stairs. Paul opened the door. They regarded each other for a long moment.

'My mother's not here,' Paul said. 'She's gone shopping.'

Cormac nodded. 'All right if I come in for a few minutes?'

They sat opposite each other at the kitchen table. The room smelled unpleasantly of damp laundry left to moulder. There were old crumbs and a sticky patch that might have been jam on the table. Paul sat with his hands loosely clasped in front of him. His hands were thin, knuckles too big for his fingers.

'I want to speak with you, Paul, because I think you knew Della better than anyone else. You told Detective O'Halloran that you and Della were very close, that you were best friends.'

Paul nodded.

'I'm not sure we paid enough attention to that, Paul. You see, that's quite unusual, at your age and Della's, to be so close to a sibling, and particularly if you're the opposite sex. It's more common for siblings to be rivals. Or for distance to creep in as you grow older, and one of you leaves home. But it wasn't like that for you and Della, was it?'

'No.' Paul shook his head.

'It occurs to me, Paul, that you might know quite a bit more about what was going on in Della's life than you told us.' Cormac kept his tone gentle, matter of fact. 'I think you may even know what it was that got her killed. And if that's the case then I'm sorry you didn't feel able to tell us earlier. I'm here because things have gotten worse, Paul. Things have become even more serious, and it isn't an option anymore, for you to tell us less than the complete truth.'

Paul's brow furrowed. 'I didn't leave anything out or tell any lies if that's what you really mean. What are you talking about?'

'You went to see Carline Darcy yesterday, Paul, didn't you? Carline told me you thought she might know something about Della's death. What made you think that, Paul? And why didn't you mention it to Garda Fisher, or DS O'Halloran when you spoke to them?'

Paul's mouth fell open. He mouthed silently for a second and then the words burst out of his mouth in a torrent of emotion. 'I didn't know!' he said. 'I didn't know anything.'

There was hectic, feverish colour in the boy's cheeks.

'But you did go to talk to Carline Darcy?' Cormac asked, very gently.

'I read about her in the paper and I thought she might know something about Della, about all the secrets she was keeping. But she wouldn't even talk to me. She just looked at me like I was crazy, and then she said something about being late, and then she just unlocked the door and went inside. She pushed it closed behind her like I was going to follow her in or something. Which I wasn't.'

'How did you know where she lived?' Cormac asked.

Another flush. 'I just Googled her,' Paul said. 'The newspaper article said she lived in a penthouse apartment on the Dock Road. There was only one apartment building on the street so I just waited outside until she came home.'

Cormac's hope of finding an answer was fading fast. 'And that was it?' Cormac asked. 'Nothing else was said between you?'

Paul shook his head but there was a spark of something in his eyes.

'What?' Cormac said. 'What is it, Paul?'

'No, it's just ... there was something weird.' He hesitated, then stood and picked up a backpack that had been left in the corner of the room. 'I think Carline had Della's laptop in her bag.'

'She ... sorry?'

'It was poking up out of her bag. Her shoulder bag. She saw me noticing it, and she got weird about it and tried to hide it.'

'How do you know it was Della's computer?'

'I don't know for sure,' Paul said. 'And if she hadn't acted all odd about it maybe I wouldn't have thought too much about it.' Paul unzipped his backpack and pulled out a slim grey laptop computer, pointed to the top right corner of the lid. 'See that?' There was a discoloured patch on the gun-metal grey lid, in the form of a female silhouette. 'This is Della's old computer. The one she had before she upgraded. There used to be a sticker there. It was a sticker of Jean Grey, from X-Men. I gave it to Della because Jean was her favourite, and Jean's a scientist too, see?'

Cormac wasn't following but he nodded anyway.

'When Del got a new computer she gave me this one, but she took the sticker off first and stuck it to her new computer. The sticker left this mark behind.' Paul tapped the patch on his computer – it was still very slightly sticky. 'The laptop Carline was carrying was the exact same model as Della's new one, and it had the exact same mark as mine in the corner.'

'I see,' Cormac said. 'You don't think it's possible that Carline simply had a similar sticker at some stage?'

Paul made a face. 'Yeah, maybe. But it's a bit of a coincidence. And she was weird about it. Why did she not want me looking at it?'

It was a fair point. Paul could have been reading too much into what might have been a coincidence. He might have misinterpreted Carline's body language in a moment that had to have been awkward and difficult. But Cormac didn't think so. Paul's thin body was rigid with tension, his dark eyes were very serious as he held the computer out for Cormac's inspection, but there was nothing of the hysteric about him. And if Paul was right, if Carline had had Della's laptop in her possession on the night she died ... well that opened up some very interesting questions.

'Tell me about Della's new computer,' Cormac said. 'You said you know the model?'

Paul described it for him as best he could, but before he was finished Cormac heard the sound of the front door opening. Eileen Lambert came into the room like an avenging angel, full of bombast and accusations. In the face of her aggression, Paul retreated into himself. There was nothing left to learn in the house and nothing to be gained by staying. Cormac left a few moments later, feeling grateful to the boy he left behind, and desperately sorry for him.

Carrie went back to the station. She'd called ahead, and Peter Fisher was waiting for her outside the interview rooms.

'Where've you got them?' Carrie asked.

'The girl's in number four,' Fisher said, indicating the door behind him. 'Mark Wardle's in number five. He's building himself up to start complaining. Wants his lunch.'

'It's not that time already, is it?' Carrie looked at her watch – it was almost 1 p.m. 'Has the Super come looking for me?'

'Not yet.'

'All right.' Carrie gave Fisher the nod, and he opened the closest door for her. Valentina sat, bare feet crossed at the ankles, on a plastic chair that was bolted to the ground. She was wearing a garda windbreaker and tracksuit bottoms over her pyjamas. Her arms were crossed and her shoulders hunched. A Styrofoam cup of tea sat on the table in front of her, a skin forming on the top of it. She looked up as they came in.

'How long am I going to be here?' she asked. Her face was pale, eyes red-rimmed. One eye was smeared with mascara. This morning's make up, smudged from crying? Or last night's, never removed?

'Are you cold?' Carrie glanced in the direction of her feet. 'We can have someone get you a pair of socks, some runners.'

'I'm fine. But I do want my own things. When can I go home?'

'You might be able to collect some basic items later this evening or tomorrow, when scene of crime is finished processing the apartment. But you're not likely to be able to stay there for some time, I'm afraid.'

'Jesus.' She pushed her hands under her thighs so that she was sitting on them. 'I'm never going near the place again, once I've picked up my stuff. I slept there all night, you know? And she was dead next door all that time. I walked over her blood for fuck's sake.' She wiped a hand across her mouth.

Carrie took Valentina's full name, her basic biographical details, then gave a nod to Fisher, who started the interview tape. 'Valentina, can you tell us where you were from say, six o'clock yesterday evening?' They had no time of death to work with, but Reilly had left her at six and it seemed as good a place as any to start. 'When did you last see Carline?'

'I didn't see her at all yesterday. I left early because I had a morning exam. I had lunch at college, then I had another exam at two o'clock. It was my last exam so after that I went straight to the bar. I was out all night, didn't get in until after midnight, and then I went straight to bed.'

'You're sure you didn't see Carline at all yesterday?'

She shook her head. 'Mark saw her in the morning. She said she was sick, she skipped her exam.' She looked from Carrie to Fisher and back again.

'You thought she was lying?' Carrie asked.

Valentina's lips were slightly parted. Her green eyes narrowed, then she shook her head. 'She might have been sick. It wasn't like she absolutely needed to sit her exams. She had enough credits to graduate without them.'

'But?'

'I thought something else was going on. She had been friendly with that girl Della at one point, you know, the

283

girl who died. I mean, not friendly enough that she should be destroyed by her death or anything. But I thought it had rocked her a bit.' Valentina hesitated. 'Look, I thought she was more upset about something her grandfather said to her. He visited during the week and Carline has been weird ever since. So when she said she was sick and suddenly showed no interest in her exams, I figured it had something to do with that.'

'How long have you known Carline?' Carrie asked.

Tears welled in Valentina's eyes. 'Since school,' she said. 'We went to the same arsey private school in Dublin. My father's a diplomat, my parents travel all the time, so I was boarding.'

'And Carline?'

'Carline was boarding because her mother was an alcoholic, and she didn't want to live with her anymore.'

Carrie paused. 'Tell me more about that.'

A snort from Valentina. 'Carline's mother has a problem with drugs and alcohol, okay? She also has terrible taste in men. Carline had a pretty shitty childhood, but who doesn't, right? As least Carls had money.'

'Tell me about Della,' Carrie said.

Valentina shook her head. 'What about her?'

'What was the nature of Carline's relationship with Della?'

Valentina made a face. 'As far as I know there isn't much to tell. They were in the same class for a while, they were friendly enough. Then Della dropped out and that was the end of it.'

'We were told that they might have been seeing each other,' Fisher said. Carrie glanced his way. She really needed time with the file; this was the first she'd heard of that suggestion.

'What, you mean like romantically?'

'Possibly,' Fisher said. 'Or it may just have been friendship.'

'If you think they were having sex you're on the wrong track,' Valentina said. 'Carline wasn't into it. I don't mean she wasn't a lesbian. I mean she wasn't into sex at all, with anyone. That sort of intimacy, it freaked her out.'

'They spent a lot of private time together,' Fisher said. 'Time alone in Della's apartment. And Carline deliberately kept those meetings quiet from you, from her other friends. Why do you think she would do that?'

Valentina didn't hesitate. She answered the question with her tear-stained face tilted upwards, chin high and angry. 'It would have been about work. It would have been about her grandfather. About her whole stupid family. To Carline they were the bloody Kennedys. Everything Carline did, she did because she was trying to earn a ticket to Camelot. Nothing anyone told her could convince her that it wasn't real.'

CHAPTER FORTY-FOUR

Carrie didn't beat about the bush. She was still horribly conscious of time slipping by. She took control of the case room quickly, pulled everyone together and updated them in unemotional terms. Carline Darcy was dead. Cormac Reilly was taking some time off – glances were exchanged at that bit of news – and she was now running the case.

'I don't want any of you reading anything into DS Reilly's absence,' she said, knowing it was useless but feeling like she had to make the attempt. 'You're all aware that Dr Sweeney found Della Lambert's body. More recently we've become aware that she is a witness to some other key evidence. For those reasons Detective Sergeant Reilly has decided it would be appropriate for him to step back from the case, and I support that decision. The timing is unfortunate, but I've no doubt you've made excellent progress under DS Reilly, and I want to hit the ground running from here.' She got a nod from an amped-up-looking Rory Mulcair and a sneer from Moira. Fisher looked confused. Dave McCarthy, usually the most cynical man in any room, leaned back in his chair, arms crossed, concern written all over his face.

'I'll be meeting the Superintendent shortly,' Carrie said. 'He's going to want answers and he's going to want them now. From this moment on we are investigating both deaths, and we need to start seeing results. Pull in,' Carrie said, and gestured with her hands, gathering the team closer to the front of the room. 'I want a recap. Let's go over what we know, see what leads we haven't run to the ground. Let's see what connections we have already made between the two cases, look at what new evidence we have as a result of this second death.' Carrie took up position leaning against the wall at the top of the room, nodded at Fisher to begin. There were a few more exchanged glances, maybe a momentary hesitation.

'Right,' Fisher said. He walked towards one of the noticeboards, where someone had already pinned a photograph of Carline beside one of Della. He turned back to the room, lay one hand flat on the noticeboard beside the two photographs.

'We know that Della Lambert and Carline Darcy were friends,' Fisher said. 'They spent time alone together in Della's apartment. We don't yet know if the relationship was romantic or platonic.'

'Right,' Carrie said. 'What else?'

'DS Reilly took a statement from Mark Wardle, one of Carline's roommates. Wardle's theory is that Carline and Della had a sexual relationship, which Carline kept secret.'

'All right,' Carrie said. 'Anything to support that theory?'

Fisher shrugged. 'Only Wardle's statement. His theory is that Carline didn't want her grandfather to find out she was in a lesbian relationship, for fear he would cut her off. Look, if you ask me Wardle's a fantasist. I listened to the recording of that interview. He wasn't very convincing.'

There was a moment's silence. Dave McCarthy shifted uncomfortably in his chair. 'Yeah, but there's the money,' he said. 'We found hundreds of thousands in Della Lambert's apartment. That had to have come from Carline Darcy and that's got to be blackmail.'

Fisher looked like he was going to argue for a moment, then he shrugged, nodded to acknowledge the point.

'Anything else I need to know before I see the Super?' Carrie asked.

'We know that Della had access to Darcy Laboratories,' Dave said. 'She had Carline's ID in her pocket. Hard to understand why she needed that, even if she was Carline's girlfriend.'

The room moved on to a discussion of the possible reasons why Carline might have provided Della with her ID, from simple left it behind by accident to more complex motivations. Carrie was only half-listening.

'Let's move on,' Carrie said. 'Where are we on the money now?'

Fisher shook his head. 'Nothing new. We don't know anything more than we knew a few days ago. Della made the lodgements herself, that's all. We've been able to confirm that through the bank's security footage.'

'Well, there won't be any objection now to getting Carline Darcy's bank statements,' Carrie said. 'Let's get working on a subpoena. If we can show a withdrawal that matches the money Della was holding or lodging we're a step closer to proving that she was paying her off.'

There were nods of general agreement, then a pause as everyone waited for Carrie to speak. But Carrie had had no time with the case. She didn't know the file, and didn't know the working theories. She needed time. Time that she couldn't take.

Fisher read the hesitation on her face. 'I think it all comes back to the lab,' he said after a moment. 'We need to confirm whether or not Della Lambert spent time there. Getting answers there has to be our first priority, right?'

He was probably right, but Carrie wanted a conversation with Brian Murphy before she tackled the fraught process of getting a warrant for the Darcy facility.

'What have we got from the Dock Road scene?' Carrie asked. 'Is the report in from the scene of crime lads yet? What about time of death?'

Moira Hanley hit a few keys on the keyboard in front of her. 'It's starting to come in now,' she said. 'Preliminary estimate of time of death is between 9 p.m. and 10 p.m. last night. Nothing else from the pathologist yet, but we've got the first of the trace evidence reports.'

Carrie gave her the nod, and Moira clicked on a document and started to scroll quickly through it.

'Lots of trace at the scene,' she said. 'Difficult to tell if any of it came from the killer until they've processed it.'

'All right,' Carrie said. 'Let's wait to hear. Anything else?'

'I've got something.' It was Rory Mulcair. 'There's a camera down the street. One of ours so it's a good picture. It's right at the edge of the shot, but you should see this.' There was excitement in his voice, enough so that the room fell quiet as he clicked and scrolled, found what he was looking for. 'Throw me the cable, will you Moira?' he said. She passed it over and he plugged his computer into the network, nodded in the direction of the electronic whiteboard. Moments later, a grainy black and white image flickered into being.

It was security camera footage from somewhere on Dock Road. The camera must have been installed high up on the side of a building. They had a bird's eye view down the length of the street; Carline's apartment building was just inside the limits of the picture. They were looking at the street at night, a handful of cars parked roadside on the apartment side of the street. The image time-skipped every five seconds. A car appeared briefly as it drove through the scene. A moment later another car appeared, and parked outside the apartment building, facing away from the camera.

'Watch,' said Rory. He zoomed the image in much closer, and the picture lost its clarity. The number-plate was too blurred to read. Rory zoomed the picture back out a little, and they watched as a tall figure with long dark hair climbed out of the driver's seat and disappeared into the building. The time stamp said that it was 9.15 p.m. 'She comes out again at 9.45 p.m.'

'Christ,' said Fisher. 'Is that the murderer? How did she get in? A key?'

Rory Mulcair shook his head. 'I don't think so. Look.' He pointed at the screen. 'You can see a crack of light. I'd say the door was propped open.'

'The time is right,' Carrie said. 'But let's keep an open mind. Rory, can you zoom in again on the car? Can we get a clearer picture?'

Rory froze the video, then clicked and scrolled and the image zoomed in, too far initially, so that the whole thing became pixelated, then further out, until he had the best available view of the number plate and the back of the car.

The number plate was still indistinct, though curves and shadows suggested certain letters and numbers and ruled out others. But the left rear brake light had a crack, and its light diffused in a distinctive pattern.

'It's a Mazda3,' Rory said. 'And is that a G? It looks like a Galway reg to me.' He clicked and scrolled, clicked and scrolled, but the clarity of the image did not improve.

'There's a crack in the brake light on the left-hand side,' Moira Hanley said. 'Look there, can you see it?'

Everyone in the room leaned closer, Carrie too. She was concentrating on the image, so she very nearly missed Peter Fisher's flinch when he turned to stare at the screen.

'Send it to the tech guys,' Carrie said. 'Tell them it's priority one. I want that image cleaned up. And Fisher? A moment with you please, outside.'

He followed her out into the corridor, and she gestured for him to shut the door behind him.

'Tell me,' she said.

She saw him think about it, consider whether or not to tell her.

'Peter,' she said.

He blew out a breath. 'It's the brake light,' he said. 'When I interviewed her, Emma Sweeney had just cracked her brake light. She drives a Mazda3 too.'

Carrie felt her stomach sink to the floor. Then she went to find Brian Murphy, and make her report.

'How did he get it so wrong?'

'Sir?' Carrie said.

'I'm talking about Reilly. You're telling me he saw the girl yesterday afternoon, and a few hours later she's murdered in her own apartment? He's supposed to be one of the best. I put my confidence in his judgement and this is the outcome?'

'I'm very new to this case, but nothing I've seen so far suggests that DS Reilly was at fault in how he ran it. There was no reason to think that Carline was in danger.'

Murphy turned hard eyes in her direction. 'Except for the minor fact that his girlfriend is the main suspect, something he either missed completely, or actively covered up.'

Carrie held his gaze. 'That evidence only came to light in the last hour. There was nothing prior to the video to suggest that Emma Sweeney was in any way involved.'

'Except that she found the bloody body in the first place!' Murphy exploded. 'It should have been you on this case from the very beginning.'

Carrie nodded. 'Yes sir, I'm sure you're right. But it's mine now and I should get on with it, shouldn't I?' She stood, unwilling to waste time on a postmortem, and asking herself why it was that Murphy had gone along with Cormac running the case from the beginning. It was out of character for a man as politically astute and as motivated by self-preservation as Murphy was. Carrie didn't dislike her boss. He'd given her opportunity when she'd asked for it, and he was relatively hands off and not, despite the evidence of the last five minutes, prone to histrionics. But she had no illusions about him. Brian Murphy never did anything without first making sure there was a better than even chance he would come out smelling of roses. So why had he taken the risk on this?

'Keep Cormac Reilly away from this case,' Murphy said. 'I don't want his fingerprints anywhere near it from now on. If he so much as makes a phone call, arrest him.'

When Carrie O'Halloran left him, Fisher returned to the case room, dragging his feet. A few heads turned but he ignored the unspoken questions and returned to his desk.

'Fisher.'

He turned his head to see Moira Hanley looking at him, phone in hand.

'Reilly's on the phone. He wants to speak with you,' Hanley said. Every head within earshot turned in their direction.

Fisher felt himself flush. 'Transfer it over here, so,' he said.

Hanley looked at the phone, then back at Fisher. 'Can't transfer it,' she said. 'You'll have to come here.'

She held out the handset. It was connected to the phone on her desk. He'd have to stand right beside her, have her listen to every word he said, and at that distance, probably everything Reilly said too, all with every eye in the squad room on him. He wouldn't do it.

'Tell him I'll call him from my mobile,' Fisher said. Then, painfully aware that every ear in the room had tuned into the exchange, he took his phone and went out into the corridor, and called Cormac back.

'Fisher,' Cormac said, answering on the first ring. 'I've been trying to get DS O'Halloran on the phone. I'm on my way in from Athenry. Look, can you check the scene reports? I need to know if they found a computer in Carline's possession. A laptop, brand is Acer, casing black, and it should have the markings from some left-over adhesive on the top right corner. It was Della Lambert's computer.'

Fisher hesitated, and the silence went on a little too long.

'Fisher?' Cormac said, his tone impatient.

'DS O'Halloran is with Superintendent Murphy,' Fisher said. 'I can ask her to call you when she gets back to the case room.' His tone was too formal. He could almost feel Reilly's antennae go up.

'What's going on?' Reilly said.

'Uh, DS O'Halloran has just been in to let us know that she's taking over the case.'

'Right,' Reilly said. 'Carrie will be running the case from here on. She'll need to make the call about bringing Paul Lambert in. And we need that laptop examined. I think what's on it will prove that Della was doing Carline Darcy's academic work. That's what all the money was for.'

'Christ. Really? But with Carline dead …' It went without saying that it was very unlikely that Carline had been the murderer.

'Yeah,' Cormac said. 'Look, Fisher, I need to get off the phone. Emma's in the lab. I don't want her near the place while all of this is going down. I want to bring her in to the station. I think the answers to all of this will be on that laptop, but we might need some help interpreting it. Emma can help us with that.'

He was about to hang up.

'No,' said Fisher. 'You can't do that.' It came out, hurried and urgent, before he'd had a chance to think through what he was going to say.

There was a long silence.

'Fisher, what exactly is going on in there?'

Fisher hesitated, glanced behind him, took another couple of steps down the corridor. He should end the call now. He could claim that he was being called back into the room, then he could wait for Carrie O'Halloran, have her deal with this mess. Instead, he dropped his voice and said, 'There's video footage from last night, outside Carline Darcy's building. It's from a distance so it's not exactly clear, but it's good enough that we can see a car pull in outside the apartment building just before the murder. A woman gets out and goes into the building. She's in there from 9.15 p.m. to 9.45 p.m., which is consistent with the time of death. The car, it's a Mazda3, and it has a broken brake light. The woman is wearing a green calf-length coat, and she has long, dark hair.'

There was a long, long silence.

'Sir, I'm sorry, but you can't go there and tell Emma anything that you learned from Paul Lambert. She can't even know that there's been a breakthrough in the case.'

Another silence. 'I'm going to hang up now,' said Cormac. 'And Fisher? When they ask you about this phone call, if you don't want to risk your job, tell them everything.'

He hung up, and all Fisher heard was dial tone.

CHAPTER FORTY-FIVE

Cormac immediately dialled Emma's number. It rang out again and again. He checked the time – 1.30 p.m. If she was at lunch she would have answered. She must be buried in the lab. He hung up and concentrated on driving as quickly as he could through the traffic. He needed to get to her. Needed to know she was safe. There was no way, just no way that Emma had murdered that girl. He would have known it, couldn't have slept every night next to a woman who could do that and not known it.

Except she'd killed before, hadn't she? Images from that scene came to him unbidden. The blood splatters on the wall and floor. The gaping wound of a throat cut so deeply that the pathologist had said the victim must have bled out in seconds. But that had been so different. That had been a desperate act in defence of her sister's life. This was cold-blooded murder. And for what? What possible motive could Emma have to murder Carline Darcy? No. This was bullshit. If that was her car in the video feed – and for Christ's sake, was he really going to convict his own girlfriend of murder on the back of a shitty image he'd heard about second hand? – then there would be an explanation.

But she'd lied, hadn't she? On the very first night she'd lied to Carrie, had said that she didn't work late often, when she was at the lab virtually every evening. It was a small lie but it was out of character. He'd known that, right from the beginning, and he'd explained it away. Had he been doing that all the way through this investigation? Finding a way to normalise things? Had he explained away every piece of evidence that could have led to Emma's door?

He called her number again, and again it rang out. He thought about her return to the house the night before, tried to remember if it had been before or after ten. He thought after. He remembered her red eyes, her distraction. He'd told her to take a shower. She'd come down afterwards and put her clothes straight into the washing machine.

Nausea crawled its way up Cormac's belly, clutched at his throat, though he forced it ruthlessly back and back. Memories of those old crime scene photographs played themselves across his mind in a grim slide show. She'd killed once in self-defence, had been deeply traumatised by it. Could that have eroded her boundaries, made murder seem like an option? But why? He could think of no possible reason for Emma to murder Della Lambert or Carline Darcy, two young women who'd had little to do with her and no motive or ability to hurt her. But the fear was so real, so overwhelming, that he felt as if he had slipped somehow sideways, so that everything in the world was slightly off-kilter. He kept coming back to the thought that Emma hadn't been herself since the night Della had died. He'd known it, and he'd let it go. Why? Why had he let things go? Cormac put his foot to the accelerator and concentrated on getting there.

Cormac abandoned the car on the verge outside the lab and made for the entrance door. He knocked and waited. Knocked and waited again. Eventually the door was opened by a man he didn't recognise.

'Yes?' he said.

'Where's Josep?' Cormac asked.

'What's it to you?' the man responded. He had dirty blond hair, too long, and a beer belly that strained the fabric of his shirt. An English accent this time.

Cormac showed him his badge, and the man – he gave his name as Roland Swaine – backed down.

'Where's Josep?' Cormac asked again.

'I don't know who you're talking about,' Roland said. Cormac gave him an *I'm not in the mood for bullshit* look and he said, 'If you mean the last guy, I was told that he went back to Poland. His mother's sick or something.'

Cormac sent Roland off to call Emma. It took a couple of minutes for her to appear.

'Corm?' she said. She was wearing a lab coat, hair tied back. 'Did you want to get lunch?'

'We need to talk,' he said. 'It's important.'

She took in his expression and didn't ask any questions, just removed her lab coat, hung it in a locker and collected her bag. As they walked away from the lab he reached automatically for her hand. Her grip on his was warm and dry, firm. Her skin was soft.

'I heard about Carline,' she said. 'John Darcy has been closeted away with Dr Murtagh all morning. Everyone's talking about it at the lab. It's just awful. That poor, poor girl. Are you okay? I'm so glad you came. I'd rather be with you than with anyone else.'

'Emma,' Cormac said again. 'Where were you last night?'

She didn't seem to have heard him at first. Then she processed what he had said and turned a puzzled face in his direction.

'What?'

'You got home just after ten. Before that where were you?' He needed to look at her, should be reading her reaction to his question, but he couldn't do it. He looked away. The silence lasted too long. Then she spoke in a low, horrified voice.

'What are you asking me, Cormac?'

'Please,' was all he said.

'Carline Darcy was murdered last night,' she said slowly. 'Are you asking me where I was? Are you asking me for an alibi?'

'Emma, please. Just answer me, all right?'

'I told you last night. I was in the lab, all night. I came straight home. What's happened? Cormac, look at me.'

'By yourself?'

'Yes.' She put her hand on his arm. He flinched, and she removed it.

'Let's talk at home. Okay? Let's just wait until we get home.'

She didn't say anything, just turned away from him, folded her arms around herself protectively and followed him to the car.

The house was cold. In the living room Emma went straight for the couch, curled into the corner and wrapped a throw around herself as if it were armour.

'Carline Darcy may have been murdered by a woman,' he said. 'There's video footage of a car pulling in outside the apartment building not long before she was killed. A woman with dark hair gets out of the car and enters the building. The car is a Mazda3. It had a broken brake light, just like yours, Emma. They haven't been able to read the numberplate yet, but that's just a matter of time. The image enhancement guys will get it.'

'It's not me, Cormac.' She looked outraged. Her voice was steady, controlled, but full of anger. 'It's not me and I don't even know who you are, if you think I could have murdered that girl. What is wrong with you?'

'Emma. I just need you to answer some questions. Please, Emma.' He was pleading. 'Fisher recognised the car. He's sure it's yours. Even the coat. He said it was a long, green coat. You were wearing your green coat when you came in last night. You have to tell me the truth now. If you went there for another reason you can tell me, but I can only help you if you tell me the truth.'

Her mouth opened, her expression was horrified. 'I wasn't there. That wasn't me. Jesus. What is going on?'

'You haven't been yourself, ever since you found Della Lambert's body. You've been having nightmares, you've been talking in your sleep.'

'I ... no.'

'You have, Em.' Cormac wanted to go to her but he held himself back. He couldn't help her if he fell all over her like a schoolboy. 'You've been off. You've been different. You've been hiding things from me.'

'Cormac,' she said, shaking her head, tears starting to well. She forced them back with an obvious effort of will, blinking strongly and scrubbing her eyes with one hand. 'You are so wrong. I can't begin to tell you how wrong you have this.'

'You have to talk to me. Please. Please just talk to me.'

'I have been having nightmares. I've been dreaming about Roisín, about that day. Except in my dreams I don't get there in time. Flynn kills her.' Emma shook her head, swallowed. 'The same dream, almost every night. I didn't tell you because I knew you'd worry. I didn't tell you because I didn't want you to think we were going backwards. I didn't tell you because I didn't want you to feel guilty about not coming home with me that night, you absolute, utter fucker.'

'Emma ...'

Emma spoke across him. 'And things have been rough at work. Nothing's coming together the way it should be, and I haven't been able to figure out why. I didn't want to tell you until I had fixed it, until things were going better. You were so caught up in your case. So fixated on making a great success of everything after what happened last year. I thought I was being *supportive*. Jesus. And all the while you're going around building a picture in your head of me as a murderer. Based on the fact that I've been a bit withdrawn, and on some shitty video footage. It's not *me*, Cormac. It's not my car.'

Cormac's phone buzzed in his pocket. It was Carrie. Eyes on Emma, he answered the call.

'Carrie,' he said.

'Fisher came to me,' Carrie said. 'He doesn't know what to do next. He says that he trusts you to do the right thing. Is he right to trust you, Cormac?'

It was on the tip of his tongue, a quick, insincere assurance. He even opened his mouth to deliver it, then found he couldn't do it. Knew in any case that it wouldn't work.

'I don't know,' Cormac said.

'You're with her now?'

He paused. 'Yes.'

'If she did this, we won't look away. There'll be no hiding it.'

Cormac closed his eyes.

'I'll give you an hour,' Carrie said. 'I'll be waiting for your call.'

Carrie hung up and Cormac turned to Emma. His phone buzzed again, and he looked at the screen. It was a message from Peter Fisher. A black and white image, enhanced, showing a numberplate. Slowly, Cormac turned the screen around so that Emma could see the picture. She looked at it, then raised disbelieving eyes to his.

CHAPTER FORTY-SIX

Cormac and Emma stared at each other. He read her reaction in her eyes. Shock. Disbelief. Horror. But no guilt. She leaned towards him.

'Cormac. Look at me. You know me. You *know* me.'

And he did know her. Knew her, and loved her, and felt the truth of her words echo through him. And yet, and yet ... The two sides of his personality warred within him. The part of him that loved her knew, absolutely, that she could never have done this. The policeman in him said that she was guilty. He had to choose.

He looked at her and knew. Emma hadn't done this. Emma could never have done this. What the hell had he been thinking? Relief made him giddy, loose, and he flopped into the chair. He wanted to reach out to her, but his mind was still going, working and working. If Emma hadn't done this, then someone was doing a very good job of making it look like she had. She was under attack. He needed to wake the fuck up and start thinking strategically. He left the room, went to the hall, where Emma's coat still hung from the end of the banisters. He took it back into the living room, spread it open over the back of the couch. There was an obvious blood stain at the hem of the coat. Emma came to stand beside him. She saw the blood and clenched her fists.

'That's just ... I don't know where that came from. I didn't *do* anything.'

'I know,' he said. 'I know, Emma.'

She was shaking her head, pale and frightened, eyes fixed on the bloodstain.

'Someone took your coat, your keys, drove to Carline Darcy's apartment and murdered her. Right now, my team, they think that's you in that video. So we need to figure this out and we need to do it quickly.'

'It doesn't make any sense. Who would do that?'

'Someone at the lab. It had to be someone who had easy access to your coat and your car keys. Someone who knew your movements and could be confident that you wouldn't decide to head for home at the wrong time.' Cormac said. He stared down at the bloodstain on Emma's coat. Della Lambert's laptop was the key to this thing.

'Della had access to the lab,' Cormac said. 'Could she have stolen something? Taken valuable or embarrassing information, something that would damage the company or an individual if it was made public?'

'No. I mean, I can't see how. Everything is locked down, all the data. You can't download anything from the lab's computers, you can't carry anything out of the building. I have a company laptop so that I can work from home sometimes, but that's encrypted and I'm not allowed to put any of the really sensitive stuff on it. And anyway, even if she did manage to get her hands on something, what would she do with it? She couldn't sell it.'

Cormac rubbed at the stubble on his cheek. 'The break-in at the lab,' he said. 'Only James Murtagh's office was trashed, right?'

'Yes. But you can't think James had anything to do with this.'

But he did think it. 'On the night that she died Della Lambert was found without a handbag, or a backpack or even a phone. Della definitely had a computer – there was a docking station in her apartment – but we never found the laptop that went with it. I think whoever killed her took it from her body that night. Carline Darcy had that computer in her possession yesterday afternoon. What if the person she took it from came to get it back?'

'What are you saying, Cormac?'

'I'm saying I think there's a solid chance James Murtagh killed Della and took her laptop, which he then hid in his office. Carline knew, or somehow figured it out, and she broke into his office to take it back.'

'And then what, James murdered Carline too?' Emma looked bewildered. 'Christ Cormac, you …'

'James Murtagh had access to your coat, your keys. He could easily have taken them from your locker and driven to Carline's apartment. His wife has cancer. Do you know if she owns a wig?'

'I don't know.' Emma was shaking her head.

'If he had access to the security cameras at the front desk Murtagh would have known that you were still safely in the lab, and he could return keys and coat to your locker with you none the wiser.'

'But Jesus, what a risk. What if I had decided to leave an hour earlier and had come out to find my coat and my keys missing?' Emma said.

'I don't think he felt he had a choice. Killing Carline was an enormous leap. Once he made the decision to do that he was long past the point of playing it safe. Besides, he must have felt the odds were good. You've been working longer and longer hours lately.'

Something sparked in Emma's eye. 'He sent me something,' she said slowly. 'Yesterday evening. Some new data. He suggested that it might hold the key to the problems we've been having lately. I spent hours last night trying to untangle it.'

'Was it?'

'Was it what?'

'A solution.'

'It was nothing,' Emma said. 'It was a dead end.'

'He used it to keep you there, so he could set you up. Christ, but he's played this well. He's smeared enough evidence around to confuse things nicely, and I am … or was, the lead investigator, which makes it so much worse. I've got zero credibility in this.' Cormac pushed his hands through his hair in frustration. 'I've fucked this up. I thought I was helping you by staying on the case, by keeping it away from you, but all I did was paint a target on your back.'

'Am I going to be charged?' Emma asked. She was evidently afraid, but she asked the question with a kind of shaken bravery that made him fiercely proud of her.

He couldn't lie to her. 'I don't know,' he said.

She nodded grimly. 'But I didn't do this and in the end we'll be able to prove it. I mean, I had to swipe my way out when I left the lab. There are cameras. When all of this is looked into, if he did this he'll be caught. James is not a stupid man. If he did this he couldn't have thought he would get away with it. Unless maybe he just doesn't care anymore. He's old. His wife has terminal cancer.'

Cormac's mind flashed to the photograph Murtagh kept in his office. The photograph of his frail, thin wife, her head wrapped in a silk scarf. He thought of Murtagh driving Emma's car, wrapped in Emma's coat, with his dying wife's wig on his head. Cormac's stomach twisted in disgust.

'He cares, Emma. He cares all right. He doesn't just want to survive. He wants to come out on top.'

Emma picked up the hem of the coat, held it so that her hands were either side of the bloodstain. She looked at him. 'I … I could wash it,' she said.

The words hung between them for a moment.

'No, Em,' he said. 'I think that would be playing into his hands. There'll be trace evidence all over your car.' He looked around the room. 'There's probably a fair amount of it in this house too. You drove the car home last night. You wore the coat. We can't undo that.'

Emma let the coat drop back down onto the couch. She shuddered, wrapped her arms around herself. 'Then what?' she asked. 'What am I supposed to do? Wait here until Peter Fisher comes to arrest me? Or make a mad dash for the airport, hide in South America for the rest of my life?' She gave a disbelieving laugh.

Cormac took her hand. 'He's underestimated us, Emma. We are going to take that fucker down. All right? We are going to take that fucker down and we are going to bury him.' Cormac saw the fear in Emma's eyes, and thought of the two dead girls Murtagh had already left in his wake. Fury boiled inside him but he tamped it down for later.

'What do you want me to do?' Emma asked.

Cormac took a moment, gathered his thoughts. 'I need your help, Em. If I'm right there must be something awfully valuable on that computer. Something he thinks worth the taking of two lives. And right now you're my best chance of figuring out what that is.'

Emma withdrew a little as she thought. She walked the room, tied her hair into a ponytail, loosened it, tied it up again. Eventually she turned to him.

'You asked me if Della could have stolen something, or if she could have found something embarrassing.'

'Yes.'

She hesitated. 'I don't know. I'm just trying to think … but I could be way off.'

'Tell me, Em. Even if it's just a thought.'

'Right, well, I've told you that the work hasn't been going well. I've thought the problem is with the mesh design. All the simulations show that it works very well. We've come at it from every angle and it works. But we're not getting the results from the prototype that we should be and I haven't been able to find the problem.'

'Okay,' Cormac said.

'What if the problem isn't with the mesh, but with the drug? I mean look, this could be completely wrong …' Emma let her voice trail off.

'No, keep going.'

'It's just, if I assume that you're right about James, and I assume that he had Della killed to cover something up at the lab, well, there are only a few options. Financial or sexual misbehaviour of some kind, or fraud.'

'And you think it could be fraud?'

'Well, Carline and Della aren't likely to have any visibility of the money side of things, and there's never been any hint of any kind of sexual impropriety. But James invented the drug. The design, all his research, it's commercial in confidence. No one has access to his underlying data. I'm just saying, what if he made it up and the girls found out?'

Cormac shook his head. 'I don't understand. How could he get away with that?'

'I'll tell you how.' Emma's voice grew more confident. 'He bloody knew that the company would throw a party at the very idea that he had designed a drug that would solve this huge problem we have of clotting around the device. He had enough seniority within the company that no one was going to look too closely at his background research, and he knew that no one outside the company would get even a glimpse of something with this much potential value. We're talking about something worth hundreds of millions, probably even billions.'

'But surely it's only valuable if it works? What would be the point of it all, if he can't sell the drug?'

'The point is that Murtagh invented the drug five years ago. It was seen as a great breakthrough, got him a massive bonus and lots of praise and attention, but it had no practical application at the time so he wasn't called on to prove that the damn thing worked.'

'Until you came along.'

'Exactly. It was the combination of my device and his drug that was the solution.'

'So then Murtagh was under pressure. You've been at the lab for a year, you've got a prototype up and running, you're starting to ask questions …'

'Carline, or, I suppose, Carline and Della, they were working on the drug side of things. They might have figured out a way to get into the background data. I don't know. Everything is so locked down at the lab but if you were determined and you had a foot in the door already, maybe you could do it. But let's just assume that they did, and they found that he'd faked it all. What if Della confronted him, and he killed her for it? Took her laptop to hide the evidence? Maybe Carline stole the computer back so that she would have proof of what he had done.'

Christ. Much of that made sense, though there were a lot of unanswered questions.

'I need to go after Murtagh,' he said. 'I need to go after him hard and with everything I've got. I need to get to him before the lawyers are called in. If we sit back and wait, all the team's focus will go into investigating you, and Murtagh will get enough time and space to muddy the waters.'

Emma was unsure. He could see hesitation in her eyes, but she sat on the couch and nodded, and waited to hear what he wanted her to do.

Cormac sat on the arm of the chair opposite her, leaned forward. 'I need whatever you can give me, whatever you know about the way he thinks, about how he would be thinking now.'

Emma huffed out a breath. 'I don't know. If I'm right, I'm trying to think about what it must have been like for him for the last few years, just waiting for someone to stumble on to the truth. It must have been terrifying. His whole career, his whole reputation on the line, and for what? A drug that couldn't even go to market?'

'You're assuming that this is the first and only time he's pulled something like this off, with this drug only. But isn't it more likely that he's done it more than once, perhaps even many times, and this just happened to be the time it mattered?'

Emma's face grew more troubled. 'It's possible,' she said. She paused. 'Do you know, before I came here I looked James up online, read all the old articles about how he and John Darcy started out. I hadn't realised just how close they were in the early days. If you read their story in a certain kind of light, it almost reads like an Eduardo Saverin tale.'

'Saverin … the Facebook guy?'

'Yes. There at the beginning, contributes a bit at an important time, then disappears into the background. That's James Murtagh. He was there side by side with John Darcy when he … they developed their first successful compound. He's named in the first patent papers filed. But then John made a refinement … an important refinement that really made the drug what it needed to be, and when the next papers were filed James Murtagh's name had disappeared. John went on to licence that drug to big pharma for hundreds of millions, at least. I wouldn't be surprised if it earned him a billion before the patent term ran out. He built Darcy Therapeutics on the back of that drug and went on to develop three more successful compounds after that. And James Murtagh just disappears into … well, into anonymous academia.'

'So how does he feel about that?' Cormac asked.

'Exactly. How does he feel about his friend and colleague leaving him in the dust? What is the lab in Galway, if not a consolation prize, and a reminder that while John has gone out and conquered the world, James is still sitting exactly where they both started.'

Cormac stood up and started to pace. 'And then Carline comes to the university. She's supposed to be the second coming of John Darcy, isn't she? Except she's just a very bright girl who is not afraid to use someone else's work to get ahead. He must have figured out that she was using Della. Christ. He must have hated her.'

'Yes,' Emma said quietly.

Cormac turned to look at her. She had sunk back into the couch, had lost a little of that vital energy. He crossed to her side, sat beside her and took her hand, a little awkwardly.

'We're going to get him, Emma,' he said. 'You just trust me, okay? This is what I do, and I promise you, I do it bloody well. I am going to get him and I am going to put him down.'

CHAPTER FORTY-EIGHT

Fisher was waiting for Carrie when she made her way back to the case room. In a quick and hushed monologue, he filled her in on Paul Lambert's suspicion that he had seen his sister's laptop in Carline Darcy's hands. Fisher had already checked and no computer matching the description had been found at the scene. He also confessed to telling Reilly about the video of Emma's car.

'I'm sorry,' Fisher said. 'It was stupid of me maybe. But he wanted to bring her in, to get her help with the laptop.'

It had been stupid of him. He'd given Cormac a heads up, an opportunity to warn Emma. But she couldn't quite bring herself to be angry. Things were moving so fast, it wasn't surprising that Fisher hadn't quite wrapped his head around the fact that Cormac Reilly was now firmly on the other side of the security glass. She would have to draw that line, make it clear to the whole team that the investigation was not to be discussed with anyone outside themselves. That wouldn't do it. She would have to be explicit, have to name Reilly as *persona non grata*. Fuck.

Carrie nodded dismissal to Fisher, and dialled Cormac's number. They spoke briefly, but he told her the truth, and without thinking about what she was doing she heard herself give Cormac Reilly an hour. An hour during which she would take no direct action, and hour during which Cormac could warn, coach, prepare their chief suspect. Christ. Maybe none of them were fit for this thing. Maybe they should hand the whole bloody case over lock, stock and barrel to an external team.

Murphy's aide appeared at her elbow.

'The Super wants you back in his office,' the aide said. His expression told her there was more.

'I just left him five minutes ago,' Carrie said.

'John Darcy's in with him, and he's brought his lawyer.' The aide paused for effect. 'He's brought Anne Brady.'

'Right.' Carrie didn't want to betray too much reaction, not in front of the aide or Fisher, but she'd heard of Brady, who was a prominent criminal defence lawyer with a reputation for ruthlessness. Why would John Darcy bring a defence lawyer to a meeting that was presumably about his granddaughter's death?

Carrie excused herself and made her way back to Murphy's office. She knocked and entered.

'Detective, come in,' Murphy said. He didn't stand and nor did the skeletal-looking man sitting opposite him. 'This is John Darcy. He took the time to come in today to offer us any assistance we may need with regard to our inquiry into his granddaughter's death. And his lawyer, Ms Brady.'

There was a woman sitting to John Darcy's right. In her fifties, with prematurely grey hair, she had a taut, focused energy about her.

'I see.' Carrie took a seat, wishing she could stand. 'I'm very sorry for your loss, Mr Darcy.'

He inclined his head. 'Do you have a theory about who killed my granddaughter?' Darcy asked. 'Was this about money?'

Carrie looked to Murphy for direction. He gave her an impatient nod.

'You may be aware that we've been investigating the murder of a young woman named Della Lambert,' Carrie said to Darcy, looking for the light of recognition in his eyes and seeing none. 'She was the victim of a deliberate hit-and-run at the university a week ago. Della was a friend of your granddaughter's. She may have spent time at your laboratory. She may have been on her way there on the night she died.'

'That is conjecture at this stage,' Murphy put in. 'We have not been able to prove that to date.'

Darcy kept his eyes on Carrie. 'What is it you're trying to tell me?'

'Just this,' Carrie said. 'I find it difficult to believe that two young women, friends, were murdered within a week of each other in Galway, and neither death was connected to the other.'

Murphy's eyes flicked to Darcy, trying to read him. That was where the power sat in the room. Murphy would be led by whatever John Darcy wanted. She would have to step very carefully. The atmosphere in the room wasn't what it should be. Nothing about Darcy's body language or his demeanour suggested grief. He looked at Carrie like she was an opponent in a game that he was determined to win, and Brady sat, a silent and hawk-like presence by his side.

'Della and Carline were friends, Mr Darcy,' Carrie said. 'But Carline took pains to keep that relationship secret. They weren't seen out and about together. When they spent time together they did so at Della's apartment. Have you any idea why Carline might have wanted to keep Della a secret?'

'Why … I don't know any of Carline's friends. Except that girl she lives with and the Wardle boy. I've never heard of a Della but why would I? You should ask her mother.'

It occurred to Carrie that probably nobody had called her yet. John Darcy had known about his granddaughter's death as soon as Brian Murphy could be sure that this time the identification wasn't a mistake, but Carline's mother was nowhere near the top of his list of important people.

'I'll do that, sir. But in the meantime, I need to ask you … If Carline had been in a lesbian relationship, would that have impacted on your relationship with her?'

Darcy recoiled. 'What? For God's sake, what are you talking about?'

Murphy shifted in his seat. Brady looked like she was about to interject.

'A witness informed us that he suspected that Carline and Della were in a relationship. The witness believed that Carline was keeping that relationship from you for fear of being disowned. Disinherited.' Carrie turned to the lawyer. 'Mr Darcy asked me if this was about money. At the time of her death Della Lambert had hundreds of thousands of euros in her possession. This is not a girl who had connections to anyone with money. Anyone but Carline that is. If Carline was trying to hide a relationship, and was being blackmailed by Della or someone connected to her as a result, there is every possibility that that somebody eventually killed her. I need to verify the evidence I have so far. I need to know if Mr Darcy would have reacted as this witness described, as he predicted. I need to ask these questions.'

Her words hung in the air. For a third time, Murphy let his eyes go to Darcy, assessing his response.

Darcy's face was pale but he was very controlled, seemed to choose each word carefully. 'Carline's mother ... I saw very little of Carline as a child. Her mother raised her, and I stayed away. I understand it was something of a ... difficult childhood. But Carline inherited a great deal of money from her father. I have other children, other grandchildren. Carline is not a beneficiary under my will and never has been.' Darcy shook his head.

'Did Carline know that?'

'We never discussed it. But I would be surprised if she had thought otherwise.'

The disdain in his voice was unmissable. Murphy caught Carrie's eye – the momentary connection between them was involuntary, both of them realising at the same time that John

Darcy hadn't liked his granddaughter, certainly hadn't loved her, and wondering why.

'You weren't close to Carline?' Carrie asked.

Darcy took a moment to think before responding. 'I didn't know her particularly well. I make no apologies for that. Her mother was a part-time model, full-time good-time girl who caught the eye of my son for half a minute. By the time Carline was born he had long since moved on but he wanted the child. He dragged that woman and my company through the courts and the tabloid papers to get her. Embarrassed me. Embarrassed his mother. Then he had the colossal stupidity to kill himself on a ski slope when he should have been working.'

'And you didn't see the child? After your son died, I mean.'

'I didn't.' Darcy's tone was cold, unapologetic. 'I was dealing with the loss of my son, the demands of running my company. Carline had her mother. What should I have done?'

Darcy clearly didn't expect a response to the question, and Carrie let the silence hang.

'The point is that I got to know Carline only as an older child. Yes, she had great potential as a scientist, but I have many scientists with proven ability working for my company.'

Carrie flicked a glance at Murphy. How far could she push this? Not far, was her best guess, not with Brady sitting in the room. And maybe not without her. John Darcy was more than capable of looking after his own interests, that much was clear.

'I have no doubt that that is the truth as you see it, Mr Darcy,' Carrie said. 'But I suppose what matters is how Carline saw it, or how those around her saw it. Would her relationship have mattered to you? If she was a lesbian, that is?'

'Who Carline went out with was none of my business. As far as I was concerned, her romantic relationships had no impact on how I saw her,' Darcy said. His expression was deadpan, giving nothing away.

It may or may not have been true. It was almost certainly irrelevant. If the blackmail theory had ever had any weight, surely that had died with Carline. But Carrie thought that John Darcy could be dangerous. She felt the need to engage in a little misdirection. She preferred to let Darcy think they were floundering. She certainly wasn't going to tell him about Emma Sweeney – it was far too early in the investigation to let any outsider know that piece of information. And so she used the Carline-Della relationship theory to distract him. His response, however, was interesting. It was clear that Carline could not have counted on any sort of familial affection from him. Had she known that he disliked her?

'You said Carline's father left her some money when he died. How much money are we talking about?'

'Her father left her his shares. They vested in her when she turned eighteen and I bought them back immediately. She was paid forty-three million euro.'

'That money was hers? She was free to spend it?'

Darcy's eyes flicked to Brady's.

'There was no trust,' Brady said. 'Other than what she paid to maintain her mother's lifestyle, the money was hers to spend as she chose.'

Carrie paused, then turned to Darcy.

'Mr Darcy, my team tells me that you are understandably concerned about security at the laboratory. The only way to access the facility is with a swipe card, and you still have to get past a security guard. Della Lambert had an access card in her pocket when she died. Your own records show that that card was used regularly right up until the day before she died. But we can't establish who used the card without interviewing your employees. We need to cross-reference entry dates for that card with the ID numbers of other employees, find out who was in the lab at the same time as whoever was using the card. Will you help us? Make your people available to us to answer questions?'

'No.' It was Brady who spoke. She dropped the word into the room as if it was an absolute, inarguable. Her cold blue eyes held Carrie's, and she offered no explanation.

'I wish to assist the investigation any way I can, detective,' Darcy said. 'But there are many considerations … the right to privacy of my employees, for example. Our confidentiality agreements with our commercial partners. I shall proceed on the advice of my lawyers. I trust you understand.'

Carrie exchanged another involuntary glance with Murphy. 'Certainly, Mr Darcy. I understand very well.'

CHAPTER FORTY-NINE

While Carrie O'Halloran was caught up with the Superintendent and John Darcy, Peter Fisher hadn't been idle. He was deeply disturbed by what they had seen on the video. He had known straight away that the car was Emma Sweeney's. It hadn't taken the enhanced photograph, which he'd risked sending to Cormac Reilly, to convince him of that. He was less convinced that the dark-haired woman seen entering the building was the same woman he had interviewed. Peter was honest enough to ask himself if that was his ego talking, if he found it difficult to accept that Emma was a killer because that would mean accepting that he had missed it. Or if perhaps he was operating on the basis of unconscious loyalty to Cormac Reilly, whom he liked and respected, and from whom he had learned a lot. The short answer was that Peter didn't know, and he wasn't in the mood to worry about it.

He was in the mood to do something.

Peter was settled at his desk in the case room when his phone buzzed. What he saw surprised him. A text, from Cormac Reilly.

Fisher. It's an ask. James Murtagh's alibi.

Peter glanced automatically around the room, saw Moira Hanley watching him. Christ, but she was a pain in the arse. Peter looked at his phone again, closed his message screen, put the phone down. Moira Hanley he didn't give a shit about, but he should tell O'Halloran about this new contact. Trouble was, he didn't really want to. This was Reilly, reaching out, trusting him. And what was he asking, after all?

Confirm an alibi. No harm in that. He didn't even have to tell Reilly he'd done it, not if he didn't want to.

Peter stood, put his phone in his back pocket, and left the case room, resisting the urge to give Moira Hanley the finger as he left. He went down a floor, found a quiet corner, and made a call to the hotel at Harvey's Point. The call was answered straight away by another Peter – 'Peter O'Toole, Hospitality Manager … no relation,' a cheery voice introduced himself in a strong Donegal accent, in the tone of one who had made the little joke a hundred times. It probably went down well with the tourists. Fisher asked his questions. He wanted to confirm again that Professor and Mrs James Murtagh had stayed in the hotel the previous weekend, checking in on Friday. Donegal Peter asked for Fisher's badge number.

'I'm supposed to wait for a warrant before I disclose guest information, but my brother's a guard, so we'll just keep it between ourselves.'

Fisher listened to the clack of keyboard keys as Donegal Peter checked the register.

'They were here all right. Checked in on Friday, left us on Sunday.'

'What time on Friday?' Fisher asked.

'No way to tell,' Peter said. 'We don't keep a record of check-in times.' More clacking. 'There's a charge for a late dinner for two to their room. That was delivered to their room around eight-thirty, if that's any good to you?'

Shite. That probably wasn't what Reilly had been hoping to hear. 'Any way to know for sure that they were both there? That they checked in together? What about cameras?'

'No cameras on the Estate,' said Donegal Peter. 'We're very into our discretion in this part of the world.'

'What about room service delivery? Whoever dropped the food to the room? Can you talk to them, confirm that they saw James Murtagh present when they brought the food?'

A trace of reluctance made its way into Donegal Peter's voice. It was one thing to check something quietly on the register, another to answer questions about guests that could be traced back. Still, he didn't say no.

'That'd be Ania Kalinski. She's not on again till tonight. I'll ask her for you, like, when I see her.'

Fisher agreed to email a photograph of James Murtagh to the email address Donegal Peter provided, then hung up.

He went back to the case room, keeping his head down, and sat and stared vacantly at his own screen for a time. Was he really blinkered by the fact that he liked Emma Sweeney personally? That he liked and respected Cormac Reilly? Cormac was the best cop he'd ever worked with. It was hard to believe that he could have missed the minor fact of his girlfriend being a dual murderer. There was something so solid about the way they were together, Cormac and Emma, like they knew each other down to the bottom of their boots. It made you want to root for them.

Peter looked at his phone. How far should he go? He didn't even know why Reilly had asked him to check it out. He couldn't text him back to ask. If this whole thing blew up, Reilly's phone records would be looked at. It was one thing to receive an unsolicited text message, it would be another if Peter was seen to be conspiring with his former superior officer.

Peter shifted uncomfortably in his seat. That thought had felt a little too slick, a little self-serving.

For a little while, he managed to turn his attention to the work he should be doing, but his eyes kept creeping back to his phone. When he found himself staring at it for the fourth time, like a teenager waiting for a message from his first girlfriend, he cursed. Fuck it. If their positions were reversed, Reilly wouldn't make a half-arsed attempt then give up the ghost. Reilly pushed every angle until there was nothing left and then he pushed some more.

Fisher logged into the system, checked the forensics reports. The report was back on the analysis of paint flecks found on and around Della's body. Paint had come from either a smart car, which Peter thought could safely be discounted, or from a BMW. Another click of his keyboard as he searched for cars registered to James Murtagh. Fisher was briefly disappointed to see that Murtagh drove a Mercedes, then ran a second search on Murtagh's wife. Bingo. She drove a BMW X5 in Mocha Black Metallic. The paint matched. Fisher sat up, took a breath. He looked around the room, half-expecting heads to have turned in his direction, but everyone was still engaged in their own work. It was too soon to share, he needed to work it up. He ran another search. There had been no report of a stolen vehicle from the Murtaghs, and no reports in the system of a burnt-out X5 abandoned somewhere. Which meant they would have had to have it fixed. No way they'd be keeping a banged-up SUV in a garage somewhere, with Della Lambert's brains all over the bashed-up bumper.

Rory Mulcair's desk was close enough that Fisher didn't have to raise his voice. 'Rory, are you finished with that list of garages? Did you have any luck?'

Rory grimaced. 'All no so far. Two body shops in Limerick, one in Mayo who said they'd call us back, but it didn't sound promising.'

'What about the North?' Fisher asked.

Rory shrugged. 'We sent a request to the PSNI on Monday. But you know yourself it's not going to be a priority for them. Chances are it'll be months before we hear back from them.'

Rory returned to his work. Fisher drummed his pen against his desk. He pulled up Google maps, looked up Harvey's Point. It was so close to the border. Reilly obviously considered Murtagh a suspect, notwithstanding the fact that his wife had given an alibi. So, assuming Murtagh was guilty, what would he have done? The man wasn't stupid. If he had killed Della using his wife's car and needed to get it fixed in a hurry, would it have occurred to him that getting the car over the border would be the safest bet? That gardaí would not be able to make direct inquiry north of the border, that they'd have to wait on the Police Service of Northern Ireland, who had more than enough of their own work to do?

The pathologist's report put Della's time of death as some time between 9 p.m. and 10, but probably closer to the earlier limits of that timeframe. He had to proceed on the assumption that Murtagh's wife had gone ahead to the hotel and checked in, maybe even ordered dinner for two believing that her husband was on his way. If Murtagh had stayed in Galway long enough to kill Della, could he have driven the car all the way to Donegal, damaged as it must have been? If so, what next? It would have been very late by the time he got there, too late to do anything with the car, but also late enough and dark enough that he could have parked the car somewhere without anyone noticing the obvious damage. Saturday morning he could have been up early, to bring the car across the border to any place that would take it.

Fisher ran a search for auto body shops on the other side of the border from Harvey's Point. There was a scattering around Enniskillen, more around Omagh. But they were franchises, attached to big-name car dealerships. Places like that kept records. Wouldn't their guy be looking for one of those small border towns, the kind of place with a population of seven hundred, but with twelve hundred people claiming social welfare, from both sides of the border? Maybe, maybe. But Murtagh would have had to find a place that could do the work immediately, somewhere that would have the paint colour, or the bumper parts to repair the BMW straight away.

Fisher sat back in his chair, absently took a sip of cold coffee, and rapidly put the cup down again. Murtagh would have wanted to stay off major roads. Fisher searched for minor roads that crossed the border, found a few possibilities, but ultimately there was only one BMW franchise within easy driving distance

Fisher took a quick glance around him. There was no one within earshot. Rory had left the room, gone for coffee maybe, vacating the desk to Fisher's left. One more glance around and Fisher dialled the number. The call was answered almost before he'd remembered he'd need to use a northern accent. When he spoke it sounded ridiculous to his ears.

'This is Constable Sammy McGinley, calling from Belfast.' *Cuhnstable Sammeh McGinleh.*

'Oh aye.' The voice on the other end sounded less than impressed.

'I'm looking for a car that was involved in a hit-and-run. Killed a young girl.' The accent was fraying around the edges now. 'Did you or any of your mates carry out any work on a black BMW, an X5? It would have been bumper work. Did you do any work like that on Saturday 26 April?' The last words came out in a rush.

There was silence on the other end of the line. Too much silence. No clicking of a keyboard. 'Twenty-sixth April?'

'Yes.'

'You're telling me he killed a young one?'

'Yes.'

'Where exactly?' The tone was very dry.

Shite. Shite. His accent had been rubbish. The man at the other end of the line had him well figured out. He should hang up. This sort of cross-border bullshit could get him into serious trouble. But garage guy had something, Fisher could feel it.

Fisher took a breath. 'Galway,' he said, in his own flat southern accent.

And now the keyboard clacking started. Garage guy checking news reports of the hit-and-run, verifying what he'd been told. A long pause.

'He was here on the twenty-sixth first thing. Tall guy with grey hair. Wanker. X5 BMW, front in bits, said he'd hit a deer. Paid extra – a lot extra – for quick service.'

Fisher's pen was racing across his pad. He was breathing fast, as if he were chasing a gouger down the street and the gouger was winning. 'And your name?'

'You're not getting my name, and you've no right to ask for it either.'

Silence. Fisher expected him to hang up, but the line stayed open. He hesitated. 'Is there anything else you can tell me?'

'Just if you ever want to catch this guy you'd better stop with the bullshit and get the PSNI out here to ask their questions the right way. And keep this conversation to yourself. I will.'

CHAPTER FIFTY

Cormac wasn't willing to leave Emma alone in the house by herself. He had visions of Carrie O'Halloran showing up to arrest her, or worse, James Murtagh showing up, knife in hand. He could have asked her to go to a friend's house, but they needed more help than that. He was going after James Murtagh, and he was determined to get him, but what if he failed? If everything went to shit Emma would need a good lawyer, and the sooner she talked to someone the better. Over Emma's protestations he called the only person he could think of, a defence attorney named Tom Collins. Despite his profession, Cormac was sure that Collins could be trusted. Collins was understandably surprised by the call, but he rolled with it quickly, suggested that Emma meet him at his offices at Abbeygate Street. They could talk things through. Emma could wait with him until they heard from Cormac, and worst-case scenario, she would be well prepared for whatever came. Cormac drove her to Collins's office, hugged her, and left her. Then he got back in the car, and drove to the university, running through everything he knew and everything he didn't.

Cormac took the turn for the chapel car park. It was jammed, so he dumped the car illegally half on the footpath, then walked down towards the lab. Cormac looked over the building as he approached it. It still looked like a World War II bunker to him. He felt sure that he would find Murtagh there, despite the fact that it was a Saturday. Things were reaching a crisis point, and this was Murtagh's seat of power, wasn't it? Cormac thought about the entrance camera, didn't want to give Murtagh those few minutes warning, that time to mentally prepare himself. He wanted to surprise Murtagh, shock him if he could, put him off balance from the start. Given the security set-up Cormac couldn't see any way around it. Murtagh would have at least a couple of minutes to mentally prepare himself, which was a problem.

Cormac walked on the other side of the road until he had passed the lab by fifty metres or so, then he cut across the road, across the grass, and right down to the water's edge. He paused there for a moment, looking out across the rippling water. The concourse building was behind him now, and anyone could be watching him from its windows. Cormac began to amble back up-river, hugging the water's edge, making an effort to look like someone out for an afternoon stroll. Moments later he was at the lab again. This time, instead of a bunker, the beating heart of the lab stood open to him through those great glass windows, as if he had taken a scalpel to it, peeled back its flesh with callipers.

That heart was mundane enough in its details. The first room was an open-plan laboratory. Two white-coated researchers were bent over their work. One of them looked up as he passed, but river-side walkers must be common enough – the man glanced at him for only a moment before turning his attention again to the apparatus in front of him. Cormac walked on. The next room was an office, smaller than the office where he had first met James Murtagh, and plainly furnished. There was a full bookcase, a screen and keyboard on the desk, a coffee cup. He wondered if it was Emma's office, though there was nothing in particular to mark it as hers. Cormac slowed as he approached the pillar that marked the end of one window, and the beginning of the next. He wasn't sure but felt that the next room should be Murtagh's.

It was and there Murtagh was, sitting at his desk, hunched over a laptop. Cormac stepped right up to the window, loomed over it, allowed his shadow to fall across the room. Murtagh was caught up in what he was doing. Whatever was on the laptop had all of his attention and it took him minutes to realise that Cormac was there. Finally, the older man turned in his chair, and visibly blanched at what he saw.

For a moment Cormac said nothing, did nothing, didn't even change his expression, just locked eyes with Murtagh until the initial shock of his presence had passed. Then, without explanation, Cormac turned and walked on, around the building and to the front door. He didn't have to wait for the security guard to open the door, but was able to follow two female employees into the building. A flustered looking Roland Swaine lurched to his feet. With bare courtesy Cormac asked to be brought directly to Murtagh's office. He was escorted back to the office. The security guard raised his hand to knock on the door. Cormac reached around him for the handle, and pushed the door open. He was very aware, in that moment, that he was about to cross a line. He was off the case, ostensibly on leave. But IA hadn't suspended him, he was still a serving detective sergeant, and he intended to use it.

James Murtagh had recovered his composure. He sat ramrod straight behind his desk, as authoritative and unruffled as a judge in his own courtroom. Cormac closed the door behind him, leaving the security guard on the other side. He pulled the chair opposite Murtagh out of the ray of afternoon sunshine in which it sat, moved it to the left, and seated himself. The laptop was gone from the desk.

'Mr Murtagh,' Cormac said.

Murtagh's face was cold. 'The appropriate honorific, *detective*, is Professor.'

Cormac inclined his head. 'Professor then. I have a number of questions. Today they will take as long as they need to take. You will sit in your chair, and you will answer them until I say I am finished. If at any stage in our conversation I feel that an answer you have given me is incomplete or an obfuscation, I will arrest you and charge you with obstruction of justice, for which you may receive a sentence of up to five years' imprisonment. Do you understand me?'

'I wish to call my lawyer. I will not answer any questions until she gets here.'

'This is not a television program,' Cormac said. 'Call your lawyer if you will, and you may tell her that you have not been arrested. I am investigating the murder of two young women. I believe that you have lied to me. That you are continuing to lie to me. If you refuse to answer my questions, if you *delay* answering my questions, you are obstructing my investigation. You are obstructing *justice*. Should I arrest you now, or do we begin?'

A moment, the smallest hesitation, then Murtagh nodded.

CHAPTER FIFTY-ONE

Murtagh called his lawyer, but Cormac refused to wait for her arrival before he began his questioning. 'You knew Della Lambert, didn't you, Professor Murtagh? You met her right here in this building, many times,' Cormac said.

'No,' Murtagh said the world coldly, clearly. 'If I met her I don't recall it. You say she spent time here and that's certainly possible. I don't know every individual who sets foot inside the doors.'

Cormac almost laughed. 'You expect me to believe that? You knew Carline Darcy was not doing her own work. Despite what you said here when we first spoke, you didn't think much of her abilities. And you expect me to believe that you felt zero curiosity about the girl who was producing the world-class work Carline was claiming as her own? That you didn't so much as shake her hand?'

Murtagh snorted. 'What are you talking about? World-class work? Someone's sold you a story.'

'You're claiming that the work was not something special?'

'I exaggerated Carline's ability when we last spoke,' Murtagh said. 'I suppose I'm as guilty as the next person of going along with the Darcy family agenda. The truth is that Carline's work was ... ordinary.' Murtagh sighed. 'You've fallen for a useful family legend, detective. The kind of thing the company uses to sell its reputation and ultimately its drugs.'

Cormac said nothing, waited. Murtagh wouldn't need prompting. This part of the story he was dying to tell.

'John Darcy is a fine scientist, no doubt about it. But his true genius, if you can call it that, lies in his ability to find the commercial value in something and squeeze it until he has extracted every drop of money. The Darcy family legend – that John single-handedly invented four blockbuster drugs – is a useful fiction, but you look at the patent filings for those drugs, detective, and you will find it's not just John's name that appears.'

'You?' Cormac asked. He allowed a little needling disbelief to creep into his tone.

'On the first one, yes. After that, many other great scientists whose work John was able to commercialise.'

'If they're listed on the patent then Darcy clearly wasn't trying to hide their contribution.'

'Of course not. John would never be so stupid. But he is listed as lead designer in every case, and it's John that people talk about, John about whom the articles are written, regardless of the degree to which he actually contributed to the work.' Murtagh was trying hard to sound urbane, a man amused and cynical about the workings of the world, but resentment curled around the edges of his words.

'The Darcy legend – a family company run by a true scientist – that legend smoothed the path for John as he built Darcy Therapeutics into the monolith it is today. Carline Darcy was a bright girl. A presentable girl. I suspect John was simply doing what he could to include her in the legend. Another family genius to continue his great work.'

'You're telling me that John Darcy sent Carline here so that he could manipulate the university to falsify her results.'

Anger flashed in Murtagh's eyes. He was happy to slander John Darcy's name, happy to suggest something here, hint at something there, but didn't want to be tied to it. That could come back to bite him.

'I didn't say that.'

'Didn't you? Tell me then, where are you going with this legend story?'

'I'm suggesting that Carline's reputation as a great scholar was exaggerated. That's all.'

'And you went along with that.'

'With what? I was asked to give her a research position here at the laboratory, which I was happy to do. She carried out basic research assistant tasks. I had little to do with her.'

'And nothing to do with Della Lambert, who worked at her side.'

'I had no reason to show particular interest in Carline's friends, detective. She should not have brought a friend into the facility, should not have been able to do so, but it seems that she did. I suppose you can hardly blame Josep for turning a blind eye.'

'It wasn't Josep who let me in today,' Cormac said.

'No.'

'Where is he?'

'He's been suspended, pending a full inquiry into the security breaches at this facility. I believe he's taken the opportunity to visit his family in Poland,' said Murtagh.

Cormac wanted to keep Murtagh spinning, so that he wouldn't have time to consider his answers, wouldn't have the opportunity to anticipate the next question. But he was losing confidence that he was going to get anywhere. Murtagh had committed himself to a course of action. He was all in now and he was undeniably intelligent. It wasn't likely that he would walk himself into a hole out of either stupidity or guilt. Maybe he should have waited, or done the alibi work himself. There had to be something there and if he'd found it he would have had a card to play now. But he was worried about what Carrie and the team would do and hadn't wanted the cloud of suspicion to hang over Emma for a moment longer than necessary. That sense of urgency was clouding his judgement.

'You lied to me,' Cormac said.

'I'm sorry?'

'About the break in. You told me that nothing was taken, but that wasn't true, was it, Professor Murtagh?'

The first suggestion of worry appeared around Murtagh's eyes. 'I don't know what you're talking about,' he said. Then he tensed, waiting, Cormac realised, for him to pull a warrant out of his pocket. A warrant he didn't have. Cormac let his eyes drop to the desk, then to the locked cupboard to Murtagh's left. He sensed Murtagh's tension mount. Christ. The arrogant fucker had brought it back here. The laptop was right here, in this office, and without a warrant Cormac could do absolutely nothing to prove it.

Cormac looked at Murtagh for a long moment, let the silence spin out, hoping that nerves and inexperience would prompt Murtagh to say something he shouldn't. But he was too smart for that. As the seconds ticked by and no warrant appeared, Murtagh's confidence grew.

'Where were you last night, between nine and ten p.m.?' Cormac asked abruptly.

Murtagh shoulders drooped in relief and he almost smiled. 'I was in bed with my wife, detective. I'd suggest you confirm with her, but she's really very unwell. Morphine, you know. You'll have to make an appointment through her doctor.'

Cormac wanted to get up and punch him, but he wouldn't give the fucker the satisfaction of a compo case. The office door opened before he could ask another question, and the temporary security guard ushered Murtagh's lawyer into the room. She was a smartly dressed twenty-something with an air of competence about her. Fuck. Cormac didn't wait for introductions.

'We'll speak again, Professor Murtagh.'

The lawyer chirped up. 'If there is a next time, detective, I suggest you contact my office to arrange a time convenient …'

Cormac didn't wait for her to finish her sentence, but made his way back through the bunker, the security guard hurrying after him. He'd come for a confession, or a lie big enough that he could use it to bury Murtagh. He'd gotten neither. Guilt and worry gnawed at him. Murtagh was confident for a reason. He was suddenly very comfortable throwing John Darcy under a bus, wasn't that worried to be heard bad-mouthing the boss. Why? If Murtagh had murdered Carline Darcy, wouldn't he be doubly wary of antagonising Darcy, a man of considerable power? Darcy would surely be eager to fully investigate someone suspected of his granddaughter's murder.

Cormac knew he was still missing something. Something that was driving all the actors in this particular play. He wanted to get out of the bunker and into the fresh air. He wanted to get back to Emma, Emma whom he'd just failed so badly.

Fuck.

Cormac stalked towards the car. He was so caught up in his thoughts that he was nearly upon Peter Fisher before he saw him.

'Sergeant,' Fisher said.

'Fisher.'

Fisher was holding something in his hand. A folded piece of paper.

'I've traced the car, from the first murder. There's a body shop over the border. A man brought a black BMW X5 there on the twenty-sixth of April. He was there when they opened up and he wanted same-day service. The front of the car was badly damaged, and the guy who brought it in had a story about hitting a deer. The car belonged to James Murtagh's wife.'

'Christ, Fisher ...' Cormac could have hugged him.

Fisher's face said there was more. Cormac waited.

'Look, the thing is, I didn't get any of this from the PSNI,' Fisher said. 'We hadn't heard a thing from them and we weren't likely to any time soon. I took a punt. I know I shouldn't have and I know I've caused us problems with admissibility and all the rest of it, but ... in the circumstances.'

'We would have been waiting a year on the PSNI. A hit-and-run in the Republic is never going to be on their priority list.'

Fisher nodded. 'There's something else. The guy I spoke to twigged that I was from the Republic.'

'What did he say?'

'Told me to get the PSNI on it, and to pretend I'd never called him. I told him it was a hit-and-run and it had left a girl dead. He copped that I was calling from down south.'

'Okay,' Cormac said. 'He was probably ex-police or ex-paramilitary. Probably knows more about procedure than either of us. I'll call a contact in the North. Someone I know in the PSNI. He'll go out, no questions asked.'

Fisher held out his piece of paper, a half-smile tugging at the corner of his mouth. 'I've an ex-girlfriend in Enniskillen PSNI,' he said. 'I called her and she called our man. She emailed through a short statement five minutes later and I caught Judge Whelan at the courthouse.'

Cormac took the paper, opened it, and read the warrant.

'It covers the lab and Murtagh's home,' Fisher said. 'Where do you want to start?'

Cormac and Fisher waited for back-up. They stood a hundred metres or so from the laboratory, out of reach of the cameras, watching to make sure no one left. It was just after 4 p.m., rush hour hadn't kicked in yet, and it took only ten minutes for the first squad car to arrive. Cormac was okay with the wait. A calm had settled now. There was nothing Murtagh could do to stop what was coming for him. The lawyer hadn't left, and he would hardly try to wipe the hard-drive with her watching him. Cormac's mind was occupied instead with thoughts of the young garda beside him. Why had Fisher taken action? There were many other tasks he could have performed that day, all equally important, and he had chosen to throw himself against the one thing that needed to be done, if his priority was to prove Emma's innocence.

Carrie arrived in the first car. She nodded a greeting to Cormac, looked over the warrant, then organised her troops. Fisher, of course. Rory Mulcair was there, Dave McCarthy, a handful of uniforms. Dave gave him a clap on the back; the others, more circumspect, sent nods of greeting his way. It was enough. They were making it clear that he was part of the team, that they didn't see him as an outsider. It was more than enough. Cormac felt a sudden, entirely unexpected, rush of emotion.

He stood back, expecting to wait, to stay outside. Then Carrie handed him a pair of gloves. 'You'll need these,' she said, and he would have grinned at her if things had been less tense.

The sight of six gardaí, four of them in uniform, brought the new security guard quickly to the door. Rory held him at the front desk. Cormac was able to find his way to Murtagh's office without an escort. Murtagh and the lawyer were still sitting there. Someone had made them coffee. Murtagh's calm control deserted him quickly. He stood almost as soon as Cormac and Fisher came in the door, gave voice to spluttering objections. Cormac handed the warrant to the lawyer, gave her a minute to read it, to explain it to her client. Murtagh was still standing behind his desk, not moving, arguing as if there was something to be decided. As if he was still in control.

Cormac took the gloves Carrie had given him, pulled them on, then took a step closer to Murtagh, loomed over him.

'Step aside Professor Murtagh. Step aside *now*.'

A final moment of hesitation and Murtagh retreated. Only one cupboard in the room had doors that hid the contents within. Cormac cast a glance across the table top, the cupboard to the left of the desk. He felt a stab of fear that he'd got it all wrong, then he opened the cupboard and there it was, neatly stacked on top of a pile of scientific journals. Cormac took it out and placed it on the desk in front of him, then turned to Murtagh, who looked utterly shaken.

The laptop was unremarkable. A black Acer, the only thing distinguishing it was a hair-line crack running along the left-hand side, and a scuffed sticky mark near the top-right corner, where someone had peeled off a sticker.

'Who owns this laptop, Professor Murtagh?' Cormac asked.

The lawyer saw what was coming. She raised her hand, an attempt to prevent what came next, but Murtagh was angry, and afraid, and beyond saving.

'It's mine,' he blurted.

Cormac opened the machine and pressed the on button. Four pairs of eyes stared at the dark screen as it slowly came to life. The last logged-in username was listed D Lambert. The password box was blank and the cursor was blinking.

Cormac turned to Murtagh, a deliberately bland expression on his face. 'Password?' he asked.

Murtagh's face creased with fury and helplessness. After a long silence he shook his head. Cormac closed the machine. Fisher would bag it into evidence. They would need to dust it for fingerprints before handing it over to the IT specialists.

'James Murtagh, I'm arresting you for the murder of Della Marie Lambert, and Carline Darcy. You are not obliged to say anything, but whatever you say will be taken down in writing and may be given in evidence. Do you understand?'

Handcuffs felt like overkill, given the age of the man, but when Fisher pulled them out Cormac didn't stop him. The fucker had killed two young women.

Fisher led Murtagh out of the room, to the sound of the lawyer assuring Murtagh that she would see him again at the station. Cormac waited behind for a few minutes. He took in the room, the awards, the beauty of the view over the river. Emma had worked here. She'd worked next door to this murderous bastard for months. He'd come so close to destroying her. Cormac let his weight fall into Murtagh's chair, sat forward and rested his forehead on his hands.

By the time Cormac left the building, Fisher had put Murtagh in the back of a squad car and sent him on his way. He walked back to Cormac, a spring in his step.

'We've got the fucker, no doubt about it,' he said, and if he wasn't grinning from ear to ear it was clear he wanted to.

'We've a way to go,' said Cormac, 'but we're getting there. Can you go in and start taking staff details? Get the lads to take names and addresses, contact numbers, ask a few preliminaries. Anyone who has good information – anyone who met or spoke with Della, or who knew what she was working on, let's get them into the station now, get their statements. For the rest, let them know we'll be in touch. And get another team out to the house, yeah? We'll need to take the car in for testing. Chances are there'll be traces of her blood.'

Fisher nodded, ready and willing. He turned to go.

'And Fisher?'

Fisher turned back.

'Thank you. That was stellar work.' The words were inadequate. Cormac was full of gratitude for the younger man.

Fisher shrugged. 'I knew she couldn't have done it. She's not the type.'

Cormac nodded, felt a pang of guilt at his earlier doubt. Had Fisher had more confidence in Emma than he had? 'I'll see you at the station, all right?' Cormac said.

There was work to do. The laptop wasn't a smoking gun. Proving it had been Della Lambert's should be relatively straight-forward, even if it took time for IT to break the password. But Murtagh would recover from the shock of their incursion, and he would be working on a story right now to explain how the computer came to be in his hands. They needed the physical evidence of the car. They needed to break Murtagh's alibi, prove that he hadn't been in the hotel room at Harvey's Point when he'd claimed to be.

And ultimately, this wasn't his case. Carrie would make the decisions from here on. She would decide who should be interviewed, and when and in what manner. He would have to accept that.

CHAPTER FIFTY-THREE

Emma was waiting for him. Cormac drove to the office on Abbeygate Street. Saturday afternoon meant there wasn't a chance of parking but he was driving an unmarked and he left it in a loading bay opposite the Mercy Convent, and walked the rest of the way. He took the steps up to Collins's office two at a time, opened the door to the conference room. Tom and Emma were there, empty coffee cups and the remains of a late lunch spread across the table. Tom was taking notes.

'We got him,' Cormac said.

Cormac didn't miss the spasm of relief that passed quickly across Tom Collins's face. 'Good,' he said. 'That's good.'

Emma opened her mouth to speak, then shook her head and swallowed. She was very obviously trying not to cry.

'I'll give you a minute,' Tom said. He stood up, gathered his papers, then paused. 'You did great, Emma.'

She snorted, half-laughed, shook her head. 'All I did was eat your food, and cry and talk around in circles.'

'You did great,' Tom said again. He put his hand on her shoulder and squeezed gently. He didn't wait for their thanks or acknowledgement, just nodded to them both, excused himself, and left the room.

And then they were alone again.

Cormac would have gone to her, if he had felt she wanted it. But that wasn't what he saw in her face. He leaned on the back of one of the chairs instead.

'Tell me,' she said.

'Fisher traced the car,' Cormac said. 'He figured out where they would have had to bring it to fix it. He spoke to a guy who met James Murtagh the morning after Della was killed. Murtagh used his wife's car to do it. The front of it was bashed in, there was blood. Murtagh claimed he'd hit a deer, and he paid for a same-day turnaround.'

Emma, already very pale, looked like she might be sick.

'It was enough for a warrant. We searched the lab. Murtagh had Della's laptop in his office. We've arrested him. He'll be questioned shortly. I think Della confronted him and he killed her to keep from being exposed. But he killed Carline Darcy for whatever is on that laptop.'

Emma shook her head. 'I can't believe it,' she said. 'That night, the night I found Della's body. If I'd gone to the lab only an hour earlier, I might have prevented it. James wouldn't have done it if he'd known I was there.'

They were quiet for a moment.

'You can't know that, Em,' Cormac said softly. 'There's no way to know that. And if you start thinking that way you'll never stop. I've made mistakes on this case, you know? I ask myself if those mistakes got Carline Darcy killed. If I'd been more aware, if I hadn't let myself get distracted by other things, could I have gotten there faster? Could I have prevented her death?'

Emma shook her head, tears in her eyes.

'But here's the thing, Em. That way lies madness. That way lies a drink problem, and early retirement, and me propping up a bar somewhere with the other men and women the job has chewed up and spat out, and then what the hell good am I to anyone? You have to let it go, right? You have to do the best you can, and let the rest go. And if you're angry, if you're guilty, you have to shove all that into the work, into your next case, so that next time you don't make those mistakes.'

He let out a shaky, hard laugh. 'Maybe you make new ones, but you try.'

A tear slipped down Emma's face, and she wiped it away.

'Okay?' he said.

Eventually, she nodded. He went to her, and wrapped his arms around her, pulled her close to him and held her, felt the warmth of her body against his, the smell of her shampoo. Tears threatened and he blinked them back. His mouth near her ear, he said, 'I love you, Emma. All right? I love you so much.'

She stayed there, in his arms, for the longest time, and he felt that maybe everything was going to be all right between them. Then she pulled back, turned away from him as she wiped her eyes and blew her nose.

'I need to go home,' she said. 'I want to shower and change my clothes. Then I'd better talk to Alessandro and see how the team are doing.' She saw the look on his face. 'What?'

'It's not a good idea for you to talk to your team right now,' he said. 'Everyone will have to give a statement, and it will be easier in the long run if you haven't spoken to anyone before they speak to the police. Afterwards there will be time for you to get together, to regroup. But for now, better to stay away.'

Emma drew a deep, shuddering breath. She was angry, he could see it, but she gave a short nod of acknowledgement. 'Then I'm going to go to Dublin. See my mother. See Roisín.'

'Emma …'

'What?'

'You'll need to give a statement too. I'm sorry.'

She looked like she wanted to slap him. 'Fine,' she said instead. 'I'm going home. You tell them to call me. I'll come in, I'll give my statement, but I'm bringing Tom Collins with me. And as soon as it's done I'm going to Dublin. If they want to talk to me again they can find me there.'

340

'All right,' Cormac said. He wanted to say more, but he was on uncertain ground.

She walked to the door, paused. 'I can't believe he did it. I can't believe he murdered those poor girls. I saw Della's body.' She stopped, swallowed against her tears. 'I can't believe you thought I could have done that.'

'Emma, I ...' Cormac began, shaking his head.

But she held out a hand to forestall him. 'No,' she said. The finality of the word seemed to strike her. 'It's going to take some time, that's all.' She opened the door.

There were so many things Cormac wanted to tell her, so many things he should say, but it all seemed too big suddenly, the barrier between them insurmountable. Only one thing occurred to him and it was little enough to offer her. 'Fisher asked me to tell you,' Cormac said. 'He never believed you could have been involved. It's why he worked so hard to find the garage, I think.'

Emma had her hand on the door handle, and her back was to him. She stopped when she heard his words, her head a little bowed. She nodded without turning, opened the door, and was gone.

CHAPTER FIFTY-FOUR

The team came back to the station, carrying with them the kind of energy generated by a successful operation. They spilled into the case room in a noisy, pat-on-the-back exchanging huddle, throwing jackets onto chairs, logging into computers and passing impressions back and forth. Carrie stood back from it all. They were releasing tension, but she felt hers ratcheting up a notch. They'd scored a goal, no doubt about it, but the match was far from over.

'Dave, where's the laptop?' she asked.

'Gone straight to technical,' he said.

'Go down there, will you?' she asked. 'Stand over them, make sure they're on it and the moment they have anything at all give me a call.'

Dave nodded and left the room. Galway had a small technical team, a couple of whom were good with computers. They were limited, though, and more challenging work had to be referred on to the specialist team in Dublin. If that was needed in this case, Carrie wanted the computer gone out of the station within the hour. They could hold Murtagh for twenty-four hours only without charging him.

Carrie looked around for Fisher, didn't see him. She turned to Moira. 'Who've we got downstairs?' she asked.

Moira was all business. 'Murtagh's in room one,' she said. 'We've put the security guard in room three.' The security guard had told them nothing at the scene, but he had priors for assault and Carrie had decided he was worth pushing. 'There were only two other scientists in the lab,'

Moira continued. 'One said he'd met Carline but had never heard of the Lambert girl. But there's a woman – Emily Houghton. She said she'd met Della more than once, even worked side-by-side with her. We've brought her in too. She's in room four.'

'All right,' Carrie said. 'Good.' She thought about updating Murphy. She'd half-expected him to appear in the case room as soon as they returned, armed with questions and looking for an update. But he'd given her some space and she should use that. Too much was in train.

'Sergeant.'

Carrie turned to see Peter Fisher, waiting for her attention. His face was taught, worried.

'Yes?' she said.

'Murtagh's lawyer has arrived,' Fisher said.

Carrie nodded, unsurprised. The lawyer had been there, at the scene.

'His other lawyer,' Fisher said. 'Anne Brady's just arrived downstairs.'

The information didn't go in. It didn't make sense. Carrie was aware that she was staring back at Fisher, mouth half open, question unasked.

Fisher nodded. 'She says she's here to defend him.'

'Come on,' Carrie said. 'I want another look at her.'

They got to the interview level just in time to see the back of Anne Brady's head as she was led into the room, the door closing behind her. Carrie ducked quickly into the neighbouring observation room, Fisher on her heels, and they watched Brady's introduction to her client through the one-way glass. The sound was switched off. The younger lawyer, her back to the mirror, half-stood in response to Brady's words. Her body language suggested an objection. Murtagh looked surprised initially, then as the conversation went on more confident. He interjected, said something to the younger lawyer. Brady didn't wait for the younger woman to react, just walked around her and placed her briefcase on the table, unlocked it. Rory Mulcair, who must have escorted her to the room, hovered uncertainly at the doorway.

'We shouldn't be in here,' Carrie said, coming back to herself. 'Come on.' She led the way back into the corridor, then turned and set the electronic lock on the observation room door. Then she turned and watched as Mulcair escorted a pissed-off-looking young lawyer away down the corridor.

'Christ.' Carrie leaned back against the wall, rubbed her hands through her hair. She looked at Fisher, seeing an ally rather than a subordinate. The last few hours had brought them closer together. He'd stretched out his neck for Reilly and had brought them a win. 'I'm out of my depth,' she said. 'I got this case about …' She looked at her watch again. 'I got it about seven hours ago. I have no clue why John Darcy would send his own lawyer to defend the man accused of murdering his granddaughter, and no clue as to how the hell he knew to send her now.' She looked to Fisher for ideas, and he slowly shook his head.

'I can't go up against Brady when I have no idea what's going on. She'll eat me alive, and Murtagh will be walking out the door by the end of the day.'

'She's just a lawyer,' Fisher said. 'She can't change the facts. Half of what we've heard about her must be bullshit anyway. Exaggerations.'

'Only half?' Carrie said.

Fisher shrugged, and they lapsed into silence. Carrie let it sit for a moment. She was thinking, thinking, thinking. Eventually, she turned to Fisher.

'I sent Dave to supervise the tech lads,' she said. 'Will you go and see what the update is? See if they've managed to get in yet?'

Fisher nodded, hesitated, then left, looking backwards over his shoulder as he left. Carrie waited for a moment until she could be sure she was alone, then she took her mobile phone from her back pocket and dialled. He answered immediately.

'Reilly,' he said.

'Cormac,' she said. 'I need you to come in. I need your help.'

There was silence on the line for a moment. 'I'm on leave.'

'It's just leave. Not a suspension.' A technicality, but a useful one.

'What's going on, Carrie?'

She'd thought about going to Murphy first, clearing it with him. But better to ask for forgiveness than permission. 'Look, just come in, will you? Anne Brady is here. She's defending Murtagh. We've got twenty-four hours and I'm not ready. I'm not likely to get ready in that time. Not Brady-ready, anyway. I need you here.'

One more pause. One more hesitation. 'I'm on my way.'

They met outside the station and walked in together.

'How is she?' Carrie asked. 'How's Emma?'

'She's okay,' Cormac said. She wasn't, but he wasn't going to talk about it.

Carrie nodded, didn't push, kept walking. He liked who she was. She was a good person, a good cop.

'Did you get anywhere with the laptop?' Cormac asked.

Carrie shook her head. 'It's encrypted. It's gone to Dublin but it will take some time.'

Shite. Another chance gone and with it the tension ratcheted up another notch. 'Are you sure about this, Carrie? About bringing me in?' he asked.

She snorted, kept walking. Cormac followed. 'You need to do the interview,' she said. 'I'll be there with you but you need to run it. You know the case better than I do.'

'All right,' Cormac said. He felt the awkwardness of the moment. 'But Fisher should be with me. You should take the obs room. If you're with me, two sergeants for one interview, Brady will know something is up.'

She didn't hesitate. 'Right. I'll get set up, let Brady know we're kicking off shortly. She asked for a pre-interview briefing ...' It was something lawyers sometimes asked for and which the gardaí were often willing to give. Briefing a solicitor pre-interview meant that the solicitor had time prior to the interview to advise their client. Sometimes it made for a more useful interview, avoiding the delays caused by multiple breaks.

'Tell her no,' Cormac said. 'She's getting nothing.'

'Okay,' Carrie said. 'So what's your plan?'

'I have to find their common interest, the link between Murtagh and John Darcy, and fracture it.'

'Do you know how you're going to do that?'

Cormac shrugged, smiled at her. 'No,' he said. 'But I'm good in the room.'

Cormac had sat in an interview room opposite Anne Brady only once before, when she'd defended an IRA bomb-maker, and that time he'd come off worse. This time he wouldn't let that happen. Not just for Emma. Not just for Carline and Della. But for Fisher and Carrie too, who had so completely laid their trust in him. Fisher took the seat to his right, low key, notebook in hand, boy scout routine ready to go. Anne Brady's cold blue eyes watched in silence as Cormac took his time setting up, settling his file just so, arranging, then rearranging the exact placement of his chair. Fisher readied the tape recorder, and gave the warning, and then he and Cormac sat, silent and waiting.

After a moment of this the lawyer cleared her throat. 'On my advice, my client will not be answering any more questions, unless you have a deal to put on the table.'

Cormac didn't look at Brady, but coolly, calmly, spoke directly to Murtagh. There was only one way to do this and that was to go all in.

'There'll be no deals for you, Professor Murtagh. You are going to spend whatever years you have left to you in prison. You murdered two young women in cold blood in order to hide a fraud you had been engaged in for years. A fraud you used to draw money and power to yourself. We have you, you see? We have everything we need to put you in jail for the rest of your life.'

Cormac nodded to Fisher, who opened a file and started to read.

'The garage attendant you met with in Northern Ireland has identified you in a photo line-up as the man he met with on the morning of the twenty-sixth. He's given a statement that you claimed you had hit a deer, and that you paid extra for immediate work to be carried out. Scene of crime have taken your vehicle into our processing unit and they are stripping it back. They have already found traces of blood which have been sent for DNA testing.'

Fisher turned a page, used his finger to trace downwards, found a place and spoke again. 'Ania Kalinski works at the hotel at Harvey's Point. She brought room service to your hotel room on Friday night, the twenty-fifth of April. Ania has given a statement. She tells us that she saw only Mrs Murtagh in the room. Your wife wasn't feeling very well, Professor Murtagh. Ania had to help her back to bed. She explained to Ania that you'd been held up, but you'd called and asked her to order dinner for both of you, that you'd be there shortly.'

'Your wife is being interviewed as we speak by our colleagues,' Cormac said. 'They are asking all about your weekend in Harvey's Point. They'll ask your wife what time you did show up at that Friday night. Will she tell the truth, do you think? I hope she tells the truth. It will be easier for her, in the end.'

'And then there's the laptop,' Fisher said.

'Yes,' Cormac said. 'The laptop.' He let the silence draw out for a moment before speaking again. He kept his eyes on James Murtagh but his attention was all on Anne Brady. He hadn't missed the fact that her laser focus had tightened even more at the mention of the computer. That was it. The reasons she was there. 'Della Lambert had a brother, did you know that?'

Murtagh's eyes held his, tight, anxious. The man was shrinking, aging right there in front of them.

'They were very close, Paul and Della. Paul was good enough to give us Della's password.' Cormac let his bluff sink in, saw the information hit Murtagh like a blow, then nodded slowly. 'I think you know what we found.' In his peripheral vision he saw Anne Brady's lips thin. She cleared her throat.

'Detective, I've recently been made aware that Della Lambert was an employee of Darcy Therapeutics in Galway. She was paid directly by Carline Darcy to carry out work for the company. That work is saved to the laptop you now hold and it is most sensitive. I must ask that no further examination of the laptop is undertaken until the contents have been cloned and that cloning has been validated by an appropriate expert. If you are not in a position to make that commitment to me now, I will be obliged to seek an immediate injunction to the same effect.'

Murtagh shifted restlessly in his seat at Brady's words.

'An injunction,' Cormac said.

'Yes,' said Brady. 'The contents of the laptop are extremely valuable and they belong to the company. To be clear, I do not seek to prevent you from carrying out your investigation, merely to safeguard the contents while you do so.'

Cormac looked from Murtagh to Brady and back again. This wasn't about covering up a fraud. Something more was going on. Cormac let the silence spin out. The room smelled only of cleaning fluid, but the air felt tainted.

'Tell me, Professor, when did Della Lambert discover that you had fabricated your test results?'

Murtagh looked at him blankly.

'Now's the time, James,' Cormac said. 'This is your chance to tell us the truth of what happened. It's not necessary. We already know what happened. I want to be clear – your cooperation will not change the outcome of this investigation. But you can choose to take the easier route. Tell the truth. There's no point in spinning this out any more than it needs to.' Cormac let a hint of the contempt he felt leak out. 'It's undignified.'

Murtagh bridled, as Cormac had known he would. He pulled himself upright in his plastic chair, then seemed struck again by his surroundings. The reality of his situation caused even false dignity to abandon him. Under normal circumstances Anne Brady would have stepped in by now. She would have interjected, objected, bought her client time to pull himself together, and offered him her confidence to lean on when his deserted him. The problem for James Murtagh was that Anne Brady was there for a very discrete purpose – she would defend James Murtagh up to the point that it was useful for her larger goal, which was, clearly, whatever was on that laptop.

'What I don't understand is why you killed her,' Cormac said. 'She was eighteen years old, without money, power, or connection. You could have intimidated her, or bought her silence. But you threw everything away. You murdered her.'

Murtagh was shaking his head. He *was* aging, deteriorating. He seemed thinner, his skin parchment-white and flaking, a tremor in his hands that Cormac had never noticed before.

The murder hadn't been a considered, thought-out plan. It had been a moment of pure fury. Cormac stared at the man opposite him, thought about what drove him. Thought about what might drive Darcy to protect him. Money. Power. It always came back to money and power.

'She did it, didn't she?' Cormac said. The words came slowly even as his mind raced. 'She found the solution. First she figured out that you'd made it all up, then she did what you couldn't. She found another solution. One that really worked.'

Murtagh stared back at him, mouth open. The truth was there in his eyes.

Cormac breathed out, a long silent exhalation.

'Della came to you that night not with a threat, but with a way forward. But she had a price, didn't she, James? She wanted you to resign. Or she wanted you to come clean.'

Murtagh's face twisted in sudden fury. 'She came to the lab looking for Emma Sweeney and found me instead. She told me that she had figured out the truth, said she wanted to offer me a chance. A chance! To go to the great John Darcy, cap in hand, and confess my sins. And she wanted me to step back from the laboratory, to hand over control to your sainted Emma.' He laughed and his laugh was angry and bitter. 'My laboratory. The laboratory that I built, from the ground up.'

'And in return she would show you her solution,' Cormac said. He was certain of it. Murtagh must have seen enough of it to know that it worked. Otherwise he wouldn't have gone to such lengths.

'I'd already seen part of it. Carline Darcy's thesis proposal. That stupid bitch submitted it to me with no clue what she had in her hands.'

'So that's when you figured it out. That someone else was doing most of her work.'

That was what had triggered him. Murtagh hadn't needed the threat to his control of the laboratory to rouse him to murderous fury. He killed Della because she was what he wasn't and could never be. She was young, and brilliant and creating, and he was old, and blind and a liar. That Carline Darcy had been part of the picture was just the final straw.

'You let her leave and then you went to your car, drove after her and ran her down. Did you doctor the company's security records? They showed that her ID – Carline Darcy's ID – was not used to access the lab that evening.'

A sneer. 'Easily done.'

And then what? After he'd killed her he would have walked back to her body, taken her phone, her computer. Planned to steal her work and pass it off as his own.

'The break-in,' Cormac said. 'That was Carline, wasn't it? She knew it was you all along, knew you had killed Della, and so you must have her computer. And Carline needed the computer too, of course. She needed the thesis Della had written for her, to try to keep up her fiction with her grandfather. So she stole it back from you. You knew that only Carline could have taken it. So you waited for a night when she would be alone and you went there and took it. Killed her while you were at it.' It wouldn't have been hard for Murtagh to figure out she was alone. He knew who her roommates were, and Cormac would have bet every cent of his measly pension that Valentina and Mark were the type to post real-time photos of their end-of-exams dinner to more than one social media platform.

Murtagh had finally shut up. He kept his mouth firmly closed and looked at Cormac as if he had just now realised the hole he was in. Anne Brady uncrossed her legs. 'My client and I need a moment to consult, detective,' she said. 'If you'll give us a moment?'

Cormac nodded. He stood and left the room, waited in the corridor. Fisher was there, face tight with tension. They said nothing, just stood and waited, until Anne Brady knocked on the interview room door, and they could go back in.

Fisher restarted the tape.

'My client wishes to confess to the killing of Della Lambert, and Carline Darcy,' Anne Brady said, in the matter-of-fact tone of voice she might use to order food at an upmarket restaurant. 'He asks that his cooperation be noted for the record.'

Murtagh buried his face in his hands. He started to cry, snivelling tears of self-pity. Christ.

'Garda Fisher will take your statement,' Cormac said. 'Make it full and frank and we will inform the court that you cooperated with our investigation. Your solicitor will have told you that an early guilty plea can be rewarded.' Cormac looked him up and down. 'You're old. You have money. They'll probably put you away in Shelton Abbey, which is a country club in comparison to Mountjoy.'

Cormac didn't feel the energy and release that usually came from putting a big case to rest. A few years in prison at the end of his life didn't feel like anything near sufficient punishment for what Murtagh had done.

As Cormac left the room, he was surprised to hear Anne Brady's heels follow him. He turned to her.

'Detective Sergeant Reilly,' she said. 'The computer, or rather, the contents of the computer.'

'Yes?'

'As I said, Della Lambert was an employee of Darcy Therapeutics. She was paid by Carline Darcy to carry out work on a drug that was the sole intellectual property of my client. The content of that laptop belongs to my client. I just want to make that very clear. It is, of course, extremely valuable.'

Cormac stared her down, but she was utterly unabashed.

'I quite understand that you will need to retain the laptop for evidence purposes, but my client would like to send a technology expert to clone the contents, to ensure that nothing is destroyed during your examination.'

'Your client?' Cormac said.

A trace of annoyance crossed over that perfectly controlled face. 'My … other client.'

Cormac took a step towards her. 'How did you get him to take the deal?' he asked. 'What else does Darcy have on him? Or was it financial? A promise to take care of his family maybe, if he goes quietly with his mouth shut?'

'I merely pointed out to Mr Murtagh the strength of the evidence against him,' she said. 'He's a sensible man.'

Cormac turned to walk away.

'Detective Sergeant Reilly,' she said. 'My client …'

'I think I've had about enough of your clients for one day, Ms Brady,' Cormac said, and he kept walking.

EPILOGUE

Emma asked him to move out the next day. Just for a couple of days, she said. Just to give her some time to think. Cormac didn't argue. He packed an overnight bag, kissed her goodbye, and found a hotel.

He waited two days without hearing from her. Two days that were, admittedly, very busy. The Henderson and Murtagh cases were ploughing ahead. Brian Murphy had made no comment about Carrie's decision to bring Cormac back onto the case. It would have been difficult for him to object, of course, given that Murtagh had confessed and given that Darcy Therapeutics were suddenly entirely cooperative. Miraculously, the very next day the company had produced hours of recorded footage from the security camera at the entrance. Footage from the supposedly non-recording camera. The company had apologised. Explained that they adopted a belt and braces approach – local security personnel were unaware that the entrance cameras at Darcy facilities did actually record, and the footage was sent to the company's headquarters in Berlin for review. The footage showed Carline and Della entering and leaving the lab together on many occasions, evidence, the company claimed, that Della was an employee. The one small positive about that particular piece of fiction was that Della's family would get to keep the money Carline had paid her, and would likely even get paid a fair bit more in exchange for signing away any claim to the intellectual property in Della's work. And that money would go to Paul and Geraldine, not their

354

parents – a local solicitor had been in touch with the station to ask for contact details for the children. It seemed that one of Della's first acts after she received the money from Carline Darcy was to make an appointment to make a will, and the will left everything to Paul and Geraldine, with an uncle on their father's side to act as trustee. The uncle was a Cork-based accountant, and seemingly a very different character to his brother. He showed no signs of being cowed by his sister-in-law and gave every indication that he took his duties to the children seriously.

It wasn't a surprise that the CCTV footage was accompanied by another request for access to the laptop, a request that Cormac had denied. Murphy hadn't overturned that decision either, at least not yet.

So for two days Cormac pushed on with the cases, chased down loose ends, worked closely with the team and felt their confidence in him grow. He made a promise to himself that he wouldn't underestimate them again. And on the third day he went to the house. He sat outside on the low canal wall and waited for Emma to come home. He could have gone in, waited inside, but it didn't feel right. That was her home, for now, and it wouldn't be his again until she wanted him there.

She came home earlier than he expected. The sun was just beginning to set, bathing the sky in an orange-red glow. She saw him straight away, parked the car and walked over, sat beside him on the wall.

'I'm glad you came,' she said. 'It's good to see you.'

The words were distant, too formal. Had there been a trace of warmth in her tone, or had he imagined it? She looked tired, worn out.

'You've been working?' he asked.

She nodded. 'Trying to unpeel the mess that James left behind. Trying to figure out the extent of the stuff he just made up. If we can define the gap, at least, maybe we can figure out how to fill it.'

'Is John Darcy there with you?'

Her face grew troubled. 'Yes,' she said. 'Did you come here to ask me that?'

'No, Em,' he said. He took her hand where she'd laid it on the wall between them. It was cold. They stayed there like that for a long moment, while he tried to figure out what he wanted to say. 'I came to tell you that I'm sorry. I screwed a lot of things up, from the very beginning of this case. I understand why you felt abandoned. If I'd gone home with you that very first night, maybe things would have been different.'

She shook her head. 'No. It might have been different, but it might have been worse too. I had already found Della. There's every chance that James would have tried to blame me either way. Except then you wouldn't have been there to fix things.'

She hadn't taken her hand away. He squeezed it again.

'I know you're upset because you think I didn't believe you ...'

'You didn't, Corm,' she cut across him, her voice low and full of emotion. 'It might not have been for very long, but you wondered, for a time, if I could have done it. I would never, could never, think that of you. And I can't get my head around that. How can there possibly be a future for us if you could conceive of me murdering two innocent people?'

He'd thought of and discarded a hundred counter arguments to this. Discarded because he knew, just knew down to the soles of his boots, that anything less than complete honesty would lose her. And he couldn't lose her. Somehow, over the past two years, Emma had become the centre of everything for him. She was the future he wanted to build towards. He wasn't sure if she could ever understand or accept the truth. Which is that he had wondered, and it had nearly broken him. And he had loved her still.

He held onto her hand like a life-line.

'I did, Emma. I did wonder. Only for a few minutes, and I was out of my head with worry for you, but I did wonder. I wondered if what you went through with Roisín had hurt you deeper than I knew. I thought about all your sleepless nights. I thought about how you came in late and upset the night Carline died. And your car was in the video. It was your car, Em.'

'Yes,' she said. Her eyes searched his, looking for something she could hold onto.

'I think you'll say you would have reacted differently, and I believe that you would have. Something in you would have seen it as a challenge to us, and you would have rushed to fight at my side, asking no questions.' The questions would still have been there, of course, they would have been there at the back of her mind. But for Emma it would have been loyalty first – fight, defend, ask questions later.

Cormac lowered his voice, held her hand firmly. 'That's not who I am, Emma. I'm a policeman. I always will be a policeman. I'm asking you to accept that we might be different, in how we act, in the decisions we make. But underneath it all, the love is the same.'

She looked up into his face for another long moment, then turned to gaze out over the water. There was silence.

'Okay,' she said.

'Okay?'

She didn't look at him but she nodded, and her hand was still tucked inside his. They sat there for a long time, and Cormac felt that the world was settling back into place.

Eventually, Emma spoke again. 'You asked me about John,' she said. 'What do you know?'

He didn't want to tell her. Not when they had begun to find a form of peace.

'Della Lambert found a solution to the drug design problem,' Cormac said. 'She found out the truth about Murtagh's fraud, then she figured out a solution.'

Emma turned to him, surprise all over her face.

'He didn't tell you? John Darcy didn't tell you?'

'No,' she said.

Cormac nodded. 'He's claiming ownership of the intellectual property. Della's design, I mean. He says that because the work was carried out on Darcy property, and because Carline paid her, the work is owned by the company. He wants us to let him have the laptop, or a copy of it at least.'

'Jesus,' Emma said.

'Yeah.'

'But he couldn't have known,' Emma said, her voice almost pleading. 'He couldn't have known about James, about Carline and Della, about any of it, until it was all over, right?'

'He did know, Em,' Cormac said. 'We can't prove it, but I believe he knew. John Darcy came to Galway on Tuesday. He met with Murtagh, then went to visit Carline. I spoke to one of Carline's roommates. She listened outside the door. She said he was asking about Carline's thesis – that thesis was Della Lambert's solution. He knew about it and he wanted it. I think John Darcy was playing both sides. I think Murtagh confessed everything, and then claimed to have access to Della's solution. He had part of it in the thesis proposal. Maybe enough to convince John Darcy, to get him on side. Darcy went along with it and when Murtagh was arrested he sent his pet lawyer in to look after his interests.'

'Oh God,' Emma said. She gave a sudden, hard shiver.

'I don't know all of the answers,' Cormac said. 'There's no reason to think that Darcy knew Murtagh was planning on killing Carline, or even that there would be some sort of violent confrontation. I'm not even sure that Murtagh meant to kill her. Maybe he tied her up and hit her to try to get her to hand over the password to the laptop, and things got out of hand.'

'He went there dressed as me,' Emma said. 'I think he knew he was going to kill her.'

Cormac nodded slowly. 'Yes.' There was no point in denying it. 'At best he was indifferent as to whether or not she lived. But I don't think John Darcy knew.'

'No,' Emma said, and her voice had hardened. 'But he didn't care, did he? If James had rolled up with the laptop and the solution in his hand John would have taken it, no questions asked, and would have protected James too, wouldn't he? To hell with his own granddaughter. She was only a girl, with nothing at all to offer him.'

Cormac said nothing. He wasn't sure there was anything left to say. After a moment he stood, offered his other hand to Emma.

'Why did he send her here?' Emma asked sadly. 'If he never cared about her at all, why did he send her to Galway, to his own lab, when he'd never taken much interest in her before then? If he'd just left her alone she'd be alive now, and happy somewhere.'

Cormac hesitated. He wasn't sure he wanted to tell her anything that would hurt her more. But Emma knew him to well. 'What?' she said.

'Darcy has another granddaughter,' he said. 'His daughter's daughter – Rachel. She would have been starting in Trinity the year after Carline. Fisher's spoken to a few people. The theory is that Darcy and his wife didn't want Carline at the same university as the girl they thought of as their true granddaughter. To them Carline was an embarrassment. They didn't want her presence to affect Rachel's social standing.'

Emma looked at him, and there was no shock in her eyes, no surprise. Just a deep, exhausted sadness. He took her hand.

'Will we go inside?' he asked.

She stood. She didn't hug him. She was too sad, and too angry for that. But they walked hand in hand across the street to their home.

She stopped him before they reached the door. 'It's over for me now, Cormac. I can't go back there, can't work at his side knowing all this. But if I walk away he gets the use of my device anyway. He wins, doesn't he?'

'We'll have to wait and see,' Cormac said. 'It's not over yet. Murtagh's hired new lawyers. He might decide to fight his confession on the grounds that Brady had a conflict of interest when she represented him. If he does go down that route he has a lot of dirty linen that he could choose to wash in public.' It sounded weak to his ears and Emma looked unconvinced. He leaned down and kissed her, leaned back again. 'John Darcy is rotten from the inside out, Emma. He'll fall eventually, if not this time, then next.' That was all he could offer her, but it seemed to be enough. She led him inside, and they closed the door.

ACKNOWLEDGEMENTS

It is hard to believe that I am here again, writing the acknowledgements for my second book. What a pleasure and a privilege it has been, writing this book with the support of a phenomenal team at the same time that *The Ruin* went out into the world.

I want to take this opportunity to thank everyone who made *The Ruin* such a success. Kimberley Allsopp at HarperCollins – Kimberley I think we spoke almost every day for a while there! Thank you for making it all so much fun. Theresa Anns, Alice Wood, Sarah Barrett, Andrea Johnson and the entire team at HarperCollins – thank you, I'm very lucky to have you. Siobhan Tierney, Susie Cronin, Millie Seaward – thank you, I'm very grateful. At Penguin I'd like to thank Alison Klooster for all her support. And Kevin Che – thank you for being such a champion of books!

I'd like to thank my editors, Nicola Robinson, Katherine Hassett and Anna Valdinger at HarperCollins, Lucy Dauman at Little Brown, and Laura Tisdel at Penguin. Every time you touched it this book got better. You have book magic in your fingertips. Thank you for all your support and your continuing belief in these stories.

Thank you to my wonderful agents, Tara Wynne, Faye Bender and Sheila Crowley. I love working with you. Love your sense of humour, your grace and your approach to the world. Deeply grateful for your ongoing support, and your patience for a writer on a learning curve!

A special thank you to my dad – my one-man marketing team in Ireland! You are phenomenal, Dad, and I love you. Also, an apology to all of his friends and family. Ahem. Thank you to Mum. At the end of the day, Mum, it's all down to you. Thank you to my siblings and siblings-in-law, Conor and Ashley, Fiona and Paul, Cormac and Nao, Fearghal and Lenka, Odharnait and Kevin, and Aoibhinn and Rob. And, in that context, thank you to Skype.

Thank you again to Kathleen and Séamus ... for all your love and support and for ongoing quality control and early reads. Very much appreciated.

Thank you to Ryan Tubridy, for picking up the book, and, when you liked it, telling everyone. Your support for writers is phenomenal, and game changing, and I'm grateful.

Thank you to everyone involved in organising the incredible writers festivals I've been lucky enough to attend this year. Thank you to Writing WA for your ongoing support.

Thank you to Val McDermid. Val, you are endlessly generous to writers coming up behind you – you don't just lower the ladder, you roll out a red carpet. Thank you very much.

Thanks to my mates, to Libby and Tim Mathew, Claire and Grey Properjon, Michael and Sara Pearson for all your support and for putting up with early morning WhatsApp messages with the latest news! Thank you to Helen Pelusey and all my friends at school, for all your support – you know who you are!

Thank you to all the wonderful booksellers I've met over the past year, and so many more I haven't met yet but who have embraced *The Ruin* and told everyone. Book people are the best people.

Thank you, Kenny. Thank you, Freya. Thank you, Oisín. You are the point of it all. The beginning and the end point. I love you.

*Read on for an exclusive preview
of Cormac Reilly's next compelling
case, to be released in 2020*

THE GOOD TURN

CHAPTER ONE

Peter Fisher was woken by movement in his bed. The room was bright – his thin curtains were no match for the morning sun. He blinked against the light, tasted the sourness of the last night's beer on his tongue. More movement. He turned in time to see a woman's dark head disappear under the covers. He lifted them, looked down at her.

'What are you doing?' His voice was on the rough side. He cleared his throat.

She stilled. 'Looking for my knickers.' A laugh in her voice.

He thought. 'I think they're on the floor on your side.'

She reappeared out from under the blankets, looked at him. 'Right. Close your eyes so.'

Peter dropped his head back on his pillow, closed his eyes, and took a moment to replay the previous night's activities. When he opened them again she was standing at the end of the bed. Her knickers were white cotton, her bra black lace. Christ but she was in great shape.

'Sneaking out, were you?'

She was pulling on her jeans now, searching for her T-shirt.

'I've got training,' she said. 'And I'm late, late, late.'

Training. She played for the Salthill camogie team. They had a semi-final coming up. Which was why she hadn't been drinking the night before, and he had.

Peter let out a heavy sigh. 'I knew if I let you take advantage of me you wouldn't respect me in the morning.'

She grinned at him, pulled her T-shirt over her head and looked around for her boots.

'You're a hard woman,' Peter said.

She sat on the end of the bed, started to lace up her boots, gave him a sideways look. 'I'd say you'll recover,' she said.

She was ferociously cute. Even first thing in the morning. He wanted to pull her back into bed and kiss her, but had better keep his distance until he found toothpaste and half a gallon of mouthwash. She might have had the same concerns. She came close to say goodbye, kissed him briefly on the cheek, then headed for the door.

'I'll see ya,' she said.

'Hey, Orla,' he said. She turned. 'D'you want to meet for lunch?'

She looked surprised. 'I'm meeting my sister,' she said. 'But … maybe later?'

He nodded. 'I'll give you a shout so.'

One last smile, warmer this time, and she was gone.

Peter considered going in search of water, thought better of it, rolled over, and went back to sleep. It was eleven when he woke for a second time. This time he made straight for the shower and his toothbrush, came back to his room to dress and straighten the bedclothes. He opened the window to let out the stale air of the night before and cold, fresh November air streamed in. It was a bright, sunny day, but there wasn't much warmth in the winter sun. He made for the kitchen. The apartment was a two-bedroom, on the second floor of a three-storey building on St Mary's Road. His roommate, Aoife, had found the place for them, had actually signed for it and paid the deposit before he'd even seen it. Which was just as well – you had to move fast to find someplace that was both decent and affordable in Galway. In his price bracket there was a lot of competition from students. Aoife could have afforded better, but they liked to live together, and she never made a thing out of it. Besides, it was two minutes' walk from the hospital, which worked well for her, though it was almost as handy for the station.

Aoife was already occupying the couch in the living room. She was wearing long pyjamas bottoms, a jumper, and thick socks, had the Saturday papers with their glossy magazine supplements spread all around her, and an empty coffee cup on the small table to her right. She raised bright eyes to him.

'You've emerged,' she said.

Peter went into the little kitchen and poured a glass of water, came back to the living room and drank it down.

'That bad, is it?' Aoife asked.

Peter shook his head. 'I'm grand,' he said.

'Did I hear lovely Orla commence the walk of shame a few hours ago? Did you kick her out?'

Peter laughed, dropped into the armchair. He felt buoyant. First day off in two weeks, and so far it was pretty close to perfect. 'She had training. We're meeting for dinner.'

Aoife raised an eyebrow. 'Jesus. Commitment,' she said.

Peter shrugged. He liked Orla. Aoife did too – she'd introduced them, on some doctors' night out. Orla wasn't a doctor like Aoife, she was a med lab scientist, ran blood tests in the hospital labs, but she knew Aoife from the social scene. He'd kissed her that first night, if he remembered correctly. Then again another night, or was it two? Last night they'd taken it further. He did like her. She was bright, funny. She always seemed happy too, and that was nice to be around, when so much of his work meant being knee-deep in human misery.

'No work today?' Aoife asked, reading his mind.

He looked at his phone. 'Not so far, anyway.' First day off in two weeks, but that didn't mean he'd get to keep it.

Aoife stretched, knocked half the papers onto the ground in the process. 'Any plans?'

'Haven't thought about it.' He should go to the gym, or for a run at least. He had the annual physical coming up. He looked down at his stomach, thought about shuttle runs and the previous night's beers. 'Do you want to go to the cinema?' There was a new Bond movie – *Spectre*. He'd heard good things about it.

Aoife looked wary. 'Maybe,' she said. 'What were you thinking?'

Peter's phone rang before he could answer. Aoife rolled her eyes, let out a sigh of exasperation.

Peter checked his screen before answering. It was a blocked number, probably the station. He pressed the button.

'Fisher.'

'Reilly wants to know if you can come in.' A familiar voice. It was Ceri Russell. A colleague.

Peter looked at his watch. 'I'm off today,' he said, unnecessarily.

'He knows,' she said. 'But the taskforce is out again tonight and they've taken four extra uniforms. Reilly says we need someone for the station.'

'Who else is in?' Peter asked. He locked eyes with Aoife, who stood and started to gather up her newspapers. Peter stayed where he was, listening to Ceri talk, not yet willing to accept that his day off had just been cancelled.

'Basically me, Reilly and Mulcair,' Ceri was saying. 'The entire taskforce is out on the raid – they left hours ago. They think there's stuff coming in by boat this evening.'

Peter stood up, looked out of the window. 'Yeah,' he said. 'It's mad how they always get a tip-off when it's a sunny day, isn't it?'

Ceri paused. 'They seemed sure this time,' she said.

Peter snorted. 'I'll be there in a half-hour,' he said. Felt her hesitate. 'What?'

'Can you stop off and make a call on the way in? It's Reilly who's asking, not me,' she added hurriedly. 'A call came in on 999. A twelve-year-old boy in Knocknacarra. He says he saw a girl his age abducted from in front of his house, about fifteen minutes ago.' Ceri's tone wasn't right for the news she was delivering. There was tension in her voice, maybe, but it was minor, office politics grade, not a voice that suggested a major operation about to kick off.

'All right,' Peter said. 'What are you leaving out?' He went to the kitchenette. Leaned against the wall. Aoife was pouring cornflakes into a bowl. He mouthed a *sorry* in her direction – she responded with a grimace. Peter went into his bedroom, phone still pressed to his ear and shut the door.

'Well, he says he saw Slender Man do it.'

Peter paused in the act of pushing off his shoes. He'd need to change out of his jeans if he was going to the station. 'What?'

'You know, the internet thing. Slender Man,' Ceri was saying. 'Look, I didn't talk to him myself, so …'

'Right. So it's a prank or a crank.' He looked at his watch. It was early enough that the traffic to Knocknacarra wouldn't be too bad. He didn't want to sit in the car for two hours on a prank call. 'Anything else?'

'His name's Fred Savage. Address is Number One, The Rise,' Ceri said in a rush, maybe relieved he wasn't making a big deal out of it.

They hung up, and Peter started to strip off his jeans and T-shirt. At least he didn't have to go looking for a uniform. He was plain clothes now, ever since he'd made the move to the detective squad. The dress code of a detective depended on the nature of the work, but for a standard day he tried for respectability. That meant slacks rather than jeans, and a T-shirt with a collar on it.

He wouldn't admit it to anyone, but despite the fact that his day off had gone down the drain, and there was a good chance he wouldn't now get to meet Orla for the promised dinner, he still felt a flicker of pleasure as he made his way to his car. He loved his job, liked that he was relied on. DS Reilly trusted him, and that proved he was getting somewhere. Maybe he was closer to making sergeant than he thought.

CHAPTER TWO

Peter didn't bother with lights or siren, other than giving them a brief flick when he got to the top of Threadneedle Road. He was in no great hurry to get in to the station, where he would likely spend the day glued to a chair, dealing with stacks of paperwork and making overdue calls. They were so short staffed that keeping the basics covered was all they could aim for and it usually took a major incident to get a trip to a scene OK'd. This call out to Knocknacarra was a reprieve – he should take his time on the drive out and back. He wondered if the dispatcher had asked to speak to Fred's parents. The Slender Man reference and the kid's name – Fred Savage sounded like a makey-uppy – had to have had her thinking she was dealing with a crank.

Fifteen minutes later Fisher pulled in outside of a mock-Tudor semi-detached. The house was painted a brisk white. A flowerbed planted with clashing orange and pink flowers formed a border around a square of well-maintained lawn. All of the houses on the street were identical, though some were better maintained than others. The Rise was not a particularly apt name for the little cul-de-sac, which had no hill at all, and no view.

The front door of number one opened before he could ring the bell, and a middle-aged woman looked at him anxiously, taking in the marked car behind him. Fisher reached for his badge, introduced himself. 'I'm looking for a Fred Savage,' he said. The woman nodded a yes and gestured impatiently for him to come inside.

'He's upstairs. I made him get into bed. Look, he's not very well. You'll go easy on him, won't you?' She led the way up narrow, carpeted stairs. The house smelled of chicken soup and baking.

'Fred is your son, Mrs ...?' She obviously knew why he was there, knew that her son had called the police.

'It's Angela,' she said. She reached the landing and opened a door into a small box room, very tidily arranged, furnished with a single bed made up with crisp white linen and occupied by a boy, small for twelve, who had a tablet clutched in one hand, and wearing a pair of Harry Potter style glasses pushed back on his nose. He looked hot, unwell.

'Fred?' Fisher asked.

The boy nodded. 'Yes,' he said, his voice not much more than a whisper. He coughed.

'You've been sick, Fred?'

A shrug. 'First bronchitis, then tonsillitis, now bronchitis again. No school for two weeks. Mum's had to stay home from work to mind me.' The boy managed to look pleased and worried at the same time.

'All right,' Fisher said. 'Look, Fred, you know I'm here because you called 999, and told the dispatcher that you'd witnessed an abduction.'

A vigorous nod, no signs of embarrassment. Fisher felt the first stirrings of worry in his gut.

'You told the dispatcher that you saw Slender Man abduct a girl. Is that right?'

Confusion passed over Fred's small face. 'I didn't say that,' he said. For the first time his eyes went to his mother's face, but it wasn't the worried glance of a little boy caught out in a lie.

'You didn't say anything about Slender Man?' Fisher asked. 'Do you know what Slender Man is?' If the boy denied it Fisher didn't relish the task of explaining. His own knowledge was limited to what he'd picked up from a few newspaper reports about a stabbing in North America. Slender Man was a sort-of digital urban legend, as best as he'd been able to make out. Something born in a photoshop challenge run on a message board that morphed into an entire mythology, given fresh impetus when two teenage girls stabbed a third to within brink of death, then claimed they'd been forced to the deed by Slender Man.

But Fred was nodding. He half-lifted his tablet toward Fisher. 'I was playing *Slender Man's Forest*,' he said. 'The app. That's what I told the dispatcher. I was playing the app before I looked out the window and saw what happened.'

Oh Christ. 'And what did you see, Fred? Tell me exactly.' Fisher kept his voice very calm. He could almost feel the thrum of Angela's anxiety from the doorway behind him.

Fred glanced towards the window. 'I saw a girl, walking her dog. Then a car came and parked a bit down the street.' Fred made a vague gesture towards the window. He was really struggling to get the words out, his voice a rasping whisper. 'A man got out and walked towards her. I didn't really pay attention to him. I thought he was going to go into Murphy's house next door. But then ...' Fred aimed another glance at his mum. This one had some fear in it, asked for reassurance.

'It's all right, Fred,' Angela said from behind Fisher. 'I'm here, and the garda is here, and nothing's going to happen to you.'

Fred shook his head before he spoke again, and Fisher formed the distinct impression that the boy wasn't worried for himself.

'He punched her in the stomach. Really, really hard. She fell down and let her dog's lead go. The dog just yapped and yapped until the man kicked it. Then he picked the girl up from the ground, and he put her into the boot of his car, and he drove away. The dog ran after the car. I don't know where it is now.' Fred sat back on his pillow, gasped in a deep breath.

There was absolutely no doubt in Fisher's mind that the boy was telling the truth. The dispatcher had screwed up, she'd mis-heard the boy, which, given the state of his voice, might be understandable. Why the hell had his mother let him make the call himself? Fisher cringed inwardly at the thought of his leisurely drive in the sunshine. How much time had passed since the call came through? At least half an hour.

'What kind of car was the man driving?' Fisher asked.

A shrug. 'I don't really know cars,' Fred said. His voice broke on the last word and he coughed, a nasty-sounding rattle. He pushed his tablet across the bed towards Fisher. 'It was black,' he said. He gestured at the tablet.

Fisher felt the blood quicken in his veins. 'Did you get a picture?' he asked.

Fred seemed to feel the futility of trying to speak. He woke the screen of his tablet, tapped on an app, tapped again, and turned the screen to face Fisher. Fisher watched as a short video played out and looped. Fred had taken it from his bedroom window. The glass through which he'd shot the video was grubby and the video itself was innocuous enough. It showed a black Ford Mondeo, parked about five metres down the street, pulling away from the curb and driving off. Peter couldn't make out anything of the driver but he could make out part at least of the registration.

Peter looked at Fred, and two very serious, red-rimmed blue eyes looked back at him. Fred mouthed one word. Sorry.

Peter stood. 'You did brilliantly, all right? And don't worry, we're going to find her.' The boy held the tablet out to him, and he took it. 'I'll get this back to you as soon as I can,' he said, and was met with a shrug.

'Did you know the girl?' Fisher asked. 'Did you recognise her, or the man?'

A shake of the head. No.

'Could you describe the man to me, Fred?'

In his rasping whisper, every second word lost, Fred described the man as tall and thin, dark hair, a beard. He was wearing slacks, Fred thought, and a navy T-shirt with a collar, just like his dad wore sometimes. Fred looked sick at the thought.

Peter turned to Angela, gave her the nod, and she followed him out to the landing.

'What was all that about a slender man?' she asked, her voice anxious.

'Just a misunderstanding,' Fisher said. 'The dispatcher couldn't quite make out what Fred was saying ...'

'He called you lot before he even told me what had happened. Then he came and found me in the kitchen, bawling his eyes out. Poor kid. He's a really good boy, you know? A really good boy.' She hesitated. 'Don't go getting any crazy ideas about his dad either, right? It wasn't him. Fred's dad lives in London, he's blond, and only a few inches taller than I am.'

'All right,' Fisher said. 'Can you give me a minute?'

He stood outside and dialled Cormac Reilly directly on his mobile.

'Reilly.'

'It's Fisher. I'm in Knocknacarra. I responded to that call.' Peter wanted to sound cool, professional, in control but he could hear the fear and excitement in his voice. He took a breath, turning his face from the phone.

'Okay.' Reilly sounded distracted.

'Uh ... the reported abduction,' Peter said. 'A young boy – Fred Savage – called it in. He spoke to control in Dublin and there was a mix-up. Some confusion. His call wasn't taken seriously but I think this is the real deal. He has video of the car driving away. I've got his tablet here with the recording on it. The recording isn't perfect but I can read a partial.'

'Give it to me.'

Quickly, Peter ran Reilly through everything he knew. His report was briefly interrupted when Reilly took a few seconds to pass on the partial plate and to issue instructions to the officers in the case room.

'I'm on the way,' Reilly said, and Peter could hear voices in the background, movement, a car door slamming. 'They're working on the partial but see if you can email the video directly to tech. If you get that done, start on the door to door. We'll be with you in twenty minutes.'

Reilly hung up, and Peter turned to see Angela Savage watching him from her front door. Peter held up the iPad.

'Can I use your wifi?' he asked. 'I need to email the video to the station.'

'Of course,' she stepped back, made room for him to enter the house.

It only took Fisher a minute to log into his own email account, attach the video and send it off, and for most of that minute he was mentally berating himself for not having done that before he called Reilly. He'd been worked up, maybe not thinking straight. Well, that was the last mistake he was going to make. From now on he was keeping his head. He waited for the confirmation that the email was gone, then turned to Angela.

'Thanks. I'll need to keep this I'm afraid, but we'll get it back to you as soon as possible.'

She shrugged.

'What can you tell me about the neighbours?' he asked, already moving towards the door. She followed.

'I don't think you'll get much out of them,' she said.

Fisher had reached the open front door. He stepped outside. There were twelve semi-detached houses in total in the little cul-de-sac, six on one side of the street, six on the other. Signs of life were minimal. Angela leaned against the doorframe, arms crossed.

'Mrs McCluskey at the end of the street will have been at home. She never goes anywhere but she's as blind as a bat and sleeps half the day. You might get a few others. But if anyone saw it they would have called you, wouldn't they? It's not the kind of thing you ignore.'

'Okay, thank you.' Peter was halfway down the driveway by now, still looking back towards Angela. Movement from the bedroom window above caught his eye. He looked and saw Fred standing there, staring down at him, looking half-afraid and wholly sick. He was pale as a ghost, with great dark circles under his eyes. Peter thought of Reilly mobilising the few officers they had left. Thought of the video, which, after all, had shown nothing much.

'Angela, what are the chances that Fred made this up?' Fisher asked. 'In a bid for attention, maybe?' He thought about the boy's dad in London, wondered how often they saw each other.

'Jesus,' she rolled her eyes. 'I've been hovering over him for the last two weeks. How much more attention do you think he might need? No, I'm telling you, he's not the type. My son's a smart, capable boy who does well in school and is well liked by his friends. There's no way he would do something like that.' She paused, glanced at the boy. 'And his name's not Fred, just by the way. That's what his father calls him, because he thinks he looks like Fred Savage. Which he doesn't.' The last said firmly. 'His name is actually Dominic.'

Angela spoke with conviction, and she didn't seem to be the rose-tinted glasses type. On the other hand ...

'That video game ... the app that Fred ... Dominic, was playing. It's definitely not suitable for a twelve-year-old.'

Angela Savage looked surprised, then gave him a hard look. 'Jesus. Everyone's a parent, aren't they? Haven't you bigger problems right now?'

Peter flushed, nodded, and got on with it.